D0240030

Dirt
Road

Also by James Kelman

Novels
The Busconductor Hines
A Chancer
A Disaffection
How Late It Was, How Late
Translated Accounts
You Have to Be Careful in the Land of the Free
Kieron Smith, Boy
Mo said she was quirky

Short Story Collections
An Old Pub Near The Angel
Three Glasgow Writers (with Alex Hamilton and Tom Leonard)
Short Tales from the Night Shift
Not Not While The Giro
Lean Tales (with Alasdair Gray and Agnes Owens)
Greyhound for Breakfast
The Burn
The Good Times
If it is Your Life
A Lean Third

Drama
Hardie and Baird & Other Plays

Essays
Some Recent Attacks: Essays Cultural & Political
And The Judges Said

Dirt Road

James Kelman

CANONGATE
Edinburgh · London

Published in Great Britain in 2016 by Canongate Books Ltd,
14 High Street, Edinburgh EH1 1TE

www.canongate.tv

1

Copyright © James Kelman, 2016

Every effort has been made to trace copyright holders and obtain their permission
for the use of copyright material. The publisher apologises for any errors or
omissions and would be grateful if notified of any corrections that should be
incorporated in future reprints or editions of this book.

The moral right of the author has been asserted

British Library Cataloguing-in-Publication Data
A catalogue record for this book is available on
request from the British Library

ISBN 978 1 78211 822 0
Export ISBN 978 1 78211 823 7

Typeset in Bembo by Palimpsest Book Production Ltd,
Falkirk, Stirlingshire

Printed and bound in Great Britain by Clays Ltd, St Ives plc.

MIX
Paper from
responsible sources
FSC
www.fsc.org   FSC® C018072

WEST DUNBARTONSHIRE	
D000046862	
Bertrams	21/07/2016
GEN	£16.99
BK	

for
Kenny Glenaan
Tony Slater Ling and Dirk Powell.

ONE

It was half five in the morning when his father wakened him. Murdo lay in bed an extra few minutes. There was a lot to think about. But that was all, thinking; he finished the packing yesterday. Soon he was up and downstairs for breakfast. Dad had eaten his and was doing the last-minute check to electric switches and gas taps, water taps and window snibs. In a couple of hours' time people would be going to school. Murdo and his father were going to America.

Then they were off, walking down over the hill and on down to the ferry terminal, Dad pulling his suitcase, Murdo a step behind, rucksack on his shoulders. Dad had wanted him to bring a suitcase too but what a nightmare that would have been.

It was a good morning, fresh and new-feeling. An old neighbour and his dog were returning from the newsagent. He saw their luggage and was ready to stop for a chat. He told long stories and Murdo quite liked listening but just now there was no time. Murdo gave him a wave. Dad had barely noticed the old guy anyway. Father and son carried on down to the pier.

A guy Murdo knew was by the entrance to the ferry terminal. His young brother had been in Murdo's class at school. The guy was working and there was no time to blether. The early morning ferries were busy. People crossed to the mainland on a daily basis to get to their work. Murdo's father was one of those and must have recognised a couple of the passengers but he didnt nod to any of them, not that Murdo saw. Dad didnt talk much anyway. As soon as they sat down he brought out his book and began reading. Murdo sat thinking about stuff. If anybody had asked what about he wouldnt have known. All sorts and everything. Soon he got up to go outside. I'm just going out a minute, he said.

Dad nodded and continued reading.

Murdo had made this ferry crossing a million times but it was still enjoyable. He leaned on the barrier seeing down towards the island of Cumbrae. Next thing they would be flying over it. But they would hardly see it because it came so close on the take-off. Murdo had only been on a plane once before, for a holiday in Spain. So that was twice, there and back. All he remembered was a happy time. What made it so happy? He stopped the thought. But it was not even a thought. The image from a photograph. His mother and sister were there.

When Murdo thought of "his family" that was what he thought about. The family was four and not just him and Dad. Mum died of cancer at the end of spring. This followed the death of Eilidh, his sister, seven years earlier from the same disease, if cancer is a "disease". He could not think of cancers like that because the way they hit people. One minute they were fine but the next they were struck down. More like a bullet from a gun was how he saw it: you walk along the street one minute and the next you are lying there on a hospital bed, curtains drawn, nothing to be done and nobody to help. The cancer his mother and sister suffered struck through the female line and ended in death. Males cannot help. All they can do is be there and be supportive. What else? Nothing, there is nothing.

That was weird, not being able to do anything, thinking of doctors and all medical science yet nothing. Murdo found that difficult. His Dad must have too. Murdo didnt know. It was not something they spoke about.

He was standing by the rail, enjoying the sea-spray, that freshness. Nobody else was there. Too blowy. Either they were inside where Dad was or else had stayed in their cars. Boats were better than planes. Even wee ones. If ever he made money he would buy one.

Even before a car he wanted a boat. With a boat ye could sail anywhere. Depending on the engine, or maybe the sails. Guys he knew had boats; their dads anyway, or uncles. It would have been great. His father didnt bother. When ye take one back and forward to yer work every morning ye dont want to be doing it in yer spare time. As if traveling on a ferry was the same as sailing a boat. It was the kind of daft thing Dad said, because he couldnt be bothered talking seriously about stuff.

Then the guy was there whose young brother was in Murdo's class at school. He already knew they were headed for America and was wanting to know how long they were away. Murdo said, Two weeks I think.

Ye think! The guy chuckled.

Well maybe it's two and a half. Murdo grinned.

The guy clapped him on the shoulder, still chuckling, took a last couple of puffs of his fag and flicked it overboard. Murdo knew it sounded daft, not knowing how long they were away for but Dad hadnt told him. Or had he? Maybe he had. Sometimes Dad said stuff and he didnt take it in. He would have had to ask to know for sure, and he didnt like asking. One question at a time.

The truth is he didnt care how long he was going away. Forever would have suited him. It didnt matter it was America. America was good but wherever. Things closed in. It was not Dad's fault, just life. Murdo was nine when his sister died. With Mum he was sixteen. People die and you cannot do a thing. All the cannots; cannot cannot. Nobody nothing nothing nobody. Cannot cannot nothings for nobody. The person is just nothing. You cannot help. Nobody can. People say how it eats inside you. It is true. That was it with Mum. Every moment of the day thinking about it from first waking in the morning till last thing at night: is she asleep or awake, and what do her eyes look like, is she seeing stuff or are they that other way, just nothing, her eyes just nothing.

People say about getting away. Yes to that. It was the best thing ever could have happened.

The ferry was set to dock. Dad was waiting for him. He shrugged when he got there. It was a particular shrug. It meant Murdo should have been there two minutes ago and should watch it in future. This was a bit daft. Ye could miss getting on a boat but not getting off. How could ye miss getting off? The ferry docked and that was that. Dad was like this when it came to stuff. Maybe he thought they would miss the train. But how could they miss the train? It was there to connect with the ferry. If for some reason it was postponed they would just jump a bus. Dad had left time for emergencies.

They walked fast with the other passengers. Some raced to get the best seats on the train. On board Dad said, You got everything?

Murdo shrugged. Yeah. He was unsure what Dad meant. Dad had the passports, the visas, the tickets; everything, Dad had everything. All Murdo had was himself and his money which was just about nothing. He went in for his phone, the pocket where usually he kept it. It wasnt there. He tried other places. Maybe it was in the rucksack: he never kept it in the rucksack.

Dad was back reading his book. Dad read books. The train started moving and the ticket-collector was coming. Murdo gazed out the window, then tried his pockets again. The idea of leaving it behind! What a nightmare. Surely not? How could he have? He couldnt. Yes he could.

Dad was watching him. Alright Murdo?

Yeah Dad.

Dad nodded, turned a page in his book. Murdo waited until the ticket-collector had passed along the train then unzipped the compartments in his rucksack one by one. Still nothing. He really didnt have it. He actually didnt have it.

Dad was watching him again. Murdo said, Dad I've left my phone. I've left it. I had it on the kitchen counter ready to take. I dont know, I just, I forgot to lift it.

Dad said, Have ye checked all yer pockets?

I'll check them again.

He checked all of his pockets again and every part of the ruck-sack but the phone wasnt there. He really had left it. Murdo said, Dad I'm sorry. I'm really sorry.

Dad nodded. A bit of peace without it I suppose.

Murdo sighed, zipped up the rucksack and stared out the window. That was him now, nothing. What did he have? Nothing. This was the first stage of the journey then there were all the rest.

The flight to Amsterdam was an hour and forty-five minutes. Then twelve hours to America! Twelve hours! Once the doors closed that was you; locked in, barred and bolted. And nothing except some stupid movie. Or else whatever, like if they had some kind of in-house sound system, maybe iTunes or something. Imagine a pill. Ye went on board and they gave you it to swallow. Next thing ye were getting off. They could hit ye on the head with a hammer. That was you out until ye got there. Memphis was the place they were landing. Although dont speak too soon. People said that. They touched their head for luck. Touch wood so touch yer head, as in a joke; which was stupid when ye thought about it. Yer head is not wood. So dont touch it for serious things. People say that too. If ye do need good luck never ever touch yer head. Not even as a joke. Murdo understood this way of thinking. Never say a thing until it is done. Dont take the fates in vain, they dont like it. Mess about with luck and it might turn nasty. Amsterdam to Memphis was a very long way. How far? Murdo was not quite sure. The lucky thing was his rucksack, it was light enough to carry on board.

Imagine the whole Atlantic Ocean. Having to swim it. Thousands of miles of water. Although if the plane crashed ye would be dead in five or ten minutes. He heard that someplace. Unless the pilot managed to land at a good angle so the plane could skite along like how a sea-plane lands on the water, and if ye had enough time ye would grab the rubber dinghy. The pilot signaling the Mayday emergency. Other boats coming to the rescue. Fishing boats and cruise-liners; all sorts; even yachts. Some yachts sailed long distances.

7

It depended whereabouts they crashed although the middle of the ocean would be hopeless. Then escaping the plane, who was sitting beside you? What if it was a big fat guy? Imagine it was an old lady, or a wee kid or a baby, they went first and might need help unless if the baby's parents were there they would be the rescuers. So it was the old lady left behind, and other old people, depending how strong they were, and the ones that were disabled and needed pushchairs. Then all the luggage in the hold, what would happen to it? The luggage would all be lost. Bobbing about on the sea. People would want to save their own stuff but there would be no room on the dinghies.

Water can be calm this time of year. It was maybe a good time for flying. Murdo liked the water at night, seeing the waves glint. Then if it was a night where ye could see all the stars. Olden day sailors used the sun and stars to guide their boat. There was good stuff online about it. The joke in school: please sir if Mercury is in Venus is it a bad day for geometry? Although things like stars and luck irritated Dad. Especially luck. Dad didnt believe in luck. He was wrong.

Ye cannot control yer health. If something goes wrong and has nothing to do with you, what else is it but luck? Genes is luck. If it is there in yer genes then that is you. People said it was "meant". That annoyed Murdo never mind Dad. It was like God decreed. God would never decree somebody dying. It was complete nonsense. What about the ones that didnt die? What was decreed for them? Were the ones that died only put here for the sake of the ones that didnt die? What was decreed for them? Was Dad only put here to marry Mum then for their daughter to die then his wife as well? Then if the plane crashed and Murdo drowned but Dad he didnt. So everything was for Dad, and God was decreeing it all for him? Is this why Murdo was on an airplane, so he would die in the crash? What about the pilot and the other passengers? Did they all die for the benefit of Dad? It was total nuts.

In a movie there was a woman in a crowded airport kept seeing this figure and it was a ghost flitting here and there. The woman knew the ghost was "for her" and was looking to find it. The ghost kept one pace ahead and the woman could never reach it till then she missed the plane. The plane crashed and was never seen again. So the ghost there was good, more like a friendly spirit. Murdo didnt believe in ghosts but spirits were different; spirit worlds, "presences". There could be a presence. He used to get a feeling when he was doing something like eating a nectarine. It was Eilidh, his sister. She loved nectarines.

★

At the Amsterdam terminal nobody in the waiting area for Memphis was from the Glasgow plane. Not one Scottish voice apart from him and Dad. Different people from all different parts of the world. Four Muslim girls too. Probably to do with school or their religion. Religions have different things about them. Maybe this was part of theirs. They wouldnt have noticed Murdo.

Although why not? People get noticed and he was a person. Imagine speaking their language. One of them could have asked a question and nobody knew what she was saying except him. Maybe they were getting hassle to do with being Muslim. And he would say something and she would be amazed and happy at the idea of this guy knowing.

In Memphis airport they kept close together. Long lines of people queued at the place for visas and passports. The lines twisted round to make use of the floor space. Cops or maybe soldiers walked up and down with guns and sticks in holsters. Some had rifle weapons cradled in their arms.

Dad touched Murdo on the elbow, thinking he was staring but he wasnt, he was looking. Everybody looks. Ye see something new and so ye look. People do that. Why not? Otherwise they wouldnt have eyes, they wouldnt see where they were going. Who to talk to, they wouldnt know. Some people were kept to one side, looking about or staring at the floor; children, everybody.

Then a security man poked Dad on the arm. Dad was annoyed. The guy knew he was but didnt care, he just gave him a look as if "hurry up hurry up".

In the carousel section the luggage hadnt arrived but the conveyor belt was moving. Murdo went in for his phone automatically. This time he didnt try all the pockets. That was that, he didnt have it. Dad should have had his own phone anyway instead of relying on Murdo. He said he wasnt, he said he was just taking a break from using phones. Fair enough for texting and making calls but for like checking information, if ye couldnt go online, it was just a problem.

People were shoving forward to get a better view of the luggage. Kids too and it was a bit dangerous. Dad kept watching in case one of the kids fell or got their hand stuck someplace.

Outside the restricted access area friends and relatives gathered; some holding cards with names written. Maybe somebody was waiting for them! Who could it be? Nobody. Uncle John and his wife were hundreds of miles away. There was an airport in a town near where they lived but only for domestic flights. They could have made a connection but it cost too much money. Dad had other relations in America but whereabouts nobody knew, only that they were there.

Signs and directions for taxis, connecting flights, buses, hire cars and trains. A big queue at the information desk. Dad left Murdo to guard his suitcase and joined the end. American people every-where, walking fast; all going someplace. Even their clothes looked different. America was not only a country but the whole continent.

Dad was signaling him. What was that about? Keep yer eye on the suitcase! Murdo signaled back to him. He dropped his rucksack on top of it and squatted beside them. Dad was right; there was bound to be thieves, even in airports. Thieves watched and waited. How could you tell a thief? Even if a guy was shifty or dressed poor it didnt mean anything.

People wore different clothes here. Plenty guys in short trousers; old ones and fat ones. Some wore cowboy hats. Ye expected rifles and ropes to lasso cattle. One man carried an accordeon-case and was wearing cowboy boots as well as a cowboy hat. The case was amazing. This beautiful design and all studs and shiny buttons. He must have done it himself; if that was the case what like was the accordeon! The music would be different too. This guy was more like Mexican or South American, so different rhythms and different dances, but some of it would be the same; ordinary walking and fast walking, and slower like a woman stepping or skipping along; or doing that bouncing step women did especially: Step we gaily on we go, heel for heel and toe for toe.

Dad had reached the information desk and was speaking to the man behind the counter who was old for a job like this, straining to hear what Dad was saying then looking at him like he didnt know what he was talking about. Dad was irritated and called something to the other information worker who was a black woman with thick glasses and grey hair. She also was old and Dad came away soon after looking as if he hadnt learned much at all. The way he strode back Murdo knew they were leaving. He pulled on the rucksack before Dad grabbed the suitcase handle.

So that was them now, outside the building, fresh air at last.

The heat was immediate, the sun striking into yer eyes and yer head; even breathing, ye were aware of the difference in air. But folk were smoking and that had an effect. It made him dizzy as a boy and sometimes nowadays he felt the same, especially if he hadnt had much to eat. Not since sandwiches on the plane. Hours ago. And when before that? Amsterdam; sandwiches again. No wonder he was starving.

A local bus would take them to the main bus terminal. Plenty queued at the bus-stop, including soldiers. Some were Murdo's age or not much older. Females and males. Maybe they werent real soldiers. Although back home you could join at seventeen and didnt need yer parents' permission. Murdo was sixteen but coming up for seventeen. He fancied the navy. Imagine Dad coming home from work: I've joined the navy Dad. But if it was his life, why not?

At the main bus terminal people were ordinary but mostly poor-looking. All ages, some with phones, sitting texting, checking stuff out, listening to music. A big screen gave information. Buses were late and customers had to be patient. Some had their eyes closed, dozing. Others stretched out sleeping on the floor. If ye were alone ye would be careful. Police patrolled and had a dog, maybe for sniffing drugs. They had guns too. Actual guns. Big sticks and handcuffs, talking to each other while they walked like having a wee laugh to each other, but watching people at the same time. Dad said, Dont stare son.

I wasnt staring.

If they look at ye just look away.

Okay.

He hadnt been staring but there was no point making a fuss. How long since they left home? Ages. Hours and hours. Maybe they could sleep on the bus. Imagine big comfy seats and just lying back, like really comfortable and just closing yer eyes. But if the bus was late what then?

They found space on a bench. Soon Dad had his book out and was reading. Murdo could have brought one. He didnt think of it. Because he didnt know he was going to need it. What did it matter anyway, it was too late; too late for that and too late for this, this and that and that and this, just stupidity, when did that ever happen, forgetting the phone, where was his head, that was the question, all over the place.

Across the side of the hall the police had stopped a guy and were getting him to open his bag. They searched inside, probably for dope. The guy's clothes were out in full view, socks and stuff, underwear. He stood with his head bowed staring at the floor. It wasnt nice.

Dad hadnt noticed. The lassies too, ye couldnt help noticing them; one with bare legs and a short short skirt, quite skinny, and guys staring and she was just like standing there.

Better not thinking about stuff. Music would have helped. A nightmare without it. There was a new system he fancied but it was impossible because of money. Everything was money. It tied in with useless old phones and headsets that dont work. Dad said read a magazine. Okay but ye still heard people talk. Murdo did but Dad didnt. Dad was oblivious to everything. Murdo needed music. So if people talk ye dont hear it, ye dont piece it together. It didnt matter when or where, yer mind just drifted, away into anything, ye didnt even know, just drifting, thinking without thinking, making his mind go in a different way, just to like go cold, make it go cold, but it was difficult, difficult, just like

Dad nudged him. You sleeping?

No.

I could have been away with all the luggage; even your rucksack, I could have lifted it off yer shoulders. I could have stolen everything.

Dad I wasnt sleeping.

Ye were.

I wasnt.

Yer eyes were shut.

I was counting to ten and opening them.

Dad sighed. Ye're too trusting. Look after yer things is all I'm saying. There's thieves everywhere.

Murdo nodded. Dad glanced up at the destination screens, closed the book and checked his watch. Come on, he said, we'll stretch the legs. There's still forty minutes. A walk will do us good. Get the oxygen pumping.

Murdo was glad to be walking but they kept inside the bus station. He would have preferred going outside, even just for a look. Here they were in America and he hadnt been outside. Memphis, Tennessee; that was the song.

They found seats on another bench near a soft drinks machine. Murdo was hungry. Dad didnt seem to be. Folk had food and were eating it on their laps. Ye wondered where they all stayed. Was it an ordinary house with ordinary rooms, a kitchen and a living room? A settee and chairs and a table. He couldnt imagine them cooking a meal like toast and beans or a boiled egg, a bowl of porridge. It really was a foreign country. An old guy passed near to them. He wore a fancy jacket with curved pockets and a string tie with big jewels like a cow's head with horns and a thing poking out his mouth – what was that? the end of a cigar maybe. He scratched his bum while he walked; skinny legs through his trousers, his shoulders hunched in. He sat down on a bench nearby then was talking out loud to himself; this wee old man. His body shape was like a walking stick. It was religious stuff he was saying. Put your trust in the Lord, put your trust in Jesus. Murdo smiled watching him.

Another man was coming past, hobbling as though his feet were bad and he called to the old guy, Amen brother amen. Maybe he was being sarcastic. Or was he a true believer? He didnt look like one; more like he was on his way to work. What kind of work? What did people work at? The same as back home, it would just be the same things; mending stuff and factories, fixing electricity and plumbing; working in supermarkets and garages, cafés. Where did they come from? Where were they all going? Some would be seeing their relatives. The old guy was talking again. His face was kind of angry. Put your trust in the Lord, put your trust in Jesus.

The funny thing was he seemed to be looking at them. Dad was reading his book and hadnt noticed, but he did eventually because of the voice. The old man raised his hand up: The Lord hath them chastened sore, but not to death given o'er.

Dad half smiled, acting as if it was nothing but how come the old man was looking at them? It was more Dad than Murdo. The old man gave him a real angry look. He said the word "Jesus" again and brought his finger down the way a teacher does.

Obviously he was cracked. Maybe he didnt like foreign people. But it made other people look across, so it was a bit embarrassing. Dad noticed too. Murdo whispered, Is it because we're foreign?

Dad shrugged. I dont know, I've no idea.

When is the bus coming?

The bus. Soon. Dad smiled slightly then gazed at the floor.

Other people wouldnt know they were foreign. Or would they? So what if they did? People think things even when they dont know a single thing about ye. Dad tried to ignore the old man but that was not easy. Then he stared straight at him. But the old man stared straight back and wagged his finger: If it be the will of *Jesus*! He will renew them by his spirit, if it be his will. Uphold them by his love, if it be his will, I'm talking the will of Jesus.

Murdo didnt like the way the old guy was saying it, and how it affected Dad. Because it did affect him. It shouldnt have but it did. And that was unfair, so unfair. After what Dad had been through he was the last person, the very last person. He believed in God too. Murdo didnt but Dad did. Murdo knew this from when Mum was in the hospice. A minister came through the wards and sometimes spoke to Dad. Dad was okay about listening but Murdo wasnt. It was none of the guy's business. How come he was even there? If nobody belonged to him, how come? He just hung about. Visiting Mum too, how come the guy visited her? A minister. Murdo would never have let him. How come Dad let him? Did he ask Dad first? Because Mum would never have asked for him. Never. Him being there like that, a stranger, and Mum lying there, not able to do anything, not even hearing him and him sitting beside her and talking about all that stuff. What did he have to do with it? Nothing. Poor Mum. Listening to him. Okay she was Dad's wife but she was Murdo's mother. Imagine he held her hand. Ministers did that. Even thinking about it. Horrible.

The Lord hath them chastened sore, but not to death given o'er. Murdo hated that kind of stuff.

★

On the bus out of Memphis he was on the inside seat, Dad on the aisle. The final destination seemed to be New Orleans but they were changing buses long before, and other changes after that. Murdo wasnt sure except they had to watch out for themselves. Dad was keeping track of things. He had all the stuff, all the information and tickets and whatever else, everything. Dad had everything. That was just how it was. He didnt tell Murdo, although Murdo could have asked. He should have, he didnt, they werent talking much.

The first stop was a wee town without a proper bus station. Nobody was waiting. The driver let two passengers off on the street. He had a smoke while getting their luggage out the side compartment then stood to the rear to finish it. Onwards again, passing alongside the main motorway then veering off on a smaller road that was quiet for long stretches. Nobody seemed to be talking, maybe a murmur from somewhere, hardly anything. Maybe they were snoozing. Murdo too. He saw a wide river and it was the next thing he saw. He surely must have been dozing. He turned to Dad, whose eyes were shut. Was he asleep? Murdo said, Dad. . .

Dad opened his eyes. It took a few moments for him to register the surroundings.

Murdo said, What river is that?

Dad squinted out the window then sat back. I'm not sure, he said. He looked again but with bleary eyes and soon closed them.

Even seeing the river! Imagine a swim. A swim would have been great. Just being on the water. If ever he got money it was a boat first. Sailing anywhere ye wanted. People had yachts and sailed round the world. They took a notion and went, and arrived at a harbour. They moored and went ashore. Anybody there? Where am

16

I? Is this Australia? Not knowing anybody and just being like free to do anything at all, anything at all. Oh no it's Jamaica. Jeesoh. A boat came first before anything.

The idea of a swim. Murdo was tired and sweaty. It had been cold before; now it was muggy.

Later they were in another town, large enough for its own wee bus station although parts were quite old and with broken windows and stuff, peeling plaster. The driver was taking a break and so could the passengers. Some lit cigarettes as soon as they stepped down off the bus, maybe went to the toilet. Others got out just for the sake of it; Murdo and Dad among them. Two people were leaving the bus and three people came on board. Eight o'clock in the evening and warm, a smell of dampness. Dad had the bus tickets out and was studying them against the itinerary and receipts. He glanced again at the tickets. Where's the driver? he said.

The driver? said Murdo.

Dad muttered, I need to check something, then headed along to the waiting area and joined the queue at the information counter.

Murdo stood a moment then followed the sign to the gents' lavatory, through a door and along a corridor at the side of the main building. A man was at the sink. He was still at the sink when Murdo finished urinating. Murdo washed his hands then put them to the hot air machine. The man was still there, and staring at him. Definitely. He was staring at him. He was. And Murdo left fast, wiping his hands on his jacket going along the corridor. He was not scared. More like nervy. This made ye nervy, stupid damn things like this. How come him and not somebody else? The guy wouldnt have done it with Dad there. Never. Only him, because it was him: oh he's young, he'll be too scared to do anything. That was the guy, that was his thinking, staring at him like that, and Murdo moved quickly because if the guy came after him, what if he came after him? Murdo would get Dad, he would get Dad. There was the exit at the end of the corridor and out he went.

Where? Where was he? On the pavement outside the bus station.

It was the wrong exit. There were two, at the opposite ends of the corridor. One kept ye inside, the other led ye out.

He was not going back in, he was not going along the corridor. So like if the guy was there. Imagine he was there. Murdo was not going in, he was not going in. He looked for the entrance drive-in off the road; the one used by the buses. It was along to the side.

This must have been the main road, where he was standing. It was long, straight and wide. The odd thing was the lack of traffic. Parked cars but none moving. Not even one. It was a Saturday night too. Maybe this was the outskirts. Oh but the sky was amazing. Murdo couldnt remember ever seeing one like this. A kind of orange into red and so very clear. Probably it had been hot during the day, and would be tomorrow.

On the opposite pavement along was a place with its name in flashing lights: Casey's Bar 'n Grill. Nearer to that a couple of shops with wide windows. Outside one was a huge wheel like from a covered wagon or else an old stagecoach. It was propped against a wall, just lying there. The pavement continued round the side of the building. A jumble of stuff lay there too. Now away in the distance a truck was coming. The typical style with the funnel. It was great to see. Murdo crossed the road before it came then watched it go, with two wee flags flying on top of the cabin.

The pavement was made of wood and when ye walked it made a clumping noise. The other shop was a pawnshop. A pawnshop! He hadnt thought of that. Pawnshops in America.

The huge wheel was rusty and mottled. From an actual covered wagon maybe. He touched it, then chipped off a flake of rust with his right thumbnail. Other stuff lay roundabout. Old farm tools made of iron, rusty and ancient-looking. All dusty. Everything. Did people ever pick them up! Did they ever buy anything!

This first shop was antiques and had two great-sized windows. Ye couldnt believe how good it was like all stuff from the old west. Amazing. Guns and handcuffs, rifles. A wide bowl contained arrow heads and another one with sheriff badges; Marshall of Dodge City, the Pony Express. Some were ordinary stars, others with circles and points. An Indian chief's headdress with feathers and like branding irons and all whatever. Round the side of the building was a plough. Behind that an open space with the front part of a stagecoach, including the bit the horses got roped into. Real stuff and all just lying there. If ye had had a car ye could have taken anything ye wanted.

Next door the pawnshop. On the window ledge lay an empty ashtray full of cigarette ends, with that fusty old tobacco smell. Good stuff. Laptops and base units, consoles, tablets; digital headsets and all kinds of phones. Old stuff too, televisions and hi-fi equipment; video cams, old-style computers. Plus big hunting knives and daggers with long thin blades. Swords too and like strange-looking things, balls and chains or something. Then farther along assorted mouth-organs, two saxophones and two acoustic guitars.

And an accordeon!

It looked okay. He wouldnt have minded a go. A bit shabby but so what if it sounded right. It sat snug between a keyboard and a bass guitar. Ye wondered whose it was? Somebody from way back. Some old guy. Probably from Scotland, or Ireland, an immigrant; maybe he played in a band. Or used to – he died and his family sold off his stuff. Because they didnt have space to keep everything; it was just a wee house where they lived. Maybe the old guy stopped playing. That happened. People can play music forever then one day they give it up. So when the guy first came to America he had to work in a factory to make ends meet for his wife and family. So he shoved his instruments in the cupboard. Maybe the keyboard and bass guitars were his too, like his own rhythm section. Murdo had three guitars, one from when he was a boy, the other two along the way. Ye started on one instrument and ended up on something else. He had a keyboard too, and he was wanting a fiddle.

Then music from Casey's Bar 'n Grill. The door had opened and two guys appeared, lighting cigarettes and continuing a conversation. A bus pulled out from the side street across the road, turning out onto the long wide road. And Murdo ran, ran, ran straight across that road into the side street entrance round to the bus park area which was empty except for Dad. Dad was standing with the suitcase and ruck-sack at his feet. Nobody else there. He saw Murdo and started walking towards him almost like he didnt recognise who Murdo was.

Murdo felt the worst ever he had. Ever. He couldnt remember anything ever worse before. This was beyond anything. Dad wasnt even looking at him, just nothing.

Aw Dad, Dad, I'm so sorry.

Dad nodded. The next bus is tomorrow, he said. He pulled out the handle on his suitcase, headed along to the waiting area. Murdo followed him, carrying the rucksack in his hand. Only two people were there. One was a black guy holding a sweeping brush, just watching them. The other was the woman at the information and ticket desk, she was black too. I need to phone Uncle John, said Dad, I need to tell him the situation.

Dad I'm so sorry.

Dad indicated a bench next to the door, and left him the luggage to guard while he crossed the floor to speak to the woman. She listened to him and passed him coins for the old-style payphone by the entrance. He went to make the phone call. Murdo just sat, there was nothing else. He came back and that was that, they were going to a motel for the night.

Dad walked a pace ahead out the bus station. A taxi-office was round the next corner; a few taxis were parked. Dad entered the office. Murdo stayed out. A guy with a beard and a turban opened the door of a car and gestured at him to get in. Murdo shrugged but waited for Dad; for all he knew it was a different taxi. The guy closed the door and folded his arms. A few minutes later Dad came out and passed the guy the suitcase. The guy shoved it and Murdo's rucksack in the boot.

When the car was moving Dad stared out one window, Murdo stared out the other. What he had done was stupid and there was no excuse. If he had known the time he would never have left the bus station; never gone anywhere except the bathroom. It was that guy staring at him. If he hadnt been there it would have been okay. He should have told Dad. He was not going to. Maybe he would, not just now.

A mile farther on he spotted a shop down a side street with its lights on. There was a porch and a couple of people stood chatting. Soon they were at the motel. This was a long, one-storey building with an open corridor: the Sleep Inn. Sleep in and ye slept in, it was clever. The guy at the reception office was young, more like a student working part-time; a black guy. He did the paperwork with Dad then gave him the key.

They walked by the edge of the carpark, along the side of the building. Their room was way towards the end. Only five cars were in the carpark. Did that mean only five rooms taken in the whole motel? No. He saw lights in a few of them so other people were here. Up on the outside corridor laundry hung on the rail to dry. Farther along two people sat on chairs on the open landing gazing out over the carpark. There were no tall buildings. No hills either. They would be seeing right over to wherever. An old man and old lady. The old lady didnt look at them but the man did and he called down: Howdy!

Murdo waved up to them: Hiya!

This was the first he had spoken to an actual American. Along at the room Dad could hardly open the door. The handle was shaky and about to fall off. Then the key wouldnt go in the lock. Then when he managed it the key would not turn. Now he had to grip the handle but it shook like it would fall off. Maybe he was forcing it too much. He stood for a minute breathing in and out. Then he got it to work. Bloody squirt of oil, he said, that is all it needs.

The room had double and single beds and an old-style television on top of a cupboard. One wardrobe. It only had three hangers inside. They werent unpacking so it didnt matter. Dad sat on the end of the double bed, still in his jacket and shoes.

Murdo checked out the fridge. He was starving. Dad must have been too. Completely empty inside; sticky patches and not too clean. The microwave was working but ponging. Although ye get pongs cooking food so it didnt matter too much. When had they last eaten? Maybe there was a takeaway someplace.

The cupboard underneath the television smelled of damp but contained cups, plates, plastic cutlery and an electric kettle. In the bathroom there was a shower as well as a toilet bowl and washbasin. The handle on the toilet bowl wouldnt pull properly. Murdo jerked it a couple of times but couldnt get it going. No toilet paper! Murdo couldnt find any. He didnt need it, but what if he did? No soap either. He rinsed his hands. And no towel!

He came out the bathroom wiping his hands on his jeans. Dad was lying stretched out on the bed, hands clasped behind his head and staring at the ceiling. No toilet paper, said Murdo.

Dad sighed.

Maybe people bring their own.

What a thought.

Murdo shrugged. No towels either.

Dad raised his head to see him. Just use yer own, he said. Dad paused a moment, then added: Did ye bring one?

No.

I told ye to bring one. I deliberately told ye.

I was keeping space.

Keeping space? What ye talking about keeping space? What are ye not goni wash? A two and a half week holiday?

Murdo looked at him.

Eh? Murdo, I'm talking to ye.

Sorry Dad.

How are ye goni dry yerself at Uncle John's? Run about the house and cause a draught?

Dad, they'll have towels.

Who'll have towels? Who ye talking about?

Uncle John and Aunt Maureen.

Murdo, we're visitors. It's called "being polite". People bring towels when they're staying with people. That's why I told ye to bring one: not because Uncle John and Auntie Maureen dont have

22

any of their own. Of course they've got towels. We're guests, and we act like guests. We look after ourselves. Things like towels, toothbrushes, toothpaste, that's what ye bring; ye bring them with ye.

Dad shook his head, unlaced his shoes and kicked them off, then stretched back out on the bed.

Murdo said, Dad maybe it's a mistake, like the guy in the office, maybe he just forgot to put the stuff in. They might keep it all in the office.

Dad's eyes were closed.

Will I go and ask? said Murdo. I was wondering about teabags as well. They've got the cups and the kettle so maybe they've got teabags too; maybe they keep them in the office.

Dad opened his eyes.

I was thinking too if there was a takeaway roundabout.

Dad raised his head again. A takeaway? he said.

I'm quite hungry.

Aye well I'm quite hungry too but it'll keep till morning.

There is a shop.

I never saw any shop.

We passed it in the taxi.

Forget it.

Dad it's not far. I'll go myself like I mean I know where it is. It's only round the corner.

I know ye're hungry son I'm hungry too. It's good ye're offering but we dont even know if it's open.

It was when we passed.

Aye well it might not be now.

The reception guy'll know. Dad they'll have sandwiches and stuff, bread or whatever, a packet of cheese; cold meat or something.

Dad sighed. Murdo, he said, I'm knackered, it'll wait till morning.

Can I not just ask the guy? He'll tell me. If he cant I wont go like I mean it's easy to do and just having a walk Dad. . . Murdo shrugged. I'm really hungry. The microwave's working too I mean like maybe I could get stuff to cook like a frozen meal. Beans and toast or something.

That's getting complicated.

Well just sandwiches.

After a moment Dad said, Okay. But nothing that needs cooking. See if ye can get a loaf of bread and the cheese separate. And teabags, get teabags.

Will I get water?

Check with the guy, maybe tap-water's okay to drink. Dad took money from his pocket while Murdo pulled on his boots. He passed him a $20 note. Will that be enough d'ye think?

I dont know, said Murdo.

Dad passed him another $5.

★

He checked with the guy in the office. The shop opened till late. He forgot to ask about toilet rolls and towels. He would do it on the way back. It was just good to be walking. Warm and with a nice smell, and different sounds; insects and birds maybe. For a Saturday night it was quiet; not like a town. No pubs or anything, cafés or takeaways; nothing like that. The houses were mostly single-storey buildings made out of wood. Some gardens were cluttered with junk; others stoned over as parking spaces. At one house music from an open window. People sat outside, laughing and talking; black people; kids too. They saw him passing.

He reached the traffic lights and turned the corner. The lights were still on in the shop. There was hardly a pavement. It was quite strange; ye had to walk on the street or else on the edge of people's gardens. Roots of trees were growing in some and ye could have tripped over. Two young guys were on the porch entrance to the shop, just hanging out; watching him. They looked about fourteen.

It was an ordinary kind of shop but with all different stuff, including magazines and books and like a medicine counter. Murdo lifted a basket and saw the girl serving. She was good-looking, with bare shoulders and a blouse that was loose. What age was she? Just about his, whatever, sixteen or seventeen. She saw him and was staring. He was white and a stranger. Other customers were black. He passed along the first aisle. He didnt know what things were there or what they cost. Some were the same as back home; same tins and packets, soups and breakfast cereals. Other stuff ye had to look at twice or else see the labels. He was thinking for sandwiches. Dad wouldnt care except how much it cost. They would save money if they made their own.

Murdo found the bread but the shelf was near empty; only wee loaves left. He took two. But for butter ye would need a whole tub of butter and that was too much. And how much cheese? Not that much. Unless there was cold meat. The cold counter had big thick sausages that looked good but maybe ye had to cook them. He picked up a packet to see and saw the girl looking across like if he was going to steal it! Ha ha. A packet of sausages. They were no good anyway if ye had to fry them. Farther along he lifted a pack of cold meat then checked out the cheese counter. A pack of ready-cut cheese-slices. Cheese was cheaper than cheese-slices but ye needed a knife to slice it. Tomatoes made good sandwiches too but ye needed a knife for them.

The girl was watching him again. How come? She knew nothing about him except he was white. Probably she thought he was American. He kept on down the aisle but his face was red now, if she really did think he was stealing. He had to lift stuff to see the price. He didnt have any option. Prices were on everything and he was able to check it against the $25. Cheese and bread, a carton of orange juice and one of milk. A packet of lettuce and a bottle of water; a wee tin of beans and a carton of fruit yoghurt.

The girl was serving a woman but looking across at the same time. So was the woman. Maybe they both thought he was stealing. If ye took too long people thought ye were waiting yer chance.

He was just working out the money. If there was change out the $25 he would buy a couple of bananas. A few were a reduced price in a basket next to the cash till. Bananas made good sandwiches too. They were overripe but would be fine inside. He queued behind the woman.

The girl's name was Sarah: the tab on her blouse said it. An old-fashioned kind of name. Murdo gazed at the floor not to look at her, then away towards the door. Really she was beautiful. A girl's bare shoulders always look good but hers really really did. And just a beautiful face. That is what ye would say. A smooth face like ye get with lassies and her hair pulled back so it was like her forehead was really smooth too, and how her neck went, then her boobs too like her cleavage, she was just really good-looking.

Then it was his turn and she ignored him. She didnt even look at him. Although he was the customer and she was the server it was like up to him, he was to talk or whatever. That was wrong. Definitely. And he was blushing again. She lifted the grocery stuff out his basket, scanning it through the machine.

Then he noticed the prices on the screen, they were different to the labels. Everything was dearer. Every single thing.

Murdo waited to see the total. It was way more than it should have been. She didnt say a word, not looking at him, just waiting for the money. Except he didnt have enough. It's too dear, he said, it's charging too much.

Huh?

Yer machine's charging too much.

She frowned at him, not understanding him. He lifted the first thing to show her, the packet of cheese, it dropped out his hand. She picked it up. He pointed to the price on the label. It says four forty-nine but the machine charged more, I watched it. The same with everything. Your machine charged more, it's just like every single thing it added on money. The total's all wrong.

She stared at him. Oh you're talking about tax, she said. You got tax on these things.

Tax?

Each one you got there it's got the price then it's tax on top. Is that what you're talking about, tax? The girl held her hand out for the money. You'll see it on the receipt.

It totalled more than $30. He didnt have enough money. He showed her the $25. You'll need to take stuff out.

Huh?

Murdo passed her the lettuce and the yoghurt. Does that make it? he asked.

Mm. She started packing the food into a brown paperbag, paused to place the two tins on a tray behind her. To the side of the cash register was the basket of loose bananas. She did a new cash total and gave him the receipt. He was waiting to see the change. A little more than one dollar in coins. How much for bananas? he said. Can I get two please?

Pardon me?

Murdo held out the change to her. Can I get two bananas please?

She packed in two bananas beside the rest of the food and pushed the full paperbag across.

Thanks, he said.

Sure. She watched him lift the paperbag. Where you from? she said.

Scotland.

Scotland?

Yeah.

Mm.

He held the brown paperbag close to his chest and exited the shop, up along the street and the main road. He started smiling. Because it was good. He felt that. Just everything. America. He liked it. It was different. Had she even heard of Scotland! Ha ha, maybe she hadnt. It was strange to think. America, an American girl. Imagine she smiled at him. Maybe she did. She could have.

Mum would have liked it here. Everything was new; away from the old stuff. Fresh air and breathing. Fresh breathing. Everything!

Murdo felt that strongly. He didnt care about stuff. School and the rest of it. They would all wonder where he was. Ha ha. Here. Thousands of miles away. It was great, just bloody great, and he walked fast: food to eat. Dad too, he must have been hungry.

It was dark by now. He remembered the toilet rolls. In the motel reception office the guy was on the computer. He had a wee pile of books beside him. He must have been a student right enough. Murdo said: We dont have any toilet rolls.

Huh?

I mean like toilet rolls?

You need toilet rolls huh?

Well we dont have any.

The guy turned and opened a cupboard door, withdrew two and gave them to him.

Do we not get any towels?

Huh, you want towels?

Yeah well there arent any.

Okay.

Are we not supposed to get towels?

Sure, yeah. Who's in the room?

Me and my father.

The guy opened the same cupboard door, brought out two towels and handed them across.

Thanks, said Murdo.

Sure.

Back in the room the television was on but he could see Dad had been dozing. Dad yawned, watching him come in the door and carry the towels and toilet rolls into the bathroom. Murdo laid the food and drink along the foot of the single bed then knelt to unlace his boots.

Dad said, Well done son.

The office guy was fine. He just gave me the stuff.

Good, said Dad. What about the shop? How was the walk? Did ye meet anybody?

No.

Dad yawned. Did ye get teabags?

Instead of answering Murdo knelt to retie the bootlaces.

Did ye not get any? asked Dad.

No but I will now, said Murdo, quickly knotting the lace on his left boot.

Dont bother.

No Dad I'll go.

No ye wont.

Dad ye need tea.

I dont.

Ye do.

I dont.

Dad, ye need tea!

Calm down.

But Dad

I dont need tea. We have needs in this life but tea isnay one of them. I'll survive. Dad lifted the towels and toilet paper and entered the bathroom.

Murdo sat a moment then switched on the television. He watched it while preparing the food. When Dad came out the bathroom he saw it on top of the cupboard. Good stuff, he said, well done.

I'll go for tea in the morning, said Murdo.

Dont worry about it.

No, he said, I'll go.

★

Last thing in the evening he went in for a shave. He hadnt done it for a while. The mirror over the washbasin was more a large flat tile but it worked alright for looking into. There were these pimples around his chin. When he shaved the safety-razor cut them, it cut off the tops. The risk was more pimples. The blood out a pimple caused that to happen. It made them spread. Ye had to be careful if ye scratched them, it could leave scars and brought plooks and boils. Ye were better patting yer face dry with the towel instead of wiping it.

Mum used to give him a separate towel. It was her told him about patting instead of wiping because wiping makes pimples spread. His werent as bad as some. But he didnt have a heavy growth. Some guys did. Dark hair meant ye shaved more. If ye were black ye wouldnt go red at all. How could ye? Then with pimples, probably it disguised them. Ye wouldnt see them as easy if ye were black. He could never imagine that girl in the shop having pimples. Girls get pimples but ye dont think of it. Sarah. It was a good name. He liked her and he could imagine her; she had good lips. People have different lips. He saw his own in the mirror and what did they look like? Thin; thin lips. A guy he knew played the pipes and he had thin lips where ye might have expected thick ones. Because playing the pipes, it was what ye would expect. Some guys were horrible-looking; gross, the worst imaginable. Yet they had girlfriends; wives and children too. So they got kissed. Gay guys kissed each other. Everybody kisses and gets kissed.

When he dried his face there were spots of blood on the towel. The usual wee cuts round his chin and neck. He splashed on the cold water again, patted his chin dry. Dad had the television on when he appeared. He looked over. Murdo said, I was shaving.

Oh.

Murdo shrugged. He sat on the bed with his back to the top end. It was relaxing watching television, except Dad kept the volume low and there were no good programmes and the adverts were like every second minute, the voices droning on, but it was comfy, and thick pillows just like sinking in. Dad woke him later. Ye're better getting inside the sheets, he said.

Murdo undressed and got inside the sheets. A while passed and he was awake again. This time it was the middle of the night. The bedside lamp had been switched off. Although the curtains were drawn light came through the underside. He thought he heard voices. The television was off. One voice mumbling. Was it Dad? Was he praying? Murdo couldnt tell, not individual words. He didnt want to listen. Dad prayed when Mum died. Murdo didnt – except only before with the pain Mum suffered ye needed to block it out, how she held his hand, gripping it, because with the pain, gripping his middle three fingers like squashing them tight, the pain she was in. Please God make her not in pain, please God. But she was, except with the medication heavier and ye saw her eyes, poor poor Mum, inside her eyes, just like hollow, a hollowness. People said, Oh ye must pray. Murdo tried it before. Not after because what did it matter. People prayed at the funeral. What for? So they wouldnt die? Oh God please make me live forever.

The voice had stopped talking. It must have been Dad. Unless it was Murdo talking out loud. Or in his sleep so he woke himself up. That happened. Dreams woke ye up. Or nightmares. Or something between. Not dreams and not nightmares, and not like wet dreams or whatever, and not music although sometimes music but weird music just like systems and things to do with planets, alien worlds and spirit worlds; worlds for dead people. Stupidities all crowding in, crowding out yer mind; the last nonsense ye heard on television, the more stupid the better. Why did they not just shut up? Some voices Murdo hated and ye wanted to drown them out.

What time was it? Who knows.

Mum and his sister, Eilidh. What world were they in? A spirit world, always surrounding you and you surrounding it. You are within it but they are within you.

★

He was awake early next morning and lay on in bed. Only a minute then he was up and the clothes on. Dad was sleeping. He didnt want to wake him. The bus was not until mid afternoon so it was okay. Dad liked long lies. The same when Mum was alive, the two of them. There were times they didnt show until after eleven o'clock. It made ye think of something else. So what yer Mum and Dad? if it was sex; sex is sex.

Murdo slugged milk out the fridge and left it at that. Teabags and Sunday breakfast. On his way out he lifted a $10 note from Dad's money and clicked shut the door. With luck he would be there and back before he wakened.

The same five cars in the carpark. A clear blue sky. Already it was warm. So peaceful. What other day could it be but Sunday! Is there something beyond enjoyment! This was more than enjoyment! No cars hardly at all. He was hearing sounds but quiet ones; insects and birds. Definitely. Mum would have loved it.

The sensation that he was seeing everything but nothing was seeing him. The road was here and him walking it. Nobody else. Not Dad and not anybody. He didnt know anybody. He hadnt seen Uncle John and Aunt Maureen since he was a baby. He didnt remember them. Who else? Nobody. Except that lassie in the shop, if ye could say he knew her. But he did. Sarah. And she knew him. Ha ha, it was true, she knew he was Scottish, whatever age she was, maybe older than him, but not much like if she was seventeen; another couple of months and him too. Ye were a man at seventeen. People said that. Sixteen is a boy and seventeen a man. Oh what age are ye? Sixteen. Wait till ye're seventeen.

Would she be there? Maybe. Although late last night and now this morning: that was long hours to work. A girl like her who was very very good-looking and like just very very pretty, she was still a girl working. So if it was long hours that was the job. Otherwise get another. Ye needed money. That was him too, he needed money, he needed to work. So he needed to leave school. Things came back to that. It didnt matter America or Scotland.

He turned off the main road, going along the side street and hearing music, the closer he got, it was accordeon. A waltz. Jeesoh.

People say about their ears playing tricks. With him it was his brains and floating away someplace thinking about whatever he couldnt remember, maybe his sister was there. He never knew until he "woke up", although he wasnt sleeping.

Murdo and the music. Walking in the beat. The beat was him walking, walking in the rhythm. Going along the street and nobody else. This waltz playing; a nice one with a real good feel, that proper rhythm there for the dance; relaxed, yeah, that was the swing, doodilladooo. That feeling too he had been here already. Or was here already. Not talking about last night.

He approached the shop. It was open. Nobody at the entrance porch. Instead of stepping onto that he kept walking, following the music round the side of the building. A few trees were here, scrawny ones. He stayed behind them, so they wouldnt see him. An old lady, the accordeon player, sitting on a chair wearing a big hat and the girl out the shop – Sarah from last night – playing washboard, stepping from foot to foot. Another lady sat next to her, not as old, but quite old.

The old lady and the girl, it was great seeing them, something just beautiful about it, seeing the two of them there in the music. The accordeon itself; cream-coloured and as fancy as ye ever would see, light glinting in the morning sun, and that brilliant sound! What a sound! That was special. That was so special.

And the girl scrubbed it along facing the old lady who nodded her head on that two three beat rhythm, glancing around at the folk watching, smiling a little but only in the music, like how some musicians did that even when their eyes were shut. This lady kept on looking, seeing the people watching, keeping her eye on them. Murdo liked that. This was *her* playing, *she* was playing. She had her way and there she was.

Murdo didnt move in case people saw him. He was not hiding, only keeping out the way.

The other woman on the porch was not so old as the musician. But what age was that? Murdo didnt know. She had a hat on too, with a fancy sort of gauze stuff trailing down the back. She sat upright with her feet firmly to the floor, moving her right hand to beat time in a sharp movement like cutting or chopping; this was her right hand beating time but it was the three beats and her wrist jerking: flicking, cutting and flicking. She could have been on drums the way she was doing it; this rigour she brought to it, which seemed to set up a response like ye sometimes hear in music:

> I told ye so, I told ye so, I told ye so.

A lot of musicians did that. They played something to you and you played something to them; stupid things:

> you should know better, you should know better
> behave yerself behave yerself
> dont you start, I told ye; dont you start, I told ye
> Naw ye didnay, naw ye didnay. I told you, I told you.

That was the other musicians telling ye, giving ye a wink and a nod of the head. It was two-way. You were on the melody. Behave yerself. That was the rhythm. The rhythm was telling ye to behave yerself. Guys Murdo played with did a lot of that for fun. And it was fun. You liked it and so did the audience and the dancers danced and off ye go, the dancers danced and away ye go, tricka tricka tricka, tricka tricka tricka.

The song ended.

Murdo wondered what would happen but nothing did happen. Somebody clapped and somebody laughed, and the accordeon player spoke to people. This was a community place composed of back gardens running into each other; some had fences and some didnt. Kids played wherever; girls throwing a ball and a couple of boys horsing around. A dozen folk were sitting on chairs, dotted about the grass. A few were standing.

The accordeon player spoke a few words to the girl then it was one, two and away they went into another. This was an upbeat number with a real driving rhythm, but in that same style again.

But then it stopped. The old lady broke off out of nothing, and spoke a few words to the girl, then played in from a couple of lines before, and stopped again, and restarted, and off they went.

They were rehearsing! Of course! It was the real stuff. Ye knew that just by listening. It was so so obvious. This old lady was special! Jeesoh, man! Murdo was chuckling, and felt like laughing!

There was a lyric this time; the old lady on vocal driving it on and jees she really was something! God. . . And the way people responded to her. They knew. Murdo couldnt make out the words, then realized why: it was French! She was singing in French! Maybe some English. The girl and the lady with the fancy gauze hat were chorusing the line endings. It was a new kind of music for Murdo and exciting how it rocked along, that humour too, and funky, just brilliant for playing, and for dancing; the kids were jigging about. Murdo chuckled then was startled to find a guy standing next to him and right there in his face; angry-looking, so angry-looking. Murdo stepped back. The guy spoke in a low grunting voice. What you doing here? Huh? What you doing here? You shouldnt be here; this aint your place.

Eh it was just eh. . .

This aint your place. What you doing round here? What you spying on us!

The music had stopped. The guy stepped forwards and pointed Murdo out to them. People were staring. Murdo was embarrassed at being caught but was not spying if anybody thought that. Why would he spy? It was music. He saw the girl at the side and tried to smile but couldnt, but he called to her: I'm not spying.

Now she recognised him and she raised her arm. Hey! I know him! He came in the store last night.

This aint the store, said the guy.

Oh he's foreign Joel. Hear him talk, he's not American.

The lady with the fancy hat said: The poor fellow! Not American! Mon Dieu!

He didnt know about tax! said the girl.

Both women laughed. The guy who had caught Murdo was still annoyed but no longer angry-looking. He was older than Murdo but not that much.

Murdo shouldnt have been there at all because it was other people's gardens. He knew that. It was just the music. I heard the music. Murdo said, I was going to the shop. I heard it and just eh – I followed it round.

The two women found this funny. The accordeonist said: Hey now children he is enjoying my music. You think I didnt see him? I saw him from early. He's audience! You think I wont see audience?

She dont get that much nowadays, said the other lady.

The accordeonist raised her hand. I saw him the moment he come in these trees there! She studied Murdo: You like the music?

It's great.

Great huh! She gazed at him.

Yeah. He shrugged. I play too.

She continued to gaze at him. Oh now, she said, I know you play. I saw how you were looking. What you play boy Cajun? You play Cajun?

Eh. . .

Come up here! she said. Murdo went immediately to the porch. You Irish? she asked.

No eh, Scottish.

Scotland, said Sarah.

It's another country, said Murdo. It's near Ireland, and the music's like not too different I mean like eh. . . Murdo sniffed, and gestured at the older lady's accordeon. I would play, he said. If ye think I mean eh if ye wanted me to I mean. . . Murdo stopped, aware of Sarah watching him and he blushed immediately, tried to stop it but couldnt. Last night she was almost angry. Now she was friends and really she *was* beautiful. Her name too, Sarah, an old name. Old names were good. The name "Sarah" was right. As soon as ye said it ye knew it was hers.

The accordeonist made a comment in French to the lady with

the fancy hat, then studied Murdo. She nodded to Sarah: Go get
him a box honey, get him the turquoise.

Sarah went to the house behind the porch.

So boy what's your name?

Murdo.

Murrdo. She grinned, stressing the "r". Well now Murrdo my
name is Miss Monzee-ay: people call me Queen Monzee-ay. Can
you say that?

Queen Monzee-ay.

This here is Aunt Edna.

Welcome, said the other lady.

Queen Monzee-ay waved at the guy who had surprised Murdo.
He is Joel, he is my grandson. Sarah on rubboard is his sister. Sarah
is my granddaughter. So now you know us. So how come you are
here?

Well I was going to the shop like I mean the store.

No now boy I'm talking here, in this place, this town. This is
Allentown, huh? How did you come by here?

Aw, well, what happened, we missed the bus. Me and my father
eh. . .we missed the bus, like that's why. We're just passing through.

Aunt Edna clapped hands. Now he's got it!

Queen Monzee-ay chuckled. Sarah returned now. She was
wearing a hat; a daft round thing, but it looked good and made ye
smile to see. She held the accordeon out to him. The top she was
wearing didnt have sleeves so her shoulders were bare like last
night. Thanks, said Murdo. He took it from her, pulled it on and
touched the keys.

Queen Monzee-ay said, Now Murdo you play how you play.

The accordeon was tuned to B-flat. He hadnt played for a while
and his fingers were not flexing right. A strange sensation too like
the skin on his fingers was too tight or something and he was
wanting to widen the gap between the tips of his fingers and the
fingernails. People were watching but he was okay. They were
wanting him to play properly. He knew they were and he wanted

them to hear. That was that, he played a jig he had learned a few months earlier. He was still with the band at that time, before Mum's health deteriorated. It was fine, he knew it was fine. Some kids were here and he hoped they might dance. They didnt but it was okay anyway. Aunt Edna applauded: Bravo m'sieur.

Queen Monzee-ay said: Want to play it again?

The same one?

The same one.

Off he went the second time. He saw her preparing to play, then she did. In she came, she played a rhythm almost like straight into him. Brilliant. Murdo played the jig a little differently now; shifting ground was how he thought of it, but it meant him doing fast steps. Mum had described it as "capering". She enjoyed it when he "capered". He sometimes did it with the band, jigging about, just depending how it went and if he was taking the lead. If he was playing a jig he was doing a jig. That was how he thought of it. Ye were not just playing for the tune ye were in it. He did it here with Queen Monzee-ay, and she played into him. Her name fitted: a real Queen, real music, real style.

She played another of hers with Sarah on le frottoir – which was rubboard in French. It was a fast number, swinging, rocking. Just so good. Queen Monzee-ay looked for Murdo coming in like she had on the jig and he was ready for it. She was fast. Thinking of somebody old, she said how she was slowing; not her brains but her fingers. Murdo didnt think so, my God. Arthritis she said but it was a joke how she said it. She was not slow at all, not lightning fast but near to that.

Zydeco was the name of the music. Murdo knew nothing about it and had never even heard the name before. He had heard the name "Cajun" but not music so much as a place, like a land or a country, the "country of Cajun". But he had never heard the word "Zydeco" before.

Sarah was laughing, and that daft hat she was wearing, just so – how to describe it? Murdo didnt know except it made ye grin, make anybody grin. More like a sailor's cap. Back home ye saw rich guys on yachts wearing them. Sarah was great. She was fun. A real lassie just laughing. That was her! She was just like special! Ye knew it! Anybody would! The real granddaughter. She was Queen Monzee-ay's real granddaughter.

Queen Monzee-ay led in on another uptempo number, with a smashing chorus line where Sarah joined in, emphasizing the Frenchness. It was sexy how they did it and it made ye laugh, really, good fun:

> Ooo la la something something
> Com si com sa something something

And Aunt Edna too, whooping and clapping, her right hand beating time, wrist jerking, the flicking and cutting movements; shouting comments in French; all just kidding on, she was kidding on and kidding him on too. He knew she was. He didnt care. It was just the best, really, for Murdo it was the best fun and he hadnt had it for a long time, for a long long time.

At the doorway of the next house a man and woman appeared and were listening. Sarah came up close to Murdo: Mum and Dad, she said.

Queen Monzee-ay wanted one from him now and he played a Canadian waltz; from Newfoundland, the nearest part of Canada to Scotland. It had a cheery effect. Sarah's Mum and Dad danced to it. Queen Monzee-ay played a harmony line and at the end she said, Hey now Murdo, see what you can do with this one. And it was another good rocking tune of her own, she called it Fresh air does you good! L'air frais fait du bien! Just add the croutons, she called.

Midway through she stepped aside, keeping a rhythm and pushing for him to take the lead, urging him on. Show me show me. She may as well have been shouting. But it was fine and in he came, using a thing he had been working on a while ago. He knew it inside out and could do what he liked with it, jazzing it up with his take on this new way of doing it. It was fine, he knew it was. Queen Monzee-ay focused on his playing, giving the briefest of smiles. She came up close and laughed, You are the croutons boy!

He kept it going then caught her signal and stepped aside. She came in where the next verse should have been and ran somewhere else. It was brilliant what she did. Her playing reminded Murdo of a guy used to play mandolin in the band. He was only there a short period but for the time he was it was one of the best times ever they had. Where he led you followed. Where to? Anywhere. Wherever he took ye! That was where ye went. His playing led ye into it, and ye got there and just jumped off. Murdo loved that, and here now with Queen Monzee-ay. She was in that league; she brought it out. It was there in ye and she brought it out.

When they stopped for a break she and Sarah did funny curtseys to him and he did a stupid kind of bow. Queen Monzee-ay said, How long you been playing the box Murdo? She pointed at the turquoise. I'm talking that one right there. You played that one before. . .!

Murdo smiled, then replied, Yeah, it's kind of good.

So how long you been playing?

Well like since I was a boy, nine or ten.

Yeah.

I'm coming up for seventeen.

Old man huh! Queen Monzee-ay chuckled. Sounded good huh, two boxes?

Definitely. Two boxes is always like well special, it can be special.

Yeah. Yeah, it sure can. When it happens son but aint too often it happens. Session this morning now it's toward a thing we're doing two weeks from now. You know I am retired!

Sarah cried: Gran you're not retired.

Queen Monzee-ay smiled.

You're not retired.

Sure honey, I can do gigs, one-off gigs.

She got to be invited first, muttered Aunt Edna.

They all invite Gran, said Sarah.

Queen Monzee-ay winked at Murdo. Blood of my blood.

Sarah said, But they do invite you they all invite you. If you see on YouTube, you dont look but if you did, these old clips and what folks are saying.

I know. Queen Monzee-ay smiled.

They all want to invite you.

Yeah and the band honey, like this time too, they want the band alongside me. I said no to that. Queen Monzee-ay shrugged, and said to Murdo, I dont mobilize the boys nowadays except it's something worthwhile, and there aint much of that these days.

Zydeco dont travel, said Aunt Edna.

Oh we get around some, said Queen Monzee-ay.

Only they dont like to pay, muttered Aunt Edna. Oh please come please come; please come play for us Miss Monzee-ay you are a legend, an all-time star of the world; you are the Queen of Zydeco music. Only we cant pay you no money!

Queen Monzee-ay chuckled. She still gets angry!

Sure I get angry. You got to live on fresh air.

Sarah's brother Joel had brought them coffee on a tray. He also brought drinks for Murdo, Sarah and himself; fizzy stuff with ice and bits of ginger and green herb leaves floating, but tasty.

Oh Aunt Edna, said Sarah, tell Murdo about the band not getting paid that time like when you brought out the "piece"!

You tell him. Aunt Edna said, I need to smoke.

Yeah, said Queen Monzee-ay, taking off her accordeon and propping it against the wooden surround. She rose to her feet, massaging her side.

Both the older ladies smoked. They lifted their coffees and moved from the porch to where chairs were set on the grass. They sat there smoking cigarettes. An older man came to sit with them and they chatted, out of earshot.

Sarah continued the story: You know a "piece" is a handgun Murdo? Aunt Edna helped Gran and the band out sometimes, like on the road? Organising the money. Joel and me grew up on these stories and they are so wonderful. Our mother told us too, from when she was a kid. Gran took her on the road.

Jeesoh!

Yeah, said Joel. All over. That was Mum's education like dives and joints and blues clubs man Zydeco and jazz and like whoh! She like. . .man, that was her, that was her education.

Murdo laughed.

You play in a band? said Sarah.

Yeah well. . . Murdo looked at her.

You always want to play music?

Murdo shrugged. Yeah

She's a writer, said Joel.

I'm not a writer.

Yeah you are.

Sarah sighed, closing her eyes. I *want* to be a writer.

She's going to do the course, said Joel. It's like a college course?

Dad says I should go to New York City but Mum says it's too cold.

She means dangerous, said Joel. New York City is dangerous.

It's not dangerous.

Mum says it is. Dad too.

Oh yeah they want the west coast, but how dangerous is that, like LA? My God! They take pistols to class.

No they dont. Joel chuckled.

Yes they do.

No they dont.

I dont care, said Sarah, they got courses anyplace you want to name; Creative Writing Programs, and it's like anything you want; poetry and fiction-writing; feature movies; documentary you know like politics; even a novel, imagine a novel! Oh my God! Sarah danced a step, then paused and sighed. Gran lived on the west coast for years. Her and the band. . . Sarah sighed. Dad says I dont need to go anywhere, they got courses here in Mississippi.

Huh! Joel shook his head.

Yeah, said Sarah, but it's the program's important Joel and they got some closeby. Dad says so. Mum too.

Oh yeah, yeah, they just want you home.

Sarah was silent for a moment. How come you are here Murdo?

Oh. Well, yeah. . . Murdo frowned.

Like here in Allentown?

Yeah. I dont know, we just eh. . .we were traveling to Alabama and that is east really; so how come Allentown like heading south, yeah, I dont know. I looked at the map in the bus station and it was like how come we landed here if it should be east?

Didnt you know this was Mississippi?

Mississippi? No, I mean like not Dad either, my father, I dont think he knew either.

Sara and Joel grinned.

Dad's doing the directions. I think it was bad information up in Memphis like us getting a bus from there then like missing the bus here; even the bus driver I mean he was not helpful.

You missed the bus here? said Sarah.

Yeah well anyway who cares.

Queen Monzee-ay was watching from her chair, and she gave a wave. Murdo waved back, and got a bad feeling in his stomach. It sounded like he was poking fun at Dad and he wasnt. He didnt mean to. It was me anyway, he said. I forgot my phone so like for directions. Murdo shrugged. My Dad's fine, he said. Really, he's fine. It's not his fault at all, it's mine. Missing the bus was my fault like I mean not his. It's just eh we dont talk that much really, being honest. My mother died eh. . . Murdo smiled. Sorry, he said, just eh. . .

Oh Murdo, said Sarah.

He scratched his brow. Yeah, quite recent, so it's. . .it's been tough I suppose really, ye would say. Dad especially because like my sister. . .

Sarah was staring at him.

God, he said and breathed in. What I mean like she died as well sorry, I dont mean to be saying this like I mean sorry, it's a long time ago like I was only nine, jees I mean a long long time ago.

Oh God Murdo.

Yeah, she was only twelve. Murdo smiled, not looking at Sarah; nor at Joel, but away way over their heads, the heads of people; almost like he was floating, his voice coming from someplace else.

Sarah's hand was on his wrist. Oh Murdo.

He opened his mouth to take in air. Joel was looking at him as well. Murdo shrugged. Just to tell ye, he said, it was a tumour, like hereditary. Through the female line. Murdo bit on the side of his lower lip. Males dont get it, he said. So the likes of me, I'm okay and Dad I mean. It doesnt affect us. It's weird with Eilidh but – my sister – even just now, I open the door and it's like I expect to see her.

Murdo grinned. She's more of a pal. I think of her like that; a pal, a pal that died. Jeesoh, sorry. Murdo scratched his head. The turquoise accordeon was where he had left it.

He made a movement towards it, he wanted to play one for Sarah. Joel too but Sarah especially. Joel wouldnt mind; brothers and sisters. Brothers and sisters were fun. This tune too, it was a fun thing he had been learning; an old fisherman's song, just stupid stuff about being fed up with the cod-fishing and then getting married and being fed up with that too if yer wife was ordering ye about all the time, so ye were like glad to go back to the fishing again. And ye had to know what a cod was like: cods are huge! And wives, wives are wives but they are girlfriends too.

He reached for the box, pulled it on and started right in on it, playing right into Sarah so she had to step back, and she was so taken by surprise she kind of shouted and it made people look. Joel laughed. Murdo sang the lyric when he played it, jigging about on the chorus. It was how he practised too. He wasnt great on vocals and didnt do it much but on this one he did.

Across the garden he saw Queen Monzee-ay and Aunt Edna smiling and clapping hands. Four or five kids returned and joined in on the jig. Murdo moved them here and there threading a way between them like the Pied Piper. It was good fun. People liked it and him being stupid too when he was singing. It didnt have to be the right words; if he didnt know the real ones make them up, just make them up. Who cares! Long ago he learned that. Half the time he wasnt singing words at all

doo doo doo, dih doo doo doo,
dih dih doo doo doo doo,
la la la, lih la la la.

As long as he kept it going and didnt stop. Never ever. If he messed up someplace keep it going keep it going, and he kept it going, some way or another. The fast-foot dance maybe. He called it that. He made it up himself. Maybe not, maybe he copied it from somebody. He liked seeing other players and how they did stuff.

He did slow walks too. Some airs he played very still, not moving hardly at all, so people focused. They had no choice, ye forced them into it and they had to do it. For some tunes they had to listen; if they didnt they would never get it, and ye wanted them to get it, and people had to be ready for that, ready to listen. Ye saw good performers and that was what they did. They led the way for the audience, they brought them along. He liked seeing the old-time players because of that and ye saw all different ones on YouTube. Sometimes ye thought "crafty", oh that's crafty, that player's crafty and ye wanted to give him a wink – maybe the fiddler because ye knew what he was up to!

Queen Monzee-ay hadnt picked up the cream-coloured accordeon. He expected she might but she didnt. Sarah had gone to stand with her and they were talking. Murdo kept it going till eventually it wasnt right, it was not right, like a change in mood; something. The kids stopped dancing and were looking.

Dad.

Dad was there. He appeared from the same end of the store building as Murdo earlier on. Murdo broke off playing, It's my father, he said, and he took off the accordeon. He passed it to Joel. Dad arrived but kept his distance. Murdo went to meet him, aware of people watching. Dad said quietly, Do you never think? Not even sometimes?

Murdo nodded.

Ye disappeared.

I'm sorry.

Just yer usual.

. . .

Let's go. Right now.

Yeah.

Right now Murdo.

Yeah Dad I just need to say cheerio. Murdo turned away from him, aware of everybody watching but that was that and he didnt care. He crossed to where Queen Monzee-ay and Aunt Edna were sitting. Queen Monzee-ay smiled and reached to shake hands with him. Instead of shaking hands she held his wrist, and she seemed to press in her fingers, like her finger tips digging into his actual flesh, and she said, Well now Murrdo you are learning, you are learning good.

Murdo grinned and she pressed in even deeper, and he blinked.

Now you are okay, she said. You can come play with me anytime. You think you might ever want to do that?

Ha ha, said Murdo.

Queen Monzee-ay chuckled, and there was that fun in her voice on the "r" stress. More than fun. *Murrdo*. She was saying the name for him and marking him with it. It was him, he was Murdo. This is what she meant. Dad didnt grasp it because he didnt know. None of it, nothing. He just didnt know. Murdo saw Sarah there and Aunt Edna, Joel too; they all knew what Queen Monzee-ay was meaning. It was only Dad didnt. He thought he did but he didnt. That was the weird thing about Dad how he didnt know things, even after this time you would think he would know.

Mum would have known.

Strange how everything was stupid. It was something he felt a lot but just now was maybe the clearest ever it had been. No wonder he got fed up. Anybody would. Sometimes it made ye angry.

Sarah was looking at him. It was hard to look back. She was so straight and honest, so straight and honest. Ye knew that immediately.

Ye did. She enjoyed everything and was interested in everything and if you did something well then she was interested in that too. Her eyes shining, and sad, how she was looking at him. Was she worried? How come? He hoped she wasnt. He was fine, it was just normal; this was life, kind of stupid sometimes; him and Dad.

Sarah's father and mother were at the back door of their house, quite close to where Dad was standing. And foodsmells were coming, like good cooking, whatever. Sarah's father strolled over to him. Weird. Dad saw him and was not sure what to do. He was just being friendly. Dad stood there waiting. It was weird to see. Sarah's father said, Hey, I'm Henry.

Dad gazed at him.

I'm Sarah's father. He gestured at the back door of their house. We've prepared some food. You and your son are very welcome to join us.

After a moment Dad said, We cant. We have to leave, we've got a bus to catch and eh. . . Our luggage too, it's at the motel and eh. . .

You talking the Sleep Inn? They're friends of ours.

Dad frowned at Murdo.

They're good people, said Henry. What time's your bus?

Ten past three.

Okay, you got plenty of time huh. I can call them.

Eh. . .

You all can pick up the luggage later.

No. No. But thanks. We have to get ready and eh you know, but thanks for the offer.

Your son here's been keeping us entertained. Henry grinned. Now we got to feed him.

No, really, we have to leave eh we just eh. . . Dad glanced at Murdo but Murdo had his head lowered and maybe didnt notice.

Henry waved his hand at Dad in a relaxed manner. Why dont my son Joel drive you there right now, go right to the motel and pick up your luggage. Then you all can come back and have some food.

No. Thanks. We need to get on.

Henry nodded.

Come on Murdo! called Dad.

Henry stepped back a pace now. Dad had started walking. Murdo followed. Disappearing would have been better. Into thin air. But he couldnt and had to wave to people because how could ye not, he had to. He did a half turn and a semi wave, but a couple of steps onward he managed to turn properly and give a proper wave and this time smiled a proper smile.

Aunt Edna gave him a big circular wave in reply. This wave summed it up and how even she stood like shoulders back and just straight, straight standing. It was like laughing at everything, Aunt Edna was laughing at everything and it was like swearing inside yer head but next time it might be outside because ye would fight anybody, it was up to you. That was Aunt Edna. Murdo had been clenching his right fist: he relaxed and allowed his shoulders to droop; it happened with the box, ye took off the box and the shoulders drooped, ye let them droop.

Dad continued ahead. Neither spoke until on the street outside Dad said, We wont bother with the shop.

They carried on toward the junction then left along the main road to the motel, not talking. Nothing to talk about. Murdo knew what Dad thought. He knew completely what Dad thought. So what? Not only was Murdo stupid he was daft. Stupid and daft. That was that.

He might have expected a row. It didnt come. Only silence. He was used to silence. Silence was good. He wanted to say it aloud: Silence is good Dad silence is good. When I am with you I enjoy silence.

Except in his stomach again, like being a kid when ye have done something wrong; the nightmare: retribution, the punishment to come, waiting for it to come and it would come, sooner or later: definitely.

Although Dad was right. Murdo never thought things through. Why didnt he? Daydreams and fantasies. Doing things and not thinking about what it was, the thing ye were doing, what the hell was it? why were ye doing it? could ye stop? was it too late?

Was there something wrong with him? Why didnt he think?

Murdo was a person who didnt think. Were there people who didnt think? If so he was one of them.

Anyway, he didnt want to think. He was happy walking. It was the fourth time walking this street and he was getting to know houses by their paintwork and fronts; the ruts in the pavement and dangerous bits where the roots of trees appeared through the ground and could trip people up if ye lost concentration. That was Murdo, concentration, he didnt have any, it was just part of thinking; better off not thinking. Nothing about nothing.

Back at the motel he stayed outside the reception office while Dad was in finalising details. He strolled along to the room and waited by the front door. On the upper floor the couple were on their chairs on the outside corridor. The old man called down again: Howdy.

Hiya, called Murdo.

Dad had ordered a taxi in fifteen minutes. Murdo was ready in five. Food in the fridge from last night. Three slices of bread and a sliver of cheese. Dad had left it for him. Murdo just left it, he didnt want to eat. He wasnt being huffy. Just the idea, he couldnt stomach it.

Ye wondered why Dad would do something like that: saying no to Sarah's father. Murdo lifted his rucksack and slung it over one shoulder. Sarah's father had been friendly. Murdo's father hadnt been friendly back; the very opposite, not even polite. It was just embarrassing. Murdo should have told him to eat the bread himself.

That would have been cheeky. But better Dad eating it than leaving it behind. Good bread and cheese. Although the bread wasnt that good anyway, it had an unusual flavour and tasted sugary. The cheese would have made it okay.

Imagine an actual meal.

Saying no to an actual meal. Why would anybody do that? Murdo wasnt the huffy one there it was Dad. What point was he making? It had to be a point. It would have been good food too, hot food. Even just to see what it was. Different people ate different meals. Americans too so what would that have meant? Good gravy and mashed potatoes maybe, cabbage and peas. Sunday lunch. Roast meat and vegetables.

That was a real meal. Murdo and his father didnt have real meals. Not nowadays, not for Sunday lunch. They didnt have Sunday lunch. They didnt have any lunch; only like toast, and soup out a tin if ye could be bothered bloody opening it. They had their meal in the evening. It was usually okay. Sometimes they had a whole steak pie bought out the butcher. They halved it for Sunday and Monday. Dad did frozen roast potatoes and peas, sometimes carrots. There was usually a football match on television. Dad liked football. Murdo did too but not so much as him.

When they reached the bus station the taxi driver drove round the other side of the bus park area. There was a restaurant. A huge big place standing on its own ground. Menus were posted outside the door, long lists of grub, all different stuff. Dad peered inside through the restaurant window. It's busy, he said. He checked his wristwatch. He peered in again. I think it's too busy, he said.

Murdo saw in the window, saw empty tables. People were coming out the restaurant and others were going in. Mostly families, mostly black people. Round the side of the building Murdo saw two cars queuing for takeaways. There was a hatch to give in yer orders.

Do ye know what ye're having? said Dad.

Hamburger and chips. Are we not going in?

It's too busy.

Aye but it's big inside. There's empty tables.

I think we're better with a carry-out son, just to be on the safe side. I know we're in good time but ye never know.

Murdo waited by the front entrance while Dad placed the order, he strolled to the edge of the pavement. This street was parallel to the main road. If he crossed here, turned right and kept in a straight line, he would arrive at the Wild West shop and the pawnshop. The accordeon would still have been there. It wouldnt have sold since last night. Unless pawnshops opened on Sundays. Maybe they did.

When the food arrived they strolled round the block eating it. Dad didnt want to go inside the waiting room until the food was finished. They sat on a bench in the bus parking area. The hamburger was okay but the chips were the thinnest ever; not even crispy which would have made them bearable. The best bit was the bun. One of these wee pick-up trucks entered. Murdo watched it circle about. This place was reserved for buses. The truck reversed into the stance across the way. The horn tooted. The front passenger door opened and Sarah was there – Sarah! Murdo was onto his feet immediately. Dad it's Sarah! And Joel too Dad look it's me, it's me they're looking for!

Joel kept the engine running. Sarah saw him and sat back in the passenger seat leaving the door open. Murdo jogged across, laughing. She had a packet for him. A present of two CDs; one from her and one from Queen Monzee-ay. Gran was talking after you left, she said, about the gig. Would you want to sit in Murdo?

What?

She's hoping you will, that'd be so cool.

She had a locket round her neck. Had she been wearing it this morning? Murdo couldnt remember. Just seeing it made ye smile. Where did she get it? Who gave her it? Was a picture inside? Ye saw them on television programmes to do with antiques. Miniature photographs were locked inside. When she talked she held onto it. Dad thinks your father could organise it, she said. Joel?

Yeah, said Joel. You come down spend the night. We'll be with friends and they got room.

Murdo grinned, whatever they were talking about, the gig. He rubbed at the edge of his mouth.

Not next Saturday but the next again, said Joel.

Sarah said, I put a note in the packet there Murdo; got all the information. I wrote it in.

She paused. A guy in a bus-driver's uniform was striding towards them. Trucks and private cars werent allowed. Over by the waiting area Dad stood by the door. Sarah spoke quickly: Gran says you played special and you played it to her – that is what she liked. Means you can play together. Makes it rich. You bring that. Dad says your Dad could organise it for the one night. Come down Saturday, go home Sunday morning. It would be so cool if you came Murdo.

The uniformed guy jerked his thumb at the exit. Joel acknowledged him, and whispered: We got to go.

You think you might? asked Sarah.

Eh. . .

Gran says so. It's enough for her what you did this morning. She said you done enough and like you will do just fine. A friend is on guitar with us Murdo, just a wonderful guitar player, just the very best, so like the four of us Murdo, a one-off night for Gran. So so cool if you came, it would be wonderful Murdo, you will let her go, she said it, your playing, she can go someplace different.

Murdo scratched at the back of his head. Sarah reached her hand to his shoulder and gave it a wee sort of massage. His eyes shut in reflex. His face went red and he couldnt stop it, couldnt have stopped it. She just

like a zinging in his ears, it was just

The two CDs you got in the packet, she said, one is from Gran and it's got her songs, them we're doing. It's from what we did this morning and maybe a couple more but not like surprises, she said to tell you, no surprises, just like what you know Murdo, that's how Gran said it, the gig's all here is what she means; no surprises. That was to tell you.

Okay.

You think you'll come? It would be so wonderful.

Murdo laughed. But what was he laughing at? What even was he thinking? He didnt know that either. Sarah's touch. His face was still red. He stared at her: the way her hair ended by her neck and shoulders, just that way the neck went into the shoulder and became the shoulder, that curve there. The locket in her fingers, then just like how she touched him, that was Sarah, jees, even just like touching.

Sarah was waving. Joel had released the handbrake, was turning the wheel and giving him a wave at the same time. Joel called out the window: Lafayette man!

Murdo held the packet. Joel waved a kind of salute and it was like a pal saying cheerio, that was him going away on a long trip. And Sarah there waving but not like cheerio forever. They would meet again. Definitely. Otherwise? Never again in his life so like that was the two of them forever and ever. How could that happen? He had only met them for one day and it was like they were true friends. Terrible.

The same woman from yesterday had been at the information and ticket counter. Dad didnt have change for the payphone and she gave him the use of her own cell phone to make the call. But he got through to Uncle John. Now they could relax. Murdo didnt open the packet until aboard the second bus. The first had been a short trip to get them someplace bigger. This second one was the longest. It was the bus after that where Uncle John was meeting them. Dad read his book until the light made it difficult. Finally he closed his eyes. Murdo waited a few minutes. When Dad looked to be dozing he peeled open the packet. It contained two CDs and a hand-written note. But before he could read the note Dad opened his eyes again. Murdo slipped the note back inside the packet.

The bus was half empty too. They could have had double seats for privacy instead of sitting together. But that was Dad; double seats for yerself was too "risky"; maybe one of them was a secret trapdoor and if it opened ye dropped down under the wheels.

At least he was on the window seat. The roads were straight and long. Imagine yer own car. Ye could go anywhere. Get away from everything. The pick-up truck Joel drove belonged to his parents but it was his to use whenever he wanted. Okay it was for deliveries to do with the family store but he could use it for other things too.

A school pal of Murdo's lived on a farm and had been driving since he was twelve. He learned on a tractor. Other boys had been driving since they were young. Back home there was a forest track led through other tracks. As long as the mud wasnt too deep it was ideal for learner drivers. Although Dad's car would have sunk, it was too wee. It was a good track for mountain bike races. Murdo had been going it a while. It led round and down through the woods to the edge of the loch. Coming out from the high trees and bushland the water always looked great, but especially with the sun making it sparkle. There was a break in the bank here out from the trees and ye could see where they dragged a boat in the old days for ferrying. There was a half demolished pier at the harbour that was used for coal in bygone days. Boys fished off it although they werent supposed to. A great song connected to when a ferry crossed hundreds of years ago taking pilgrims to Iona. The ferry was more like a rowing boat. It only went when travellers wanted it. They had to signal from the other side. In winter they swung a lantern. The song was about a young guy called Lachlan Cameron getting hunted by Campbells. Murdo knew the song well. Really it was a pipe tune. The young guy was badly wounded and they captured him. They were going to hang him at the town of Inveraray where they hanged people for the government. Lachlan managed

54

to escape before they took him. He hid under an old upside-down hulk, a beached fishing boat at the head of the loch. One of the lasses from the village found him. She was out walking and heard his agonised breathing. She brought him food, even although he was a different religion; either a Catholic or Protestant and she was the opposite. After three days and three nights she helped him onto a rowing boat across the loch but she wasnt able to row him over for reasons to do with her own family. Maybe they were loyal to the Campbells. Whatever it was it meant she wasnay able to help Lachlan further. It was brave of her taking the chance and angering her own parents. The crossing is quite far but if ye were used to rowing and had a good boat then ye could manage it. But ye had to know what ye were doing. The water changes round there. Two lochs meet so the waters are deep and treacherous because of the currents and ye wouldnay want to swim. It was a wild wild night when Lachlan set out. If he made it to the other side he promised to send the lassie a letter. She never got a letter so Lachlan didnt make it and was never seen again. Did he escape to freedom? Maybe he rowed away someplace else and dragged the boat ashore, hid it in the bushes. It was easy done. There were thick thick woods where Murdo lived. Ye would just make sure ye had a good spot and a good landmark. The song ends without telling ye if he made it over. Did the boat sink? Did Lachlan drown? That was the story for the lassie from the village. She *knew* Lachlan was dead. Otherwise how come she didnt get his letter? If he was alive he would have sent it at all costs. But maybe not. Murdo didnt know whether the guy would have sent it. Maybe he wanted to turn up and surprise her. The worst thing for the lassie was if Lachlan sent the letter and other people got it and just burnt it without telling her. So he was alive and she never knew, and he never knew that she never knew but just maybe that she didnt want to hear from him again, she had found another guy. That is what he would think. It was a sad story. Except the wee cheery ending, because nobody found the rowing boat, so that was a hope. If ever Murdo had money a boat is what he wanted, above all. Never mind a car. . . With a boat ye could take off anyplace, anyplace at all, it was up to you, just wherever. Imagine a lassie too, like a girlfriend and she was coming with ye, there would be nobody there except you and you could just like whatever, even a swim, like nude, you could just dive in and that would be that, just her body and ye would be swimming together and diving down, her floating past ye and her nude body just stretching

It was dark now and ye could see faces reflected in the windows. A couple of folk had their individual reading lights switched on. Apart from that not much, country or town. Who knows where, he couldnt imagine anything, and didnt want to anyway, it was a waste of time. Dad wouldnt do anything.

Murdo took his head away from the window. He had been leaning against it to feel the cold, then the vibrations, he would end up travel sick.

The idea of the gig with Sarah and her grandmother. It was straightforward except with Dad it would never happen. Never ever. Ye could even feel sorry for him; sometimes Murdo did. In this life things go. What did he feel, right at this very moment? Life was ending or something. Because it was all just stupid how things happened. Ye met people then it was gone. A lassie like Sarah too. Lassies touch ye but when it's a certain way, just a certain way, ye just kind of like. . .it's something, ye could shiver. That was how she touched him. What did it matter anyway? It was gone and that was that. Only sometimes, Why me? That was what ye thought. Ye meet people and they have lives, but you dont.

TWO

Past midnight and deserted. They were seated on a bench at a bus-stop, luggage by their feet; the second bus dumped them here an hour ago. No bus station, just this bench at the outside wall of the drop-off point. Uncle John still hadnt arrived. There was an old payphone but Dad couldnt make it work. Maybe nobody could. He was back trying again. He managed the coins into the slot okay but whatever else he was doing it just wasnt happening. He saw Murdo watching and replaced the receiver, stepped away from it.

Dad will I try? asked Murdo.

Instead of replying Dad walked to the edge of the kerb and stared one way then the other.

But with payphones ye had to do everything in sequence. When ye put the money in and when ye dialed the number was important. Maybe Dad was doing it in the wrong order. Plus the area codes. It was only a wee town. Maybe ye needed to key in different codes like for cities closeby or else if it was a different state. Maybe it was. Then if there wasnt much light to see and there was hardly any light here; only one lamp, plus the moon!

Maybe Uncle John's car had broken down someplace. That happens. People get breakdowns. What if he had had one in the middle of nowhere?

Dad was still staring down the road. Maybe he hadnt heard. What did it matter, it was Murdo's fault anyway, them being here. That was missing the bus. Then disappearing this morning when he went to the shop and heard the music. If he didnt need the teabags he wouldnt have gone to the shop. So it was the teabags' fault. But it was Dad wanted them.

Murdo settled his elbows on his knees and pulled up the hood on his jacket although it wasnt cold. It was calm and peaceful. Ye noticed the breeze, that wee whisshh, whisshh. That is how calm it was. Just sitting there on the bench. That was good anyway, having benches. It was too wee a place for a waiting room but at least ye could sit down, then leaning forwards, yer elbows on yer knees and just staring at the ground, and the ground was like anywhere in the world. Ye could forget everything.

What happens when ye get mesmerised? The way sounds connect in yer brain. Ye hear sounds. Him and Dad on a bench and nobody walking past. A ghost town. People in their houses and all the doors closed. Windows all shut. Yet sounds were here. The wind at night blows in from the hills or from the sea. Thunder miles away and the sounds. What comes in yer ears? These wee passages and tubes.

Something does. Then what happens? Connections. Memories maybe. Not just memories. Ye go someplace in yer brain. Back home they lived up a hill at the back of the town and there were no sounds except country sounds: the fields and the hills; the forest, the river and the lochs; the sea itself. Lying in bed at night and ye cannot sleep and have to close the window: how come? oh it is too noisy! But the sounds arent loud it is only because ye hear them. You: you hear them. So ye just have to not hear them, then ye can go to sleep, instead of floating off in yer head.

A science teacher played the class music to do with rain and water. Big dollops of rain on a corrugated roof; soft pattering on a shallow pond; a rushing river; drip trails on a pane of glass. People were impressed but it wasnt as big a deal as all that. The fiddle makes the sound of a train blowing in from a distance, disappearing into nothing. A mouth organ did as good a train sound as a fiddle. Trains coming and going. Ye could do stuff on accordeon too, or plucking a guitar string. It depended who was doing it and what they were doing it for. But it was always people doing it: Take away the people and there wasnay anything. That included computerised sound-systems, multi-track mixing and whatever, it was still you had to programme it in. The teacher was right about that.

But it was obvious anyway. Trains never arrive any place. Only the person. A train is there and then it is there and inbetween it is there, and there, and there it is again because it doesnt go anyplace. A person never goes anyplace, it is only the train. The train moves and the person arrives. "Doh" starts and "doh" finishes. When ye get to doh ye arrive, ye have arrived. And take off if ye want!

That was Murdo right now, he felt like that. The world moves but you dont, you are still sitting there.

Music helped ye work things out. From "rain" to "train" ye added a "t". Then there was "tee" as in la tee doh. "Tee" is always getting someplace and never arrives, not until "doh". "Tee" needs the "doh". "Me" stands alone.

What sounds do people make?

The sound of Mum.

Did Dad make sounds after she died? Murdo didnt, he couldnt. Didnt because couldnt. Couldnt couldnt. Whoever could would. He couldnt. His head didnt work. Only for stupid stuff. What was a hospice? He didnt know. Imagine that. Ye have to be dying. The doctor tells ye, Oh ye have to go to the hospice.

But I dont know what a hospice is.

It means you are dying.

Oh.

Dad told Murdo the night he heard the news. Murdo had a night off from hospital and was fooling about with a couple of pals. He came home before eleven o'clock, intending to make toast and tea then skip upstairs to his room except Dad was waiting by the door, waiting for him. They sat down at the kitchen table. Dad wasnt looking good. He was trying to be okay but wasnt good at all. It was just like jeesoh ye knew something. Eventually Dad spoke. Mum's being transferred to the hospice. He stared at Murdo then gave a wee smile.

Oh Dad that's brilliant!

That is what Murdo said: brilliant. The exact opposite from what it was. He thought hospice was good. He thought it the next thing up from a hospital. He thought a hospice was where the patient went as the next stage in the recovery process. Go into a hospice and then go home after. Could ye get more stupid? How could a person be so stupid? So utterly utterly just the stupidest most stupidest

Dad didnt know he had misunderstood and it was about two days before Murdo realized the truth. Nobody told him. It was how people reacted when they heard him say it. It was like Oh God. . . And Murdo saw their faces.

Imagine seeing into somebody's head. A surgeon does it but only for bones, brains, arteries and stuff, not to see actual thoughts or hear what somebody is thinking. Inside the head is the skimpiest imaginable bit of noise, like the weest tiniest particle possible. It begins from a thought in the brain which sets off a vibration. These vibrations add to the noise of the world. Dad's too; sitting on the bench; this wee town in America; staring at nothing; his arms folded and mouth open – it was, it was open. Dad sat with his mouth open; an old man! He wasnt staring at nothing, but into the distance, the street out of town. In his head it was the same as in Murdo's: Mum and Eilidh. Dad and Murdo, Mum and Eilidh. Two and two: two alive and two dead.

At the funeral the Minister was talking about God's creation. Created and cremated: the letter "m" turned the live creation into the dead cremation. "M" for Minister, "M" for Mum, "M" for Murdo.

Some letters can be good. Murdo liked "b" and "s" and "z" but not so much "d"; "t" was okay. Dad was "t" for Tom. "M" for "mee" was good as in doh ray mee. "Mee" is a cheery note. Not for a death. Ye make that sound deep in yer throat; mmmmmmm, a humming sound, going on and on and on. It can last forever. But when the breath is gone the "m" is gone.

Murdo leaned his elbows back on his knees and sat forwards, staring at the ground.

Soon after came the police patrol car. This was the third time. It passed slowly, the cops staring at them, just like out a movie; quite scary. The car looked heavy and powerful. Probably they were suspicious characters. If they made a wrong move the cops would arrest them. If they tried for a getaway they would catch them easily or kill them. They would! If they thought ye were dangerous. Maybe ye werent dangerous but so what, if they thought ye were: bang bang, Aaahhhhh. Oh he is innocent. Sorry, I shouldnt have killed him.

A 4x4 approached. One of these solid big things, built like a tank.

Uncle John! said Dad.

It was. He had the window down and saluted them with his arm outside. Another man was with him. Both wore baseball caps. He did a U-turn, pulled up beside them and jumped out.

Tommy! Uncle John laughed loudly and grabbed Dad for a cuddle, slapping him on the back. It was strange to see. Dad just stood there but he was laughing too. He never gave cuddles except to women. Murdo didnt expect it either but the same happened. Uncle John grabbed him by the shoulders: cuddle thump thump thump. Then he stepped away, looking him up and down. Murdo Murdo I was expecting a wee boy for God sake what age are ye now, ye're near bigger than me! Jees Dave look at the size of him.

Dave was the man with him. Uncle John grabbed Murdo by the shoulders once again: cuddle thump thump thump: Tommy Tommy, what age is he! Honest to God I was expecting a kid! How old are ye son?

Sixteen, coming up for seventeen.

God love us! My own big sister's grandson Murdo that's who you are! She never made it but you have. Uncle John laughed then shook hands with Dad a second time. Tommy son I never thought to see ye. I feel weepy! He sighed, then introduced the other man. A good friend. Dave Arnott. Got the Macdonald blood in him. Eh Dave!

Dave smiled and shook hands with Dad then Murdo. Uncle John meanwhile lifted Dad's suitcase. Dad said quickly, That's heavy.

Uncle John gave him an amused look and hoisted it into the boot of the 4x4. Although much older than Dad he lifted the suitcase easily. Murdo made to shove his rucksack into the boot but Dad did so instead. Uncle John closed the boot and showed Dad into the front passenger's seat. Dave and Murdo were for the rear. Murdo sat on the side behind Dad. While they were finding the seat-belts Uncle John said: Tommy son, how in hell you ever end up in Allentown, Mississippi!

Dad sighed.

Uncle John laughed. One for the storybooks eh!

He drove in a relaxed way, chatting to Dad with one hand on the wheel, shouting occasional comments back to Murdo and Dave, while the radio played country music. He lived in a small town someplace on the outer regions was how he described it: I call it Scotstown. Every second person ye meet. Take Dave's family now the Arnotts, they been here since forever, eh Dave?

Couple of hundred years, said Dave.

Hear that? Puts us all to shame! Then you got Macleods, Macleans, Macsweens, Macaulays, Johnsons – Johnson's a Scottish name Tommy?

Yeah.

Just everywhere ye go!

Dave turned to Murdo. You got Arnotts and Macdonalds round where you come from?

Eh yeah, I think so.

The old Macdonalds! cried Uncle John. They were the ones with the farm; eh Murdo boy!

It was the Battle of Culloden that ended it for the Macdonalds, said Dad. They were forced to leave the country after that. They would have been wiped out otherwise.

Jees yeah! Hear that Dave? Wiped out! Then ye got the other one, Glencoe. Right Tommy?

Yeah. And before that the Covenanters.

The Covenanters! Uncle John called over his shoulder.

They got a homecoming two years from now! replied Dave.

When Dad didnt answer Dave Arnott looked to Murdo for a comment but Murdo was not sure what he meant. Dad was knowledgeable on history and politics but he wasnt.

Later no one was talking. Uncle John had increased the volume on the radio. It was for one particular song, loud on mandolin. Bill Monroe! he said. His people now they hail from the Outer Hebridee Islands Tommy, you believe that? Bill Monroe! Come from the island of Lewis. Uncle John started singing along on the chorus: I'm on my way to the old home, a place I know so well.

He knew the song but not the words and continued in a doo doo doo doo doo style. He stopped soon and chuckled. That's us Tommy son! On our way to the old home! Hey Murdo! You sleeping back there?

Nearly.

Nearly! Uncle John laughed.

★

It was past two in the morning by the time they arrived. Murdo enjoyed that drive. He didnt remember Uncle John too well but there was something about being here and traveling a road ye had never been before with this old guy from yer own family. Murdo's granny was Uncle John's big sister. That gave Murdo a nice feeling too, seeing the parallel with himself and Eilidh. When Uncle John spoke about his sister ye could see how much she meant to him. His own wife was Aunt Maureen. Murdo met her back when he was wee but couldnt remember anything about her. Her and Uncle John had two sons living in other parts of America: first cousins of Dad.

Aunt Maureen had gone to bed but left sandwiches for them

on a plate. Uncle John put on the kettle for tea. Dad just sat there, he looked exhausted. Murdo said, Mum would have loved it here Dad wouldnt she.

Dad smiled.

Uncle John was Dad's relation by blood but Mum would have loved the adventure. Plus the house; detached bungalow-style with a basement, comfy and with wee ornaments and fancy-looking things. All of it, Mum would have loved it.

Murdo was put in the basement. When Uncle John told Murdo he said, Great. Uncle John laughed and slapped him on the shoulder. Aunt Maureen had guessed he would choose that because it was what boys liked.

But for Murdo it was only because it was out the way of things and he could relax and not have to bother about stuff. There was one big room and two wee ones and the stairs down opened into the big one. A mattress was on the floor but Aunt Maureen had prepared it like a bed with sheets and a duvet, and left two towels neat and folded on top of it. That was the towels. Ha ha to Dad. People gave ye towels if ye were a guest.

With his two sons long gone Uncle John wanted to develop the basement properly. He hadnt got round to it yet but would in the future. A question of time, he said. Most of the space was taken up with furniture and stuff; cupboards, wardrobes and different types of tables; big polythene bags bundled together. Uncle John had shifted stuff to create space for Murdo roundabout the bed area but it was difficult to walk without banging into something, and the same in the two small rooms adjacent. But it was still good, and private too: Murdo liked that.

Dad had brought him a bottle of whisky as a present. Uncle John examined the label: Very nice indeed. I'll enjoy this. He stuck it away into a cupboard and brought another one out already opened. He poured wee ones for him and Dad and added a drop of water. Yeah, he said, you got relations everywhere Tommy. Now Molly Mulhearn, my own mother's first cousin, we called her Auntie Molly, ever hear of her? she was a great old character.

Uncle John carried on talking. It was good interesting stuff but Murdo was too tired. The thought of getting into bed! Dad too must have been tired. And what about Uncle John himself? He had been working all day then come to collect them, and tomorrow morning it was back to work – in six hours' time! How do ye cope? asked Dad.

I'm used to it, he said.

Murdo smiled, smothering a yawn. Although past retiral age Uncle John had worked in the same full-time job for years, and traveled long distances. It had to do with maintenance, warehouses and stores, and clean bright offices too; factories and stores and a long long way away but nice because fields and valleys and clean bright offices, warehouses and the stores, he hadnt been able to get time off with the high maintenance, working weekends and all sorts was a sore point. Here they were, Dad and Murdo, and Uncle John was having to work. He had tried and tried but they didnt let him. Ye would think after all these years but no, they couldnt manage without him because like high technology was high maintenance, if ye couldnt go right it was disasters all round to do with everything, just everything and it was only him knew the ins and outs. Uncle John had stopped talking. Murdo opened his eyes and smiled. Uncle John was grinning. Away to yer bed son, ye're out on yer feet.

I was just. . .

Ye were snoring!

I wasnt, I'm fine.

Away ye go.

Okay.

Dad smiled, he was sipping at his glass of whisky. Uncle John rose from his armchair and gave Murdo another cuddle thump thump thump. Take a sandwich and a glass of milk down with ye, he said.

Are ye sure?

Oh never say that in this house son! Aunt Maureen left them

67

there to be eaten so ye better eat them. Ye're in yer own house and ye've got to remember that. She'll give ye what-for if ye dont! Ever heard of Geronimo?

The Indian Chief, said Dad.

Now ye're talking Tommy that's yer Aunt Maureen! Uncle John sat back down and lifted his whisky.

Murdo was glad to get downstairs and close the door. He ate the sandwich then undressed, put the glass of milk at the side of the mattress, switched off the lights and was in between the sheets immediately.

Where was the glass of milk? The dark was so intense. His eyes adjusted eventually. Only the one wee window, high up where the wall met the ceiling.

There was an old smell too. Maybe dampness. And a constant sound like wind swirling faraway, then a rushing sort of hollow noise, making ye think of outer space; these stories where the astronaut is sucked out the door and into orbit; currents of wind sucking ye out, except maybe ye dont get that in space, if everything is just the same then how can there be wind, there isnt any and there cannot be any. Or else things would move. Everything would move. But everything does move, everything does move, roundabout you. So it is the opposite of the wind, the wind inside out and you just filling a gap, sucked in filling a gap.

★

He was staring at the ceiling, staring at it for ages not knowing anything. But then was looking about. Wherever he was, he remembered; and pulled the duvet to his chin. Sunlight through the wee high-up window at the ceiling, a narrow strip of window. Up at ground level. This was the basement. Here they were. They were here! Murdo was out of bed at once, pulling a wooden chair to beneath the window. Not much space to walk. He stepped up on the chair to peer out but would have needed a step ladder to manage.

The one drawback: the basement had no toilet. He had to use the bathroom at the top of the stairs; the one for the main house.

The packet given him by Sarah lay next to the rucksack. Inside was the note and the two CDs. The one by Queen Monzee-ay and her band was a "greatest hits" compilation. The other was a selection of stuff. Murdo switched on the light to read the note. The gig was a week next Saturday at a place called Lafayette, 9 p.m. and the venue was the Jay Cee Lounge, which sounded like a bar, but that was okay. Murdo unpacked the rucksack to see what clothes he had brought. Probably not enough. Jeans and two shirts, joggers and T-shirts; a pair of shorts that did for swimming; underwear and socks. His idea was to wash stuff for the second week. He folded and stacked his clothes on top of a cupboard.

He had no idea of the time except he was starving and needed the toilet. When he opened the basement door he heard voices drone. He went upstairs but the bathroom door was shut and somebody in showering, probably Dad.

The voices came from the open-plan kitchen/dining area which was enormous compared to back home. But only Aunt Maureen was there, behind the kitchen counter watching television while preparing food. A weather report was showing. She became aware of Murdo suddenly and she laughed and came to meet him. Oh Murdo!

He laughed too like as if they knew each other already. But they did, they did know each other. You are Murdo, she said. Of course you are!

He made to shake her hand but she gave him a great cuddle instead, then stepped back to look him up and down. My Lord, she said, you are the spitting image! You are. She cuddled him again. You are the spitting image!

Who of? asked Murdo.

Everybody! My! How long since I seen you now son huh? What are we talking here is it ten years?

I think it's eleven.

Eleven. My Lord and you are the spitting image!

There was a choice for breakfast. He took a banana and a plate of cornflakes. There was a big table in the dining area but also stools at the counter. Murdo said, Will I just eat here?

Sure.

Murdo sat on a stool. Aunt Maureen chatted between doing her work and watching the weather report. This television channel was devoted to the weather and nothing else. All different aspects of that. But it was interesting. Hurricanes were coming in the direction of Florida. Real hurricanes. They could cause bad damage to people. They got it tough down there, said Aunt Maureen.

In Florida?

Oh yeah.

Murdo hadnt known that. Usually Florida was a holiday destination. People with money went there for their holidays. So this was new information. He hadnt realised how big America was. Amazing difference in temperatures. It could be 130 degrees someplace then minus degrees someplace else. Blizzards and heatwaves, tornadoes and torrential rain. In California they had a place called Death Valley. Temperatures there were the hottest of all. Death Valley. You could go and visit. One of Aunt Maureen's sons lived in California and had kids of his own, so her and Uncle John were grandparents.

Murdo had thought she was Scottish but she wasnt. Her family was American "from the beginning". Except going back further, yes, they were some kind of Scotch-Irish people. I dont bother too much about that, she said, except if I know them or if it is somebody's folks but not like old ancestors from way way back. So how about you now Murdo, how was your traveling, all the way from Scotland, how did you do that?

We went on the plane via Amsterdam in Holland.

Holland huh!

Then to Memphis here in America.

But you got a boat someplace?

Yeah, where we live it's like an island. It isnt but it's like one, ye need a ferry over to the mainland. Then the train to get the plane.

Well now there you are!

It was a long journey.

Sure it was, said Aunt Maureen. The place we would like to see now your Uncle John and me, that's Hawaii. We were on the west coast last year visiting the children; drove up Seattle way, my Lord, the sunset there huh, it was just so pretty, that's the ocean. Got talking to folks and they said about Hawaii, how we would love it down there.

Hawaii! said Murdo.

I been three times to Scotland, huh. Three times. Yeah. No one ever come here. Never. You and your father now you are the first. Aunt Maureen frowned. You surprised about that?

Yeah, I am.

Well it is true son and I wonder about it too. I dont say it to your uncle but I do.

Murdo heard a door closing. That's Dad out the bathroom, he said and got up off the stool and went through.

He returned to finish his cornflakes. Aunt Maureen was watching the weather channel. Gale force winds and a coastal town; huge waves blowing in over a wide road, guys taking selfies, jumping out the way of the water. A woman talked into the camera about damage to roofs and trees snapped in half and smashed onto cars crushing people. A total nightmare. Murdo carried his empty cereal bowl to rinse clean at the sink. You dont do that, said Aunt Maureen.

Murdo grinned but upturned the empty bowl on the draining board. He said, Is it okay if I go outside?

Huh?

Is it okay if I go outside?

Son you go where you want. This is your home and your family. You go ahead and you just do it. Dont go asking me.

Thanks.

No thanks about it.

It was bright in the dining area. Glass doors led from there to the patio and garden. He swallowed the last of his orange juice, rinsed out the tumbler and upturned it next to the empty bowl. Aunt Maureen, he said, I think people would love to come here. Honest. They would love to come. It's just they cant afford it. It costs too much money. Otherwise they would. They definitely definitely would. It's smashing here.

Aunt Maureen smiled.

Honest.

I hear you Murdo.

The dining room doors opened directly onto a wooden patio. He headed outside. It was a good size of a garden, bounded by hedges tall enough to block off the neighbours' view, but cluttered with junk; old-style garden furniture and children's outdoor toys mainly, including a chute and swings, and a scooter and a bike with a wheel missing. There was an old garden shed too whose roof looked set to collapse. He prowled around. A football. What a find! It needed air but could be used. He kicked it around, tried a few keepy-uppies but soon stopped. So very warm and with the clear blue sky. Ye forgot about the sun how good it felt. This garden was so so different from Sarah's but enjoyable in its own way. Ye would appreciate the privacy too, if ye wanted to sunbathe, and it was good for that here, definitely.

★

Murdo had returned downstairs and shoved on his swimming shorts. It was a new pair bought for coming here and they acted like ordinary shorts as well as for swimming. Between two cupboards in the corner of the room he found a stack of books on the floor by the wall. The first one he lifted was cowboys and indians and it looked interesting. He took it upstairs. Aunt Maureen found a huge towel for him. More like a blanket. He had to pass Dad outside on the patio. There was like a roof here; spars of wood across the top gave shade. Dad was at the table reading.

Down by the far hedge Murdo spread out the towel on the grass, took off his T-shirt for a tan and lay down on his front.

Dad hadnt noticed him anyway. Although maybe he had and it just didnt register. When Dad was reading he switched off from everything. Murdo didnt. He wished he could. His concentration wandered for nothing, away thinking about stuff, until then he "came to": Where am I? Dad tried to get him to read books. Once he started he enjoyed it but it was just starting. The one he brought from the basement was good. Okay, cowboys, but a not bad story and he was quite enjoying it: Cherokee Indians and settlers.

After a while Dad called: Alright there!

Hi Dad, yeah!

Watch out for the sun!

Okay.

Too much of it isnay good.

Yeah.

They went back to reading again, then Murdo stopped and lay on his back, shielding his eyes from the sun. Later Aunt Maureen appeared from the house and called him onto the patio. A tray of sandwiches and a coffee each for him and Dad. Usually he didnt drink coffee. The smell put him off when he was young and he hadnt quite got over it. The only thing worse was cigarette smoke. He opened the slices of bread to see inside. Cheese salad.

Dad waited until Aunt Maureen had gone, and smiled. What ye looking for inside the sandwich?

I was just seeing what it was. Cheese salad. . .

So what would have happened if it wasnay a cheese salad, would ye have sent it back to the chef?

Murdo smiled, but Dad lowered the book. Seriously? he said. I know it's just a habit.

Well that's all it is.

Some habits are good son but some arent. The bad ones are there to be broken. Somebody gives ye a sandwich ye dont open it up to see what's inside. Know what I mean? It's actually bad manners. Think about it.

Murdo sniffed. Dad resumed reading. Murdo lifted the sandwich and the coffee, about to return to his spot in the garden. He hesitated then sat down at the patio table. He didnt want Dad thinking he was huffy. He bit into the bread. He wasnt even hungry but Aunt Maureen made the sandwiches especially. He had to eat one. Anyway, better for cleanliness to eat at the table. That would be Dad. If ye dropped crumbs at a table ye could wipe them up whereas in the garden, if ye dropped them on the grass ye didnt see them again.

Although birds came to peck. That was good if ye fed the birds. But what about the crumbs that landed on the earth? causing wee tremors. Insects would feel it. As soon as the food landed that would be them. The earth tremors would tell them. Hundreds of insects arriving from miles around; there they were, heads poking out the soil: snap snap snap. If they missed the grub they ate one another. Insects didnt worry. Did they even know who was who? That's my granny I better not eat her. Or if it was a lower species of insect, they would eat them. Insects fed off one another.

Dad had finished his sandwich and lowered his book onto the table. He lifted the coffee. I take it ye're not missing school!

Ha ha.

Dad was smiling.

I never want to go back. I dont Dad. I really dont.

Aye well there's things we have to do in life Murdo, we dont always want to do them.

Not school though.

School. Work. You go to school I go to work.

I want to go to work.

Dad sighed.

74

I do. I want to go.

Ye will soon enough.

Aye but Dad I really want to, really. I do.

So ye keep telling me.

Because it's true.

Dad shifted on his chair, raised the book and gazed at it for several seconds, then lowered it. Where's all this come from? he said. Ye've only got a few months to go and that's you.

Dad

Less than a year.

Murdo groaned.

One year.

Dad it'll no work like I mean it wont.

What ye talking about?

Me at school Dad it's not working, it's hopeless.

Oh God.

It's me. I'm just like – I'm hopeless.

Of course ye're not hopeless. Ye're not hopeless at all.

I am.

Ye're not. What ye talking about?

Well what I mean I'm not able to do it. I hate it. I really hate it and I just – I cant do it. I wish I could but I cant.

Ye're bright enough.

Dad

Ye're only repeating this year because how things have been at home. It's nothing to do with being stupid or hopeless or some such nonsense, it's because of what's happened, it's because of like just. . .the past year and Mum being ill Murdo. Just stick in. Stick in. Ye'll catch up.

I wont Dad.

Ye will. Then next year it's college.

Aw Dad.

Ye're only repeating this one year. That's all.

Dad

Naw. No more.

Dad I'm only saying

Dad groaned. He looked at Murdo. Murdo shrugged. He lifted the remains of the sandwich and stood, shifting back the chair. He didnt feel like the coffee but took it anyway.

Dad said, Watch ye dont burn. It's into the mid eighties.

Murdo nodded, returned to his spot on the grass. Dad glanced across but Murdo pretended not to notice, lifted the cowboy book and lay down on the towel. He stretched out on his front, the sun on his back.

He turned to his page in the book. It was good having an actual ordinary book and ye just marked a page and whatever. Quite an interesting story too. But he wanted back down the basement. Except if he went it was being huffy. It wouldnt occur to Dad there was a reason, like music, thinking about music. Okay if he had a headset or something but when ye had nothing, jeesoh. Really it was playing, he needed to play. He really did and he couldnt. He wanted to and he couldnt.

That was Dad: Ye cannay bring the accordeon.

How come! How come he couldnt? How come Dad didnt let him? What was the big problem? It was just stupid. It wasnt like Dad had to carry it. God, just bloody hopeless. He got up from the grass and left the book on the towel, strolled past the patio and through into the dining area; whatever Dad would think, who cares, he would think something.

★

Uncle John returned from work near 6.30 p.m. Dad had gone to his room a while ago. Murdo was helping Aunt Maureen lay the dining table. Back home he cooked most of the weekday meals. Sausages a lot of the time or beef mince; potatoes and peas, beans. Dad did it Friday nights and the weekends. Friday night was fish and chips Dad bought out the chip shop. Most meals they ate on their laps watching television. Here Aunt Maureen laid out the dining table. Different food in bowls so ye could help yerself; meat and vegetables, piles of potatoes. If ye wanted more ye could get it and it wasnt a fuss. If ye wanted bread ye could take that too. Different from the bread back home but better tasting than the stuff from Sarah's shop.

During the meal Aunt Maureen flitted between the dining table and kitchen but took part in the conversation. She was a brilliant cook. She acted like she wasnt but she was. She called it home cooking but what else would it be? Ye lived in a home and ye had the cooking so it was home cooking; food ye could eat and just relax.

Dad and Uncle John were drinking wine; Aunt Maureen and Murdo had orange juice and water. Dad wouldnt have minded if he had asked for a glass. A wee one would have been fine but just now he was more thirsty than anything. Uncle John was talking about the early days and how life was okay around here even when things werent so elsewhere. Work hard live good. It's how it's been since I got here all them years ago. How long mother?

Thirty-eight years, replied Aunt Maureen. I met you thirty-seven; we been married thirty-six.

She's the brains in this family!

People got two jobs, sometimes three. Aunt Maureen pointed at Uncle John. He always had two.

Uncle John shrugged. It's the work deal round here.

Not always it aint.

Well most always.

The boys were little you had three.

Is that not a lot? asked Murdo.

Tell him that, said Aunt Maureen.

Uncle John was aware of Dad looking too. Well sure three jobs, if that's what it takes. Nobody comes in forcing ye; ye want to work ye work. Bop till ye drop Tommy boy ye just get on with it.

Dad smiled. Uncle John paused, about to add something, changed his mind and sipped from his glass of wine. He glanced at Aunt Maureen. I wouldnt have called that one a job now if you're talking the bread delivery truck.

So what would you call it mister, huh? You drove all night through. Me and the boys never saw you.

One nightshift! That's the job she's talking about, one nightshift.

Every Saturday night Sunday morning. Twelve hours straight you worked, so dont tell me.

Uncle John grinned, jerked his thumb in Aunt Maureen's direction.

Oh yes now you gotta make fun of it; seven days out working.

It was only for a year or two. Uncle John winked at Murdo. Young family son, your Dad knows what I'm talking about.

Three jobs, said Aunt Maureen, we hardly saw him.

Uncle John reached for his wine and gestured with it to Dad. Dad raised his own glass in reply, and they clinked them. Uncle John looked to Murdo: Sláinte mhath son.

Sláinte mhath, said Murdo.

They clinked glasses. Aunt Maureen joined them. Dad raised his glass again, and gestured to Murdo to raise his: they held them aloft. Dad said to Uncle John and Aunt Maureen: This is just to you two, from me and Murdo, thanking ye both for having us here.

Definitely, said Murdo.

Och away and behave yerself! grunted Uncle John.

Naw, said Dad.

It's a real pleasure for us, said Aunt Maureen.

Dad was looking embarrassed. He noticed Murdo watching him and smiled. This was the most relaxed Murdo had seen him for ages. Murdo felt it himself. Here ye were free to relax. Back home ye werent. Back home was the house and everything in it. Everything. Every last thing. Everywhere ye looked it was Mum not being there and ye could not get away from that. Never. How could ye? Never ever.

Dad was looking at him. Murdo raised his head.

Uncle John and Aunt Maureen were in the middle of a conversation. Something about Uncle John not getting the time off. No need to raise that now, he said.

Yes there is. Aunt Maureen turned to Dad. He walked into that office Tommy, he confronted them. Huh! That is what he did. He let them know what he thought. After twenty-two years! Huh! They wouldnt give no proper time off! His family from Scotland! No now dont you tell me! said Aunt Maureen to Uncle John. Mister, you are hurting!

I'm not.

You are hurting.

Bloody hurting, I'm not.

Oh now!

Sorry, but I'm not.

Aunt Maureen shook her head. Them boys coming here and you not being around. . .!

I will be in the evenings.

They dont make it easier for you is what I am saying. Lord knows they could help it along, but they dont, no sir.

Why not? asked Murdo.

Why not huh? That is a fine question son. You say it to him and he might listen. I say it and I am a critical woman.

Uncle John winked at Murdo. Aunt Maureen stared at him. Finally he said: Three times I went into that office. Three times. They still didnt give it; said they needed more notice.

More notice huh!

Because it's a busy time.

In there's always a busy time.

I'm just saying what they told me.

The favours you've done them!

Eventually Dad said, It's being here that's important. I'm not interested in rushing around places. It's having the break; relaxing. Sitting in the sun. We dont get any sun, where we come from!

It's true, said Murdo.

So dont go worrying about us. I dont need to go any place except here where I am. I'm here and it's great.

Uncle John nodded. We'll see, he said, we'll see. He smiled suddenly. Ever hear of the Cumberland Gap?

Yeah, said Dad.

They wrote a song about it, said Aunt Maureen.

Uncle John winked. Her family!

Now it aint my family mister but I know what you're thinking!

The conversation continued on family matters; old people from way back. Dad knew some of their names. Back home he hardly ever spoke about his family so it was interesting to hear. Murdo knew much more about Mum's side because she used to talk but Dad hardly ever.

They helped clear the table, passing the things to Aunt Maureen who stayed behind the kitchen counter, emptying bowls and arranging leftover food inside the fridge. She piled the crockery and cutlery into a dishwasher. Dad made a joke about back home him being the dishwasher.

They moved out to the patio before it got dark. Uncle John had returned into the house and came back carrying a tray with two beers, two tumblers of whisky and a jug of water. Before long Murdo's arms were itchy; him and Dad both. Dad was scratching his head too. Mosquitoes. They were here first, said Uncle John, them and the Cherokee Indians.

Dusk's a bad time, said Aunt Maureen, you got to cover up your skin. Bare arms are no good.

Uncle John shared out the drinks with Dad. You want some orange juice? he asked Aunt Maureen.

No we dont, she said and lifted her teacup, winking at Murdo.

Does he drink a beer? Uncle John asked Dad.

Dad said nothing. Murdo answered, I'm happy with orange juice.

Good for you, said Uncle John.

He's a boy, said Aunt Maureen, you're forgetting that.

Well I'm not forgetting it. Uncle John pushed a beer to Dad. Trouble with this place, he said, ye need a car. You should've brought yer licence Tommy! Then ye could get out and about.

Dad shrugged.

What about buses? said Murdo. Is there no buses?

Uncle John smiled. If there are son nobody knows!

So do people just walk?

They do that slow running kind of thing, said Aunt Maureen.

Power walking, said Uncle John.

Not power walking mister that's fast walking.

Jogging.

Aint jogging. I dont know what you call it. I see them doing it at the mall. Round and round they go. They dont buy nothing, they go there for the walk. They all got partners.

Partners? said Murdo.

Yes sir. They go in two's. Three's a crowd son that's the old saying. Aunt Maureen chuckled. My Lord!

Uncle John laughed. Dad was smiling. Uncle John raised his glass but instead of sipping the whisky he stared at Dad: Why didnt ye all come those years ago, when ye had the papers and everything? Uncle John waited a moment. It was your father.

You talking about when I was a boy?

Yeah. Your mother would have come. It was him made that decision. She didnt get the chance. Uncle John sighed. I know she would have come Tommy. You know why I know that? Because she told me. Uncle John sat back in his chair.

Aunt Maureen said to Murdo, Your mother was a lovely person.

His grandmother, said Dad. She was Murdo's grandmother Aunt Maureen. She was my mother.

Oh of course she was Tommy I am so sorry! Yes and she was a fine lady. She took us to church. That was the parish church and it was Scottish Presbyterian right there in Glasgow.

Well where else would it be? chuckled Uncle John.

She was good fun, said Murdo. I remember her.

Dad glanced at him. You were only a child.

Yes but I remember her.

Do ye?

Yes Dad, really. She made me laugh.

Aunt Maureen was quiet a moment. That is a beautiful thing to say. I hope somebody says it about me.

Och of course they will, said Uncle John.

She's in a better place now. Aunt Maureen reached to Dad to hold his hand, and she stroked the back of it. Like your own sweet girl, the good Lord knows, she's walking with Jesus.

Dad hardly moved, except his shoulders a little. Uncle John swallowed a mouthful of beer.

She is, replied Aunt Maureen.

Uncle John smiled when Murdo glanced at him. When Aunt Maureen said "girl" she wasnt meaning Eilidh it was Mum, Mum was Dad's girl, his girlfriend, his wife. The one "walking with Jesus" was Dad's mum, Murdo's granny.

Murdo hadnt thought of it before, just how close they were, Dad and Uncle John, and Aunt Maureen.

Uncle John patted Murdo on the side of the shoulder. You've had hard knocks Murdo boy, that's what ye get in families. So you got to stick together. Folks get hit by things, tragedies and whatnot, they stick together.

Aunt Maureen peered at Murdo. Oh now he is like his mother?

You talking his mother or Tommy's?

Both, she said.

Uncle John laughed and she did too but it was how Dad laughed! That was the real amazing thing. Dad just burst out with it like a real actual laugh! The three of them laughing away. Murdo laughed seeing them. Uncle John went off talking about some old guy, a distant cousin. Alabama in the old days. Kentucky too, where Aunt Maureen came from. Then a bird landed on the grass a little way down. It walked about. Not hopping, walking. It was weird-looking, with a long tail and a bluish purple colour. Uncle John was saying about another of the old relations, Uncle Donald, who married a woman from Knoxville called Molly.

Related to the Mulhearns, said Aunt Maureen, their daughter married a Gillespie and moved to Arizona.

He was a character, said Uncle John.

He was a mean nasty old man. That's why his family left; soon as they were old enough.

He had a hard life.

Huh! Aunt Maureen shook her head.

He did.

Dont go excusing him now you know how he was to that poor woman.

Yeah and I'm not excusing him. Uncle John continued on about Uncle Donald and how he was and Aunt Maureen too, who knew the old woman involved. Dad was listening, and seemed to know the people or maybe had heard of them or something and was enjoying it in that relaxed way Murdo hadnt seen for a long while.

That bird was still there, pecking about in the grass. It had a strange face. At the same time ye could see how the face of a bird can be like the face of a human. There was a famous painting of a man with the head of a bird. This one had bright eyes squinting about. Squinty and sharp equals mean and nasty. Maybe it was a human thousands of years ago. Some believed the spirit of a dead person flitted into an animal, a bird or a fish. Or an insect. Some Indian chiefs wore headdresses made of feathers. Uncle John was talking again. Murdo got up from the chair, attracting Dad's attention to point towards the house. Dad would know he meant the bathroom. But when he exited the bathroom he went downstairs to the basement; he just needed a break.

The basement was the best space possible. Okay it had no air conditioning but so what? The privacy and just like how it was yer own place; ye couldnt beat it. Although the light was so so dim. Heavy shadows, ye wondered about spiders' webs. That was the trouble being low down; things could crawl onto the mattress.

Uncle John had said about cockroaches and how not having air conditioning was a good thing, otherwise they would have been worse. Murdo thought maybe he was kidding but Aunt Maureen said how insects needed moisture and dampness, same for mosquitoes. Dont put ponds in yer garden. Unless ye want mosquitoes. Mosquitoes bring the birds. Ye can shoot a bird. Makes a stew.

★

Next morning he stayed longer in bed. He was awake then back asleep. People said about jet lag so maybe it was that. He needed a shower but was starving. Dad was in the garden when he came upstairs; Aunt Maureen sipping coffee at the kitchen counter. Murdo moved about getting his breakfast. A hot day was forecast. Murdo hoped there was a beach nearby but there wasnt. Up country was a big valley where people went with lakes for swimming and water sports. Uncle John planned on taking them the weekend after next. This coming Saturday he had something else planned if things went right at work and no emergency call-outs.

Aunt Maureen made a pot of coffee. Even the smell was strong. She said to try it like she did: half and half milk. He was happy with fruit juice. She poured an extra coffee: Hey Murdo you take this out to your father?

Of course. I was just like – yeah, of course.

That okay?

Of course, I was just eh. . .of course.

Nothing, he was just nothing. Dad didnt see him come through the doorway, didnt lift his head from the book until the coffee was on the table. Then he looked up: Okay?

Yeah.

Good.

Dad reached for the coffee. Murdo returned to the house. While closing the glass doors he saw Dad lower the book and clasp his hands behind his head. He rinsed the breakfast bowl and spoon at the sink then downstairs to the basement, straightened out the sheet and duvet. Murdo did most everything back home, including super-market shopping and laundry. One time making the bed he discovered the bottom end of the sheet was full of stuff; dandruff and old skin, flakes and flakes of it. Every night in life the body sheds skin and the movements ye make while sleeping causes it to reach the bottom, plus yer feet trampling it down. Ye flapped out the sheets and dust microbes were everywhere. Sunlight beamed through the ceiling window and picked them out like in funnels. Each time ye moved millions scattered into the air. Ye coughed and spluttered just to see it. Skin. Flaking old skin, dandruff, showers and showers of it.

Hold yer breath!

Except ye couldnt. Breathe or die. Imagine a lassie seeing it, she would just look at ye. Beyond disgusting.

Maybe beetles lived off it. Parasites and living organisms. Back from the beginning of time. Some things were prehistoric and would have been here since the house was first built. Way before that, back when the Cherokee Indians pitched their tents. In this land the white man was the stranger who killed the Indians. Right where Murdo slept was their land, beneath this very house. Imagine a door leading down, if there was a cellar deeper than that, way way beneath the foundations. If it was a movie it would lead to some gruesome dungeon linked to unsolved terrors and murders beyond imagination. Hellholes and maniacs with chainsaws. Folk getting chopped up and sawn in two. Or black holes, ye open the door and fall to yer doom. If it was a proper black hole it turned a body inside out.

Murdo returned to the stack of books he found earlier, and discovered another stack beside a cupboard; sci-fi tales and detective stories and a few religious ones, with pictures to illustrate the stories. Then inside a cupboard and stuck in at the back were more books, ones with sexy covers. Sexy inside too, jees, that would have been the sons. Ye would read them but not so people would see so like private viewing ye would hide them. Obviously. Murdo opened one and sat down on the mattress. Ye could just about read but were uncomfortable shifting about trying to see better. The light was too bad to be true. The high-up window didnt give enough and the position of the ceiling light didnt help.

Maybe there was a bedside lamp. Stuff was piled into the two small rooms. Cupboards, boxes and bags. Old-style blankets and sheets; clothes and shoes but also plates and bowls, cups. Kettles, pots and appliances with these American-style electrical plugs that were so flimsy-looking ye would worry about explosions; and two electrical extension cables, one forty metres in length.

Even a torch! If there was one he couldnt find it. He stepped over boxes to check out other places. Another cupboard; he knelt down and on the bottom shelf found an old-style top-loading CD hi-fi. He wiped it down with the edge of his T-shirt. No radio but two extra compartments for cassettes; one was for recording. Imagine it worked. Maybe it did. Why not?

The plug was the usual two-pronged thing. He looked for a point and pushed it in. The set-up light came on.

He got the two CDs Sarah had given him and put the first on immediately. It worked! Fast and rocking. Queen Monzee-ay! The tracks she played on the porch. He blasted the volume till jeesoh, people would hear! He turned it down at once. He unplugged it and sought an electrical point nearer the edge of the mattress. He found one and plugged it in, keeping the volume low. The second CD was all different musicians, all accordeon-led. Just brilliant; amazing-mazing stuff. Murdo lay down on the mattress to listen. That sound quality too, the wee sisssss, ssssses. That additional stuff on the old audio system: zzzzsih, sihhh, zzzzsih, different from MP3s, like picking up remote audio pointers. Guys looked for old vinyl records to get it even more. Sometimes it was good but other times ye didnay want it. They said it was better with the interference, like hearing a band live. But it wasnay a band live; just yer own ears connecting, surrounded by audio waves out the machine, with you at the centre – the minutest spec, think of that sonny boy, infinity plus 1. Forgive us our sins and trespasses. Jees, that was Milliken the maths teacher, lessons on compressed data. No such thing as interference. God is great. Infinity plus 1. God is greater. But it was true with the sounds, it wasnt interference.

Oh but it didnay matter now anyway he had the music. He felt it so strongly how he could just relax, relax. Breathe properly. Not being able to play drove ye nuts. But when ye could listen! At least ye could listen. Yer eyes look and yer ears hear but what sees and what listens? Yer brains. Ye listen to the music but "you" is the brain. The brain listens, the brain works.

That was the truth. Every night in life. Lying in bed and all the stuff going through yer mind whether from a gig or a rehearsal, how things worked and if they didnt work. If somebody was out on something, ye had to put it right. You could be asleep but yer brains werent. All these times Murdo woke up and had to jump out of bed and write down, "guitar in more" "fiddle to shut up" "bass too thump thump" "space space space". What did that mean, "space space space"? Murdo knew.

Then having to stop it all and go to school and listen to silly crap nonsense from people all younger than ye. Just shit, bla bla bla; guys all looking at each other and if their hair looks cool or what, what kind of shoes, what kind of trousers; talking about the same stuff all the time and even lassies like it was the same one they all fancied, aw look at her look at her, check her out!

Murdo was sick of it. Ye just want to laugh. Then if a girl does look at ye, like a real look. Ye think they dont but they do. Girls look. That was Sarah in the shop when she saw Murdo: Who's that?

Me, shouts Murdo! Me!

Who are you!

Ha ha.

Sarah was tough. Then ye knew her and she wasnt. How she was in the shop taking the money, just tough! Then Sunday morning, how she was then: beautiful. But she was beautiful on Saturday night too.

She knew nothing about Scotland. Not even where it was. It was only England she could "see". Murdo said to think about the top of England. She couldnt. That was weird. He was the only Scottish person she knew. So if she didnt know Scotland, where did she think he came from? Nowhere. He didnt have a country, it was just him. Murdo. The gig in Lafayette. Oh Murdo will come. As if it was up to him. Probably they thought that. Oh ask Murdo and he will come. How will he get there? Oh somebody will drive him. Who? His dad or his uncle. Maybe his auntie. Oh here he is, here's Murdo. Hiya Murdo. All ready to play, and his accordeon sent from Scotland. Oh he got it air mail express delivery, where's the gig!

Ha ha, if that was true. Oh Dad are ye going to drive me? Oh yes, where's my driving licence. I left it in Scotland. Maybe we can get a train or else a bus. Do buses go to the gig?

Playing with Queen Monzee-ay was another world. The trouble was Dad knew nothing. It never would have occurred to him about the old lady sitting there that she was a beautiful beautiful player, just a brilliant musician. He didnay even hear her playing! When Dad arrived Sunday lunchtime she was sitting having a smoke.

What did that mean anyway? a brilliant musician. For Murdo to speak about music with Dad he would have to start from the beginning, the very very beginning.

★

Later somebody was coming downstairs. Murdo reached quickly to stop the music, was lying on his side when the door clicked open. Dad. In he came. Murdo pretended to be sleeping. A glass of orange juice balanced on a book near his head. Dad would lift it in case it toppled. A sexy book with a sexy cover. That was it without a lock, people just walk in. Dad waited without moving. Murdo opened his eyes and looked about.

Hey, he said, ye coming upstairs?

I fell asleep. I was just eh I was reading.

Hey, said Dad, ye coming upstairs?

Of course Dad yeah.

Dad nodded. Ye done it last night as well.

Done what?

Ye disappeared! Ye left to go the bathroom and ye didnay come back. When we were in the garden. I looked in later and ye were snoozing. We were expecting ye back and ye never came back.

I was just tired I mean I fell asleep.

Ye could have fell asleep later Murdo it would have been nice if ye had come up the stair. Uncle John and Aunt Maureen were looking to say goodnight. It would have been good if ye had been there for them. For Aunt Maureen especially. That great meal she prepared.

Dad I'm sorry.

Yeah I know son but that's the reality. It's not anything to be sorry about. Ye just have to think about things. It's a kind of respect; ye respect the person.

Dad I do respect them, what d'ye mean! They're great, Aunt Maureen and Uncle John are great.

Well they like you son that's for sure. Dad stepped to the door but then paused there. He looked again at the old hi-fi. Its set-up light was showing. Is that a CD player? he asked.

Yeah.

I thought I heard music.

I found it in the back room.

Huh!

I was playing it low.

Right. . . Dad was looking at the CD player again.

It was lying in a cupboard, said Murdo.

So ye just took it?

Murdo gazed at him.

Did ye ask Aunt Maureen?

. . .

Did ye ask Aunt Maureen?

Dad what about?

About taking it.

No. I just found it I mean I just found it, it was lying in a cupboard.

If it was lying in a cupboard ye went looking in the cupboard. Know what I mean son ye dont find things lying in cupboards. Not without looking inside: ye went looking inside. Which isnt a nice thing to do, being honest about it. Ye dont go into people's houses and look about in their cupboards. It's not something ye do son, not in people's houses. Ye're here as a guest. Ye should have asked first: that's all I'm saying.

Sorry.

It's no a question of "sorry".

Well I am sorry.

It's for future reference Murdo that's how I tell ye these things. Dad closed over the door. The creaks of the footsteps up the stairs; the bathroom door opening then shut and snibbed.

Murdo had waited a moment then stretched out on the mattress again, clasping his hands behind his head. He didnt want to go upstairs yet. But where else?

Nowhere – except down through the dirt.

That was the trouble with the basement. Ye were already in the earth. On the ground floor wee chinks of light came in but not down here. At night the dark was like the densest black ever. Ye could have been floating in outer space, falling backwards, so ye couldnt see what was roundabout, just looking up the way and like how ye never look up the way, ye never do. Ye always think about sideways like how the universe goes; a straight line going on forever but horizontal, never up and down like vertical, so infinity again. Discovering America, that was tides, going sideways and thinking sooner or later, going sideways ye're bound to hit India.

A different world. That was America. Ye thought ye knew it from the movies but ye didnt. How the Cherokee Nation was till the white man came and stole the land. People fighting and dying. Men, women and children and the stuff they leave behind. Soldiers, cowboys and indians, slaves. Black people. Chains and prisons, getting hanged. Wee babies. Martin Luther King and the cops just battering and killing people. Alabama and these places, and here ye were. People had their beliefs. Were any of them right? They couldnt all be right. Except they believed them. Even that stupid bird

although it wasnt stupid.

Of course it wasnt, just a wee bit unusual how it looked at him, if it did. Murdo thought so. Whatever a person was to a bird. Birds didnt know. Maybe some do, like a parrot. If you were interested in a bird the bird would be interested in you. Cows saw people as giants. Some animals only saw black and white. Bats were blind. If ye had a pet bat it would know ye by the sound ye made. Every person has a different sound, a different face, a different voice. The instruments they use have the same sound but how people play them makes the sound different. Birds too. Birds look at ye. People say "bird-brain" but that is the last thing. Birds are clever. Back home it was seabirds squawking, big gannets and gulls; oystercatchers, guillemots, ducks; all kinds, it depends where ye were. Ye heard them calling to one another. The same sound going all the time, just repeating and repeating be careful be careful

> Here comes a stranger, a stranger,
> Here comes a stranger.
> Here comes a stranger, a stranger,
> Here comes a stranger.

Aunt Maureen was in the lounge area when he came upstairs; the television on. Murdo had thought she was cooking but here she was knitting, sitting on one side of the settee with a knitting box beside her, a cup of tea set closeby, and a magazine near enough to read. On television the islands in the Caribbean Sea were illustrated in diagrams relating to storms; and the Gulf of Mexico too, and the weather coming in from there: tornadoes. He called: Hi Aunt Maureen.

Hey Murdo. You have a lie-down huh?

Yeah.

Your Dad was saying.

I thought ye were cooking. . .

Yeah son I'm having a break.

Murdo walked to sit on Uncle John's usual armchair. Is that tornadoes?

Tornadoes, sure; low-risk in this state. You go to Texas now you got it bad, up through Oklahoma. Here you're talking hurricanes, coming in from the gulf shores – you heard of Orange Beach?

No.

We got a coast here you know, but they squeezed us out. Look at a map son you'll see what I'm talking about. Got a map book someplace. Wherever it is! Aunt Maureen laid down the magazine and her cup, lifted her knitting and a knitting pattern book; she glanced about the room.

Murdo watched the Weather Channel for several minutes. The focus had moved now to New Mexico and Colorado, Arizona into California and the coast down there, the long peninsula into the Pacific Ocean. So they had good sea there, then the Gulf of Mexico and the Caribbean too, and the Atlantic Ocean. It was interesting. Good stuff about America he hadnt known. All the places. Aunt Maureen, he said, I was wondering about walks roundabout here?

Walks?

Walks, like where people can go.

Oh walks huh. Sure. They got a park. Aint much of a drive. During the day is good. There's some funny people go in the evenings.

Yeah but what about round here? Just going a walk?

You want a break son huh! We got you cooped up. How long you been here a day? Aunt Maureen smiled, paused a moment in the knitting.

Honest Aunt Maureen I wasnt meaning that.

We'll go to the mall tomorrow son that's the plan. Got some things to buy for tomorrow evening, got some people coming over. What they call a pot-luck, you know what a pot luck is?

No.

That's some of the cooking I'm doing now, for the pot-luck. You'll see. Kind of nice. Neighbourly. I got some things to pick up. You'll like the mall. Got all kinds of stores, all the big ones. Hey now Murdo they do the power-walking there! Folks older than me. Round and round they go, elbows flashing. You see their elbows? They'd knock you for seven.

I was just meaning a wee walk, just round the streets.

You need to get out son that's what you are talking about. Temperature's up now though, pushing on eighty, be hotter than that in an hour. Evening's better; early morning: people go early morning. What about your father, you ask him? Him and your uncle's going for a beer later. He's taking him to a bar.

To a bar?

Aint fair huh? Got to be twenty-one for that. Aunt Maureen glanced up from her knitting. I got a friend takes buses. She takes buses everywhere.

I thought there werent any.

Oh there's buses son; of course there's buses. I dont go on them. But she does. Then she dont drive. I always did.

You! Did ye! Murdo chuckled.

You surprised about that! Since I was twelve years old.

Twelve years old!

My Daddy taught us all. For when he got too drunk to, like

the song says. Aunt Maureen paused. No, he didnt get drunk hardly at all except with your Uncle John there now, he liked your Uncle John; for as long as he knew him. My Daddy's people were from Kentucky, him and his old father came here to work, talking about my granddaddy now Murdo we called him Poppo. My Lord! Aunt Maureen nodded. It's poor people goes on buses Murdo. You know what that means? Huh? Taking chances is what it means.

Murdo shrugged.

Now son you dont know what's going to happen. And who's there. You dont know anything about that either.

Yeah but Aunt Maureen if ye need something in a hurry and ye dont have a car, like I mean if ye cant afford a taxi.

Aunt Maureen continued knitting. I hear you, she said.

Have ye got a local store here, a local one?

Sure.

How far away is it?

Too far.

So do ye not go to it?

Not much.

Murdo shrugged. I would go, if ye needed anything. It's me does the shopping back home. I always walk.

Oh you do?

Yeah. I dont mind at all. I quite like it. Except if it's raining like heavy, if it's lashing down.

Lashing doon! Aunt Maureen chuckled.

Well it does lash down. Murdo grinned. So then ye've got to take a bus. Seriously but, if ye ever need anything I mean. . . He shrugged.

I hear you son.

*

Aunt Maureen said about poor people but that was them. They were the poor people. So why not a bus? They came on buses

94

from the airport so why not now? People worried about things happening but things happened everywhere. So if ye were too scared to go out did ye stay in the house forever? Ye read about hermits from the olden days, usually for a religion and they were communicating with God. They lived on their own completely, away in the woods or in caves at the side of mountains; maybe rocky coasts. How did they eat? They didnt work and didnt go to shops. They didnt want to meet people. They lived off the land, they ate insects and plants. Maybe they caught a fish or killed a rabbit or a squirrel. Or a deer. But if ye dont have a gun how do ye kill a deer? Ye would have to jump on its back and strangle it. Unless ye trapped it, ye could lay traps. There was plenty deer back home. Early morning they come down to the loch for a drink, so ye would hunt them there, if ye were allowed, like Dad said, it was rich people owned them and rich people that shot them.

Squirrels and rabbits.

Fish!

But if ye had no boat and nothing to catch them with? Ye used yer bare hands. Ye lay down with yer hands submerged and waited for a fish to swim over, then fast lifted it up.

America was fine except the sea, he missed the sea. Back home ye could always get out and get away, away from everything.

It didnt matter where ye were if ye were stuck in the house, and the garden was the house. For Dad it was Heaven: sitting in the patio reading a book. Not for Murdo. What did ye do in America? I read a book. Tomorrow was Wednesday. From last Friday six whole days. Nearly a week.

In the distance the sound of wood being sawn, just the ordinary sound of the saw: brooop brip, brooop brip. It was right for the setting if ye were outside; thinking of settlers cutting down trees to build log cabins.

Murdo was out the garden when Uncle John came home from work. He worked on maintenance and part of that was being ready for emergency call-outs. It was a boost to his wages and he had been doing it for a long while. The big news was for this Saturday coming then the weekend after next.

Saturday was what they called "The Gathering". Although it had a church connection it was good fun according to Uncle John, keeping alive the history and culture of the Celts. Stalls and raffles, home baking and prizes and competitions; all different stuff and finishing with a dance in the evening. Some old Scottish guy had left instructions and a sum of money so it would happen year in year out. There was a wee chance Uncle John might cancel if a work emergency arose, but if nothing happened by Friday night they would be off Saturday morning. If something happened while they were away they would text him.

The really big news was the weekend after that: they were giving Uncle John the Friday off and guaranteed no call-outs Saturday and Sunday. This meant he was free Thursday night through Sunday evening, so they could plan something good. They were speaking about it at the table. Murdo just listened. There wasnt anything to say. It led into the usual conversation about relations. Uncle John was talking about his sister's husband again – Dad's father – blaming him for not emigrating when Dad was a boy. If Dad disagreed, he didnt say anything. Murdo was ten when the old guy died, his grandpa. He sang comic songs and folk songs. Murdo had a memory of him, like not so much funny as cheery, but in a kind of angry way. That was the memory: he was an angry old guy.

Uncle John carried on talking but stopped when Aunt Maureen arrived. He kept his lips closed tightly and drew his fingers across, zipping up his mouth.

Well I hope so, she said, meals are for eating.

Uncle John made the gesture of unzipping his mouth then repositioned the food on his plate. Potatoes to the right and meat to the left. How else ye supposed to do it? he said, and winked at Dad and Murdo who were already eating.

Aunt Maureen sat for a while without touching hers. She did

the same last night. Murdo wondered if she was saying a Grace to herself. Maybe she just needed a break after cooking. She had her own style of eating too like she didnt want to open her mouth too wide. She used a knife only when she had to. She cut up her meat into small pieces then laid down the knife and ate with the fork, and after most every mouthful she wiped her mouth with a napkin.

Towards the end of the meal Uncle John looked out a bottle of wine and displayed the label to Dad. Local produce, he said and offered Murdo a small glassful.

It's too strong, said Aunt Maureen.

Och no it's not.

You tell me huh! You see that Tom? He calls it local like Alabama well it aint Alabama. That is a wine from my own home state. That is a Kentucky wine.

Uncle John smiled. Sure it is mother but you wouldnay call it strong. Down the wine country they'd laugh ye out of town.

Oh they would huh? You telling me?

I'm talking about strong drink.

You think I dont know about strong drink? My Lord.

Uncle John smiled. What d'you say Tommy? A wee one for Murdo?

Eh. . . Dad frowned a moment.

I dont really want one, said Murdo.

Ye sure son? One means nothing.

If it means nothing why take it? asked Aunt Maureen.

Because it's tasty.

Oh it's tasty alright.

How do you know?

I know.

Uncle John gestured with his wine glass. Now this lady here; you know she has never tasted one drop of the cratur in all of her born days? What do ye make of that? And her father, if ye knew her father. . .!

He was no drinker.

Not at all. I'm not saying he was.

Sure he liked a beer, well so what? a beer huh, what's a beer?

Nobody's saying nothing about that. I was only going to say about old Poppo.

Oh now my granddaddy huh? You got something to say there? Nothing bad.

Yeah you got that right mister. You dont know one single thing bad about him. Not about him you dont.

Nothing bad at all. Just fun. Uncle John chuckled. Old Poppo distilled the stuff.

Aunt Maureen glared at him. You cant keep your mouth closed.

That tradition is in your blood my lady is all I am saying.

Aint in my blood! She clasped her hands together on the table and glared at him again.

Uncle John sipped at his wine. Her granddaddy was called Poppo. A real mountain man. Coonskin cap and all that.

Oh now be quiet.

Him and her father took me hunting one time.

More than once, said Aunt Maureen.

More than once mother sure, I'm talking this one time the old man shot the bird! You know what I'm talking about. How old was he?

He was seventy-three. Aunt Maureen laughed and smothered it quickly.

Yeah, said Uncle John. We were going through the land up from some marshes, nearby this little pond.

The bird pond.

The bird pond yeah, that's what they called it.

That's its name, said Aunt Maureen.

Yeah, and a great pond too, something different about it; all weeds and rushes, frogs jumping; all of that, the dogs were with us.

You have two mister, huh?

Two beauties, yeah. See now they were looking to scare the birds out the weeds and the undergrowth so they would rise up and we could shoot them. Well not me so much. I didnay have a gun.

You couldnt shoot huh?

Not then I couldnt.

You learned mister.

I did, yeah. So we were walking, just watching the dogs, they're gone about a hundred yards on, two hundred, and away separate from each other Murdo, that's how they did it, the dogs trained into it.

Aunt Maureen nodded.

They scared out the birds. Just them being there. I dont know quite what it was, but then one rose up from the marshes.

Aunt Maureen sighed, shaking her head. She smiled at Murdo then looked back to Uncle John, rubbing at her mouth.

Round the side of the pond near to where we were, he said. Not over our heads but not too far away in distance this bird rose up, a good-eating bird, just rose up into the sky and old Poppo just whohh turning and raising the rifle, aimed a moment: boom! I thought he had missed. Ye've missed I says. He didnay say anything. Ye've missed I says. No now son I aint missed he says I aint missed.

Aunt Maureen laughed, smothered it again and blinked, then laughed again.

Uncle John was shaking his head. I aint missed he says.

Aunt Maureen had a napkin wiping her eyes. Uncle John was laughing just as much. Dad too was laughing. Murdo too, seeing it in his mind's eye, Uncle John just young, and there was the bird and the old guy with the gun. In the middle of laughing Aunt Maureen managed to speak. Oh the poor thing, she said, the poor thing.

The story hadnt ended. Uncle John waved to quieten everybody down. Aunt Maureen pointed at his meal plate: Finish your food mister. You drink that wine and you forget to eat.

Okay. He smiled, took a sip of wine, calmed enough to carry on: I thought he had missed. I did. I thought he had missed.

You thought that huh? Aunt Maureen winked at Murdo and Dad.

The bird was just up there and Poppo had his shotgun down now back in his arms – you know how they hold it – just standing looking up.

What was my father doing? asked Aunt Maureen.

Oh your father, he was the same, just looking up. But he was smiling, he was smiling. Oh yeah and he told me to wait; wait he says, just wait now John you see up there, you just keep looking.

Aunt Maureen nodded; her eyes closed a moment and she had her head lowered. Uncle John touched her on the wrist, and said to Dad: Me and him got on Tommy; he was a good guy.

Dad nodded.

Uncle John smiled. And old Poppo there, the bird with its wings flapping. No son he says I aint missed. The bird with its wings; flap flap, flap; flap flap, flap, till then it stopped, it stopped flapping.

Poor thing, said Aunt Maureen. What about the dogs mister?

Oh man the dogs, yeah, they were waiting too, running in wee circles, not taking their eyes off it. It was up high too. How high would it have been? forty feet? Sixty feet! I dont know, it was high. I'm telling you that bird; that bird gave its last flap and dropped like a stone. No son I aint missed it.

My Lord. . .

The dogs raced each other to get it.

Did they? said Aunt Maureen.

I think so. What a shot but! And ye know something else? they didnay think it anything special.

No sir.

I came home wanting to talk about it and people just looked. Her mother and people, they just looked.

Aunt Maureen grinned. They made fun of you huh?

They laughed at me!

Sure they laughed at you, can you blame them? I cant.

All the time we were there, the first time your aunt here took me home, all they did was play tricks on me. Naw but it's true, yer bloody sisters!

Hey! Hey now!

Yeah well they did!

Aunt Maureen peered at him. Yeah well you always always got to talk. What's your name huh? what's your name is it Scotch oh Scotch oh my oh my my. . .! Aunt Maureen frowned to Dad. He went round every one of them, where we lived, all our neighbours; every one, what's your name now is it Mac, is it Scotch is it Irish.

They thought I was bloody IRS!

Dad laughed.

Hey now I was young, young and proud. You would be exactly the same standing there far from home. A wee Scottish boy, that's all I was; what did I know!

Aunt Maureen made a face at him, and drawled out: Glaaaassgoww, I'm from Glaaassgow. Oh yeah we got family there says Becky, in west Kentucky we got family!

Uncle John grinned, but didnt speak. Aunt Maureen hardly had touched her food while he was speaking. She studied her plate now; moments later she got up from her chair, lifted the plate and left the room. It left a silence. Uncle John watched the door for a while. He said to Murdo. She's talking about her sister Becky.

Murdo glanced at Dad.

Uncle John added, She's dead now.

Oh God, said Murdo.

It's a couple of years ago.

Murdo shook his head.

Good people? said Dad.

They took me in and gied me a life Tommy, know what I mean, what did I know, a wee boy from Glasgow. Uncle John swallowed a mouthful of wine. He said to Murdo: How's the basement son?

Good.

Aye, she said ye'd like it down there. Uncle John smiled. So did the boys! One time me and yer Aunt Maureen were gone overnight they threw a party. First half hour thirty kids arrived. Fun and games eh! Other kids came and they didnt let them in. They had a pitched battle. We came home and what do you think? a window broke, two chairs smashed to pieces; broke tumblers, broke plates, broke damn everything! Uncle John turned to Dad. So what did I do? I turned the whole goddam space into a storeroom. No more party time.

Well fair enough, said Dad.

Yeah fair enough, that kind of behaviour; they were too big for it. Hurting their mother. They did hurt her. We trusted them and they let us down. You put the trust in kids they got to earn it, and go on earning it. That's growing up.

Uncle John sighed. Your cousin Calum's out in Silicon Valley Murdo, that's three thousand miles away.

Whoh!

People forget that. Ye cannay just get up and go.

Not like the old days.

Not the old days either son, that's here to Scotland. That's wagon trains, crossing the Sierra mountains in the middle of a bloody snow storm. Uncle John stopped. Aunt Maureen had reappeared with a pot of tea on a tray, milk and sugar. She set it down on the table. When she was seated she said to Uncle John, You talking about something?

I was just saying about California, that time we visited. We drove the length of that coast; Seattle down through Santa Cruz; central California. That's a beautiful coast too, ye might no think it but it is.

You talking about the boys?

Not really no.

Aunt Maureen sighed. Feuding runs in families.

I know, said Dad.

Uncle John winked at Murdo. Me and the boys had a bit of a fall-out. . . Uncle John swallowed the last of his wine and glanced at his wristwatch: What d'ye say Tommy? Still fancy a beer?

Eh. . .

Aunt Maureen peered at Uncle John. You fit for driving?

Uncle John smiled.

★

It was relaxing after they had gone. Murdo helped with the clearing up then sat in the lounge watching television. Aunt Maureen came in for some of it but mostly she stayed around the hallway, doing cleaning and tidying for the people coming tomorrow evening. Then she came into the lounge with the vacuum cleaner. She gave him a big smile then battered on with it. He could have done it for her but she didnt want him to, like as if he didnt know how to do it properly! Who did she think did it when Mum was ill? Murdo did all the house chores; all the tidying, everything. Even the garden. Dad was like Uncle John with traveling; seven in the morning till seven in the evening.

Murdo left her to it. Downstairs he switched on the music and looked out a couple of the books he had found. He went back upstairs to see if he could borrow a bedside lamp. Aunt Maureen got one for him. It made all the difference. He positioned it close to the electrical point where he had the hi-fi. Now he could turn off the main light, get onto the mattress and just read and play the music. In between the sheets was even better; as good as back home. Not any better but just equal to it. Although the books were better. Back home he hardly had any apart from children's ones from years ago. If he wasnay playing music he did most stuff online. Not games so much, not nowadays. He used to but then stopped, like he just lost interest and kind of gave up. It was boring. People went on and on about games, then ye checked them out they were just like hopeless, going over and over the same routines till yer head was buzzing with it. Some folk needed music. Murdo was one of them. Music keeps ye sane. People said that and it was true. More true was it kept ye safe. But he needed to play. Listening was good but wasnt enough. Even proper listening.

Murdo did "proper listening". That was what he called it. He listened and took stuff in. Only if things are on yer mind. Even ye concentrate hard, they creep in, and where does it take ye? Wherever, just anywhere. Listening to music takes ye places, and ye go these places, letting in the music, how the music comes in on ye, washing over, ye think of tides, like a slow tide, an evening tide.

★

Then he was needing to be someplace else, he really really had to be and it was so so urgent, just so urgent, traveling on from there wherever he was going but to this place, where it was, and black people, and brown people too, wee people and skinny people, just people everywhere. Cowboy hats and funny-looking jackets; flip flops and big boots. Skinny girls with bare legs and blotchy skin with purple patches, the muscles in their legs hard-looking. Ye walked in the bus station and there they were; maybe they were ordinary, maybe they werent, the ones looking, who are you looking at; short skirts riding high up too so if they came up further, further and further. Maybe they were prostitutes. Ye saw guys staring and the lassies didnt care or else stared back, short short skirts and legs stretching. They were just there and if guys looked at them they didnt bother. Maybe they did. How they dressed: sexy and tough. Ye tried not to look. Cops were there. Dad too, although maybe he wasnt and it was just him himself and slow along the corridor, who are you looking at staring at me? That was them, sexy, but they would just say whatever, Murdo, seeing the lassies, and that one seeing him, just how she shifted, how she stood, shifting, seeing him, short short skirt and him just looking to see, seeing her: and her looking at him like that, who are you looking at, and her legs just like short short skirt just beautiful, stretching up, her thighs there and just like raising her skirt was she raising her skirt? maybe she was, seeing if he was there if he was looking, if he was seeing; he was, her pants tugging down, and even if she wasnt wearing any, she wasnt wearing any, maybe she wasnt; and he was looking and seeing and she knew he was, he was there and she saw him, it was him she was looking at, and he was just like – because with her short skirt riding higher, that was her too just seeing him, looking at him and just seeing him, and still doing it, she was still doing it and it was him, she was looking at him.

He was awake and on his back lying there. The dampness.

He raised himself onto his elbows. A sliver of light through the ceiling window. He had to go to the bathroom. He lay back down.

He had to go.

What time was it? It didnt matter. He reached out for the bedside lamp; dampness and sticky. He got up from the mattress, left the basement door open to light the staircase. In the bathroom he used toilet paper and cold water to wipe clean the semen. That was it if it touched the sheets or the duvet. A wet dream because he wouldnt wank. But wet dreams were terrible because ye didnt know, they just happened and there was nothing ye could do, it was always just like wakening up, oh I need to go I need to go and that was that ye came, it was hopeless.

Back downstairs he left on the light and was in fast between the sheets, but without switching on the hi-fi. It was a thing that happened so that was that and ye would dry in the dampness. Stupid jumbles not even making sense. Ye just hug and the girl fits and if yer bodies fit then they fit. Ye see the shapes, ye dont need to because it is like ye are built for it, ye just fit in and the girl takes ye in, just sliding. Oh jees. The lassie fits into you and you fit into the lassie. That is the design: male and female.

Sarah too, not to think of her like that, because like her family, if ye know somebody's family, ye dont want to think of her that way like bodies and yer arm round her pressing her in, nude, and just feeling her and if she's pressing

★

They were going to the shopping mall. Aunt Maureen had booked a cab for 11 a.m. It was good to be going but Murdo's head was elsewhere. He put his shoes on at the door and went outside to wait on the porch. Dad was already there, sitting on the bench by the wall. Taxi's due, he said.

Right.

Dad noticed he was wearing a T-shirt. Maybe ye should put on something else, he said.

Dad it's fresh.

Yeah I'm not talking about that, it gets chilly in the mall because of the air conditioning, Aunt Maureen was saying. People catch colds; they

Murdo didnt wait for the next bit. Back in the house he took off his shoes and downstairs to the basement. He switched on the music to a particular track he was listening to. It was on the second of the CDs, the one with the other musicians. Just the most soulful sound ye could get and an accordeon too it was a knock-out.

A sound like that, ye just didnay expect it, just how he had it, he really had it. In learning a tune there was "a thing to get". Once ye "got it" you were fast away and could go at it and play to it and do most whatever ye wanted with it. It was not only the tune but a certain thing that gives ye more than that. When ye got that ye could go with it. Anywhere at all. Ye were just free and could do anything.

He took off the T-shirt, found a proper shirt and put it on – and took it back off, the waste of a shirt, wearing it to a mall. It was Joe Harkins said about "the thing to get". Joe played mandolin and was pretty brilliant. He played with the band for a few weeks. Mum

106

was there and coming to gigs at the time so that was a year ago. She liked the sound they were getting. She said it was different.

It was different: Joe!

People said he was a cool guy but it was the way he pushed ye on. And ye had to go with him. Ye had to. It was the real stuff and ye knew it was. There were good clips of him on YouTube but what ye saw was what ye saw and not like how it was from the inside. Ye didnay get that anywhere, that was like inside their heads. Ye had to play with people for that.

Joe was out on his own. Ye got left behind if ye werent careful and if that happened too much it was like Joe shut down, he went cold. If he had to go alone he shut down. That was bad, a player like Joe. Ye didnay want that happening. Imagine a band where the lead guy stops in the middle and says, I'm away home.

Ye got that tingle playing with him and ye didnt forget it. How could ye? Why else would ye be doing it? Ye thought that to yerself: this is a real band. That is what ye felt. That was Joe. When he was there ye had to go for it. Once ye got it ye could go for it all, just bloody go for it all, so like ye were bursting, and ye would see Joe maybe nodding his head, eyes closed.

Murdo! Murdo!

The taxi. Dad shouting on him from the top of the stairs.

It was true but, if ye couldnay cut it with Joe maybe ye couldnt ever, and that is how ye would be. Murdo put the T-shirt back on and grabbed his jacket, switched off the hi-fi and went fast upstairs. Dad waited by the front door ready to lock up. Aunt Maureen was in the cab. Sorry about that Dad. Murdo pulled on his trainers.

Dad nodded.

In the cab he sat next to the driver who yapped on about space museums and railway museums and drive-in movie houses that were as good as anything ye could find anywhere and served traditional ice-cream, glancing over his shoulder at Aunt Maureen as though ice-cream interested her in particular.

The road was complicated with roundabouts and flyovers. They had three and four lanes for traffic and drivers on the inside drove faster than ones on the outside. The worst was a guy whizzing along in and out, not bothering even to pamp his horn. Aunt Maureen called from the rear: Look at that. One finger on the wheel.

According to Dad the aisle seat on the bus was preferable to the window seat because ye didnt have to look out. It was too stressful seeing the crazy drivers. The driver didnt say anything. He heard Dad's voice and knew he was foreign. The nearer to the mall along both sides of the road were restaurants and free-standing stores. Different buildings; some fancy-shaped with round roofs and new-looking red bricks. Dad paid the fare. Aunt Maureen didnt want him to but he did.

They walked between department store buildings and it was good shade. Hot but not too hot. Aunt Maureen led them into one huge store, straight through and out the other side, into the main shopping area. Two huge-long floors of department stores. People going round and round. Women with babies and kids; old people too, and power-walkers. In one place there was a huge imitation rocket ship. Kids climbed to the top then slid all the way down on a chute. Other entertainments; an ice-rink and either two cinemas or one, and did they have an indoor golf course? Aunt Maureen said they did but it sounded fantastic. She didnt come much to this mall. When she did she made the most of it. She had favourite stores and shops and enjoyed going in for a look. Most were for clothes and fancy household items. For the pot-luck tonight she needed plastic cutlery and napkins; paper plates, paper cups and paper glasses. After eating ye just dumped everything into the bin.

After the first couple of stores Murdo stayed outside. So did Dad who had brought a book and usually there were seats. Up on the first floor Murdo leaned on the barrier seeing over and down to the ground level. Along was a larger-than-life model of a guy playing electric guitar. It was fixed at the entrance to a store. Surely a music store? Murdo couldnt quite make it out. Hey Dad, he said, look! A music store!

Dad glanced up from his book, shifted on the bench to see. Murdo pointed down and along to it. Ye think I could have some money I mean eh. . .?

Dad paused a moment. Okay, he said. He took dollar notes from his pocket and peeled off a $10. Much ye talking about?

I dont know.

Dad peeled off another $10 and passed him the $20. He stood up and peered over the barrier. Below was busy with people but the model of the musician was visible. Dad said, Ye sure it's a music store?

Well what else?

Dad shrugged. Why dont ye wait till Aunt Maureen comes back?

I was only going for a look.

Yeah. She'll be here in a minute.

. . .

Murdo she'll be here in a minute. Then we'll come with ye. One minute. Just one minute. I dont want us missing each other.

Murdo nodded.

This place is massive son.

Yeah. Murdo made to hand back the money. Dad looked at the two ten dollar notes. Naw, he said, hang onto it. As soon as Aunt Maureen comes we'll go.

Dad I'm not bothered.

Aw for God sake.

Really. I'll go another time.

Dad sighed. Murdo held out the money. Here, he said.

Right, said Dad and took it.

Murdo turned from him, leaning his elbows on the barrier. Dad sat down and opened the book. It was good to read a book. Dad liked doing that. What did Murdo like? Nothing. Nothing was good. Nothing was the best of all. Dad gave him nothing and that was what he wanted. From Dad anyway. Who cares? He saw the shop and out it came. He just opened his mouth and out it came, the first thing in his head. Better not talking at all.

Aunt Maureen reappeared. She chatted while they walked. Murdo stayed a pace behind so it was Dad she was chatting to. The next store had no seats. She left her bags next to where they were standing. Dad took out his book and was reading in the space of two seconds. Two seconds. Murdo stood still. He could only stand there. People scream. He didnt. Memories of boyhood, shopping with Mum and Eilidh and the agony, the agony. Stand there and be quiet. Be quiet. Stand. All ye could do. Clothes and clothes and clothes, and clothes and clothes and clothes – and that smell and how the lights were, the glare, people banging into ye. I'm goni scream I'm goni scream I'm goni scream. Although he might have slept, here, if Dad had allowed it. Dad wouldnt. He could read standing up but sleeping was barred. Ye could read but not sleep. Bad manners.

He could have brought a book. The cowboy one, he could have brought that. How come he didnt? Because he was going out. Stay in the house if ye want to read. In is in and out is out. Ye didnt go out to read a book. What about a sexy one, if he had brought that?

Before long Aunt Maureen was there. Murdo and Dad carried bags for her. A couple she carried herself. There's things in them I dont want bashing, she said.

They headed along to the food court. There was a choice of places. A Mexican one looked good. Mexican's spicy, said Aunt Maureen. Your Uncle likes spicy. That's why he's got the bad stomach. She led them to an empty table by a delicatessen. Once upon a time you got a real bit of dinner here, she said. Not now you dont. A sandwich is good for me. See if they got turkey Tommy, or chicken.

Murdo? said Dad.

Is it a sandwich?

Whatever.

So a sandwich?

Dad stared at him.

Tuna please. Or cheese. Chicken. Murdo shrugged.

So ye dont have a preference?

No Dad, just anything, thanks.

Dad walked to place the order. Aunt Maureen was checking through her purchases and receipts, and talking at the same time: Some folks spend their lives in here, huh. Then you got the walkers. Twice round the mall then it's lunchtime, another twice and that's them done their day's exercise. There's folks come here in the morning dont go home till evening. You believe that? They spend their life right here. Dont buy a thing; they just walk about, dont do nothing. Dont work. Nothing. They got their entitlements, you know what entitlements are son?

Murdo didnt reply and Aunt Maureen's attention was distracted by two young women arriving at a nearby table, one pushing a buggy with a baby inside. They were maybe from China or a country roundabout there, both wearing tight jeans. They didnt look over but just sat down, fixing the baby. Aunt Maureen wasnt quiet in talking so they could have heard what she was saying. Maybe they were just walking about, like if Aunt Maureen was referring to them. Maybe they thought that. If they did they were wrong, very wrong. Aunt Maureen would never have said any such thing, and now was away talking again.

The elder girl lifted the baby out of the buggy. The baby didnt laugh but stared at the mother – if she was the mother. Aunt Maureen was saying about how things used to be when this mall was first built and how it had changed so much. But she stopped talking. It was the baby, how she stared at the baby, even like she wanted to lift it up. Jees, imagine she did, just reaching to lift it. Oh my, she said, he is a beauty. He is a true beauty, that is what he is.

But she kept on staring. The young women exchanged looks. They were more like girls. The younger one fingered her necklace.

She was about Murdo's age. He could see the side of her face and just like the position she was sitting, as if she could maybe see him out the corner of her eye and how she was fingering her necklace again. How come? She was sexy-looking. That was the truth. Was she going to look at Murdo. Maybe. Maybe she didnt because with Aunt Maureen there and talking. Dad too, Dad was back, distributing the stuff, sandwiches and drinks, napkins, plastic forks. Extra salad with the cheese sandwich, and potato crisps. Murdo took his sandwich and gobbled it down fast. A lumpy bit stuck in his throat. He took it out to see. An orangey kind of thing. He left it at the side of his plate, drank some juice.

Dad looking at him. Murdo bit another piece of the sandwich. He wanted to leave the table but if he went too soon it was like he was still in a bad mood because of the music store. And he wasnt. He really wasnt, he just wanted away, just to walk about, on his own, he just wanted like – his own space.

He needed to tell Dad about the gig. Sometime he did. If he didnt he wouldnt know about it, and that wasnt fair. Okay if Dad said no, but he needed the chance.

The young women were chatting together, and Aunt Maureen too, to Dad, but including Murdo in it, just stuff about how it used to be way back. Murdo smiled, a kind of smile, if it was a smile. Smiles are just whatever, ye give one.

★

They were home by two thirty. Dad and Murdo offered to help Aunt Maureen prepare and she told them not to bother. It's a pot-luck, she said, nobody's going to worry too much. Then at four thirty her friends Josie and Melissa arrived early and helped her prepare the dining-room area. Melissa was Dave Arnott's wife. Dave came later with his daughter and son-in-law and their children.

People all brought food in bowls ready to eat. This was the pot-luck side of it. Ye came and ye took pot-luck. Whatever people brought was what ye ate. It was a good idea. Most were neighbours but a few had traveled a distance and were maybe connected to the same church as Aunt Maureen. The food was spread out on the dining table; some of it on the side cupboards and kitchen counter. Murdo was hungry but nobody was eating.

The women stayed around the kitchen and dining area while the men were outside on the patio and garden, drinking beer out bottles and smoking if they smoked. Two conversations were on the go with the men. Dad and Dave Arnott in one: Uncle John in the other. Murdo sat roughly between them but was glad Uncle John drew him in to his. It was difficult in company with Dad and people at the same time.

Uncle John was wanting to talk about stuff to do with Scotland, and not family stuff. Murdo was glad. Ye get it out yer head then it is all back in. An older man held onto his hand. Yeah, gotta be brave. Before him Aunt Maureen's friend Josie gave him a hug and said, Oh now son she's in a better place! talking about Mum, which was the kind of thing drove him nuts. It wasnt just daft it was worse than that. Although she was being nice, of course she was, obviously, and ye just had to act like it made sense, although it didnt, it was just like mental madness.

Oh yes isnt she lucky, passing on to a better place. He should have said that. At school the Headteacher broadcast a message of sympathy "for Murdo whose mother has passed on".

Passing on to a better place. The coffin is pushed into the furnace. Oh isnt she lucky. Maybe we can all go! After death comes life. A dead person going. Death comes after life and life comes after death. So death is not death.

Two kinds of life: before death and after death. After-life is after-death. Dead but not dead is vampires. The undead. Then Hell with all the demons. Imagine that was true. That would be the "unlucky soul", oh the unlucky soul, he's dead and going to Hell.

What if ye do something good in Hell? Do they take ye out and put ye in Heaven? What if ye do something bad in Heaven? Do they take ye out and put ye in Hell? How do ye get from one place to another?

Uncle John and the men were talking about work. To them it was interesting. Murdo would have skipped downstairs but it was too early for that and would have annoyed Dad. But it was okay to leave the company, surely?

He stepped down from the patio, and walked to where he did the sunbathing. It was good here; a thick hedge and a high hedge so if ye wanted shade from the sun ye could get it. The earth was hard, and dry grass, different grass. Ye think of grass all being the same but it wasnt.

On parts of the hedge it was like dew had already gathered. Slimy stuff, soapy. Cobwebs glinted. Whatever spiders they had here, probably various species, maybe poisonous ones. Murdo had gone online before leaving Scotland and there was this tiny spider could fire a line of mesh twenty-five metres across a river. Although maybe that wasnt Alabama. He walked on a bit to where the hedge thinned out. Ye could have made a hole to crawl through, and escape. Except if it landed ye in the next door neighbours' garden. Uncle John said the buggers were liable to shoot ye stone dead, and would be justified in a court of law because you would be seen as an intruder and they would be protecting their property.

Two of Dave Arnott's wee grandkids appeared less than ten feet away. Murdo pretended not to see them, two wee girls. He bent to study the grass. He picked out one stem and concentrated on it. He held it so that they could watch. He parted the stem of grass midway along the centre, aligned it within his thumbs and blew into it. A slight rasping noise was all it managed. He tried again but it wasnt working and he dropped the grass stem suddenly, as though frightened by something in the hedge. Jeesoh! he said.

The girls stepped closer. What you looking at in there? said the elder one.

Ssh.

What you looking at?

A tiny wee creature.

They were puzzled. They maybe didnt understand his voice. It's a tiny tiny animal, he said, pointing in behind the leaves. It's in there hiding.

The girls looked to see and the bigger one crouched to peer in. Murdo looked from one to the other and put on a scary voice: Maybe it is not so tiny. Maybe it is a big giant bear. A big big giant bear. . .!

The girls shrieked. Murdo made big eyes at them, and stepped closer, raising his hands: A very very big. . .big. . .big big bear. Waaaahhhhh!

They laughed loudly and raced off a short distance. Murdo also laughed. The two girls approached to see what he would do next. They saw their father strolling down from the patio, a phone in his hand: Dave Arnott's son-in-law, who lifted a ball on the way and threw it over their heads. They chased after the ball while he strolled on, studying the phone. He stood a moment then called to Murdo: How's it going?

Fine.

You John's relation?

Yeah.

So what you work at?

I'm still at school.

School, huh. Okay. You like it?

No. Murdo chuckled.

So uh where you from? you from someplace?

Scotland.

Scotland, huh. That's like a long trip?

Murdo shrugged. Had to go from Glasgow via Amsterdam, then non-stop to Memphis.

Memphis; cool. The guy snapped his fingers. Oh now, I got it, the bus connection! You stayed over Allentown, Mississippi?

Yeah. One night

One night huh. You see a white face?

Murdo looked at him. After a moment he said, Do ye mean eh. . .a white face in Allentown like did I see one? Do ye mean did I see one?

The guy didnt reply; his attention drifted from Murdo and over the other end of the garden, where his daughters were playing near a broken-down shed. The guy said, Ever been to Shreveport? One time I was like headed down the I-20, landed in Yazoo City. Yazoo City man they all play the yazoo there.

Pardon?

We got relations in Shreveport, on my own mother's side. Her people come from Oklahoma City. Moved to Shreveport like way way back, a long time ago. He stepped sideways and gazed around the garden. His daughters werent in sight. Girls must have gone inside huh, looking for food.

Murdo nodded.

Hey you listen to Pete?

Pardon?

Pete Marshall? You dont get Pete where you come from, WROT? Radio?

No, I dont think so. My Dad would know.

Oh now Pete's real funny; a real funny guy. He tells it like it is, he thinks something he comes right out and says it. He's got like a political line to gospel man he'll let you know it. He wont pull back on that.

His attention was distracted. The girls had reappeared by the broken-down shed with an old hosepipe. The older one flung the heavy end of it in the direction of the younger one and it would have hurt if it landed. The guy frowned. You got kids?

Me. . .

He suddenly pointed his finger at Murdo. I know you! I know who you are! Oh man I know you! Hey man I'm Conor, you're uh

Murdo.

Murdo yeah: you got the little girl passed on. That is the saddest thing. He moved as if to shake hands.

I think ye mean my sister. Murdo said, Ye're mixing me up with my father. It's my father's daughter that died, she was my sister.

Your sister, yeah. Okay. I got that. And your mother huh? Yeah, I got that. Man that is the saddest thing ever. Old Dave was telling me about that. Your sister and your mother. Yeah, I got that now.

Conor reached to shake Murdo's hand. He gripped it and didnt let it go. He kept on gripping it, so so tightly, just staring in at him and his eyes piercing, piercing in like how people say, his eyes "pierced" like a sharp point digging in to make a wee hole to see in behind yer eyes behind yer skin, not into yer mind but someplace else, if there is some kind of other place there and a thing inside it, eyes piercing their way in. That was this guy Conor. He kept his grip on Murdo's hand and Murdo couldnt take it away. That was the horrible thing. He didnt try to but knew he couldnt. This damn guy, he was too strong. His grip was too strong and bloody powerful and it was horrible. It was even painful! Jeesoh. His eyes too! He was just a nutter.

He stopped it and let go Murdo's hand, patted him on the side of the arm. Murdo didnt rub or massage his hand but he folded his arms. He kept looking at the guy and was not going to look away.

You are John's nephew. I know who you are. Your name is uh. . . Murdo.

Murdo, yeah. Moved here from Scotland huh. You got Tom too? He's my father.

Yeah. Conor slowly nodded his head. Sister and mother, yeah. . .that is the way of this world. People dont know it. They never know it! I'm talking what's in store for them up yonder. He pointed up to the sky. The future is what I mean. We walk this road and what do we see? Nothing. A road is heavy with blood and we see nothing. A blood-stained road and we are as blind men.

That old road is mapped out man we just dont like read it, we dont see the signs man. You dont see a thing how can you read it? You need to see a thing before you can read it. Aint possible otherwise Murdo.

Murdo watched him.

You think life is fair?

What?

You think life is fair?

Who me?

You, yeah: you think it is fair?

Me? Do I think life is fair?

Let me tell you man it aint fair. No sir. You expect that you are misguided; you are seriously misguided, one seriously misguided human being.

Out the corner of his eye Murdo saw Uncle John on the patio again, laughing at something. But Dad wasnt there, maybe he was in getting food. Down the far side one of the wee girls was tossing a ball onto the roof of the shed. Murdo hoped Conor would notice so if he did it would shift his mind from wherever, so he would go away.

He patted Murdo on the side of the arm again then glanced at his phone, scrolled down for a moment. No sir, you dont read the signs you will stay blind: deaf, dumb and blind. What you got to do is grow up, you got to grow up. I'm talking here: Conor tapped the side of his head. And here. . . tapping his chest.

Then he smiled as if everything was just friendly conversation and it was Murdo's turn to talk. That was like ha ha, did he honestly believe Murdo was stupid enough to fall for it? It just made ye angry. He would never have spoken like that to Dad. None of the men. He wouldnay have dared. Just Murdo. Murdo was a kid. Say what ye like do what ye like. Now he stepped towards Murdo as though to shake hands with him. Pleasure talking with you, he said.

The real pleasure was him going away. Murdo would like to have said something but said nothing. It was the wee girls ye felt sorry for.

Bad manners and good manners. Good manners is being nice to them with bad manners. You fit into them and all their crap. Gab gab gab. So all ye can do is nod yer head. Murdo was sick of that. They could speak and you couldnt. They had the right; you didnay. That was this life, all the shit stuff ye ever could get. Imagine the worst, then a plus 1. Ye were to talk but not talk. Not to talk but talk. That summed it up. Oh hullo yes it's a nice day Mum's got a tumour and she's dying. That was the funeral too, people speaking to you but you werent to speak to them except Yes, I'm fine. Everything's good, Mum's in the coffin, bla bla bla.

Back home ye would go home. I hate this party I'm away.

Where was Dad? Down in the garden slugging a beer. Him and Dave Arnott – old Dave, that was what Conor called him.

Uncle John had the bottle of whisky out which Dad brought him as a present. He was showing it to the other guys. Dad in the background, Dad smiling. Old Dad. It was good seeing him in company. Mum used to worry. Oh is he going to be okay? She wouldnt be there to look after him. Dad could get upset, too upset, too angry. Mum worried. Murdo should thank his lucky stars Dad didnt manage to many gigs. What a nightmare if he had! If anybody spoke when Murdo was playing. Dad wouldnt have coped with that. He would have gone round the dancehall telling folk to shut up and listen. That was Dad, according to Mum. Here he was part of the company. That was unusual. Him and Uncle John, they just chatted about stuff to do with the family and back home in Scotland how it was going to be for the future, for politics and for religion and football. Uncle John liked hearing about Rangers and Celtic, especially Rangers beating Celtic – and Clyde and Partick Thistle too and Hearts and Hibs and Aberdeen and all the teams because ye didnt get anything about it in the States, only English teams, Spanish teams, French teams, German, Italian; what happened to Scotland? That was the issue. All the old players. Uncle John loved that and Dad could do it.

Murdo wished he was home. Here ye couldnay breathe. Space

and hills, the sea. Imagine a boat and just like getting out on the water. Nothing big, just breathing, Oh I just want to breathe I'm away on the bike, Ardentinny or someplace, just great.

At least the garden was here. Without the garden he would have been trapped.

He was hungry. A couple of the men were eating. He would have to talk to people and he didnt want to. How was he feeling? Maybe angry.

No. Like he had been in a fight. Imagine a fight. Battered, that is how he felt, and lying down is what he felt like doing. His bed preferably but the grass would do except the mosquitoes. Always worse when the sun set and it was that now. He wanted down the basement and couldnt go because it was bad manners. Dad. Dad this Dad that. But at least he was relaxed. Here he was just in company with the other guys, and that was something. Really, it was: Dad, relaxed. Dad relaxed Dad relaxed Dad relaxed. Ye could imagine it a tune, jazz cornet, nice and bluesy mellow, Heyyy. . . Daaad. . .yeahh. . .Daaad. . .heyyyy. . .yeahh. . . Or that classical guy on solo piano, that slow rippling.

Usually it was Dad nervy. If Murdo had been in the company then poor Dad, he would have been watching for everything; if somebody told a joke and used swear-words in the telling, or if it was a joke about sex like if the guy was too open about women or if it was like homophobic or racist. Back home there were two brothers lived along the street from them. If Murdo and Dad were together it was a minor disaster meeting them downtown because they got so excited about football and everything was "fuck" this and "fuck" that and Dad couldnay cope because Murdo was there and Murdo couldnay cope with Dad no coping with him and it was like yer nerves just got so so frazzled – frazzled was a good word, making ye think of sizzling ends snapping about on a hot plate. Sausages!

People were to get food when they wanted but so far he hadnt been able to. A couple of the guys had chicken legs and plates of a salad sort of rice thing and French bread. Crusty French bread was great.

Murdo cut through the garden, round the far side of the patio and along the driveway, past the 4x4. He could even go in there and sit. Uncle John left the door open. Instead he walked round to the bench on the front porch.

He sat down on it. Ye could actually see the mosquitoes! That way when the light hits at a certain angle and ye see them all going crazy. Bats would come out. They had twelve different kinds of bats here. They fed on mosquitoes. Bats were like spiders: ye were glad to see them. If it wasnay for bats ye would get eaten alive. That was midges back home. Teeth-bodies. If ye zoomed an image of one online it was like the worst pre-Jurassic terror-beast imaginable: a flying Velociraptor, all teeth and snapping outside yer window. Millions of them. All zig-zagging. Did they ever bump into each other. Maybe they did. Although sound and radar working in the one system. Airwaves. Everything all over the world; all connected. Billions of connections, all avoiding one another. Each on its own individual path or trail. More like a trail because some of it ye make up as ye go along. Whereas a path is laid out for ye. Ye follow a path like ye follow a tune where ye cannot deviate: ye have to play it the way it is always played. Always the same and always the same. That was the one way always the true way.

Murdo hated that style of playing. Of all the hate he hated that was the most, because it was the worst. Maybe not the very worst.

Guys spoke about jazz but it is not just jazz, ye can make a trail out of anything, anything at all. He did it with the "Blue Danube Waltz". For Mum, making her laugh. She told Dad and Dad said, We'll call it the "Grey Clyde Waltz". She laughed at that too, the quiet laugh she had. Nobody else in the world had that one, like a gurgle up from the throat and tiny air bubbles beeble beeble beeble – some kind of thing, ye could never have got that, be be be be, how did ye get that? And then it was gone. Mum was gone. So that was her laugh gone too.

So if it was a racist joke did it mean the guy was racist? Maybe. People said things. They did it at school too like they were testing ye. If ye laughed ye were racist if ye didnay ye werenay. So are you racist? No, I was just testing you.

Sorry Dave but yer son-in-law is an arsehole.

Naybody else bothers. You get angry and everybody else thinks it is okay. Oh look at Murdo he's angry, how come he's angry! Oh he likes that lassie, if he didnay like her it would be okay, just like a black face in Allentown, what is that? so what, people have thoughts that are just like the craziest craziest shit. They dont even know ye but think things about ye. Oh I'll say it to him he looks easy. How come?

At the same time ye got sick of it, just sick of it, and away from here before somebody came. He got up and tried the front door but it was locked. He had to pass round the back entrance in through the patio. He gave Dad a wee wave in passing. Women were there by the kitchen counter and the dining room table. He continued through to the bathroom. The door was locked. He walked downstairs, and shut the door, and if there had been a snib on the door he would have locked the thing! He felt like a Cherokee Indian. This was his place and here he was buried, except buried alive.

★

The knock at the door, however long after. Half an hour. It was Aunt Maureen. Murdo blinked. He had the music low but kept off the light. She said, I want you upstairs son you got to meet the women. They want to meet you.

She waited outside the door. Aunt Maureen. Sometimes he felt he loved her. She loved him. He knew she did. That was an amazing thing.

There were seven women, cheery and friendly-looking, and a

baby slept in a buggy. Aunt Maureen named and pointed out each of the women: Josie and Melissa, then Liz, Emma-Louise, Katherine, Ann-Marie and Nicole who was Melissa's daughter. Josie said, Hey Murdo how are you?

Fine.

Murdo's always fine, said Aunt Maureen. You ask him that's what he'll say. I'm fine. Oh I'm fine. She dragged a dining chair to beside her own near the fire-surround: Now Murdo here's grandmother was John's sister. Her name was Effie and she was a beautiful lovely person. She took us to church there in Scotland, it was the Parish Presbyterian. Murdo here's got some fine fine memories of her. That right son?

Yeah.

John's been trying to persuade him and his father to come stay permanent.

The women looked at Murdo, waiting for him to speak. But he knew nothing about this. Nobody had spoken to him. So it should have been Murdo to ask Aunt Maureen the question. Liz said, So you want to come live here Murdo?

Eh. . .

A big step huh?

Murdo smiled.

It aint plain sailing, said Josie. You got the red tape nowadays.

Sure but the family connection, said Aunt Maureen. Plenty others get in dont even talk the language.

You got that right, said Josie.

Aunt Maureen indicated one of the women: Liz is Welsh.

Way back in the mists of time, said Liz. I dont cling to it.

Sure, said Aunt Maureen. John says Scottish half and half but his boys aint half anything they are American.

Family's important, said Emma-Louise.

Huh! said Josie.

What you saying family dont count?

No now I aint saying that, just not like it was. It dont pay to be ordinary. Come from India and it'll be okay, come from Vietnam and Haiti, Korea, Russia what do they get, tax free for five years? WIC, food stamps!

My Lord. Aunt Maureen reached to hold Murdo's hand for a moment.

Emma-Louise said, So Murdo how do you like being here?

I do.

Oh you do huh!

Yeah.

Another of the women laughed, Ann-Marie. It's his voice! she said. I love that voice. Is that the Scottish voice?

Well what else is it gonna be? asked Emma-Louise.

I dont know! Ann-Marie laughed again.

Aunt Maureen was squeezing Murdo's hand, and she kept a hold of it. She looked around the women. Him and his father have had it tough, she said, I got to say. You all met Tom, huh, his little daughter passed on? Murdo here's little sister. Now his mother, his own sweet mother, poor soul, she's with Jesus now.

The women gazed at him. He was going to say how Eilidh was his big sister and not his little sister.

Sure hard to take, said Emma-Louise. Didnt you say it's hereditary Maureen?

Through the female line.

You'll have the memories Murdo. Josie nodded. Oh yes you will, she said.

The others smiled, expecting him to say something, but what about? He couldnt say anything. Memories. He didnt want to say anything about memories. Eilidh wasnt a memory. He had taken his hand out from beneath Aunt Maureen's; he folded his arms briefly. He wanted to speak but was not going to except like it had be cleared up otherwise

otherwise what? It just wasnt true and it was Eilidh. Murdo said to Aunt Maureen: She was actually my big sister Aunt Maureen like I mean she was coming up for twelve when she died, I was nine.

Huh? What did I say?

No just eh she was my little sister, but really she was older, she was my big sister. She was a great girl Aunt Maureen. I dont like people talking about her.

Oh.

I dont mind if I'm not there. It's only like when I'm there, as soon as they speak, she disappears. It begins with her then she's gone.

Well you dont have to talk about her now son.

Murdo kept his head lowered, not looking at the other women. Aunt Maureen was squeezing his hand again. It's because memories, he said, I dont like that about memories. It's just what I feel, memories are for other people. They arent to do with me and her. I think about her every day. Ye know I mean every day. I mean every single one.

Oh son.

It's not memories, she's just here. Murdo glanced at the other women. They were listening. Ye hear it in songs, I'll always be with ye, and it's true. Eilidh is always with me. She was my big sister and she is my big sister and it makes ye cry thinking about it. I know it does. Murdo shrugged. I cant help it. I cant stop it and I dont care. If she wasnay there when my Mum died I dont know what would have happened. It was Eilidh got me through it. Not even my father, he couldnt have managed it, never. It was only Eilidh. Murdo shook his head and he stared at the carpet. It doesnt matter about God and Jesus and that stuff, I'm sorry, people say about passed on and she's with Jesus, I'm sorry but she's not, she's with me. Me. She had her own life. It was her unique one. My big sister, she was a great girl and a real person. She's my big sister, that is what she is.

Murdo was not going to cry but he felt like it. So now he had spoken. That was that. He wished he hadnt but he had. That was Aunt Maureen.

Because she was a great lady. The best auntie it was possible ever to get. Imagine being annoyed at Aunt Maureen! Never. That was ha ha ha, never ever ever. Only he needed to say it about Eilidh. Otherwise it was not her. If it was not Eilidh he didnt want to talk. She was not a memory. If he spoke about her like she was one then she was. She wasnt, she was his sister and a real girl, a real great girl; that is what she was and never never never, he was not ever ever going to let it go. Why should he? Ye just get angry, so so angry, bloody talking and talking, people talking.

That was that and nothing more. The women looking at him. Then Josie about her own family – not from the old days, she didnt like the old days; she was saying about a farm she knew and some of the women were smiling and joining in talking so like Murdo could just go quiet, close down, ye think of closing down, and seeing Melissa looking at him and her daughter too like how she was just staring and as if it was him she was staring at, and he looked back at her, just seeing and it was like him, it was him she was staring at, how her blouse pulled back too it was like her skin through it, her actual skin, because it was just like so thin white the material and even like her nipples like it was her actual nipples

twinges and twinges

she was shifting on her seat, changing how she was sitting – Nicole – she blinked a couple of times and something or other he didnt know except just blushing he was blushing oh God he was blushing if she was staring at him: she was.

It was not actual "staring" at all, she was just waiting for him to speak.

Murdo sat forwards on the chair. They were expecting him to talk about what Emma-Louise had said. What had Emma-Louise said? Melissa too, looking at him, encouraging him. It was nice of her. Dave Arnott's wife. Nicole was her daughter. If she saw him blushing. She must have. Aunt Maureen touched his hand: It was your Uncle Robert son huh? Didnt he go checking it out?

My Uncle Robert. Yes eh. . .

It was hereditary huh?

126

Yeah. He said how the tumour never came to men. So they werent doing the research. If it was reversed roles, and the tumour only affected men then they would have done the research. Especially if it was rich ones. They would pay the money to save their own skin. My Uncle Robert said that.

Emma-Louise said, Doctors here dont do their work.

That is a fact of life, said Josie.

A sick person's got more chance seeing the Governor of this state. What do they give you? A nurse is what they give you. Least that's what they call them. But they aint nurses, not proper ones like what you would say, a nurse.

You got that right, said Josie.

My own mother was lying there, Emma-Louise said. She was skin and bone. Were they cleaning her? No they were not. Can you believe it?

I can believe it, said Josie.

They would not clean her and would not feed her. My Lord that was a hard hard time. Sure we got support, but not from them.

The door opened and the two wee girls entered. Their father was behind them. Nicole was up from her chair and peering at the wall clock. She leaned to see into the baby buggy. The two girls came to Melissa who was their grandmother. Nicole was their mother, she was the guy's wife. He stayed by the doorway, phone in hand.

Emma-Louise continued talking: Not one sip of water did they give her; they denied it to her. I wanted to give her a drink and they would not let me. I told them. I said you know all this is? It's money, you all are cutting corners, running down costs, you think I dont know that! I know it.

The younger woman had lifted up the baby and was sniffing its nappy. Liz winked at the other women and called, She dry Nicole?

She is. Nicole tucked the baby in between the sheets.

Liz called to Conor: How's your mother keeping Conor?

Good.

Liz smiled. Conor had raised his head and glanced around the room, passing over Murdo. Then he looked back at Murdo as though seeing him for the first time. He folded his arms, but stood there quite relaxed. Mister Cool. That was the way he was standing. If the women didnt see it. Acting like he was the big boss showing them all! He had tried to bully Murdo in the garden and now he was doing it here. In front of everybody. The guy was a bully. It sickened ye. Guys ye have never seen in yer life before and they still try to bully ye. They dont even know who ye are like ye could be the best fighter in the whole world! They dont know anything about ye but they still try to bully ye, and they do bully ye. This guy bullied Murdo in the garden. Now here he was doing it again in front of all the women. Murdo was young so he thought he could get away with it. So arrogant, totally stupid too because ye dont know who ye are talking to. Somebody could take out a gun and shoot ye.

Aunt Maureen touched Murdo on the wrist. A woman who hadnt spoken before was attracting his attention. Murdo smiled at her and she said, How do you like it here Murdo?

I like it fine.

You do huh?

Yeah.

Well we sure like having you here, she said.

Murdo grinned, although he needed to get away. Only because he was edgy. He got up from the chair and said quietly to Aunt Maureen. I'm going through for something to eat.

Aunt Maureen gripped his hand for a moment.

Melissa and the wee girls were with Nicole and the baby now. Conor stood to the side of the door to let Murdo through. He might have escaped downstairs altogether except he thought to grab some food on the way. Uncle John was in the kitchen. He had a beer tucked under his left arm and was manoeuvring two heavy-looking trays of food toward the edge of the kitchen counter. One held platefuls of chicken pieces and sausage rolls, and the other piles of sandwiches. Murdo took the tray with the sandwiches. He held the dining room door open for Uncle John, followed him to the patio table. They set down the food. Thanks Murdo boy. . . Uncle John winked while ripping a beer from the pack. Thirsty work this talking! he said to the men seated there. Know what they call it back home? Blethers. Ye're blethering. Ye're all blethering. Some people's a believer, I'm a bletherer. Eh Murdo?

Murdo grinned.

Uncle John glared at him. Insubordination! He gestured at a spare chair.

I'm going to go through just now.

Aye aye cap'n. Uncle John saluted him.

Down from the patio Dad was with Dave Arnott who was speaking to him. Dad listened but was watching Murdo at the same time. Murdo gestured at the trays of food, lifted two sandwiches and continued on into the house. People were in the kitchen and dining area, he walked through and downstairs.

★

He heard the bathroom door close and his hand reached to the volume control but it could hardly be lower. Back home he could blast it! Just blast it.

Here was here. Here is where he was. He couldnt stay down forever.

Where's Murdo! Oh God maybe he's fallen down a pit! There's a black hole below the basement and he's fallen down! Ohhh dohhhh ohhhh ohhhh. Scary! "Fallen-down-the-pit" music, a cello, ohhh dohhhh ohhhh ohhhh, scraping yer knees, ohhhh ohhh ohhhh, dohhh dohhh dohhh.

Although if he had had a guitar, a guitar would have been good. Anything at all. What he was missing was being able to play. There was the music store at the mall, if there had been any instruments.

A whistle or a mouth organ. A kid's keyboard, a xylophone. What did ye get for twenty dollars?

Foot creaks from above. He lowered the volume again. But there couldnt be any lower, except minus 1, the infinitesimal of the infinitesimal, so ye screwed yer head right down further and further, the furthermost deepest down point ye ever could, then minus 1, so what ye picked up wasnt sound as we know it, just data beyond audio, just like lines lines lines and no lines, no lines, no lines, a string series like DNA, so low it was unique, nobody nobody nobody – especially Dad. Otherwise "face the music".

Ye did something wrong and ye faced the music. Music was the punishment! Imagine the punishment! Bad behaviour! Go and listen to music! It was so stupid. That was life.

If life was fair, ha ha.

The opening to the next track made him smile. The repartee; the musicians having a laugh; drummer and lead calling to each other. It was special. Ye wanted to turn it up louder, louder, louder, for them sitting upstairs and what was happening under their nose. A bully bossing people. Dave Arnott's son-in-law. Uncle John's pal. He was Dad's pal too; and nearer Dad's age than Uncle John's. That was the bully, Dave Arnott's son-in-law, his daughter's husband, he was a total bully. A coward as well as a bully because bullies are cowards. Maybe he bullied her. The kids too; the wee girls and the baby. Imagine he did. And Dave allowed it? How come? Dave was a big guy and could just have battered him. Murdo would have battered him. Dad too. Dad wouldnt have allowed it. If he knew. Murdo could have told him. Although what was there to tell? Murdo was there and the guy was saying things that were horrible. Ye wouldnt say these things to people except if ye could get away with it, like if the person ye were talking to wasnt going to tell ye to shut up, just bloody shut up. That was what Murdo should have told him, Just shut yer fucking mouth. Murdo should have said that and he didnt, he just let him get away with it. Grow up, grow up, you are just one stupid fool. Murdo was just a nothing and he was going to say whatever, just like whatever, anything he wanted because what was Murdo? Nothing. A young guy not worth bothering about. Oh who is he, just like from a foreign country, he's nothing. A guy talking down to ye like that. Murdo let him. That was the sad thing.

Imagine letting him. Murdo did. Was it bullying? It was bullying. The things he said, he would never have said them to somebody else like if it was somebody to fight back. Murdo didnt fight back. The guy didnt think Murdo would fight back and that was that because Murdo didnt. So he got bullied, the guy bullied him.

How could ye allow it?

Ye hear the sizzles and sissssssss; outer audio points not getting picked up, ever more compressed; mp-3, mp-4, -5, -6, -7 and ever on to where -1 is an algorithm, another system altogether, another universe; forget awesome, awesome is human, awesome is stupid. Way way beyond. Ye dont see so ye dont witness. Although ye still know, ye still know; the stillness. He was not asleep,

a while later,

but hardly awake.

If he was he didnt know it. Not awake and not asleep. Not dreaming. So thinking. Only he didnt know it. Thinking but not thinking. Whatever time, who knows time; something in his head anyway, whatever that was, now gone. Things go. How many tunes in the world disappear forever? How come ye lose them? Ye cant just get them down and like have them there so then ye can just whatever, ye can just play them.

Ye got jittery. Things in yer head. Could ye get them out? Ye couldnt, these people bully ye during the day and are into yer head at night. At school too like as a boy, it was happening to ye and it was all ye thought about, every minute of every day, bloody bully, Murdo would have battered him, just picked something up and crashed him over the head with it. Having a wife like that, wee kids. It was just like amazing how a guy like him, how he got away with it. Dave's daughter was great. Murdo hadnt been looking at her, if anybody thought that. When somebody looks at you then you look back. She looked at Murdo so Murdo looked back. Although it was not that kind of a look. Imagine it was. She didnt talk much but listened to everything and was beautiful. Guys would say that. She was. Just natural too. What age was she! An actual woman, and she was looking at him, and her blouse, how it came onto her boobs and ye couldnt help see the colour, how they were shaped in the material, pulling tight and her nipples, how she didnt speak and just listened, listened to everything, just looking, and her hand to her mouth, rubbing the sides of her mouth, her lips. It was so so natural. Even her blouse like white and silky. She wasnt dressed up although she seemed to be. Just how she looked, she just looked good – sexy, ye would say that, an actual woman, jeesoh, it was just how everything, like when she was sitting there too ye couldnt help seeing how her boobs were like jeesoh ye saw the shadows into the curve just so natural, everything.

★

Next day clouds were there; white clouds on a blue sky. Back home it was grey on grey on grey. Aunt Maureen said rain was expected later. She was in her room and Dad wherever, Murdo didnt look. He went upstairs with the cowboy book he was reading, heading for the lounge. But when he opened the door there was Dad in the armchair nearest the window, the best place in the house for reading. Dad called: Hi!

Hi Dad. Murdo was about to leave again.

I thought ye were downstairs?

I came up.

Good to see ye reading!

Yeah it's eh. . . Murdo held the book up for Dad to see the cover then hesitated by the doorway.

Are ye sitting down? asked Dad.

Okay. Murdo went to the settee.

I heard yer music. I just mean I heard it, I'm not being critical.

Sorry Dad I was keeping it low.

I'm not saying it was loud. Dad marked the page of his book and closed it. And I dont want to keep getting onto ye. It's just last night there we go again, ye disappeared. The people were going away and you werent there. Aunt Maureen and Uncle John's friends and neighbours; ye should have been there to say goodnight.

. . .

They were looking for you.

I didnt know. Otherwise I would have come up. I didnay hear anything.

Yeah well nay wonder with the music.

Dad I was keeping it low.

Yeah ye said.

I was.

Even if ye could change the tune son know what I mean?

It's two different CDs.

Is that a fact, ye wouldnay know it with that same beat all the time.

Zydeco Dad, it's a style of music, that's what it's called. That's how ye get it sounding the same.

Dad smiled for a moment. Murdo shrugged and studied the floor. Dad said, I'm only smiling.

Yeah well that's the music it is. That's the drive, it's the accordeon; the accordeon's driving it I mean it's just. . . Murdo glanced at him. Dad it's good. Once ye know it. It is Dad, it really is.

I believe ye.

There's actually a wee festival coming. All different bands. It'll be fun Dad it's like a week on Saturday in a town called Lafayette. It's not too far I dont think. That's how come I'm listening to it so much it's because I'm learning it. So it's not just listening.

Right, listening and learning.

I know ye dont get it. Other people do.

Good for them. Dad raised his book and opened it.

Dad I'm not being cheeky.

Glad to hear it. Dad turned a page in his book and read for a few moments, then he lowered the book. What festival is this?

Music Dad, it was Sarah; mind the lassie that came to the bus station with her brother?

Ye're talking about Allentown, the people ye met in Allentown?

You met them too.

I did, yeah. Dad nodded.

So what's wrong?

Nothing's wrong. Nothing's wrong Murdo.

Well because ye're not saying anything. Is it because they're black?

Pardon?

. . .

Pardon?

Is it because they're black?

Because who's black?

Murdo looked at the floor.

What do ye think I'm a racist now? Is that it?

Dad

Eh?

No.

It would be pretty poor if ye did. Dad raised his book again but lowered it immediately. Something's bothering you. I wish ye would say what it is. Eh?

Murdo gazed at him. We dont really go anyplace. This is the seventh day since we left Scotland.

It's Thursday. We've been here since the early hours of Monday morning.

Yeah but we left Scotland last Friday Dad that's a week.

Well I'm just glad to be here son I dont know about you. Relaxing and taking it easy. Away from everything. I thought you would have appreciated that, getting off school – you hate school so much this is you getting away from it. I enjoyed last night Murdo, it was a good wee night, meeting people and talking. And it'll be a good day on Saturday too. Dad shrugged. What I'm saying is that's fine for me, the way things have been, I'm not that bothered about going anywhere.

Okay Dad but getting out a walk.

Yeah a walk, okay.

So it's okay if I go a walk?

Of course, if that's what ye're wanting to do. I dont object to ye going a walk. Dad nodded. The only thing I will say is tell me where ye're going.

Dad if it's only a walk how will I know? I mean like I'll no be going any place. I wont know until I get there. Unless the shop. Aunt Maureen said there was a local one.

It's miles away. It's miles away Murdo.

Is there not a garage? I thought there was a garage, like I mean they'll have a wee shop for milk and bread and whatever, newspapers and coffee. I could go there.

Dad looked at him.

I'm not saying I want to go there.

I thought ye were.

I wasnay, it's just like somewhere to go.

People pass through gas stations Murdo. All kinds of people from all everywhere. Ye dont know who ye're talking to, there's a lot of crazies about. Guys drive with guns in the glove compartment. Road rage here son they pull a gun on ye. Ye get yer head blown off. You want to hear some of the stories Uncle John tells.

Dad

I'm just saying ye've got to be careful.

So I cant go for a walk?

For God sake Murdo dont make it a big deal.

Well it is a big deal.

No it's not.

It is.

It isnt.

Dad it is.

Jesus Christ!

Well ye always get upset!

No I dont.

Ye do. Then it ends up a row.

Dad was silent for a moment. I just worry. What's there and who's there.

Dad it's only a walk.

Things happen on walks.

What things?

Ye're not that thick. As ye keep reminding me, ye're sixteen years old.

Exactly! I could've got married months ago Dad I could have been a father by now.

Oh aye who's the lucky girl!

Dad I'm only saying. It was Mum made the joke. You were there when she said it, I would make ye both grandparents. It was her said it Dad it was Mum, it wasnay me.

Oh jees Murdo.

Murdo stared at the carpet. Neither spoke until eventually Murdo said, She would have liked it here.

Yeah only for a holiday.

But she would have liked it.

Yeah.

I know she wouldnt have wanted the racism. She would have hated that.

Yeah, well. . . Dad nodded.

Definitely.

Dad shrugged. Racism's everywhere son.

Yeah but is this not the worst? lynching people and civil rights and stuff; Martin Luther King. Ye even hear about it at school.

Well that's the old times.

Yeah Dad but the cops battering people and killing them? Murdo gazed at Dad. I was wondering that, like how come Aunt Maureen and Uncle John are living here?

Dad smiled.

I mean like here, in Alabama?

That's simple son it's work. Aunt Maureen's from Kentucky and there wasnt any work. So they moved here. People need to work. That's how they leave one place to go to another. Uncle John left Glasgow and came here then he met Aunt Maureen.

Yeah but Alabama?

It's not just Alabama that's racist son ye've got all these other places.

New York!

Yeah New York. Dad sighed. He shifted on the armchair to look directly at Murdo. Murdo held his look. What is it ye're trying to say son? D'ye think it's just here ye get racism?

Dad

Is that what ye think?

No.

It's racist everywhere son. Just like Scotland too. Dont act like ye dont know.

Dad I'm not acting like anything.

This isnay some class at school son this is the real world; this is what ye get in the real world. People are different all over but that's what ye learn when ye grow up. You're talking all the time about how mature ye are and then ye come out with stupid stuff like that. So is it Aunt Maureen and Uncle John then because they live here? Is it them that's racist?

What?

Is that what ye're wanting me to say?

Never. Never. I'm not saying that at all.

The trouble is son you dont know what ye're saying. Dad shook his head and turned from Murdo.

Murdo sat still. Dad had his book opened and was studying the page. Murdo waited. Dad continued to study the page. Murdo got up from the settee, lifting his book. He left the room without looking back, clicked shut the door behind himself. He headed along and into the bathroom. He washed his face and hands without looking in the mirror then dried and opened the door gently. Nobody there. He stepped out and downstairs.

He had left his book in the bathroom. It didnt matter. He sat down on the mattress. Then the fast clumping down the stairs. Murdo sat there. The door opened and Dad.

He stood by the side of the bed. He said: Murdo, if you have got something to say, say it.

Murdo looked away. Dad stepped around the end of the bed to face him. Stand up, he said.

Murdo didnt.

Stand up!

Murdo stood up and nearly smiled. He looked at the floor. He folded his arms and unfolded them. Dad said, Tell me what it is?

What what is? I dont know what ye mean.

Dad stared at him

Honest Dad I dont know what ye mean. Murdo put his hands in his pockets then took them back out.

Dad said, I only asked ye to say where ye were going. That's all. And it's because I worry, I worry.

Yeah I know Dad but really ye shouldnt because I cant go anywhere anyway so what does it matter it doesnt matter. Really, it doesnt matter.

What are ye talking about?

Murdo folded his arms.

What are ye talking about?

I've got no money. Murdo rubbed round the sides of his mouth. What I'm saying: I dont have any money.

What d'ye mean?

Murdo shrugged.

I give you money.

Yeah but not for myself. Murdo shrugged again. Like only if I need it for something. I dont have any money of my own. Know what I mean Dad I dont have any money.

I give ye money.

Murdo unfolded his arms and turned his head to look away. Dad, what I'm saying, ye never give me any pocket money; like ye never ever give me any pocket money. What about pocket money? Ye never give me any pocket money! Murdo shook his head:

Pocket money Dad ye just never ever. . . Pocket money, it is fucking pocket money Dad. . . Murdo was clenching his fists. Ye never. . .ye just. . .ye never ever give me any damn bloody pocket money and I dont know what to do I dont know what to do I'm just I'm stuck. I cannay go out even a walk Dad; I cannay go out; I dont have even one dollar, one dollar; I cant even buy a packet of chewing gum Dad nothing, I cant buy any damn thing and I cant do any damn thing. . . Dad. . . Dad I cant do anything.

Murdo was shaking now and tried to stop it, pushing down his hands by his sides, clenching and unclenching his fists; taking a deep breath.

Dad turned away.

I'm sorry, I'm sorry Dad. Dad it doesnt matter.

It was Mum dealt with pocket money.

Yeah.

I mean. . .

Yeah Dad sorry.

Ye need to remind me, if ye just could remind me.

Okay Dad.

I dont want us to fight. Whatever happens son I dont want us to fight. I mean me and you. Dad reached out his hand and clasped Murdo's shoulder. Murdo had his head lowered.

Dad went away soon after. Murdo laid down on the mattress, eventually switching on the music, just quietly, a beautiful number that was so so easy, going along someplace, the damp leaves, branch roots, smelling the woods, the loch water.

That evening Uncle John drove with Dad to the local bar which was about three miles away. They werent so strict as back home on drink-driving where Dad wouldnt have taken even one bottle of beer. Here Uncle John drank three or four which according to him was "nothing".

Murdo was glad when they went. It was good for Dad getting out and good for Uncle John too because whenever did he get the chance? Never. Dad being here was special for him. Once they had gone he sat with Aunt Maureen in the lounge watching television. She picked out a magazine from a magazine rack at the side of the television. Murdo knelt down to check through it, and found a book called the USA Road Atlas. It was full of maps. An actual book full of maps. Every page was a map, and followed on from the page before, or ran into the page coming after, just like online if ye were scrawling or zooming in someplace. It was just a brilliant old book. Murdo flourished it aloft. Aunt Maureen glanced at it. Huh? she said. Oh you want to go someplace Murdo?

Murdo grinned, sat back on the settee with it and began from page one. It gave a clear idea not only of the roads but the land itself; mountain ranges, rivers and lochs. The book had generalised maps and the downtown centres of the major cities. It was brilliant. Just scanning map pages and seeing the names of actual towns. Their very names! Murdo had to read them out to Aunt Maureen. Honest, he said, it is just amazing. Look! Gretna! Imagine Gretna! Elgin! Jeesoh, Elgin. McKenney! Cadder! Aberdeen! Aberdeen, actual Aberdeen. It's all Scottish names Aunt Maureen. Glasgow!

Glasgow sure!

Highlands! Jeesoh. Highlands?

Huh?

A town called Highlands. An actual town!

What is so wrong with that?

The Highlands is a whole place, not just one town.

Maybe it's a different Highlands.

Well yeah of course but one town!

Reminded the old people of home I guess.

Well yeah but – Phil Campbell! What is that is that a town? Phil Campbell? An actual town?

Sure it's a town.

But it's a guy's name! Phil Campbell!

Aunt Maureen shrugged. They all go there. All the Phil Campbells. One year a bunch of them came from the west coast of Canada.

Jeesoh!

You want the tourists to visit get a fancy name!

Do they come from Scotland too?

Well now I cant say there son.

There would be hundreds of them if they did. Imagine it! all the Phil Campbells! Murdo returned to the map and saw Millport. Millport! A Millport on the map. Millport. Aunt Maureen, that's right beside where we live, Millport, it's an island along from us; Millport's the name of the town!

Huh!

We used to go there. My pal's uncle's got a boat and Millport is a place we sailed. There's a great pier for jumping in the water. We used to do it.

You did?

It was great, just great. There was a chip shop there as well and if ye were hungry, ye always were, if ye were swimming, so it was great, ye went in there after, whatever, fish and chips. It was just smashing.

Sure sounds good.

All the different names. It's great!

Aunt Maureen chuckled. That's the old people, she said.

Rome: look! Rome!

Rome Georgia, sure: Rome Georgia, Athens Texas, Paris

Tennessee. That's the jet set Murdo. You know that one? Aunt Maureen sang:

> Oh we're not the jet set
> We're the old Chevrolet set.

You dont know the song? Rome Georgia, Athens Texas. Aunt Maureen chuckled. It's fun. You got to listen to it. They got an Athens in Alabama too. You look and you will find it there.

Murdo didnt answer. He was seeing the very town itself: LaFayette. He studied it. LaFayette. There's LaFayette. Aunt Maureen, he said, I'm just seeing it here.

Sure. Aint far from Chattanooga.

So it is close.

Yeah it's close. You got cousins in Chattanooga; Gillespies – unless they all went west. Used to get on a train there took you down through Huntsville. Did that train go over to St Louis now? I think it did. Chattanooga's Indian; they got a song.

> Pardon me boy
> Is that the Chattanooga choo choo?

Aunt Maureen stopped. Something going down the line, track twenty-nine. . . She frowned. The Dixie Line son you ever hear of that? Back then it was famous. It's gone now more's the pity. People dont know. You ask them and they dont know, my Lord, in the old days, they had to drive them coaches onto boats, had to stop the train. That's how they crossed the Tennessee River. Now it's for tourists. Aint got one for ourselves. Son it is beautiful up there. They got the Lost Sea Cave. You ever hear of that?

No.

You didnt hear of it?

The Lost Sea Cave. Never.

Huh. Son they got a whole underground sea over there, up by Sweetwater.

An actual sea under the ground?

They got boats go on it. If you like boats.

Boats!

Sure. We could go there week after next. We aint fixed any plans yet. Got the long weekend huh, so we're going somewheres that's for sure. Aunt Maureen glanced at the clock on the wall, made to rise from the armchair. I'm going to make a hot chocolate son what about you you want one?

Can I make it for you? asked Murdo.

No you cannot.

Murdo rose from the settee and walked with her to the kitchen. Things tied in. Amazing how it happened. When Sarah said about the gig she made it seem like it was easy to get there. How easy? Now he knew. She said him and Dad could stay overnight with friends but if it was as close as this maybe they wouldnt need to, they could just get a bus home. Maybe they had their own friends, their own family relations. But that wouldnt matter if they drove home after. Or like a bus. There had to be a bus. Ye think a bus goes to LaFayette? he said.

Aunt Maureen chuckled. You like buses huh!

Well I just mean like. . .

You got a notion for it. It's mountain country; good country. They got resorts. You go skiing back home?

No.

Calum does. He goes skiing Murdo. You dont think of snow in California huh, but they got snow alright, they got mountains. Him and his wife now they got a good size of a house son they'd put you up any time; you and your Dad want to visit there. Any time. Got two children of their own, younger than you. That's your first cousins Murdo. My Lord, they would love to see you there.

Is John there too?

John? Huh. Aunt Maureen smiled. You ask the questions.

I was just wondering.

Sure. Well no, he aint there. John's in Springfield, Missouri, that's

143

where John is – little John as I call him. Him and your uncle now one's hammer and one's tongs.

Murdo smiled.

Yeah, only it aint so funny. Aunt Maureen lifted her mug of hot chocolate and held it to her cheek. She turned to Murdo and touched his hand. She had switched on the Weather Channel. Now she switched it off. I'm going in my room a bit, she said.

Aunt Maureen would you mind if I took the Road book downstairs with me?

My Lord Murdo I do not want you saying that kind of thing! Makes like you are not family and yes you are family. This is your home and you do what you want. Aunt Maureen brandished her fist at him.

Sorry Aunt Maureen.

She nodded.

*

Murdo's concentration was on the book of Road Maps. Maybe ye didnt have to go through Chattanooga at all for driving, if ye could pass through the wee towns. Except if it was the bus and folk were getting off. That was his recollection of buses coming from Memphis.

Noises from outside, tyre noises on the gravel. Uncle John's 4x4; him and Dad back from the pub. He got up off the bed, shoved a chair under the high-up window and stepped up to see, but would have needed a step ladder to see properly.

The bathroom door closed. Murdo undressed swiftly, switched off the light and got into bed, expecting footsteps down the stairs and Dad chapping the door to see he was okay. Why would he not be? Vampires attacking, creatures from the depth coming to drag him down.

He thought to put the light on after but his head was gone

because of the gig and the idea of that, if it was even possible. Surely it was? Even just "possible".

If he couldnt he couldnt. He said he would so really he had to. Otherwise he would let people down.

Amazing how black it was with the light out. Ye couldnt see a thing! Better with yer eyes shut. If ye were in the dark too long with yer eyes open ye got that weird feeling like things closing in; the land coming together and shutting ye in. An earthquake and the ground cracks, you fall in, aaahhhh, trying to cling on, the dirt crumbling. Scary.

He switched the music on, playing it quiet. Playing it quiet was listening to it quiet, and made it different. But full-sounding.

The truth is Dad knew nothing about music. So nothing about Murdo. He heard him play in his room, and knew he was in a band, or had been before Mum was ill.

No point talking.

Maybe Aunt Maureen would come with him! She could drive, she could hire a car.

He shifted on the bed. Moonlight through the wee window; it angled, making the ceiling itself a kind of map made out of papier-mâché, all the bumps, lines and cracks. Imagine a marker pen and tracing it out, following the lines, circling the bumps for mountains and lost valleys, lochs and rivers. Contours. Ye could trace them with yer tongue on the roof of yer mouth, the way sometimes Murdo drew things, sitting on a bus and an old man's head from the seat in front. Then Mum, he didnt want to draw Mum, how she was sleeping, that way she was, the changes; these changes in her face.

Poor Mum.

Murdo thought things that were totally private. Nobody ever got to know. Not even himself in a weird way. It all mixed in without working it out. Then later something came out. Maybe while he was sleeping. Not dreams, just whatever. Thoughts working their way through. Sometimes he got angry and shouldnt have.

It was just life. Dad met Mum; if he hadnt Murdo and Eilidh wouldnt have been there. Different parents different children.

★

Early next morning Murdo heard the gravel crunch beneath the wheels of the 4x4, then it had gone. Uncle John was on his way to work. Murdo lifted his jacket and walked upstairs, collecting his boots from the rug at the front door, treading past Dad's bedroom and through into the dining area. He tried to unlock the dining room exit to the patio but it wasnt locked. He opened it and stepped outside. Aunt Maureen was there in the garden. Hey Murdo!

Aunt Maureen! I'm just going a walk.

You're early?

So are you!

Huh. . .? Oh, Mister Impatient!

"Mister Impatient" was one of her names for Uncle John. Most every morning Aunt Maureen was up along with Uncle John and sat with him before he went to work. Murdo hadnt thought of that.

He intended walking in a square. The streets roundabout were wide and straight, up and down and side by side, so it was easy walking. The houses neat with trimmed grass lawns, no front hedges. The lawns stretched to the kerb at the edge of the pavement, if ye could call it a pavement; the grass came right down to the kerb. It was like walking on somebody's grass. Uncle John said about a boy getting shot dead for crossing somebody's garden. That was hard to avoid. If ye didnt walk on their grass ye would have had to walk on the street.

Surely that was wrong? If there was no actual pavement. Beneath the kerb was a curved drop and a stank to fend off a torrent of water, for when they had floods. Flash floods. They spoke about them on the Weather Channel.

While he was walking a pick-up truck backed out of a driveway.

A big man in a check shirt was at the wheel. Murdo had to stop in his tracks to let the guy out. The guy looked at him as if it was Murdo's fault. On the main road only a few cars passed. A woman walking a dog. Another woman walking a dog. No sign of a bus-stop. If there was a local bus it maybe would go into the city centre. From there there would be buses to everywhere.

It was so peaceful! Then a sudden feeling that he liked it here. Nobody knew ye. They didnt know ye were alive. They hardly even saw ye. It was like a new life! He was on his own and going about. Whatever it was, whatever he did, it was him. That was the feeling. This was the outside world.

Although in a weird way it wasnt. Because he was here. It was an outside world but he was in it. The inside world was in his head. Nobody went in there but him. Murdo grinned: a song in his head, a great one by Beau Jocque.

> Ah forty down, a forty down,
> a forty down down down down down
> dig it down

It was true but Alabama and here he was. It was him and nobody else. Only Beau Jocque, and his brilliant band, swinging along.

Murdo chuckled. So if he was here so was Sarah because it was her gave him the compilation.

He just felt good. So good. Life was good. It was his life.

The idea of that: whatever, just whatever! Where was the accordeon, he needed the accordeon!

True but, ha ha. Back home he would have played! He needed to play, he was wanting to play, he was going to play, and with Queen Monzee-ay. And would tell Dad. He needed to tell him.

He strode on now, power-walking round the block and there was Aunt Maureen's house in whatever – half an hour?

He walked along the driveway to enter the back door. Aunt Maureen had gone. For breakfast he lifted two bananas, poured a glass of milk, returned downstairs, opened the Road Atlas. Chattanooga wasnt far, if ye had to go through it by bus then it was a case of taking a right into the state of Georgia, over the mountains.

He needed money. Not a lot. He didnt like asking Dad for anything, but that was that and he would have to.

Two accordeons made it special. They got that deep-sounding full thing that can be the best. Ye clenched yer fist thinking about it, and ye could feel it in the big muscle at the top of yer arm. Ye got that tension, a quivering feel to it. Dreams are dreams but this could happen. It was up to Murdo. Queen Monzee-ay *knew* he could do it. Of course he could. Ye just did it. Ye went ahead and ye did it.

Ye got the lead in and it was fine. By the weekend after next Murdo would have the set in his head. Then with the box. As soon as he got the box. He needed to get the fingers moving. Some proper playing. It would come. But the sooner he had a box the better. That pawnshop in Allentown. Maybe there was one in Chattanooga, or in Huntsville. Buying one out a pawnshop was okay. If it played it played. Ye tried it first. Ye would never buy one without playing it. Especially an accordeon, it would be bloody useless, like it had to be ready so if the reeds needed cleaning, there was no time for anything. A special glue, beeswax. The wax of a bee.

That was life. Everything for something.

There was nothing to worry about. Queen Monzee-ay *knew*. As soon as she heard him play. Even before! She said she knew when she saw him standing beside the tree! That is the truth! She said that. Just the way he was watching. But that was true. Watching means taking it all in. Ye see the person and then ye watch him. Oh there he is! Ye see the whole person. So watching means seeing all the bits and pieces; how he stands, how he moves, how he listens, how he looks. Queen Monzee-ay saw all that.

She was lead so he was playing to her. Relax, settle down. Then if she asked him for one. Probably she would. In Allentown for the first time he played "Blue Skirt Waltz". How come? Just because turquoise, that was the accordeon. Then for a girl, a blue skirt dancing. Put on yer blue skirt and dance. Girls dance in that certain way. When ye see a girl's legs, a girl is dancing and there are her legs. Murdo liked to see them. That is that, just the legs dancing, there is the girl, her legs, look! Jees! Beautiful legs didnt go on and on until one peak, if they were beautiful then that was the peak, that was like music where one thing was this and another thing was that but how could a polka be better than a waltz! it was just the most idiotic thing could be said. A girl's legs were beautiful but hers were more and hers over there were more and more; that was like beautiful legs + 1, beautiful legs + 2; just stupid nonsense, so three legs were better than two. Daft stuff.

★

Aunt Maureen had come from the house carrying a tray and called to Murdo who was sunbathing at the rear of the garden, lying on his front on the beach towel and reading the Road Atlas book. He had left the hi-fi in the room. There was a cable and lead that would have stretched back into the house, although Dad was there. Anyway, the book, it was just amazing like how ye could trace all where the roads went and the land between and even the distances, it told ye some and ye could work out others, and follow roads all the way up or else across. If ye stayed on the Interstate 75 ye landed way up in Detroit or else the other way it was down the very southernmost tip of America in a place called Mangrove Swamp. What a road! That was interstates. Roads going inbetween all the states. That one was like all the way north to all the way south.

And interesting roundabout LaFayette and Chattanooga up to Sweetwater where the underground sea was. Mountains and stuff, national parks. They were talking about the weekend after this one coming, when Uncle John had the Friday off. Murdo was thinking if he did go with people on the Friday and they went up someplace and stayed overnight or whatever, maybe he could still make the gig on Saturday evening because like it was the same motorway road and there had to be a bus, surely. Or else hitching a lift. People hitched lifts. Ye were just careful. Stay overnight with Sarah's family then Sunday morning Cheerio and that was him back to wherever, Sweetwater, or Cumberland Gap where Uncle John's old uncle somebody used to live years, years and years ago, and Uncle John's old uncle somebody was Murdo's old uncle uncle somebody plenty times removed.

Murdo closed the Atlas book and got up from the big towel. Aunt Maureen had settled the tray on the patio table and chatted with Dad for a while. She returned into the house and Dad was back reading. He didnt look up when Murdo arrived. So Dad hi and all that I want to play a gig and it's at LaFayette in the state of Georgia. Gulp! Pardon? What did ye say! You heard! Ha ha. Better saving yer breath. If it was later wait till later and dont do it sooner.

Dad was engrossed in his book. Murdo would have to talk first. Ye have to in this life. This is this and you are you. Although Dad knew he was there. Murdo had lifted the glass of orange juice. Dad, he said, I was just thinking there about the music. Just eh. . .

Dad nodded.

Like the way it is for me, how I do it, if I dont have an accordeon or guitar or like whatever.

Dad half closed the book.

I'm not talking about other people. Just myself Dad. What I do I listen. I listen and just kind of – I dont know if it's taking it in. Only it's something I do Dad I mean if I'm bursting to play and I cannay I mean that happens too, I'm bursting to play and I cannay. So I've got the music to hear. Just hearing it the way I'm hearing it, it's like learning, although I'm just listening like I hear it and I learn it. It's just the way I do it Dad so I mean that's just how it is.

Dad smiled.

No just because like with the music Dad I just seem able to

take it in. Maybe other people dont. Like even in school, my head is like just going through everything I mean everything Dad just whatever like thinking about stuff if maybe there's a tune I'm working on. You go to work and I'm up there in my room. Before I go to school: that's what I do and sometimes I just forget where I am Dad just like doodling about on the guitar or else like I jam in Dad ye know like I've got some old music I stick on Dad ye know what I do like how I jam in, and I just forget everything. I forget everything.

Murdo stopped talking and was looking at the patio floor, a wooden floor; spars; the earth down below. Echo echo echo, thud thud thud, solid earth: thud, pwohhhh, thud

Dad was listening to what Murdo was saying.

What was he saying? It was all daft. Even the name: Chattanooga. Dad wouldnt let him play the gig. This is what Murdo knew. He wanted to laugh but only in a stupid way. Because he was an idiot. Sixteen years of age. It was all just insanity. School. Who cares. The teacher said about Mozart when he was seventeen, Court Musician, what does that mean? Murdo just wished something, he didnt know what. Disappearing. Things dont change. Not in this life. If they do then what? Nothing. Himself standing there, the swimming shorts, sun tans, he just went red.

Dad said, That festival son. Ye were saying about it?

Yeah, it's near Chattanooga.

Right.

But the festival's LaFayette in the state of Georgia; it's over the border in the mountains, ye see it on the map, it looks great, just a wee town. Aunt Maureen knows it. They've got a museum. I think we've got relations there unless they moved out to the west coast, like California.

Dad smiled.

So did Murdo. No he didnt. It was just ha ha. Except his stomach didnt feel good.

The bird that fluttered, the bird that looked at him. Imagine a bird looking right at ye? Did birds do that? That was like a Cherokee Indian bird. It was there and just looking, what ye doing here, this is my place.

The biscuits on the plate. The glass of orange juice. The glass was cold. He lifted it and held it in his right hand; wet, the condensation. It was cooler in the patio with the overhead kind of wooden spars thing that was like a roof, so ye didnt get sunburnt.

Ye sitting down?

Yeah. Murdo sat down at the side of the table.

Dad smiled, looking towards the house. Aunt Maureen had appeared. She stopped at the table. She scratched her head, puzzled about something. She was looking at Murdo. Murdo smiled. Hi Aunt Maureen.

Huh, she said, now what did I come out here for? She peered at Dad. My memory son what's happening!

Dad said, I'm as bad.

You are huh!

Murdo glanced at Dad.

Aunt Maureen smiled at the biscuits and stuff on the table, was about to head back into the house. Now Murdo, she said, and wagged her finger the way a schoolteacher does giving ye a row. Are you alright? she said, That is what I am asking.

I'm fine.

Is he Tom?

Yeah. Dad smiled.

Mm. Aunt Maureen frowned. You too now what about you?

I'm fine, said Dad.

Everybody's all fine in Scotland huh?

Murdo grinned.

You doing the ironing? asked Dad.

It's been piling up on me.

Can I give ye a help? Murdo asked.

No, she said, you cannot; you cannot give me any help one little bit! She took his hand: Not on vacation. You're on vacation son. You watch that sun now, she said, you are warm.

He knows, said Dad.

I only do it for twenty minutes.

Half an hour ago, said Dad.

Well it wasnt half an hour, said Murdo, then he smiled at Aunt Maureen who was looking from him to Dad and back again.

Give me a hug, she said to Murdo. He got up from the chair and moved to her. She held him close to her and sighed. Murdo son, she said and hugged him again. It was a real cuddle. This is the kind Aunt Maureen gave.

Queen Monzee-ay wouldnt have been as good at it. Neither would Aunt Edna. But was that true? Maybe it wasnt. If it was their own family of course they would be good. If it isnt yer own family it is just a different cuddle. Aunt Edna would have been good at it, just depending. Cuddles can be weird. A wee cuddle from one was a big one from somebody else. Dad hardly gave any. Uncle John's were all slap slap slap slap. Some guys thumped ye hard. Dad cuddled Murdo at the funeral, and other times too. All the cuddles of the day at the funeral. There couldnay be any more cuddles. But then how Dad shook yer hand, sometimes that was like a cuddle.

Aunt Maureen was saying something about the weather. Dad said something back to her and ye could see about him, how with Aunt Maureen, Dad was the same as Murdo. Dad thought about Aunt Maureen in the exact same way. She was just the very best, really. What else? Nothing.

It was strange. Murdo didnt care about stuff. There were things in life people cared about. He didnt. Ha ha is what he felt.

No point talking. Even how Dad was there with his book and Aunt Maureen just like how she was doing everything.

She was a real aunt. More than any blood. What was blood? Blood was nothing. There couldnt be a better aunt. She was talking to Murdo now. Protecting the dog, she said, he went out to find it, took shelter in the car.

God. . . Dad shook his head. You hear that Murdo?

What was it again?

Boy just found there with his dog, said Aunt Maureen. He was protecting it; went in a car for shelter and the car got flattened. Tree fell right on top of it, snapped apart. Oklahoma.

Jees, said Murdo.

Aunt Maureen looked from Murdo to Dad. Protecting the dog. My Lord his poor mother, no rhyme nor reason there huh!

Murdo said, That's the thing in America, people die from the actual weather.

Sure they do.

The actual weather.

Not in Scotland huh?

No. Except maybe like climbing accidents on mountains, snow avalanches, or else like drowning maybe if ye were out on a boat but not actual weather like I mean where people die. No. Not like floods and twisters and whatever.

You didnt know that huh?

No, said Murdo, I dont think people do know that back home.

Dad said, Maybe some do.

Aunt Maureen lifted the plate of biscuits. You didnt eat any, she said.

I did take one, said Dad.

I was going to, said Murdo.

You got your orange juice son huh?

Yeah. It's like real oranges, better than we get back home.

Aunt Maureen suddenly wagged her finger at Murdo. Oh now, she said, I know what it was. I got the question for you Murdo, church on Sunday. You go to church back home?

Dad was looking.

You want to come one time with us? Uncle John and me? We're going Sunday morning. You think you might come? Would be nice if you did.

Murdo smiled and nodded.

Well you think about it, she said.

Okay Aunt Maureen.

It was all mixed up. Aunt Maureen was great. She was just great. It was Murdo who wasnt. He was a horror, the things he thought about, horrible thoughts, horrible horrible, just the most horrible.

His voice too, he didnt want to hear it again, ever. If Aunt Maureen was going to church on Sunday then maybe, maybe he should even just think about it, just think about it. He didnt care about any of it except just her, Aunt Maureen, it was her, it was just to go with her. Murdo didnt care about meeting other people, nice ones or not. If Aunt Maureen was meaning guys his own age or else girls, ones who went to church.

It was daft. Murdo would meet people and he wanted to meet people, and if he went places he would. He would meet people. So if that was church like a place to go then okay. So maybe that would be something. If Dad didnt go. Maybe Murdo would, if Dad didnt.

But why? if he didnt believe. Dad believed, Murdo didnt. Murdo had his life too, his own space. The basement. Dad had his room. This was Murdo's. So what was wrong with being in it? Jeesoh, if it was his? How come it was like a big deal to spend time in it? If Murdo hadnt had the basement this whole holiday would have been a punishment. Anyway, it was not a holiday. Who would have called it a holiday, nobody. Coming here was recovering from a bereavement. Ye were bereaved and had to cope. Mum dying was a bereavement. Murdo had to cope and Dad had to cope. It was not a punishment. People look at ye and think it to themselves: Oh the poor boy lost his mother, what did he do to deserve that?

Nothing. Nothing to deserve it and nothing not to deserve it. She just died. That was Mum, tumours that live on and kill females. Males have theirs. Things are how they are. Never mind God and Jesus. Aunt Maureen was the best but that was her. She had hers and Murdo had his.

Her and Dad would be talking. The boy's just lost his mother.

Oh well I've lost my wife. Yes but your mother? Not as bad as your wife. Losing your wife is worse than losing your mother. No it isnt. Yes it is. He's having to cope. So is everybody. Murdo is a young man. A young man is not a boy: a young man is a man. So if he is a young man then he can go where he wants and just act like whatever.

So what if nice people go to church? Who wants nice people! Ones who praise the Lord and are so welcoming to everybody? What is nice people? Do bad things not happen to them? If bad things happen are they so nice?

The idea of innocent people. They hardly live then they are dead. Ye wonder about that. If God makes people dead is that Him punishing people? If it is yer nearest and dearest is that God punishing you? Who else could it be? With Mum it was like ye must have done something very very bad. Ye think it to yourself because how else? If ye sinned it must have been badly, very very badly. Yer sister then yer mother. The very worst of all. So if things happen for a reason what is the reason?

People talked about sinners, "we are all sinners", but it wasnt true. Maybe Dad believed it. A believer believed. Was Eilidh a sinner? Murdo was sick of that stuff. We endure hard knocks and it is for a reason. God knows the reason. We dont know but God does. Maybe Jesus does. The blood of the lamb being redeemed. The lamb was Jesus. Through the blood of Jesus who is our blessed saviour, our living redeemer, by the shedding of his blood our sins are washed away. Blood-stained roads and blind men walking. Josie. Josie was Josie. Aunt Maureen's friend. They were believers. That old guy in the bus station, a walking skeleton. Cracked.

Imagine a baby. A sinner! So crazy, so so crazy. That guy Conor must have thought so and it was his baby. So that would be his sins. The sins of the father is like punishment for the children; two wee girls and a baby. A baby only had to be born. As soon as it was born it was like doomed. That was how it worked. Maybe Dad thought the same. Mum was dead because Dad was a sinner.

That was Hell if it was his fault; so Hell was now and not after ye were dead. On the road not seeing the signs. A blind man walking. That was Murdo, not seeing the signs. He thought she was getting better. That was the worst stupidity. She was not getting better and was not going to get better. Murdo didnt know that. Nobody told him. Naive childishness. He needed his father to tell him. How stupid. He knew she was badly ill but actual dying. The very end and she couldnt get out of bed. Imagine. Ye imagine it, how do ye imagine it, just a smile, not the breath to say Murdo, holding onto his fingers.

★

Late Friday evening after dinner they were sitting on talking. Uncle John folded his arms and stared into Murdo's eyes for about five seconds. Murdo smiled then stopped. It was a staring contest. They kept it going for several more seconds. Murdo stopped first although he didnt have to. Uncle John relaxed. You ever think of staying here? he said.

Oh now, said Aunt Maureen.

Murdo glanced at Dad.

Uncle John raised his hand at once. Never mind him son I'm asking you. Do you think you would ever ever consider it?

Both Dad and Aunt Maureen awaited his answer.

No, he said. I only mean I wouldnt consider it, because I dont know. It's not a thing I mean it wouldnt be me making the decision.

Aye but son if it was you?

Dad had risen from the table; he took his empty teacup through to rinse at the kitchen sink.

Murdo said, Yeah but Uncle John it wouldnt be me making the decision.

What is this boy a politician! called Uncle John. Then he reached and trapped Murdo's wrist on the table. Ye're no getting away with it. Out with it! I've heard yer Dad, now it's you. If it was your decision what would it be? Would ye stay or go? Eh, stay here or go home?

Murdo smiled, then chuckled.

Uncle John laughed and pointed at him, turned to Aunt Maureen. Murdo looked from Dad to Aunt Maureen and back to Uncle John. It was true. It was just true and he was saying it out loud.

Uncle John called to Dad: Did ye hear that?

I did, said Dad, returning to the table.

Aunt Maureen was smiling, and Uncle John said to her: Mind you old Jimmy Shand was good! Uncle John winked at Murdo. So how much is an accordeon? he said. They expensive?

Aye, said Dad, the kind Murdo likes.

Well if they're good quality. Murdo shrugged.

Italian, said Dad.

What is that a joke?

Murdo said, They make the best accordeons.

You're kidding me on son! The old Eyeties. Did you know that? he asked Aunt Maureen.

Well mister their music is beautiful. You forgetting that?

No I'm not forgetting that. I'm just saying, it's not something ye would think. Music aye, okay. Not musical instruments. You liked the big guy mother.

Well who didnt huh! Pavarotti.

Aw great opera, said Dad, I can listen to opera. Dad smiled. Any day of the week!

Murdo said, Mum liked opera. It was Mum liked opera. Opera is what she liked. It was her. Murdo looked again at Dad. It was her liked it Dad.

Of course. Dad smiled.

Murdo looked away. Opera was Mum, always Mum. Murdo couldnt believe Dad would say stuff like that. Great opera. Did he actually say that? What about ordinary opera?

He stared at the table. Dad was looking at him but he couldnt return it, couldnt, couldnt look at him. He glimpsed Aunt Maureen smiling to him and tried to smile back but couldnt. It was too bad. Dad was saying something, whatever Dad was saying, whatever, something.

But that was Murdo, he had to leave the table. Because otherwise – he just had to leave.

It wouldnt have been crying. He didnt cry. Even if it started he was able to make it stop. Not blinking. If ye blinked then it ran down yer face. It was getting yerself cold. Ye had to just be there and not do anything except make it not happen and that was how ye made it not happen, by not doing anything, nothing. That was how Murdo managed it, getting yer head out and just like not being there in the company: although ye were; ye went side on to it, making yer mind wander, if ye could think of something, just yer mind, going places. In school he did it. Or wherever, on a bus or the ferry – him and Dad going home on the ferry from leaving Mum in the hospice damn bloody hospice, every damn bloody night Dad in the ferry lounge and Murdo outside unless it was gale force and the rain too too heavy, the spray battering yer face, spattering it. Murdo needed that. Ye think of the song because he would have swam over, and the seas were wild, he didnt care about the seas, he would swim over and over and over, but that was it now, Mum, she would be with Eilidh.

He heard Dad doing something, maybe just moving on his chair. And Aunt Maureen saying, You boys have had the worst time.

Murdo gazed at her. Aunt Maureen.

Ye thought about it and it was true. Him and Dad. They had had it the worst. It couldnt get worse because it was the worst already, it was the worst there had ever been and they were in the middle of it. What ever could be worse. And Dad too, Dad too. Murdo said, Dad. . .

Dad smiled.

Murdo got up from the chair and went down the basement. He

didnt switch on the light and didnt put on the music. He wanted to hide. People couldnt hide.

He kept off the light.

This was the densest. Here ye were blind.

A quiet kind of swish, swish. Flying cockroaches? But Uncle John said they buzzed. How serious was he? Murdo wasnt sure he had ever seen one, unless it was the big black ones with the thick body. Ye think of things slithering. Burying into the earth.

It was just life, ye think of life, how everything changes. This long long period of stuff that isnt good, where nothing is good and ye always get taken back into it, can never get out it, reaching out and ye cannot get what it is; expecting it to leave but it never does; ye wake up and it is there again, ye get the moment where things are good and even ye forget; ye forget it all and expect the normal stuff but it doesnt happen and ye are back inside it; Mum is not at the door telling ye to get up or ye'll be late for school; that is not going to happen, never, and it is just you, a wee speck spinning.

Life was different to what ye thought. Dad would just be whatever, worried, he worried. He was just coping same as Murdo. The two of them.

More time passed. Murdo could not stay downstairs. He went upstairs to the bathroom.

Dad was alone in the kitchen. He had started on the clearing up, and was glad to see Murdo. He didnt say anything but Murdo knew he was. Murdo said: I was doing the clearing up Dad. I told Aunt Maureen I would and eh I mean it's not really you to do it.

Okay.

Murdo moved past him to the draining board to make a start. Dad had already stacked the dinner plates in the sink and filled it with hot water. I'm not using the dishwasher, he said.

Me too.

Ye have to wash stuff twice if ye do.

I know, said Murdo.

Okay. Okay. . . Dad left the kitchen, maybe going to his room or else to get ready. Maybe him and Uncle John were going to the pub. Murdo would be glad. Being in a pub would be interesting.

Better being outside seeing stuff, just looking, walking about.

Murdo had his hands in the soapy water. There was a wee back window directly above the sink. A tree blocked most of the view but it was still great seeing out. He didnt mind cockroaches anyway if that was the swishing sound. Insects were everywhere. Spiders' webs and all sorts. Who cares. Murdo didnt. Never ever. People thought thick woods and dark forests were scary. They didnt like going into them. Murdo did. Murdo went into them. Even as a boy, ye might say forcing himself, he forced himself. That was Eilidh, after she died. Murdo did funny wee things. He went into the woods and sat next to bushes and trees; creepy crawlies down in the dirt, damp earth, muddiness. The sun never reaches these places. No grass but roots and remains.

Dad's bedroom door was shut. Murdo chapped it. Dad opened it. Murdo said, Dad, I'm sorry.

Och away. Dont worry.

Dad

No. Ye're right; what do I know? Opera. I dont know a damn thing.

Dad it's my fault.

No it's not.

It is.

No it's not. Dont worry. Dad came out from the bedroom and closed over the door. They returned to the dining room. Murdo entered behind Dad and Uncle John and Aunt Maureen were peering across at them.

THREE

The Gathering was a two-hour drive away, more than a hundred miles distant. They left the main highway and were onto a smaller road that had a number instead of a name and went along at the foot of a mountain. Aunt Maureen thought it was known by the name of a ranch. From there it was onto a rocky road that was more like a wide trail. The cars were parked for free in regimented rows down one side of a big field. Attendants were there to guide the drivers. Once parked ye crossed and walked a tree-lined track and in through a wide gate where they took entrance fee money.

Ye werent allowed to bring in food or drink of yer own, and no guns either. Uncle John had advised them earlier: Dont take yer six-shooter. Posters were pinned onto the trees; some serious, some for fun:

ALL CONTESTANTS PAY ADMISSION

IF RAIN WEAR A HAT

NO REFUNDS ON BOUNCY CASTLE CHARGES

ALCOHOLIC BEVERAGES DESIGNATED AREAS

BEWARE FUND RAISERS

SAVE A SMOKER — DONATE A LUNG

KIDS UNDER (~~10~~) 2 GO FREE

In the evening a dance was scheduled for the Marquee Tent which they called The Hielan Fling. The entrance payment entitled ye to attend that plus the afternoon music event. Dad wanted to pay but

Uncle John wouldnt let him. The people at the entrance passed out information flyers. Murdo took a few and put them in his pocket. A large poster advertised The Wee Bairn Games (0–5). Another advertised a Hunt the Sporran Competition. Some of the Kids' Competitions finished before they arrived. It had been going since 10 a.m. and was now about 12.30. A Dance Competition for Girls was split into age groups. Jig Dancing I: (3–5), Jig Dancing II (6–11), Jig Dancing III (12–17), Jig Dancing IV (18+). Uncle John made a joke to Aunt Maureen about entering the last group. Quite a few girls wore Highland dance outfits. Adults too, wearing fancy Scottish clothes, tartan and kilts. One woman in from the entrance gate knew Aunt Maureen and was delighted to see her. Aunt Maureen introduced Murdo and Dad as her nephews from Scotland. Murdo liked her doing that. They chatted together and they walked on slowly, waiting for her to catch up. No sooner did she catch up than she saw another woman and went to meet her.

Sally Rose, said Uncle John. She's an old friend of yer Auntie. That's the last we'll see of her. Look for Josie too, because she'll be roundabout. Then who else? Quite a few, I dont know, church people. Uncle John chuckled and winked at Murdo. She's in her element son. Just watch it with the religious aspect. Nay wisecracks!

. . .

Dad glanced across.

I'm only saying to watch it son. Uncle John winked. Whatever ye said to the women, just be careful.

Dad smiled. What did ye say? Eh? Murdo. . . ?

I dont know Dad, I dont know.

They had stopped walking and moved to the side of the track to let people pass along. Was it about religion?

I dont know.

Och it's nothing, said Uncle John, me and my big mouth.

Murdo looked at him. He couldnt remember a single thing at all about whatever he was supposed to have said except if it was personal stuff about the family, talking to Aunt Maureen maybe.

But if he had said something it wouldnt have been a joke, not like a joke. Never. If Uncle John thought that. . . Wisecracks? What did it even mean? Jokey comments? He would never have made jokey comments. Never. Horrible even to think. Aunt Maureen and her friends. Never ever.

After a moment Uncle John said: Maybe I've got the wrong end of the stick. It was when ye were talking with the women son, the pot-luck night; did ye no say something? Emma-Louise and them were talking about it later. Am I wrong son? asked Uncle John.

. . .

What was it ye said? asked Dad.

Kids running along the track toward them, past them, making for the main area. People everywhere, everywhere. Dad tapped him on the arm. They stepped sideways to allow the kids past, running past.

Murdo kept his head lowered. Dad was waiting. Murdo didnt know. He didnt care either. Dad whatever. Dad whatever all the time. Murdo's stomach was that weird way again. Twisted. That was how it felt. Uncle John said something. Murdo didnt hear. Dad said something back. Murdo didnt hear that either. Dad saying: We'll walk.

Uncle John held up his right hand. Murdo son, I've got the wrong end of the stick.

Murdo shook his head. I dont know Uncle John I might have said something like eh I dont know, I might have said something when I was in talking with Aunt Maureen and them or else if they picked me up wrong. But I would never have said any jokey thing like wisecracks. Not to Aunt Maureen. Definitely. Never.

Uncle John said to Dad: It's me Tommy. I've got the wrong end of the stick. I'm just a dumpling. Murdo son I'm just a dumpling.

It's okay.

Do people still call ye that in Glasgow! They said it when I was a boy. Ya bloody dumpling! That was what they called ye! Worse!

Murdo smiled.

Dad was just watching. But it was Murdo's fault for over-reacting.

Uncle John was feeling bad and it was for nothing. Quite soon after he saw men he knew, men in kilts. Aw look, he said, old Charlie, I'm goni say hullo, and off he went.

The people going along the track; fat and thin, young and old; the usual. Dad and Murdo continued walking. The temperature into the high seventies. Dad had his hands in his pockets and was just looking about, relaxed. Murdo said, Dad.

Yeah?

What Uncle John said there about wisecracks. I dont know what he was meaning because I didnt say anything like that. Nothing like that. I would never ever have done it. Jeesoh Dad Aunt Maureen, she's great. I would never ever say anything to upset her and like her friends, never.

Yeah I know. What it is Murdo, just keep yer own thoughts. Ye might have an opinion about religion and ye're entitled to it. But be wary. There's things here ye dont want to talk about; politics and that, the racist stuff. People dont think the same. It's like back home Rangers and Celtic, Protestants and Catholics, ye're aye the opposite. Whoever it is ye're the opposite. If it's all Catholics you're the only Protestant, all blacks you're the only white. The ones ye happen to be with they're all one thing but you're the other. So ye watch what ye say. The best thing is say nothing.

Murdo nodded.

Ye okay?

Yeah.

Ye went awful white there. Green. I thought ye were going to faint son and I havenay seen ye do that for a while. Dad smiled. I used to do it myself.

Yeah.

Dad chuckled and went into his pocket, took out a twenty-dollar bill and pressed it into Murdo's hand. I meant to give ye it earlier.

Thanks Dad.

See how it goes. If ye need more come and ask. Dad pointed

along to the various stalls and tents down the side of the field. Have a wander, he said.

Will we meet someplace? Murdo asked.

Och we're here all day, we'll bump into one another.

Yeah.

There's the music on too then the dance tonight. So ye'll no be disappearing. Dad clapped him on the shoulder then went one way. Murdo went the other, away from the main stalls and towards the far side of the area, to the edge of the field on the other side of the tents, way away from everything.

It was very warm now and he felt more like lying in the sun than trying stuff at the stalls. The scenery too; rock formations and mountains, it was so so good seeing the mountains. Ye got rivers here but not the same lochs like back home. Probably it was true what they said about Scotland: if it wasnt for the rotten weather it would be the best place in the world. Although Alabama too, once ye got to know it. Aunt Maureen said it was a beautiful state. Except where was the sea? Ye were hemmed in without it. They didnt have any except that wee bit of coast at the Gulf of Mexico.

He found a shady place. A sort of red dirt but the grass was okay. He lay down, using his jacket as a pillow. Jet streams far far in the sky. Three, four, maybe five trails. Where were they going? They already were here. Back home ye saw a plane high in the sky and it was headed for Canada. Low in the sky was England. He browsed through the leaflets he had lifted at the entrance. Global Hunger and people in prison all over the world. Good people, Christian people, suffering hard knocks, miseries and tragedy. Open your Eyes, and Open your Mind. Most was religious stuff but quite interesting. One gave information on the history of the "Henry Craig Gathering". Henry Craig had donated the use of this place annually. He was long dead but people kept the tradition and traveled from all over.

Although based on the Highland Gathering it was not trying to be a real one. It took from the ceilidh and was an ancient ideal going back into the mists of time. Horsemen rode round the land with the fiery cross held aloft, calling the clansfolk to order. They had the clan obligation to entertain their rulers, kings and chiefs. They sang songs, told stories, danced and took part in athletic games. It was like a tax. People had no money in those days so the kings and chiefs took a percentage of their fish and farm produce, and their whiskey too which was known as uisge beatha, "water of life". Their descendants still brewed it to this day only nowadays they called it "moonshine".

The thud of a football.

Down the field boys were playing football and two girls with them. A kickabout would have been great, even in the sun. He shoved the leaflets back in his pocket, got up and wandered among the stalls and tents. Seeing the price of stuff. Dad had given him the $20 but did that include food? He was starving. One place sold beer but one bottle alone was $7. Other stalls sold food. People sat outside drinking, eating and chatting. At a place farther along Uncle John was sitting with two older men. He was smoking a cigarette! Uncle John! Murdo hadnt seen him smoke before.

He hung back, unseen, then went sideways between stalls.

Here they sold stuff with Celtic themes. Kilts, Scottish whisky and buckled shoes. One stall had stained glass and decorative jewelry. Swords and shields; dirks. Scottish Irish. The culture of the Celts. The folk doing the selling were dressed in the old ways: kilts and fancy shirts, leather waistcoats. Some had long hair and blue clay designs on their faces. Mixed males and females. All ages. Plenty wore Highland outfits. Girls wore short kilts. Some of the older ones were very very good-looking. Really pretty and their kilts were like the shortest, the very very shortest, and just great legs. Socks and tunic outfits. White lace on their blouses; ruffles and sashes.

Older women wore the kilt too, and tartan waistcoat tops, tartan shawls. All different hats and wee umbrellas to keep out the sun. Guys mainly wore kilts or shorts. There werent many in his age group. They wore kilts with shirts, T-shirts and vests, had tattooed arms. Cowboy hats, baseball caps, bunnets, berets and Glengarrys. Their T-shirts had printed references to Scotland but other stuff too; one said "Hands off the Ocean" and another "Hands off the Presbytery"; one had "FBI" in big writing then underneath "Federal Bureau of Integration". A man and a woman had identical T-shirts saying, "Hi I'm Phil Campbell". Imagine saying hullo, I saw yer town on the map.

Three old guys chatting together wore kilted outfits in the official style with the traditional curved jackets, and shirts and ties too, thick socks with dirks poking out. Skinny legs and knobbly walking sticks. Maybe they were officials. They looked like the high-up ones that did judging at the real Highland Games.

One of the tents did face painting. Kids and toddlers were having the Scottish Saltire painted on their faces and on their hair round the back of their heads. Some had the Scottish Saltire at the front and other ones round the back, the Confederate flag. Ye could research yer family history and discover Scottish Heritage; the Battle of Bannockburn and Culloden; posters of Braveheart. One said "King Arthur: Scottish?" The American Constitution, the American War of Independence, Remember the Alamo and the American Civil War.

Girls selling ye religious stuff. Although they were smiling they were not having a laugh. One held lottery tickets up to Murdo. He shook his head, expecting her maybe to say more but she didnt, she went away to somebody else. Even if he did buy a ticket, if he won a prize, how could he collect it? He should have said that to the lassie like if he was back home in Scotland what happened, did they post it to you? She would have gawped at him. Oh is he an alien! She probably hadnt even heard of Scotland. Although surely here she would have! Anyway, he didnt have money for lottery tickets.

Stalls and tents along the way offered prizes for throwing a basketball and firing slug guns at targets. $5 a go!

He found a place where ye could "score a goal!" – ye kicked a football into a bucket for $3. If ye scored two out the three shots ye won the prize. Murdo was going to try it. They had the same game back home. Ye had to chip the ball rather than kick it. Ye were lucky to land it in the bucket at all. Even if ye did and the ball hit the bottom it bounced back out. Ye had to land it in so it hit the back and swirled roundabout. It was very very difficult. Even if ye managed it the only prize was a gigantic football the size of a huge belly; more of a balloon than a ball. Probably only worth about $3. He passed on. Near the beer tents were the usual stalls where ye won prizes on games like bingo and tombola. The one thing missing was music. He couldnt find one stall. It could have been instruments or CDs; just something. Folk were selling raffle or lottery tickets supporting good causes. Mostly they were religious, talking about religious aspects of life; Christ on Calvary, the Day of Reckoning, Saved by Grace. Some of it Murdo didnt know. He knew the words but not what they meant – The Truth of God Is the Judge. Churches had individual names: Live Oak Biblical, Back Creek Historical, Ray of Light Reformed, Tyson's Ridge Glad Tidings. They would have been Protestant. Catholic churches would have had the names of Saints. Back home they would, although maybe here was different.

Then a black guy! He spoke to folk as they passed by the tent. He had an African voice. Another black man was with him, and three black women, and white people too. Pictures of Jesus and little children all different races and colours. That was so unexpected and great to see.

But what had he expected? No black people at all.

One of their posters was brilliant: Music is the Glory of God.

They had T-shirts for sale: Redemption, Freedom, Forgiveness. Murdo was going to take their leaflets but when they didnt move to give him one he didnt offer. Some posters and pictures were not paintings but photographs of stained glass; stained glass and four girls killed

– four girls killed. Murdo read the poster, not getting too close. Four girls. A bomb did it. A bomb at a church. Was that true? It had to be true otherwise it wouldnt have been there. Four girls and killed. Four girls. Murdo stepped back from the stall. He was going to take a leaflet but didnt. Was it true? It had to be otherwise

how could it not be? Otherwise it wouldnt be there. Jeesoh! Four girls killed. Four girls killed! Murdo walked on. Imagine Sarah. She would have got angry, so so angry, just so angry. She would have talked to the black people. What happened? But it said what happened, a bomb. If ye were black ye would have been so so angry. But white too. If ye were white, what would ye feel? What did he feel? Not like talking. Maybe to Sarah. Except she wouldnt have been here, she wouldnt have come. Queen Monzee-ay! Never. Aunt Edna! Ha ha.

★

A sign at the entrance to the marquee listed the times of the day's events: Declan Pike – 3 p.m. Session – 5 p.m. Hielan Fling: Doors Open 7.30 p.m. Round the sides of the marquee families and small groups of people picnicked on the grass. A few dogs were jumping about. A collie was off the leash and two boys were running with it. People wore kilts and T-shirts and the males had Glengarry hats. The buckles on their leather belts looked the same design. A couple of the guys had the same face-paintings as the kids. One had "Sons of Red Eagle" printed on his T-shirt.

Uncle John was there, smoking another cigarette. He saw Murdo and waved him over. He was sitting with old guys underneath a massive umbrella. He saw Murdo and held the cigarette aloft. A filthy habit, he said. Now I'm asking ye son, at all costs, dont tell yer Auntie Maureen. Or I'm a dead man.

The other men laughed.

I only do it once in a blue moon and this is the blue moon,

bom di bom bom. One of these days I'll stop it altogether. He pointed at one of the other smokers. He's the rascal gave me it! Temptation saith the Lord. Uncle John covered his eyes with his other hand. Get Thee behind me!

Uncle John put his arm round Murdo's waist and drew him forwards. My nephew Murdo, all the way from *Scatlin*.

We're the Neighbourhood Watch! said one of the men.

Grandpop brigade, said one.

Your Dad passed here twenty minutes ago, said Uncle John. He thought this was a union meeting. These guys dont know what a union is. It's a train line right! Union Pacific. The old Dixie line. Uncle John took a drag on his cigarette then stubbed it out, turned to Murdo: You see the Alamo stall son?

Eh. . .

Look for the Alamo stall. See the Scottish names! Four maybe five born Scotsmen all fought for Texas. Same with the Confederate army. D'ye see the Civil War stuff? Scots, Scots-Irish. That's Ulster. Plus you got the ordinary born Americans with Scottish names. All the way through you got them. That'd be something for the schoolkids if ye set them a project eh, count the Scottish names.

Sounds like a lot of fun, said a man.

Uncle John chuckled. Then he stood to his feet and groaned, rubbing at the small of his back. He stepped away from the group, side on to Murdo so that his actions were shielded. He put his hand into his hip pocket, withdrew money and slipped it to Murdo.

Aw Uncle John. . .

Go and have some fun.

Ye dont have to do that.

Behave yerself. Just stick it in yer pocket.

Thanks, thanks a lot.

Mind now with yer Auntie, about the smoking. Dont say a word. Whatever ye do, ye must not.

Murdo smiled.

Uncle John was dead serious. Mind now.

Definitely.

Uncle John gripped Murdo by the arm and whispered: Forget about that religion carry-on, what I said to ye earlier on son I got it wrong. Completely wrong. You know what a dumpling is? I'm a dumpling. Okay?

Of course.

Uncle John smiled. He gazed at Murdo and was going to say more but instead clapped him on the shoulder. Away and have fun. He said, There's boys kicking a ball about by the way.

I saw them. They're a bit young.

Ach join in anyway.

Murdo grinned. Uncle John sat back down with his pals. Murdo checked what he had given him. One note. A fifty! Fifty! Jeesoh! Murdo stopped and examined the note. $50. One note for fifty dollars. Uncle John. $50. Jeesoh. Plus Dad's twenty equalled seventy. Seventy dollars.

He was starving. Things were expensive. Weer stalls were better. At one two lasses were getting served. One fair hair and one dark; both in Hielan dance outfits. Maybe they had been in the jig contests. Probably. Short kilts. Amazing how short, long socks high up.

They were friendly to the woman serving as though they knew her. She was an older lady and had on a shawl, although it wasnt tartan. Or was it? Maybe it was an old style. Ye felt that about the Gathering, they were like old style, from bygone days.

At the side of this stall the price list for food was broken into individual items. Not actual meals but there was savoury stuff, pies and bun things; plenty donuts. In bigger writing it read:

$6 FOOD-PLATE FOR HUNGRY BEAVERS

$8 FOOD-PLATE FOR HUNGRY BEARS

$12 FOOD-PLATE FOR HUNGRY HORSES

Murdo waited behind the girls. American voices. The lady returned their change and they lifted their plates. They half turned, watching to see what Murdo would do. He wasnt sure what to order except he was hungry. There wouldnt have been much difference between what a horse would eat and a bear. Except four dollars. Bears might even have been hungrier than horses. They could tear a person limb from limb. A horse didnt. What did a horse eat? Murdo couldnt think. Oats? Did they eat meat? Maybe they were vegetarian.

The woman was waiting. I'm just wondering please what ye get, said Murdo. I mean like the difference between the plates, if ye take the six dollar or else the eight?

Huh?

The two girls had walked a little farther off, but were listening. Probably the lady hadnt understood him. Murdo said, I was just wondering please about the actual food? Do I choose it or eh. . .

The lady smiled suddenly. You Maureen Simpson's nephew?

Eh. . . Yeah I mean eh my Aunt Maureen.

From Scotland?

Yeah. Murdo grinned. Simpson was Dad's mother's name before she got married.

Well now, said the lady. She signaled a man seated to the other side of the stall. Murdo had noticed him but didnt think he was part of it. He was older too and thin-looking wearing a baseball cap, sipping a cup of coffee or tea. A slogan on the cap read Duncan Bizkitz Outlawd. Duncan Bizkitz. Him there's Chess. I'm Clara, Clara Hopkins. Now your name son?

Murdo Macarthur.

That's right, yeah. Thank you Murdo for coming here to our table. The lady waved at the food and passed him a wide cardboard plate.

Thanks. Murdo peered at the food, moved a step to the right, seeing the various stuff. He stepped along and paused, then returned. Eh. . . he peered along at it all again.

Here, she said and took the plate back off him. She began putting food onto the plate herself, not asking him but just doing it. Murdo was glad. She was giving him a real pile.

Get one aboard afore the plate sinks! said the man, pointing at the donuts.

He's Maureen's nephew.

Huh?

Come all the way from Scotland.

Oh yeah. . . Guess you must be hungry son.

Yeah, thanks, said Murdo.

Dont say thanks to him, said the lady, he's joking. She settled a donut on top then passed him the plate.

Murdo was waiting to hear what it cost. She checked what she had put on the plate then checked it again. She hesitated then jerked her head sideways, looking away from him. He waited but she ignored him, as if she didnt know he was there. He knew what it was. He was just to go away. She didnt want him paying.

The man shifted sideways and bent towards him like he was going to say something but he didnt. He sniffed and sat back on the chair, folding his arms.

Murdo said to the lady: Thanks very much.

Uh huh, she muttered.

Murdo balanced the large plateful of food between both hands and walked away. He looked to see the two girls but they werent there. Then he did see them, heading toward the tents at the side of the area, maybe for a sit-down on the grass.

★

Murdo was in the marquee before three o'clock and it was almost empty. He sat by the end of the third row, along from the corner of the stage platform. He had food on the plate and was sipping water out of a paper cup. He had forgotten to buy a bottle at the stall and didnt want to return for one. Unless he could have paid. He would have preferred that. It was too awkward if she didnt allow it and would have looked like he only went there to get it for free. So he looked to buy one elsewhere and found a church tent dishing out free water. They had big containers of it and served it in individual paper cups. It was good and would make people think about their church; ones like Murdo who were not one way or the other.

The entrance to the marquee was from the opposite side of the space where he was sitting. Ye walked in and the stage was to yer left, a raised platform. The main seating all lay to the right. A line of tables went down each side. Down from the stage was a fair-size space for dancing.

It was still quite empty when the musician arrived, Declan Pike. He wore a beard, long hair and a baseball cap, jeans and a leather jacket. He stuck his sunglasses into a pocket then moved about by the mic, checking things out, positioning a chair nearby the mic stand. In one band Murdo played with a standing joke with the older guys was technical support at small venues. There never was any! Ye would turn up at a church hall and somebody would ask the wee woman making the tea: Where's the sound man? and she would faint. That was the joke. They didnt have any sound man here either but the PA worked.

Folk had come in by now and sat in various places. The musician noticed them. He gave the impression he was pleased to see them. He adjusted his guitar and started tuning. It was twenty past three already. Maybe he was waiting for more. He took off the guitar and propped it against the chair by the mic stand. He pulled out a pack of cigarettes. People watched him. He gestured with the pack, patted his chest as if to apologise and headed towards the entrance, withdrawing a cigarette as he went.

A few more arrived. People sat dotted around. Sometimes for a wee audience ye wished they would all sit together at the front. When they were all wide apart it just seemed what it was: empty. Although what does it matter, ye just play. The musician switched on the mic when he returned. He peered up at the overheard sound speakers and called to a couple of folk at the back. You all hearing me okay?

Nobody replied that Murdo could hear but he nodded so they must have done. Then he battered straight into "Johnnie O'Breadislea" taking Murdo by surprise! Quietly in but full-sounding every note like how ye want, and a particular quiver he was getting too, taking ye right into the story. One song and whoh! Murdo might have been first in with the clapping. The musician was surprised. He looked across and grinned. Murdo felt a bit daft but at the same time who cares. The guy introduced the next one about coal mines in Kentucky, and a wee town getting destroyed by a big company. It was strong. This one had a good chorus. He had a hard voice, occasionally rasping, but it was fine. The music piped through the system to speakers outside the marquee entrance and more people arrived. The musician called to them: Afternoon!

An older man answered: Afternoon!

He was bald with a wee white beard and wearing a waistcoat with bright colours. The musician noticed, pointed out. I like it!

This old guy paused a moment: Oh you do?

Yeah.

Well now I'm glad of that son might of gone home if you hadnt.

People laughed. The old guy then offered the musician a beer. But it was good fun, a nice atmosphere. The musician introduced himself, Declan Pike – call me Declan – and how he came from these parts but was now living in Houston, Texas. Part-time musician, full-time oil-worker.

Murdo liked hearing this. Guys back home did ordinary jobs too. Ye felt with him that he was trying for songs that were real. Stories from life. That style and voice of his, saying about the next song, written by this guy down in Texas who got shot dead in an argument over a welfare check. A slow track and that guitar just barely doing anything, ding, ding, telling the story, hear a verse, ding, ding, perfect spacing. And when he sang it he *had* the audience, they were just engrossed. Really it was a beautiful song, and strong applause from the audience. Aunt Maureen was among them.

Murdo hadnt seen her since they first came in. Josie and another woman were with her.

The older man from the foodstall stood by the entrance, still wearing the Duncan Bizkitz baseball cap; he held a fiddle-case under his arm. The musician had noticed him and given him a nod while affixing a harmonica onto the guitar.

He had a good attitude. Some musicians act blasé, making it cool to ignore the audience. This guy didnt do that. He looked straight at people. A group of younger guys in kilts and Glengarry hats had a table along the side and he called to them: How's it going boys?

They looked at him, surprised.

He was about to set off on the next number then gazed at the roof and spoke in a stagey growl: It's the goddam daylight man I aint used to no daylight.

Some of the audience laughed. Aunt Maureen wouldnt have liked the "goddam". He saluted somebody at the entrance now, a woman who was standing with people – Dad too, Dad was with them. They made their way into seats near Aunt Maureen and when they were seated the woman was next to Dad and she was saying something to him. Dad bent to hear what she was saying – it was weird, his head was quite close to hers. Not touching, it was just weird. Murdo couldnt remember seeing him sit beside a woman before.

Declan had begun on the next song, a join-in one about the railroad. A few people knew it. The old guy with the fancy waist-coat punched the air with his fist clenched, caught up in the story and angry.

Seeing people angry about a song. Ye didnt get that much. Murdo had never heard the song before but thought of the train cars down from Chattanooga having to cross the Tennessee River on boats. Ye could imagine all sorts.

When the song ended Declan adjusted the mic a little, and called to the man with the fiddle-case: You want to help me out here

Chess! Then he introduced the song while Chess approached the stage:

Any Macphersons in the company? It came out like "MacFIERCEsons" the way he said it. There were a few jeers and laughter in reply but no Macphersons. My mother was a good Appalachian girl, he said, Macphersons was her people, come from Scotland some time. All dead, most of them, far as I know. Hanged them. Damn near wiped them out altogether huh! That's what the next song's about. Guy robbed the rich to feed the poor; yeah, Robin Hood. Was Robin Hood Scottish? No sir, he would not wear no green uniform! Declan chuckled into the mic. Scotch joke right?

A few in the audience laughed but most seemed not to know anything, but Murdo knew. Robin Hood couldnt have been Scottish because he wore a green uniform. Protestants blue and Catholics green. Murdo looked to see Dad. It was the kind of stuff he hated. And hearing it out in the open made it strange-sounding and childish.

Chess was now on stage and with his fiddle at the ready. Declan pointed at the slogan on his baseball cap: Duncan Bizkitz Outlawd! Them's the politics I respect! Old Duncan now, he was a good old boy, fought a good fight and what happened to him? turned him into a goddam franchise.

Applause and some laughter.

Yeah, now, you all know another Macpherson? General James B?

People were quiet. The younger guys in the kilts and Glengarrys were staring at him.

Yeah, nothing worse than a Civil War, brother against brother. James B fell in the struggle for Atlanta, killed by men under the command of the bold John Hood; a hard man, a one-legged man; them two boys both Scotch descended, one north, one south, same class at West Point. Macpherson had the brains, helped Hood pass his exams. But Hood had the savvy. Declan spoke into the mic: You talk about your Beauregard and sing of General Lee;

but the gallant Hood of Texas he played Hell in Tennessee.

Yeah! called somebody, and another gave a loud piercing whistle, some scattered applause but then silence. And Declan continued: Another of the bold fellows there, Ould Paddy Clebourne from County Cork, Irish as the day is long. And a Protestant! Yeah. Some man the ould Paddy fellow. You all know he annoyed the bossclass? Asking them to emancipate and arm the slaves? Declan paused. Confederate Army General asking them old armymen to dish out guns to the slaves, free them and their families. Yessir, aint that a man.

Declan chuckled, glanced about the audience. Moral to that story: life is complicated. Okay! Listen up now, this is the bit makes me smile, some of them rebel boys – Scotch, Scotch-Irish, Ulster-Scotch, whatever you want to call it – they put their own words to this song. Folks been trying to track them lyrics down, cannot trace a single line. The men are gone so's the words they wrote, commemorating the time they shot down James B. Macpherson, made him one Union soldier that did not go

marching through Georgia.

He had sung the last line and it was to a tune Murdo knew from back home to do with Protestants fighting Catholics. Declan looked about the audience again. No sir, he said, they stopped him dead in Atlanta.

Declan did his stagey growl into the mic: Good talking here in my home state. Cant get talking this way in Texas boy they would string me up. All them songs are histories. Lyrics I sing written by whoever, I dont know, tune goes back seventeen hundred or thereabouts. Right Chess?

Chess nodded, adjusting the fiddle.

"Macpherson's Farewell", said Declan leaning in to him, and added, Shoulder to shoulder.

They exchanged looks then Chess did four scrapes of the bow. Four scrapes. How did that work? Sad but not sad, not like for crying. This was straight-talking how Chess played it: here is the story this is the story, and in Declan came with it:

Fareweel, ye dark and lonely hills,
far awa beneath the sky
Macpherson's time will not be lang,
On yonder gallows high.

Farewell. Getting put to death on the gallows. This became a fight too. But what was the fight? Murdo didnt know. But that is what he heard. Tough was Macpherson's life and tough how he led it. Murdo knew the tune well but this was different how Chess played it and the song like how Declan Pike sang it. It was a thrilling thing and not a lament like a farewell: more of a big and loud "Cheerio guys", a shout: "Cheerio guys!"

Just dealing with the problem, that was Macpherson. Hullo and cheerio. Up on the gallows awaiting the drop. People waiting to buy yer fiddle. Guys ye knew. Ye were maybe having a beer with them the night before. Now here they were, wanting yer stuff. Oh you're going to be dead in a minute so give me yer fiddle. Fuck you. Maybe yer clothes too, jees, the olden days; people had nothing. You go your way they go theirs. Families and friends split down the middle, you go one way yer pals go another.

Ye expected one thing in music then it was away someplace else. How did it happen? But it did. Everything was in that song how these two guys played it, and the men fighting and the women suffering and all everything that happened, all just stupid. They were telling ye and if ye didnt like what they were telling ye then hard luck.

It was special, so so special. Murdo was lucky, how could he be so lucky like just being here and just like everything, everything. He was wanting to play, it would have been good to play. He got up onto his feet and that was that, not looking at anybody; kept his head lowered, stepping to the side of the area, having to go round the back to get out.

There were plenty gaps in the audience. Less people here than Murdo thought. Maybe a few had gone earlier. He didnt look too closely in case Dad was looking, he just needed away.

★

Stalls and tents mostly were closed now; people shifting things into cars and pick-up trucks. The places doing business were for food and drink. The busiest cooked bar-b-que. Folk sat inside or on chairs outside, having a smoke and drinking beer, laughing and talking. Their voices carried. People had gone home and would return for the Hielan Fling. Most but not all. Ones who had traveled a distance would be staying during the in-between time.

Today was the first gig he had been to in ages. Since before Mum died. And being in the audience was good. That strong effect it had inside ye. The music into the body, connecting ye. Sound wasnt just mental it was physical, made up of these tiny wee parti-cles just like anything else; yer hair and yer teeth, yer socks and shoes; yer entire body: sounds were part of it.

The field at the other side of the Gathering area. Murdo had been walking and arrived here without knowing. Earlier on boys and a couple of girls were playing football. At one stage the ball trundled towards him and he did six keepy-uppies, then passed it back. The boy who collected it did a weird flick trick with the ball between his ankles, then kneed it to one of the others who trapped it on the upper part of his foot. So ha ha to you!

It was true but, Murdo wasnt good at football. Dad was a lot better. Dad played for actual teams when he was a boy. He used to come out with other dads. They played in a patch of spare ground down the street where they lived. The boys and the fathers together. That was fun.

It was still hot and Murdo had the jacket slung over his shoulder. He only brought it for the pockets. He reached the fence at the far end of the field. There was a break in it. He could walk through. Beyond was a clump of trees. Ye could cut through here and be away altogether.

The sound of a helicopter; there in the sky circling. Where had it come from?

He kept walking. Cattle! Cowboys riding through gulches and canyons. In the old days in Scotland ye got cattle drovers from the Highlands driving the herds down to the big Glasgow market, cutting open the veins in the cattle to let out blood for food; mixing the blood with porridge oats.

Cattle look at ye. Captured and chopped. What happened to the horns and tails? Hamburgers and sausages. A lassie in school said how all the disgusting bits made hamburgers. She was a veggie, but what she said was right enough. She had her own style, and her own laugh too; a real laugh, sounding like a gurgle or something, and ye could make her laugh.

That certain way a lassie laughs. Guys can make them laugh. Ye make a lassie laugh, that would be special.

Imagine walking through the trees. Imagine he had brought the rucksack and his stuff was all inside, so ye could just like head off into the mountains. Maybe that was the way to LaFayette, marching to Georgia, that would be him, and Murdo laughed. There by himself, he did, he just laughed; not for long.

What time was it anyway? Who knows. There was a lot going on about America and a history to this place too, the south. Horrors. Ye just didnay think about it.

Declan Pike's playing was excellent but that other side too, how he performed and how some didnt like it. That was politics. Some clapped and thought it was great. Others didnt seem to, maybe they hated it. Imagine hating music. It wasnt music it was what ye said. But if what ye said was in the music, if it was part of the music, so like it *was* the music. . . . So then they would hate the tune, hate the words and hate the singer.

★

Murdo strolled towards the marquee. A big truck was parked behind it. Guys were unloading musical equipment in through a rear entrance. A Scottish Country Dance Band was providing the evening music. Murdo heard music, not via the speaker system but from inside. The session: he had forgotten about it; scheduled between the afternoon and evening events. People chatted by the front entrance. More smokers. It would be good to smoke. Ye could just disappear and nobody worried about how come ye were disappearing: Oh he's away for a smoke. That would be great in school. Imagine the teacher. Where is everybody? Please sir away for a smoke.

The session took place not on stage but in the audience area. Chairs had been shifted to create a space. Declan was there on guitar, sitting on a chair and finger-picking. Chess Hopkins was with the guy in the fancy waistcoat and other older people. They hadnt long been started and people had drifted away, including the family. Murdo moved to a chair on the fringes. Declan sang another then passed his guitar to a man who sang a folky song about animals. It was good fun for a session. He did another then Declan took back the guitar, did a country-style song with little flourishes here and there. He laughed a lot in his playing and ye felt ye were sharing a joke with him. Some players never smile let alone laugh. He looked for Chess at the end of it. You about ready? he asked.

Yeah, said Chess then hesitated.

He was looking for the fiddle. Murdo had seen it; it was near the raised platform, placed parallel to its bow on a chair. He waited a moment but Chess wouldnt see it from where he was sitting. Murdo rose to collect it, also the bow which he held upright while walking. Fiddlers were fussy how ye held the bow. Murdo once got a severe row about it. A fiddler with a bad temper, it wasnt unusual.

Chess watched him. Murdo handed them over. Chess said, Thanks son.

I saw them when I sat down, said Murdo.

You did huh. Well I'm glad you did.

Instead of going back to his old seat Murdo sat on the edge of the main group. He had a fiddle at home but for learning only. Nothing like the one belonging to Chess. What was it about fiddles? His made ye smile! Macpherson on the scaffold. Imagine ye were there and he threw it high in the air. Whoever catches the fiddle gets to keep it! Everybody scampering about.

A couple more drifted in. Younger ones were way to the side. Four of the kilted guys in the Glengarrys returned to their same table, not far from the raised platform and talking quietly, not to distract from the music. This was like back home. Nobody expected people to stop talking, just not to be rude. Only if they had too much to drink their voices got loud. Then it was hopeless.

Another one new to Murdo. So much of this was new to him. Soon enough Chess was in on the fiddle and Declan was whistling. The song called for whistling. There was religious content but it was okay. More joined in on the chorus which amounted to whis-tling the tune. Not as easy as ye might have thought. People had a laugh doing it. Good fun. The young ones at the side were trying to whistle and stare each other in the eye at the same time. What ye noticed with a song like this was how it brought people into the company. At the end ye seemed to know the ones sitting next to ye.

A discussion started about the song led by the bald guy with the wee white beard and the fancy waistcoat. He said it was an old tune from bygone days; somebody else said it was new. They looked to Chess Hopkins for an answer but he didnt give one. Declan was yawning, leaning his elbows on his guitar. He yawned again, then made to rise from his seat.

Chess called to him: You know "Bonaparte's Retreat"?

Declan was in the act of bringing something out of his side jacket. I got to have a smoke first.

Guitar's only an add-on anyhow, said Chess.

Oh you think so! said Declan in the stagey growl he used in his performance.

It's a distraction.

Declan grinned, raising the guitar over his head, seeing a place to lay it. Declan hesitated, seeing Murdo who wasnt too far from him. He gestured with it towards him. Murdo shrugged, took the guitar from him.

Declan had reached into the pack for a cigarette then strolled to the exit. The woman was there who had been in Dad's company earlier. She and Declan exited together. Murdo sat with the guitar on his lap. He knew the makes of the good ones. This wasnt one of them. Yet it was very very good, just like whatever, it didnt have a name.

People were waiting for Chess. Murdo saw how they paid attention. When he was ready he spoke out the corner of his mouth: Old Napoleon now watch him go, he's on the retreat again.

Murdo knew the tune but different to this. The funny thing here was the actual feel Chess was getting. Murdo wondered what it was, but then obvious, it was Scottish. Was it Scottish? Murdo hadnt heard it played this way before. But he knew it and knew what to do with it. He was keeping time, tapping his fingers on the body of the guitar and whatever like he was ready to play, and he was ready to play, he was. Chess looked the question at him, how if he did want to play then that would be fine. Murdo slipped the strap over his shoulders. A wee rhythm just, to let the fiddle go. Murdo played that in, keeping it on keeping it on, watching and hearing what Chess did and going with that, a swing forwards now the fiddle was freed up.

Chess didnt look anywhere. Some look at things and some dont; some close their eyes. Chess didnt close his but neither did he look at anything. His playing was different. Maybe an older style. Murdo didnt hear playing like this much. But he liked it; there was a swing and a swagger, just happy who ye were, that was Chess and his baseball cap. He wasnt a busy type of player but he did stuff and ye could see how his head and his upper body, his neck, that control he had. Everything was measured. Ye knew he could burst out. Any time, he could explode right out. He didnt.

Murdo kept it on except a point when he veered off a fraction, brought about by something Chess did that knocked him out, but it was only that fraction and he got through. The guitar was a help, whatever it was. It had a mark like a signature so probably it was hand-made.

The tune ended. Chess nodded to Murdo who grinned. He caught sight of Aunt Maureen, hand to her mouth and gazing at him, sitting with people near the back of the marquee. Uncle John was there but Dad wasnt. Chess chuckled, tucking the fiddle under his arm. He wagged the bow at Murdo. I know what you did!

Yeah I missed that wee bit.

You did too!

I caught it though.

Yeah you caught it, you caught it. Chess wagged the bow at him again, called to the old guy in the fancy waistcoat: Hey now Bill he aint heard of no Bonaparte! Who in heck's Bonaparte, that's what the boy wants to know!

Murdo knew fine well who Bonaparte was.

Dad was by the marquee entrance. Murdo hadnt seen him arrive. So during the song. So he must have heard a little of it. He wouldnt have been too surprised. Maybe he would have been. He didnt come much to gigs. Uncle John would have enjoyed hearing Chess.

That old style making ye think of ancestral relations from bygone days. Mum too, she would have liked it.

Chess shifted on his chair and called to his wife Clara who was one of those at the back: Hey Clara you going to sing one?

Clara looked like she was surprised by the question. Chess said, What d'you think, you want to do one here? Maureen's nephew from Scotland?

Chess winked at Murdo. Clara leaned to say a word to Aunt Maureen then rose from her chair. She stepped along the row to the side and walked down and along to sit closer to Chess, within the main body. She smiled at Murdo. You doing okay son?

Yeah.

Thought you might want to sing, Chess asked.

Okay.

"When I Die"? Chess knocked up the side of his baseball cap, scratched at the side of his ear and said to Murdo, "When I Die" son you know it?

Eh. . .I'm not sure.

Chess nodded. You'll get it.

Murdo glanced at Clara who smiled.

I dont play on this one, said Chess.

You dont play on it? said Murdo.

Chess said, I sing a little. He glanced sideways, laid the fiddle and bow on the empty chair next to him. You'll get it, he said then looked at the ground, composing himself.

Also he was waiting for Clara. Her eyes were shut. Then she moved her head side to side and seemed to relax. She began the song and immediately was there in it, her voice so distinctive, so clear, so powerful. The word "steel". "Steel" for strength, staying strong; strong from the beginning and strong at the end: wherever that was. This voice would not stray, it was there on the path. She had "steel" and she gave this to the song. Chess entered from the beginning, replying "when I die" to each sung statement; Clara repeating the "when I die" to begin her next statement:

> when I die I'll live again
> because I believe
> and have found salvation
> *when I die*
> when I die I'll live again.

It may have been a hymn. Probably it was. An American one maybe; so ye wouldnt have heard it back home. Chess was looking to Murdo, directing him: come in as soon as ye like. And Murdo found he could, plain and speedy.

Mostly Clara sang with her eyes closed but when she did open them they seemed to fasten on somebody in particular, so the person knew they were being looked at. It reminded Murdo of something, but what? he couldnt think what. Eventually others came in on the line-endings:

> when I die I'll live again
> hallelujah
> because I'm forgiven
> my soul will find heaven
> *when I die*
> when I die I'll live again
> hallelujah

When the song ended Clara smiled to Murdo and gave a wave to Aunt Maureen, a relaxed wave. Aunt Maureen looked pleased and happy. Chess said, That was nice son. We do one more huh?

Murdo looked for Declan before replying. He rose from the seat to see better. Uncle John gave him a cheery thumbs-up. Murdo grinned. Declan was standing beside Dad by the entrance. The woman was also there. Murdo called, One more?

Declan saluted. Dad was just watching. Murdo adjusted the guitar. Chess said, We'll do "The Lost Pilgrim" son.

"The Lone Pilgrim", said Clara.

"Lone Pilgrim", yeah. . . Chess pointed out Murdo to the

company. This is Maureen's nephew from Scotland, Maureen and John there, you all maybe know that?

Murdo, said Clara.

Chess had raised the fiddle, he leaned to speak quietly to Murdo. I'll give it a good-size of an introduction son; you come in when you are ready. Just you take your time. We take it all the way through and back again. All the way through son. That's for Clara huh? So it's right for her. You know what I'm saying, we got all the time here.

Yeah.

Chess sniffed. We need you in there. Two introductions, three, it dont matter. Okay? When you are ready, we'll hear that nice guitar. You okay now?

Yeah.

Okay. Chess said to Clara: Just wait till the boy comes in Clara. We'll take it through and just you know. . . Chess shrugged. Clara nodded.

Twice on the introduction and it was needed. Murdo watched and listened and eventually he could come in; that bit trickier than earlier. Chess was watching till when Murdo had it he returned to the beginning so they could play it through together, fully.

So it was right for Clara. It was Clara. Of course it was Clara! Murdo could have laughed. Everything was Clara. Chess needed Murdo there for her. It had to be right for her. Of course it did.

Then it was.

Her singing and nobody else.

In the story she sang she came to the place and what kind of place was it, she was singing the place; a place for the beautiful souls. So it was another hymn, like the last one. Murdo knew them now as hymns so if they were like songs, actual songs, the other name for them was hymns. This was people's hymns. What are hymns? hymn? "a hymn"?

He didnt catch the words. He wasnt bothered about them. Beautiful souls. Memories and cheerio, goodbye beautiful soul goodbye, lost souls and finding souls.

Murdo was playing the song and when the song ended he waited, guitar on his lap, while people clapped. Clara was smiling up to Aunt Maureen. Murdo looked for Dad but couldnt see him. Declan Pike was coming towards him. Murdo stood up to lift the strap up and over his head. Declan patted him on the shoulder. Hey! he said.

Murdo handed him the guitar. It's a beauty, he said.

Declan took it from him. Yeah.

What is it?

Huh?

What kind is it? said Murdo.

Declan growled: The good kind.

Is it got a name?

No sir, it aint got no name. Declan said quietly, Hey now what about Clara Hopkins? Aint she the lady? Man, she is something. Aint heard her sing in a long time. How d'you manage that! Clara dont sing nowadays! You got her singing son! Declan patted him on the shoulder again then prepared to leave.

Aw, are you going? asked Murdo.

Yep. I been playing a while. I need a beer. Declan repeated this in a growl: I need a beer. There's a tent back there doing barbeque and they're getting me a steak. I'm talking a steak. You eat steak?

Steak?

You dont know what a steak is?

Murdo grinned.

Declan studied him a moment then wagged his finger at him. Now boy I asked your father that same damn question and he said the same damn thing back to me: Steak? That's what he said, steak. I says, You eat steak? Steak? he says, Steak? You boys from Scotland and you dont know what steak is! Declan stepped back a pace to study Murdo properly. You dont know the history of steak in this country?

The history of steak?

Shame on you! Declan chuckled, turning away. He gripped the guitar-case and saluted the people sitting around. Some acknowledged this, others didnt notice. The old guy in the fancy waistcoat gave him a clenched fist salute and called: I worked on that railroad son. I worked on it!

Oh you did huh?

Sure I did. And you know what? they didnt murder me.

Declan laughed. He had a cigarette in his mouth already. He paused to speak with Chess and Clara for a few moments, then headed to the exit. Aunt Maureen was closeby, sitting with people. She saw Murdo looking across and waved to him. Murdo waved back. His jacket was lying on a chair. He didnt even remember putting it there.

★

The dance proper began at 8.00 p.m. It wasnt late but when ye were hanging about it was like the distant future. If Murdo had been with guys then okay but he wasnt. Nobody to talk to and nothing to do. That is how it was. Find a chair, sit on the grass, go for a walk. He had gone for a walk a few times, got to know people's faces, and they looked at him. How come he's here again?

The stalls and tents shut long ago. Only actual foodtents were open and more for meals than snacks. No sign of Dad. Maybe he was in with people. Folk had bottles of wine and it looked expensive. He would have preferred a bag of chips or a hamburger maybe, something to eat while ye walked. Maybe ye didnt get chips.

Younger people were over by the field but not the two girls from Clara Hopkins' foodstall and he wondered if they had been at the session. Maybe they had gone home. Probably they had, if their parents had been there; no choice. Time to go home and ye went. That was the unfair thing about it, if ye wanted to meet people, ye werent able to. They come into yer life then go out.

He had reached the exit by the parking area. This was outlaw land; ye could imagine their hide-outs in the mountains; secret canyons. The road coming here was dirt and stones; probably a trail from the old days. If ye didnt have yer own transport ye couldnt come. How did people manage? That was the thing with America, how did ye get places?

A family coming towards him; a man, a woman, a boy and a baby. The baby bounced along on the man's shoulders. They wore ordinary clothes but the woman had a tartan shawl across her shoulders, pushing the baby buggy with the boy hanging onto the side of the handle. Murdo moved aside to let them pass. He wasnt going any farther, otherwise he would exit past the pay-to-enter table. Although nobody was there taking money so he could just walk back in again. He returned along the path. Declan appeared, with the woman who had been talking to Dad. The guitar-case was slung round his shoulders. The woman was talking and gesturing with her hands, but stopped when she saw Murdo. Declan shook hands with him. How's it going? You doing okay?

Yeah.

Doing good huh? You know Linda here? My driver?

Linda ignored him and gave Murdo a little wave.

Declan said, Linda here dont approve of the Gathering. Declan chuckled. She dont care for the kilt.

I care for it, said Linda.

Not on men you dont.

Certain men.

Certain men! Men with thin legs?

Murdo smiled.

It's not a joke, she said.

Murdo flushed.

Linda said, Sorry, not you.

Declan said, She dont like being here Murdo.

Not with them I dont.

Declan said, How about you now did you enjoy the day? Bit of fun huh? Declan swung the guitar-case to one side and brought out his cigarettes.

Yeah. . .the music, what you did, it was strong.

Thanks. Declan gazed at him, then nodded and lit a cigarette. Thanks, he said again.

Linda groaned, closing her eyes. These people hated what you did!

Hey now! Declan raised his hand.

What you said and what you sang. Every last word! You know who I'm talking about.

You're talking some and you got some everywhere. I dont take "these people" Linda, "these people". These some are my people and they are your people.

Oh God. Linda shook her head, stepped farther along the path, before stopping.

I get worse down Texas any night of the week. Any night at all. Declan glanced at Murdo. They throw knives down there.

They hated what you said! called Linda.

They did huh! Got to be doing something right then huh! Declan smiled. He said to Murdo: They still dress like that in Scotland Murdo?

Murdo smiled. Declan raised his eyebrows.

No, said Murdo, no. They dont. Maybe some right enough. Usually it's just guys at a football match or rugby maybe like international games. Or else like weddings: guys wear them to get married.

Special events huh?

Yeah.

Do they carry the fiery cross? called Linda.

I dont know. I think it's just traditional. Christenings as well. Murdo smiled.

Declan had shaken his head. Linda said, Hey I'm sorry. That was real fine playing.

Murdo gazed at her.

Real fine. Linda smiled. She turned from them and continued walking.

Declan said, Accordeon you play huh?

Yeah.

Your father was saying. Declan nodded and made as if to say something more, then nodded again, looking after Linda; he raised his hand in a farewell.

Murdo started to speak and stopped. Declan waited. No, said Murdo, I was just wanting to ask eh I mean have you ever heard of a music kind of event in a town LaFayette?

Well sure I have if you're talking Cajun music.

Murdo grinned.

You are huh. That is what you're talking about.

Yeah! And Zydeco?

Sure, yeah, that's Lafayette. Declan chuckled and signaled to Linda to hold on a minute. She stopped along by the exit, at the pay-to-enter table.

. Near Chattanooga? asked Murdo.

Chattanooga. . .?

I dont mean in it but near to it.

Aint Chattanooga son.

I saw it on the map.

Chattanooga!

I thought it was quite near I mean if it's just like well if ye're going down the interstate road and that's you crossing into Georgia.

Georgia! Lafayette aint in Georgia Murdo! No sir, that's a whole different Lafayette. Spell that one with a capital F: L A capital F. Declan growled. Got its own history there boy! No sir, one you want is Louisiana: Lafayette, Louisiana. A different state altogether son. You're talking Cajun music, you're talking Zydeco music. Whoh now! Declan shook his head, chuckling, inhaled on his cigarette then dropped it and ground it out.

The state of Louisiana?

You got it. What you planning a trip? That is one nice little festival.

Murdo grinned.

You take care now Murdo.

Thanks.

Yeah. Declan continued along the path; he and Linda walked on together. Murdo returned to the main area.

Dad was at a foodtent, sitting at a table with Aunt Maureen, Uncle John and people. Murdo kept out of view. Dad would have wanted him to come and eat food with them. He didnt want to. He wasnt hungry – he was but he wasnt. He wanted to go home. It would be good hearing music. He was just wanting to lie and just – just listen.

Murdo didnt care if Dad went with him. He had already said it was stupid. If he went he went and if he didnt he didnt it, was up to him. But Murdo was going. If he wanted to. He would go if he wanted to. He did want to. So he was.

Seventy dollars. Yesterday he had nothing. It was how yer life went. Up one day down the next.

Murdo skirted round the blind side of the food tent, down the central part moving in the direction of the marquee. A girl stood in front of him. She had a phone in her hand and a flyer. Two others were with her, wearing leggings and blouses. The tallest had a white flower in her hair. The first girl was smaller and thinner but sharp the way she was looking at him; a lot of freckles. You sign your name for me? she said, holding the flyer out to him. With her other hand she held up the phone for a picture. Murdo glanced at her then signed the flyer. Is it okay? she said, indicating the phone.

He shrugged. She moved to take a selfie with him. She took another photo then studied his signature on the flyer. You from Scotland huh?

Yeah.

You go to school here?

Eh no. In Scotland. He looked at the other two.

You go to school in Scotland! The girl grinned to her pals who were watching. He goes in Scotland. She squinted at his name on the flyer. What does it say? she asked.

Just my name.

Murdo, she said, not including Macarthur. She passed the flyer onto her pals. You play in a band, like a real band? Somebody said you did.

Who?

Somebody.

Was it my Aunt?

He noticed the other two girls and it was the one with the white flower in her hair – she looked away, she had gone red, and turned so it was hard to see but it was easy to see, she had gone so very very red, like a pink, the pinkest red possible; and himself too jeesoh he couldnt stop it, he was blushing too. He lowered his head.

What age are you? asked the first girl.

He made to leave.

What age are you? she said, hitting his arm. Sixteen huh? You sixteen?

Murdo looked at her.

Huh! She laughed to the other two: He's sixteen!

The girl with the white flower walked away. The third girl followed her. The first girl pointed after them to Murdo and mouthed something which he didnt understand, then rushed to catch up with them.

Stupid blushing, he couldnt stop it. People's lives werent like his. That is what he knew. Girls didnt know about him, except he didnt say funny stuff or whatever, because what are ye going to say, what are ye going to talk about? If lassies are to smile, oh it is a girl, ye should get her smiling. Guys say that. But what about! People found TV programmes funny that he couldnt even look at, and wanted to cover his ears and just block everything out; these stupid old guys making their stupid jokes round a table and people in the audience Oh ho ho ho. Ye felt sick hearing them, yer actual belly, oh jeesoh man I'm going to puke. How come people laughed? Probably they had to, probably it was like an order from the people in charge. Oh ye have to laugh even if the jokes are stupid, this is a TV programme and people are watching all over the stupid world. If ye feel like dying, ye still have to laugh.

Maybe they didnt get told. Maybe they just laughed. Folk did laugh. Ye spoke to them about nothing at all and they laughed. In the supermarket ye asked somebody stacking the shelves, Where is the cheese please, do ye have any cheese? Oh yes it is the next aisle! and they laugh at ye.

What for? Weird sounds breaking up their breathing, that is laughs. Imagine an alien and ye heard people laughing: weird noises from nowhere, uh uh uh uh uh, ah ah ah ah ah, hih hih huh hih hih huh, he he he he he, ho ho ho ho.

What did it remind ye of? Noises in the jungle. After midnight down the woods, insects and animals; all different ones.

What age were they? Thirteen or fourteen maybe; not fifteen, Murdo didnt think so, although she was good to look at, her with the white flower, hot; and a nice thing about her too like if ye were poking fun at her, if ye tried, probably she would not let ye or else would poke fun at ye back. The flower made ye think that. Her blushing made ye think about poking fun at her, but the white flower meant she could poke fun back at ye. Otherwise how come she was wearing it? That was lassies. Although he wouldnt have poked fun at her anyway. He didnt even know her. Even if he did so what because what did ye talk about? If something was funny, so she would smile. Ye wanted her to smile and not be sad. The world was sad but if ye could smile, maybe ye could, if ye could say something to her. Something funny, but ordinary too, and it would make her smile, a thing to make her smile.

★

He could have gone home. Right now, he could have. If somebody asked What would ye rather do? Go home, I'll just go home. Back to Scotland? Yeah. Jeesoh ye like Scotland? Yeah – even the bad bits!

But why go home? Oh God so he could play so he could play, so he could get ready. He just needed to play, play play play, to practise, to practise; the fingers, just the fingers. He felt that with the guitar, he needed to just like play. . .!

Home tomorrow then back next Saturday with the accordeon, his own accordeon. All he needed was the plane-fare. Dad, any money!

Ha ha.

Imagine but! He would go home to come back. Home to come back.

Why not? If he had money. People did that, like musicians, to get yer own stuff. If they needed it. Why not?

The marquee was closed. He hadnt expected that. People were preparing it for the dance. Okay. It was quite quiet. He heard shouts from somewhere but it just sounded like people having a laugh. That was twice today lassies looked at him, counting the ones at Clara Hopkins' foodstall. They looked at ye because ye played. Mum laughed about it, if it was a gig and she saw a lassie standing or whatever, like smiling or just like whatever, looking at Murdo.

Even playing sometimes ye could see a girl's face, if she was looking at ye. Then it was like what are ye going to do? If she waits behind. Just go outside with her, or what? Other guys did, they said they did and had sex and all that. So they said, some of them. If ye believed them. Some of them ye did. Other ones ye didnay, just the usual crap boasting shit.

Murdo hardly talked after a gig anyway. Sometimes he forgot where he was. Usually he was tired. People maybe were wanting to chat. He just nodded as if he was listening but most times he wasnt. He couldnt concentrate; the conversation going on and on. Sometimes he needed to get away, outside the actual venue. A fiddler in the band smoked hash and he would be somewhere. Murdo just walked round the building. One time he did it and the venue was a church hall. When he went round the back it was a graveyard and the fiddler was there smoking and jumped out his skin. Telling the guys later he called Murdo Count Dracula! Standing there having a smoke and out he comes like up from a coffin.

But it was funny. Ye got a laugh in bands. Murdo missed it, he missed playing, missed the company, having a laugh with the guys.

He kept around the edge of the area. Much of the space was empty now, cleared of tents and stalls. The marquee was still closed.

He didnt want to go in until the band started. People would be sitting about. Then it was Oh there's Murdo, and saying hullo and all that, Oh you're Murdo, hullo. Hullo back.

It was okay if it was Aunt Maureen, he could speak to her. Uncle John too. Dad would want to know what he had been up to and where had he been? Ye disappeared again? I didnay disappear Dad I just went a walk. People go walks. I was just walking, just like whatever, what does it matter.

*

Inside the marquee the tables had been shifted to accommodate the dancing and two rigged together as a sandwich and refreshments bar. Beer was available as well as soft drinks. It wasnt as busy as people expected but it was still okay and a cheery atmosphere. Dad and Murdo sat with Aunt Maureen and Uncle John who had managed to get a table down the far side. Dad had given Murdo another twenty dollars which made $90 all in. He still hadnt spent anything.

The musicians came from someplace up near Canada. They played ordinary Scottish-style country dance stuff but it was lively and brought people onto the floor, and ye had to respect that. They were playing a medley of reels when friends of Aunt Maureen and Uncle John stopped to say hullo, and pulled over chairs to sit with them. They hadnt been at the pot-luck night. The conversation was to do with how things were at the Gathering, not as good as years gone past and how things had changed. They were talking about traditional country dancing. Uncle John made a comment about the dancers that made them smile. He called to Murdo: The Hielan Mishmash son eh!

Murdo grinned.

Tell us what it is?

Eh. . .

Murdo's a musician, said Uncle John. Accordeon son eh?

People gazed at him. Aunt Maureen was smiling. Dad smiled too.

You play accordeon? asked a man.

Yeah.

The Hielan Mishmash! Uncle John chuckled.

Murdo said, It's just where people dance but they dont know what they're dancing and just like clump about. He shrugged and drank a mouthful of apple juice. They were waiting for him to say more but what else was there?

That was Dad. Dad must have told Uncle John about it. The Hielan Mishmash was the name the guys gave country dancing back home when people just clumped about the floor. Take your partners for the Hielan Mishmash! They didnt know the steps and just pushed, pulled and twirled roundabout with plenty of hooching, hand-clapping and feet-stamping. Why not? Who cares if it is a reel, a jig, a waltz, a two-step or a polka, or a jive, if ye were there for a good time. It wasnt school.

People could be snobbish about Scottish country dancing and that included musicians. Ye had to play this, that and the next thing and ye could only do it in a certain way. Up to a point okay but ye needed room for yer own take. Even traditional stuff. If something was necessary ye did it. It was good when ye heard a tune ye knew and it turned into something else; it started from there and ended there, but where did it go in between! That was the fun, that was exciting.

This band werent like that. They did the usual. The usual was good, just maybe not all the time. Except for dancing, ye had to have dancing.

At the table Aunt Maureen said how nobody was calling the moves like happened in the old days and people were agreeing with her. But sometimes back home they still did it. It was good fun. Take your partner by the hand, lead them down right to the band, turn and curtsey how do you do, clap clap hands and boogie boo; the twos step up now threes and fours, back you go straight down the floor – everybody moving in a neat formation. Murdo spotted the couple with the Phil Campbell T-shirts on the floor. Ye felt like saying, Hullo, how are ye, I've seen ye on the map. He pointed them out to Aunt Maureen. She made a sad gesture at the band and at her own ears. The music was too loud for her. She called a question to him: You enjoying yourself son?

Yes.

She had asked him twice already. But he was. Dad had asked him as soon as he sat down. Probably because he didnt have anybody his own age. Uncle John asked him too, Ye enjoying yerself son? Yes. So how come ye arenay dancing! Why dont ye grab a lassie!

Uncle John seemed to think ye just went up to a girl and said, Hullo may I have this dance? If ye did they would just look at ye. Probably they thought he could dance. He couldnt. People think ye can because ye play the tunes. But ye cant. You just play the tunes, they do the dancing. Musicians dont dance. That was the good side of the Hielan Mishmash: ye just got up and that was that.

The conversation shifted to the music from this afternoon, not the event with Declan Pike but the session that followed with Clara, Chess and Murdo.

Guitar isnay even his instrument, said Uncle John, it's accordeon! Is that right son?

Murdo sipped at his drink. Yeah, he said, I suppose.

Aunt Maureen was smiling. So was Dad, but half looking at the table at the same time like he was a bit embarrassed.

Eventually Uncle John and one of the men went to the bar to place an order. A beer would have been good. Maybe Uncle John would buy him one. He had made a joke about it earlier on.

The one thing missing was a pal, so ye could just hang out, go for a walk or whatever, check things out. Then if ye did see a lassie, usually there were two together, so if a pal was with ye it made it like a foursome. On yer own it was pretty hopeless. Ye dont usually get "one girl". A lot of "one guys" but lassies go in twos. Ye cannay ask one and not the other. Three together made it okay for one to ask one so if it was like the three girls from earlier on ye could ask one. Two would be left behind but that was okay. If the one with the white rose was there maybe Murdo could ask her. Maybe.

Aunt Maureen was chuckling, enjoying something Dad was saying to her − about Murdo, Murdo as a boy. Dad was talking about him. Another woman was listening to what Dad was saying and she peered at Murdo.

Murdo smiled at her, then got up and went a walk. He knew what Dad was telling them about, it was actually a story: The boy who fell down the pit.

Murdo headed across past the refreshments bar. It wasnt an actual pub so maybe there were no age restrictions. A beer would have been good. But $6 a bottle! That was what they were charging. He could have bought one and taken it outside to drink. Murdo continued along, skirting the dance area. People stood around the exit, smoking and toing and froing the portable toilets.

Outside it was quite deserted beyond the marquee area. Most every stall and tent had been taken down. This made it possible to see over to the carpark which was only a fraction full compared to the afternoon. Those who operated stalls and tents had disman-tled them and just gone home. Murdo strolled for a little bit. It was kind of odd being here, in this landscape, the Scottish country dance music blaring through the external speakers, though it wasnt blaring and didnt carry all that far.

When he returned inside Uncle John was by the entrance, chatting to a couple of older guys who were both wearing the kilt. Murdo! he said. Where've ye been? I was looking for ye!

I was only out a minute!

Ye're aye disappearing!

No I'm not.

Uncle John put his arm round him and drew him closer. My nephew from Scotland, Murdo.

Hi Murdo, nice to meet you. You know the isle of Skye?

Yeah.

I went over three years ago with my wife and daughter. It was wonderful.

The other man pointed at the kilt he was wearing. This is the Macleod tartan. You know the Macleods?

Yeah.

I'm a Tormod. There's Torquils and Tormods.

Okay, said Uncle John. He smiled at the two men and led Murdo a few paces off. He spoke quietly: So ye enjoying the music son?

Yeah.

What do ye think of the accordeon player?

Yeah. . . He's fine.

Uncle John held him by the elbow. Ssh, he said, I had a wee word with him. Ye're alright for one. Just wait till the break. Then you go up.

Murdo hardly heard.

Uncle John said, I asked him for ye.

Murdo nodded.

What I'm saying son I asked him for ye. I'm talking about doing one on the accordeon. They'll be taking a break in a minute then you go up. Uncle John smiled.

No. Thanks but eh no.

It's fine son ye just go up during the break.

No what it is Uncle John, really, I'm not eh. . .

Son it'll be alright, it's no anything to worry about.

I know, I mean I just eh. . . I would rather not.

Uncle John gazed at him.

Is that okay?

Of course. No bother at all son, it's only if ye wanted to. The guy's happy to oblige. Ye would just go up at the break. Uncle John said, Nobody's forcing ye!

Thanks.

It was only if ye wanted to.

Thanks Uncle John.

Uncle John patted him on the side of the arm, then returned to the company of the two older men.

Murdo walked along by the rear of the marquee. A row of chairs was lined closeby the canvas with a passageway between it and the second end row. The good thing back here was the shadows. Only the dance area was brightly lit. He might have sat down except it was tricky finding free space. Couples sat together and ye were too close to them. They would think ye were trying to whatever, listen in.

The idea of playing one, it was not on. There was nothing wrong with Uncle John asking, it was just impossible. He was still there with the two old guys, now standing aside to let pass a woman with a laden tray. Ye could see her smiling, so he had made a jokey comment. Uncle John was good. He tried to help and make things happen for people. Maybe Murdo could have played.

He couldnt.

Aunt Maureen was talking to Dad now. More stories. Dad glanced roundabout, probably wondering about Murdo. Where Murdo was sitting was quite shadowy and Dad wouldnt have seen him. So this was him disappeared again! That was Dad, disappeared. The story about "The boy who fell down the pit". It was one Dad told them when he was wee, him and Eilidh. He would have been four, so Eilidh seven. It was one with a moral to it. Ye were not to wander off or bad things would happen. The wee boy in the story used to wander off by himself and his Mum and Dad were fed up giving him rows about it. One day he went into the forest and fell down a pit. Help me help me! Get me out! Nobody heard his screams. His Mum and Dad thought he was lost and gone forever. He was trapped down there for days and he had to eat worms and spiders and beetles. All the creepy crawlies. He had to eat them all or starve to death. Except not the frog! He would not eat the frog. There was a frog down the bearpit but the boy wouldnay eat it. Frogs come from tadpoles and the boy liked tadpoles.

Murdo knew that was right because he liked tadpoles as well. Eilidh didnt. She was like Oh of course he would eat it. Why wouldnt he? Of course he would! That was Eilidh. He would have to eat it else he would starve to death! If it was France he would eat it. People eat frogs' legs in France. They nibble them.

Are the frogs wearing them? said Murdo.

Good question, said Dad who told it to Mum. Are the frogs wearing their legs when people nibble them?

The boy didnt eat the frog because the frog was his pal, and nobody would eat their pal! If he had he would never have got out the bear pit. Because that was how he escaped. He climbed on the frog's back and out they hopped. It was a good story. Dad used to tell them. Even if he gave ye a row; after the row was over and ye were getting put to bed he sat down with ye and told ye a story, Murdo and Eilidh, just the two of ye there and him sitting, and quiet, ha ha, that was Dad.

Last song before the break: A Dashing White Sergeant. Some knew the steps but most didnt. Ye could learn if ye wanted. The web was full of these instruction videos. But who cares? Ye want to relax and not have to go and do stuff.

What was interesting here was how the fiddle took the lead and that gave it an American feel. Murdo thought so. But it might just have been hearing the fiddle, thinking of Chess Hopkins – it wasnay

Macpherson played the fiddle on "Macpherson's Farewell", it was him. The fiddler here was nowhere even close to Chess Hopkins.

But so what, if he was doing his best? Maybe he was.

There was a sadness in music. Even if it was cheery, or supposed to be cheery, ye still heard it. Even The Dashing White Sergeant.

★

During the break he walked about. He was back at the table when the band began a medley they introduced as "The Happy Hoedown". There was a cheer and an immediate rush for the floor when people heard the opening tune. They grabbed partners, whooping and punching the air.

A man had been talking to Aunt Maureen and Dad and they were straining to hear what each other was saying. Murdo wasnt trying to listen. He couldnt hear anyway. The man had a beer in one hand and kept giving angry looks at the band. But it wasnt the band's fault. Dad and Aunt Maureen seemed to agree with the man but surely if people wanted a conversation they should have shifted to the back of the marquee? Uncle John was away doing that, sitting with a couple of men at the side, but that was them. Most people wanted to dance. They were there for a good time. What was wrong with that?

A woman was heading towards Dad, coming straight towards him. There was no mistaking this; stretching out her right hand, her forefinger pulling and beckoning him to come to her. Murdo hadnt seen her before. Aunt Maureen called to her: Hi Ruthie!

The woman seemed not to see Aunt Maureen and was wagging her finger at Dad like she was giving him a row. It was quite, in a way, comical, seeing Dad like this. But weird. When she took both his hands and yanked him up off the chair he allowed it. He smiled at Murdo and Aunt Maureen like Oh I'm helpless, I'm helpless. Then he was on the floor with her and standing,

209

they were looking for a gap, then they were dancing. Dad. Dancing.

Murdo sipped his juice and watched how he was doing it. He knew a few of the steps. The woman was good. She looked to be leading Dad, holding his waist and guiding him through bits. They stayed on the floor for the next dance too.

That was something, Dad, imagine Dad.

One tune the band played was the "Ballad of Glencoe". Murdo could have grabbed the accordeon for that. He could sing it too:

> Oh cruel was the snow
> that sweeps Glencoe
> and covers the grave o' Donald

It was a waltz. Dad was still there with the woman. Aunt Maureen was gazing at dancers too. There was a spare seat next to her. Murdo moved onto it. Hi Aunt Maureen.

Well hi Murdo you enjoying yourself?

Yeah.

It's nice.

Yeah.

And he was enjoying himself. Although nothing was going to happen. He knew that. It didnt matter. Being here was great and just seeing everything, how everything was. Okay if he had had a pal they would have had a laugh, maybe chatted to a couple of girls or whatever.

Dad and the woman danced past. Aunt Maureen smiled seeing them. Ruthie Lawrence, she said.

Later Aunt Maureen was still smiling. It was another tune by then. Just that way she was looking at the people on the floor, that smile, smiling to see them. Murdo could have drawn her, if he had had a pen or a pencil, to try and get how she was looking, this way she was watching the dancers like even she wasnt watching them at all but over the tops of their heads, and her eyes and just below the lines there, that was the lines from smiling, she did smile, worrying too. She didnt dress up much but tonight she had.

And this necklace she was wearing. She had on this necklace and it was like sparkling, really sparkling. Murdo hadnt seen it before. Maybe she hadnt worn it before. Not during the day anyway. Definitely not. Maybe it was diamonds? It could have been. Murdo leaned to her. Aunt Maureen, he said, that's a brilliant necklace.

She squinted round at him.

It's really. . .it's just, it's really really nice.

He still gives the presents Murdo, he still manages to do that. Aunt Maureen smiled, fingering the necklace.

Do ye fancy a dance? he said.

Huh? You want to son?

Please, yeah, if eh. . .

I dont mind. Aunt Maureen stood to her feet carefully.

That's great, he said. She put one hand out to him and he held it, walking with her onto the floor. Ye're looking great, he said, I think ye're just. . .

Aunt Maureen frowned.

No, he said.

Oh yeah you can flatter huh! It's a family trait I reckon.

Murdo laughed. When they were on the floor they stood by the edge. He put his hands to Aunt Maureen's upper arms. She glanced at the other dancers. What is this one? she asked.

I think it's a jig.

Huh, I thought it was too.

Aunt Maureen I've got to say, I'm a hopeless dancer.

She nodded. We'll try a two-step Murdo, a fast one. One two shuffle, one two shuffle but kind of fast. You wont fall down. Jigs is kind of tricky.

She adjusted his hands and waited, looking to see a space; they set off. Aunt Maureen slowed to a stop. Now Murdo you're going backwards, she said, dont you go backwards: you got to lead me; you are the man here.

Okay.

Dont watch the floor too much.

Yeah but if I kick ye?

Dont worry about that, she said. Where I come from people wear boots and it dont stop them. Throw the sugar on the floor and off they set. You know what a clod hopper is?

No.

You dont huh. They got them clogs and go hop hop hopping along.

People were coming and Murdo was going to side-step away but Aunt Maureen kept him on the same track. She was good at dancing. He had expected that. They danced a path round the edge of the dance area but were not going as well as all that. They seemed to be then lost the rhythm. It was Murdo's fault. Aunt Maureen smiled. You just got to concentrate Murdo, that's what it is.

Murdo felt his hands sweaty and was aware of them on her dress, his hands maybe gripping her so they creased the material instead of just holding her, palms and fingers. He wasnt sure if Aunt Maureen noticed. She was humming under her breath. Murdo kept going, one two shuffle, not thinking too much, one two shuffle, one two shuffle.

★

Late night on the road home, the 4x4, Uncle John driving, Dad in the front passenger seat, Aunt Maureen and Murdo in the rear. Murdo was awake but must have been dozing. Silence but for the hum of the car engine. Uncle John and Dad talking, they were talking. Not now, and no radio. Murdo yawned. Aunt Maureen had noticed and smiled, then gazed back out the window. The silence continued until Uncle John said, Of course he's Irish. . .

I thought he was American, said Dad.

Talking family, he's a descendant.

I thought his mother was from Glasgow.

Aw yeah, from way back but Declan! Know what I mean that aint Scottish. Who's called Declan? It's Irish. A name like that. Oireesh. He's Oireesh. I dont know about her; the woman he came with.

Linda, said Dad, I think she came with other people.

Mm.

Aunt Maureen called: Lives in Springfield Missouri Tommy; same as your cousin John. I know Linda, she is one nice girl, and she knows young John too.

Dad twisted on the seat to see round at Aunt Maureen. Aunt Maureen winked at Murdo then was staring out the window again.

Cousin John was Uncle John's elder boy, the one he didnt talk to. But Aunt Maureen talked to him. Two days ago Murdo had come out the bathroom after a shower and she was on the phone to him. Murdo heard enough to work that out.

Uncle John had started talking again but more quietly now and Murdo had to shift on the seat and strain to hear.

We saw a television programme, said Uncle John, Irish–Scotch or whatever the hell, Scotch-Irish! I was angry watching it Tommy, so would you have been. King James and all his rebels right enough. Dont call me Scotch. I tell them that in the bastard work, ye want Scotch go to the bastard pub. Excuse the language, he said. Uncle John sniffed, but an angry sniff. Call me Scottish, that's what I tell them, I'm not Scotch, dont call me Scotch. I get a bit annoyed the way everything here's Irish, know what I mean – Oireesh!

Dad spoke quietly. The guy's from Alabama but Uncle John. He only works in Texas.

I've got nothing against him – whatever he is, dont get me wrong. Only it aint a thing to talk about; not in that company. You got to know who you're talking to. Religion like that! He's a bloody singer! He's paid to sing! That Billy Boy stuff, Protestants and Catholics and all that. In the name of God Tommy what century is he living in! Know what I mean, it's insulting. Uncle John glanced at Dad. How does he know anyway?

He works beside Scottish guys. Dad said, Offshore, there's a lot of Scottish guys work offshore; he hears the banter.

Banter! Uncle John shook his head.

Murdo looked to the rear-view mirror but couldnt see his eyes. He sat back on the seat now. Dad knew he was listening. Uncle John was silent. That was something how he didnt like Declan. And other people didnt too. That was what upset Linda, and she got angry. Declan just laughed. He took buses everywhere and made jokes about it. He said he appreciated buses because he wrote songs traveling on them. Nobody wrote songs driving an automobile. Declan said that, if they did they would crash! Everybody has a laugh but Declan had a good one. There was a quality to it; the same when he was talking between songs. It fitted in with that stagey growl he did, kind of macho but like a kid-on, dont take it serious.

Aunt Maureen was dozing.

They were passing through a built-up area. Uncle John was doing his cheery wee whistling now, hardly making a sound other than the breath escaping, how it escapes sometimes like how with the pipes the bag expels air, the breaths, huh hih huh hih huh hih, and the drone, that drone

FOUR

On Sunday afternoon Dad came out to the patio carrying a book and a coffee. Murdo was sunbathing at his usual spot in the garden but closer in to the hedge for shade. The hi-fi and US Road Atlas were closeby. He lowered the volume and exchanged a wave with Dad then returned to the book he was reading, one about a guy who came back to the town of his birth after years in an army stockade for a crime he did not commit. The sheriff of the town hated him because of a thing from childhood. It was good, set in the state of Arizona.

Dad hadnt opened his book, he was just sitting there. Usually he would have been reading in the house before coming out and was carrying on where he left off. Sometimes he read while he walked. That was Dad, a major reader. Murdo reached to turn down the hi-fi volume again but would have been as well turning it off altogether. Ye wasted brain energy trying to listen and this interfered with the music. It was worse than frustrating. It seemed a lack of concentration but it wasnt concentration at all. Ye did concentrate. It was just some of it went in the wrong direction. Or else it was a different concentration; concentrating to concentrate. Real concentration was where ye didnt have to think about it, yet took it all in.

The temperature was into the eighties now. Aunt Maureen had said it was going to be hot. Her and Uncle John had gone to church. Before leaving she came downstairs to see if Murdo had changed his mind. It was awkward saying no. But he hadnt said yes in the first place so it was not like he had changed his mind.

He carried on reading. Later Dad was coming towards him, carrying a chair from the patio. Is company okay? he asked.

Murdo grinned.

Dad gestured at the book. Any good?

Yeah.

Dad nodded, he sat back on the chair, closing his eyes into the sun. This is the life, he murmured.

Neither spoke for a while. Murdo moved to lift his cowboy novel but stopped when Dad spoke. The thing with church, he said, at one time, ye would have had nay option but to go. Whether ye believed in it or not. It's still the same in some places.

Back home, said Murdo. Stornoway and these places.

Yeah but here too son it depends on the community. Some of Aunt Maureen's friends, if ye didnay go to church they would send round a doctor, they would think ye were ill!

Murdo smiled.

Seriously, they're strong on the church and ye just have to watch it.

Fundamentalists. . .

Not fundamentalists Murdo that's where ye're wrong. They're just ordinary people.

Well Dad I saw their leaflets at the Gathering and like some of the things they were saying I mean they were just kind of – kind of silly. I'm not being cheeky.

Are ye not?

No.

Good. Ye know son I've got to say, maybe you dont know, how proud Aunt Maureen and Uncle John are of ye.

Murdo shifted on the chair, shaking his head and breathing loudly.

Honestly, said Dad, I think that was a wee thing about church ye know, I think they were wanting to show ye off! Because of yesterday, when ye were playing the guitar. One of their friends said they were "spellbound"; that was the word. Telling ye son that's a real compliment. It's a good compliment. It's the kind of one people dont say unless they mean it. Really. That was you on guitar too. . .! God imagine the accordeon! Ye would have blown them away!

Murdo looked at him.

Naw but ye would have! Dad grinned. I'm no kidding ye son ye would have blown them away!

Dad I'm no wanting to blow anybody away.

No

Really, I'm no wanting to blow anybody away. Murdo sat forwards on his chair and was saying, It's only to play with them Dad not to like beat them. How can ye beat them, ye cannay beat them, it's daft saying it. Know what I mean, it's just daft like it's just eh – it's daft. Murdo shook his head. Sorry Dad. I only mean like. . . I'm sorry.

Dad smiled. I'm no used to being called daft. Eh?

Murdo had lowered his head, was staring at the patio floor; and the edge of the table almost was white in places because where the sun, the way the sun affected it.

Dad clasped his hands on the table. I'm no used to being called daft.

It's just ye see it was Chess led me. Chess Hopkins Dad he's brilliant, he is just brilliant. Him and Clara, it's just like great great music, just great. Clara is special; she is so so special. Like playing with them Dad, just playing with them. . . Murdo shook his head.

Aye well you're special too. Dad looked away.

Murdo closed his eyes.

Ye are son.

Dad it's not the same.

It is the same. Ye are. People thought that. That is what they thought. And they said it too. You disappeared! Dad smiled. I only wish. . . If ye had played the accordeon son, when ye had the chance. I mean ye had the chance. The band would have let ye play. Uncle John asked them and they said aye. He asked them for you. They said aye. It was you said no! Dad sighed. I'm not getting at ye. I just. . .I dont understand it. Usually ye play at the drop of a hat.

No I dont.

Yeah ye do, if anybody asks.

Not anybody.

Och yes ye do. Ye're aye ready to give them a tune. Dont get me wrong, it's nice that ye do. Ye did it with the black family. That's what ye did with them. Ye did. I was there and saw ye.

No ye didnt Dad.

I was there.

Murdo smiled, shaking his head.

What do ye think it's funny?

Murdo stopped smiling.

They ask ye to play and ye play: Uncle John asks ye and it's Oh no. No. Dad stared at Murdo. That's what ye said to Uncle John, No. Right there on that bloody dance floor in front of his friends. He's gone to all that trouble asking the boy on the accordeon then you turn him down! I couldnay believe it! I couldnay! You have the cheek to turn him down!

Dad sat back shaking his head then sat forwards again and wagged his right forefinger at Murdo. It's nothing to do with being bloody black so dont start that nonsense. You played for them but not for yer own family. That's the point I'm making.

Dad

What did ye mean to hurt them? Eh? Did ye? You hurt Uncle John. You hurt him. And when ye hurt him ye hurt me; ye hurt me and ye hurt Aunt Maureen. That was a family thing Murdo. It goes deep. The same going to church. You had another chance and ye didnay take it. Aunt Maureen was wanting to show us off. We're her nephews from Scotland. It's a big deal.

But you didnt go either.

That's right.

Well?

She asked you first.

Yeah but she asked ye Dad she asked ye!

That's right she asked me, of course she asked me. She asked you and you said no then she asked me, and I said no. If you had said yes I would have said yes.

. . .

Ye didnay, ye said no. If you had gone I would have gone.

So ye wouldnt have left me in the house myself?

That's one way of putting it.

So like ye cannay trust me?

Dad gazed at him.

Murdo shrugged.

I trust ye son but things happen.

What things?

Aw never mind, said Dad. Uncle John and Aunt Maureen will be home any minute.

Murdo turned his head. I've got my own life Dad. If I play I play. I play if I want to play. If I dont want to play then I dont play, and that's that.

Exactly, ye've summed it up. Dad sighed. Look son when Uncle John asks ye to play the accordeon ye play the accordeon. That is what ye do. This is family, it's a family obligation. It wouldnay have been hard son, not for you. Ye play that accordeon like a champion so ye should have played it for us. Just like ye played it for the black family. I still cannay get my head round that one! The first I heard ye play since Mum died. Coming round the back of that house. The middle of nowhere and all black people. And there ye are playing for them! Dad laughed briefly, then shook his head.

Dad

Well it's true.

Dad it isnt, it isnt true at all. I wasn't playing *for* them. Not *for* them. I was playing *with* them. You only came at the end, so ye only heard me, ye didnt hear Sarah's granny.

Dad smiled.

Dad she's famous. She's a famous musician. Queen Monzee-ay, she's a famous famous musician. Ye shouldnay bring her down.

I'm not bringing her down.

Ye are.

I'm not. I resent ye saying that Murdo I really do.

She's a great musician.

I hear ye.

She's playing that festival I was telling ye about.

Dad groaned. Nobody's heard of any music festival except you. LaFayette's just a wee town. Uncle John's drove through it a hundred times.

Yeah because it's a different Lafayette. The one I'm talking about is in the state of Louisiana. There's different Lafayettes. Declan told me. Declan Pike.

I know who he is.

Yeah well I mean he's a musician. Murdo shrugged.

Yeah so that explains it then eh! Dad stood up from the chair shaking his head.

Dad

Dont Dad me: you think you know the world son and you dont, you dont. Dad turned from him and lifted the chair. He strode onto the patio, dumped down the chair and continued into the house.

Murdo watched the door close. He sat a little longer then collected his stuff, returned to the house, and downstairs to the basement. He closed the door and lay down on the bed; but jumped up at once, took off the shorts for a pair of joggers, grabbed a T-shirt and pulled on his trainers. He found the money in his jacket pocket, extracted a $20 note, and upstairs two and three steps at a time, needing to go fast fast fast. Dad was in his room with the door shut. Murdo passed along, heading for the back door but stopped there. He returned to Dad's bedroom door. He called, not too loudly: I'm going a walk. Just round the block. I'll not be long.

He didnt wait for an answer. That was that and he was glad. Down from the patio to the side driveway exit, out onto the pavement, he kept walking. Very very glad. Of course Dad would worry but it was his fault. Dad was Dad. He was angry now but would worry after.

Worry worry stupid worry, stupid stupid worry worry.

Only if he had said "Dad". He didnt say "Dad". He should have said "Dad". I'm going a walk Dad, just round the block Dad, I'll not be long Dad.

He would worry because he always did.

Murdo glanced back over his shoulder. He wasnt there! What a thought! Ye could imagine it, Dad running down the street, Murdo Murdo come back come back!

Although he couldnt stay away too long. Definitely not. Aunt Maureen and Uncle John would be home soon and would worry if he wasnt there.

A street corner ahead. He turned along it, seeking a landmark. Houses had the flags of America and Alabama, one or the other or both. The one for Alabama had the same Saltire design as Scotland but a red cross on the white background instead of a white one on the blue.

People worried. How come? Because it was a row caused him to leave the house. Oh I hope he doesnt do something daft! Ye could understand it but not too much. What would he do? Run away and never come home! It was daft. Dad was Dad so it was not like forever and ever. How could it be?

Only if he had said "Dad": I'm going a walk Dad, Dad I'll not be long, so then he would have known it was okay and not to worry. It was just like he needed to get out the house. Ye couldnt stay in forever just because ye worried about getting lost. Then what happens? Ye're dead. Here lies Murdo Macarthur who never went out the house. Stupid worries. How can ye live?

I'm just going a walk. Well dont disappear! Although roundabout here it was quiet streets. Maybe nobody did walk. That was Uncle John's joke, people were feart in case they got shot as an intruder. So they went to parks or the shopping mall. But without a car how did they get there? They had to walk. To go a walk ye had to walk. Unless a taxi. But if ye were saving money? Maybe they hitched. Some would. Poor people didnt have a choice so it was like ye had to hitch. Or else ye were stuck. Imagine being stuck. If ye were in America. How could ye be stuck! Ye would go nuts. It was like so vast, it was just like so so big!

Seeing the Weather Channel ye thought it was too big, icy wastes and summer suns. Then ye saw the Road Map book and it was like Oh I could go, I could just go. Getting to Lafayette, Louisiana would have been easy with a car. There were different roads ye could take. Imagine a driver's licence and not using it. That was Dad. How could ye have one and not bring it? The easy route was straight south to the town of Mobile then along from there. Ye passed through New Orleans then the town of Baton Rouge. Lafayette came after that. But if ye went sideways to Allentown, Mississippi for the first stop it was still quite easy; Yazoo City and after that Jackson. The maps made everything closer; go east to Savannah or west to San Diego. But ye could if ye had a place to go. Murdo did. Cousin Calum was in California.

Jeesoh Aunt Maureen! Her relations were everywhere! That was the amazing-mazing thing. Anywhere ye wanted. Just like if ye wanted to disappear, if ye did. Sometimes he did. Life made ye think it. Money wouldnt matter, twenty dollars or no dollars, ye just went, if that was you, ye just went, if ye were disappearing. Or like – whatever.

The lawns here were right down to the pavement and didnt have any hedges. No people hardly at all. They were maybe all at church.

Murdo walked on. Walking was good. Walking was the best. Walking was just the very very best. How it quieted ye down, quieting yer brains. Brains. Murdo's brains, quietened. Walking alone, no sound, nothing.

Sunday was church day. So is Monday Tuesday Wednesday Thursday and Friday if it is my class sonny boy! Milliken the maths teacher. Ye went for maths and he gave ye the bible. Compress yer head sonny boy. All days are church days. Interference does not exist, interference is data. All moments are moments of God. All time is God's time. A right-angled triangle made of three right angles, think about that. Infinity. All circles are lines and all lines are a point. The way, the truth and the life. All points are the one point. Infinity. And God is greater than that. Plus 1. And God is greater than that. Nothing gets beyond Him. Go to the web and dive within, reach into the depths. You are the minute-most spec.

People thought he was nuts. Murdo heard another teacher call him "staunch", Oh Mister Milliken is "staunch", his beliefs are "staunch". So ye had to respect him. Forgive us our sins and trespasses. Keep us from temptation and grant that we may rise each morning freed from danger whole in health. That was "wanking", everybody knew that.

A man with a dog. The dog on an extension lead. Murdo walked to the inside in case he got tripped up; ye had to step over the lead. The man ignored him. An Alabaman, if that's what they are called, Alabamans; Alabamans and Alabawomans. Some guy on television was making the joke, Ala Bama and the Forty Thieves. Uncle John hated it: Childish stupidity.

The guy with the dog was the first walker Murdo had passed. And he looked across at Murdo. Because Murdo was the first walker he had seen. You see them but they see you. Think of that sonny boy.

Different for dogs. Dogs are the same anywhere in the world. They just see a person; there's a person; Scottish, Aborigine, Iceland, woof woof.

Just quiet; trees and quiet. A good place for walking. The hedges were round the back gardens but not the front; just these lawns, the grass shorn.

Ahead was a big church with a real tower. It looked old but how old could it have been? Red bricks and a square-shaped tower; fancy windows, and pillars, solid-looking. People were in the parking areas. What if Aunt Maureen and Uncle John were there and spotted him? Never.

But maybe. Maybe counts. Count a maybe.

Murdo was round the first corner. People ye see. Nobody is nothing. He continued along this street. It led to a main road, and round onto the pavement there was a bus-stop, an actual bus-stop! It had a bench for people to sit.

Aunt Maureen and Uncle John knew nothing about buses but here was a stop next to the actual church. Maybe they went to a different church.

Now Murdo recognised the road. It was the one to the mall. At the bus-stop an information board listed times, destinations and links to other bus routes.

How far had he walked? Twenty minutes or half an hour. How far was that? Not round the block anyway. Then the same back to the house. Dad would worry.

$90: forty from Dad and fifty from Uncle John. Ye could get an accordeon for ninety dollars. Or twenty, it depended on the accordeon. How much for bus tickets? That was the one thing the information board didnt list. A bus here would take ye into the main bus station, then it was from there to Lafayette, Louisiana. Then if ye came back it was the same money. So bus-fares and accordeon. Unless he got a drive from Uncle John or somebody. Dad, if Dad had his licence. Maybe he could phone Uncle Robert. Uncle Robert could go to the house and find the licence; send it express delivery. It would have been here in two days or three – Scotland to America, four maybe.

So Dad could have hired a car. That would have made it a brilliant holiday. Everything would have changed.

What a life. Murdo was glad to be walking. Shopping malls opened on a Sunday. No matter about church and everything else, people lived their life. It was their life to lead although people acted like it wasnt. Oh I thought it was my life? Oh no, it belongs to him over there, yer father. He has two, you've got none.

Other shops ahead. Not the shopping mall; ordinary shops in their own ground with their own wee carparks. And cars were there so these shops were open as well. Of course they were.

He stopped walking and about-turned.

How long had he been gone? More than an hour. Round the block? Some block. Dad would be glad when he walked in the door. Glad, sad or mad. Everybody has their own life. If he wanted to be angry, it was up to Dad.

Murdo felt like running. Oh but never run son never run, they might get the wrong idea. That was Uncle John. Then they'll definitely shoot ye. It was okay if ye were an athlete or like jogging but not an ordinary person.

Not one child either. That was what Murdo noticed. Not even in a garden. Where were the kids?

The mall!

Or church – the praying voices. And the kids twisting up to see the adults, wondering how come their eyes are all closed? Droning on and on and on, how come? What's wrong with the adults? What are they doing? Oh forgive us Father, hoahh hoahh hoahh, Gohhhd oahhhhh, forgive us oh Father please please oahhh hoahhhh oahhhhh Gohdddd. What is happening what is happening? Is it the big bad wolf! Oahhhhh oahhhhh. Look out and be careful. Close your eyes close your eyes! Oahhhhh oahhhhh. Quick! Quick quick quick! Oh Father Father God Almighty thank you thank you for keeping us safe through the day that is gone and now we pray Thee to watch over us through the coming night oh God the coming night when it is all dark and shadows fall and mysterious knocks and noises if the big bad wolf comes chapping the door.

Chap yer own door!

He kept to the main road on the way home, remembering the turn-off to Aunt Maureen's house. He entered by the driveway, round the side garden. Dad was there on the patio, wearing a shirt and trousers instead of jeans and T-shirt. He moved fast when he saw Murdo, coming towards him. Murdo stopped. Dad clapped him twice on the shoulder. Good son, he said, we're going for a meal. Did ye bring a shirt?

A shirt? Yeah I brought a shirt.

I mean a proper one?

Of course a proper one.

Fine. Away and change. Dad sighed. I'm just saying.

Okay.

Uncle John and Aunt Maureen are getting ready.

Okay Dad.

Downstairs Murdo plugged in the hi-fi immediately; but didnt switch it on. He stood a moment, then sat down on the edge of the bed. He stretched out, staring at the ceiling. Of course he had brought a shirt and of course he would wear it. Going for a meal with Uncle John and Aunt Maureen: of course he would wear it. Go and put it on, is it a proper one. That was a row. Did people need rows?

Dad just had to speak. He didnt have to but he did. That was Dad. How come he even wanted to eat? He couldnt have been hungry. He didnt go anywhere except the patio! People work then they eat. Things happen and they dont eat.

Dad said a meal but did that mean best? like as if Aunt Maureen and Uncle John would notice, even if he wore a T-shirt. T-shirts were a joke. How long did Dad wear one before sticking it into the laundry bin! a bloody week? Murdo should have said it to him, Dad change the T-shirt you are bloody minging.

Murdo sat up, then was onto his feet and rummaging around to find the shirt. He had brought two: ordinary and best. Proper was best. First a wash. He jumped upstairs to the bathroom, checked his face in the mirror; ye could see the actual bristles. He peered at his eyes, again at his eyes, almost a smile. Mum; not Eilidh.

He didnt even need a meal. That was the truth; he didnt want to go. If he could just say it! What is wrong with saying it? I'm not going. I'm not going. No Dad sorry, I dont want to. I've got like things to do and I dont want to go anywhere. I really really dont. He said it aloud: I'm not going, I am not going. No Dad. No, I am not.

Of course he was. Aunt Maureen and Uncle John. Of course he was. They were wanting him to go, and if he didnt? Oh he was going of course he was going, he was starving. Starving.

They were waiting for him.

★

The restaurant was called the Home-Run Deli and was their favourite one. It was not like a deli the way ye would expect it in Scotland. It was a big like barbeque place full of all different kinds of food for sitting in. Vegetables ye hadnt heard of. All kinds of ribs, chops, pork, ham, lamb, chicken and steak, and one called "joints", and a lot of fish. They had music every Wednesday from teatime until ten at night; bluegrass and country. Uncle John and Aunt Maureen liked it too but especially the atmosphere is what they enjoyed. It's down home, said Uncle John.

They wanted Murdo and Dad to try different things and explained what some of it was, and eat whatever caught their fancy. Murdo was starving and so was Dad. Much of it he didnt know – "grits" – but they also had pizza and lasagne. "Grits" is porridge with cheese, said Uncle John.

No sir mister, said Aunt Maureen who only wanted a sandwich; she called it a hot sandwich and ordered mashed potatoes to go with it. It was Kentucky food instead of Alabama food. That was the point she was making. She winked at Murdo. He was not sure what to eat but eventually he went with lasagne and fries – chips. Dad and Uncle John had steak but with mashed potato instead of chips. Uncle John made a joke about Murdo and Italian food to go with Italian accordeons, then ordered beers for himself and Dad, orange juice for Aunt Maureen and Murdo.

Aunt Maureen's sandwich was the best thing. Murdo would have got that if he had known. It was not really a sandwich at all but with turkey and bacon and toasted cheese; tasty-looking.

It was good with Aunt Maureen and Uncle John. They were cheery and kept things going. The usual stuff; family and Scotland and bits about Kentucky and places. Uncle John did the talking on America. Aunt Maureen listened as if he was speaking about things she didnt know. He came out with daft sayings – "A slap on the face with a wet kipper". People laughed at that but what did it mean? Nobody knew. Old sayings from the old days. A song about Davy Crockett, born on a mountain top in Tennessee, played the fiddle at the Alamo. Scottish background. Everything was Scottish background. Aunt Maureen made faces behind his back. Let somebody else talk, she said and she nodded at Murdo. Uncle John grinned at him. Murdo said: How far is California?

What? Uncle John looked at him.

Aunt Maureen smiled.

Murdo said, Well I was just thinking like the idea of Cousin Calum like I mean driving across, if we went to see him.

Huh! said Aunt Maureen.

Uncle John sighed. Murdo son, how many miles in a day can ye drive?

I dont know.

Five hundred? Uncle John glanced at Dad. Eh Tommy? Okay. Divide it into three thousand and that is yer days.

Wow, said Dad.

Six. A minute a mile, said Uncle John. You want to go faster go faster.

Aint safe, said Aunt Maureen.

No I'm not saying to go faster, only as an estimate, just working it out a mile a minute as a guide to distance.

Six days! said Dad.

Three thousand miles. Uncle John shrugged. Then if you're going north Tommy. . . Calum's in Oakland.

Murdo would have asked about Louisiana too but not with Dad there. But knowing about California meant ye could compare it. Six days to California, how many to Louisiana? The Road Atlas book was brilliant for calculating. They had a page where the distances between places was laid out in miles and kilometres. Straight south to Mobile and turn right. Left to Orange Beach on the southernmost tip which sounded brilliant the way Aunt Maureen spoke about it; a great beach where ye could swim and just enjoy it all; the Gulf of Mexico.

For Louisiana ye continued right past New Orleans and all the way until just before Texas, that was Lafayette. The gig was nine o'clock Saturday night so that was early Saturday morning he had to leave, very very early, the earliest. Except that was for ordinary driving in a car; not like buses with all changes and connections and sitting about waiting then like what happened from Memphis if ye missed a connection so an overnight stay, so then ye would miss the gig. So it had to be Friday. It could only be Friday. Except that was Uncle John and the trip to the Tennessee Valley. So what happened there?

Nothing. He would just tell Dad. Sorry Dad.

Although Aunt Maureen was saying about the weather, it was turning bad the next few days. Maybe they would postpone the trip! If it was like a downpour why would ye want to go? Nobody would. It would just be like nightmarish boring crap, stuck in a tent looking out. The whole weekend. So they wouldnt go and it would be postponed, so then they could go to the gig. Why not? They could. They would love it! If they went they would. They wouldnt but.

They wouldnt go.

Why not?

Because it didnt happen. People didn't do things like that. Imagine they did but. And Dad was like Oh Uncle John the weather is too bad for the Tennessee Valley, maybe we can go to Queen Monzee-ay's gig instead!

Ha ha right enough.

But why not! if it was his own son playing? Wouldnt that be something? That would be special. Here we are in America and Murdo's playing a gig. Aunt Maureen would love it! So would Uncle John. He just needed an accordeon. So he had to get one, and he would get one, and knew where to get it.

Aunt Maureen and Uncle John were enjoying the meal. Just being there was a good thing and occasionally they stared around the place as if they hoped to see somebody they knew. It would have been nice if they had; here's our relations from Scotland, showing them off.

$90 wasnt enough. Dad would give him more if he asked. Maybe he would. Although what did it matter, if he wasnt going. Instead it was the Tennessee Valley. It was all arranged. Uncle John was getting the day off especially. So dont waste yer breath son totally impossible and if something is impossible it is just not possible so why even talk about it dont bloody talk about it it is just a waste of breath. Fine for you wasting your breath, but not for other people, not if ye're a guest, and that is what you are son a guest! So shut up.

They were going up country, mountains and rivers and boats, fishing and just everything – friends coming with them, all for a good time and like overnight and whatever, tents or else a what-do-ye-call-it, bungalow thing made out of wood, sort of cottage, logs

just everything, everything.

So he had to go. Although he was not going to. He couldnt. The gig was on and he was playing it. He said he would and had to. He gave his word to Sarah so like breaking yer word, how could ye if it was like manners, good manners, that was ha ha ha, breaking yer word. It was fine when it suited Dad, not when it didnt.

Queen Monzee-ay was expecting him and had her set worked out for the two accordeons. So that was that.

Unless the weather. Torrential rain. Maybe it would be postponed. But if it was they would just go someplace else. It was their last weekend together and Uncle John had wangled the day off. So Murdo couldnt not go. That would have been the worst of all for Dad. Everybody doing things for ye, and then ye say no, just like a slap in the face. A family matter, the same as the Gathering and not playing the accordeon. Family comes first. Being a guest. Not knowing what guests do. What is a guest! Are family guests? Family is do as yer told. Same with guests. Murdo had to go with them. Otherwise

Otherwise nothing.

Dad was asking a question. He was going to the bar and was asking him what he wanted to drink. A big pint of lager Dad ha ha ha.

Please, he said, maybe an apple juice.

Did he even want an apple juice! Why not a glass of wine! A jack and coke, guys drank that.

Dad had got up from his chair, going to the bar or else to find a waiter. He stood there looking about. Uncle John pointed to the other corner of the large room: the Men's room. Over there, he said.

Dad headed across and as soon he had gone Uncle John was up and over to the end of the bar, and to the cashier's desk where a wee queue had formed. He was still there when Dad exited the Men's room. He saw Uncle John. The two had a disagreement. It was in good spirits; not loud enough to embarrass people. Dad wanted to pay the bill but Uncle John was insisting and insisting. Uncle John won. When they returned to the table he led the way. Dad followed with more drinks which included two whiskies. Uncle John was speaking to Dad over his shoulder. That's how we do it here, he said.

I wanted to pay something, said Dad.

Huh! said Uncle John.

Aunt Maureen looked from him to Dad, then to Murdo. Uncle John and Dad were sitting down now. Dad taking the drinks off the tray. Uncle John said to Aunt Maureen, He's the guest. I dont want him paying.

Dad smiled. Well Uncle John I have to pay something.

Uncle John immediately sat forwards, almost up off the chair, and he glared at Dad: You paid the goddam tickets!

The force of this shocked Dad, and Aunt Maureen cried: Oh now mister!

Sorry. Uncle John closed his eyes.

Murdo looked again at Dad who was staring at the table but now had raised his head, gazing at Uncle John.

Uncle John said, Sorry. I'm sorry. He clasped his hands on the table and was still. He glanced at Murdo and smiled a moment but not cheerily.

Whatever it was, not paying the tickets, what tickets? Not the plane tickets, Uncle John paid the plane tickets. What other tickets? The bus tickets?

Uncle John shifted on his chair and said to Dad, Sorry about that Tommy.

Och! Dad shrugged. Not at all.

Aunt Maureen sighed. She smiled, looking around, and said to Murdo: You like this place son?

Yeah.

You want to come for the music now, they have some fine musicians play here.

Murdo nodded. Eventually Uncle John raised his whisky glass and paused with it. After a moment Dad raised his. Uncle John said to Murdo, What is it ye say again son is it slàinte mhòr or slàinte mhath?

Eh. . . Usually just slàinte, or slàinte mhath.

Some of them here say slàinte mhòr.

Do they?

Yeah. Uncle John glanced at Dad. Slàinte mhòr, it's just one of these things that they say.

I dont know it, said Dad. Mhòr is big.

Yeah, said Uncle John. Big whisky eh!

Yeah. Dad smiled, sipping the whisky. It's a nice one.

I like it, replied Uncle John.

Aunt Maureen said to Murdo, You're thinking about the drive home son huh? You worrying about that? Aunt Maureen was opening her purse; she withdrew the car keys. This what you're worried about? She jerked her thumb at Uncle John, and snorted: You think I'd let him drive huh? You want us to land on top of Old Smokey?

Murdo grinned. I wasnt thinking that at all!

Oh yeah! Uncle John chuckled.

I wasnt!

This guy sees everything! laughed Uncle John.

Dad smiled, looking from one to the other. Aunt Maureen closed her purse. Dad said, I knew ye were a driver Aunt Maureen but not the 4x4, I didnt know ye drove the 4x4.

Oh you didnt huh!

No!

Aunt Maureen touched Dad on the wrist.

Murdo said, You liked driving the wee car Aunt Maureen.

Yes I did son thank you for saying. Scoot here and there huh.

Uncle John smiled, but didnt say anything. After a moment Aunt Maureen glanced at him: Dont go blaming yourself now mister we had to sell it.

Yeah.

We didnt have the choice.

No.

Aunt Maureen nodded, and said to Murdo, He dont want me going on buses Murdo.

Murdo smiled.

But Aunt Maureen frowned at Uncle John: So how am I to get any place huh? Cant go on a bus and aint got no car.

I know, replied Uncle John.

You dont know mister: stuck in the house. What happens when these boys go? Huh? What happens then?

We'll miss them. Uncle John sipped at his beer.

Sure we'll miss them. Sure we'll miss them.

You'll go down in the dumps. Uncle John winked at Murdo.

I wont, said Aunt Maureen.

Is that a promise!

Oh now you want to promise to phone Springfield, Missouri? she asked.

Uncle John gazed at her.

After a few moments she winked at Dad, jerking a thumb in Uncle John's direction and she said, He thinks I dont know about walking Tom! I walked them mountains when I was a girl and I can keep walking them.

Uncle John frowned, I'm not saying a word.

No sir, she said.

On the road home Murdo sat in the front passenger's seat. He was not sure whether to speak to Aunt Maureen or not and was wary of disturbing her concentration. Her gaze rarely strayed from the road ahead and it seemed like her preference was silence. In the rear seats Dad and Uncle John didnt speak hardly at all.

★

Be sociable.

What is "be sociable"? There was nothing wrong with lying down. That is what bedrooms are for, ye go to relax and just like escape. Sometimes ye needed that. Not having to talk to people. Putting on the music. Reading a book or anything at all. Nothing at all. Why has it got to be something? Think about nothing. So what if it was the afternoon? Ye need yer own space. Bedrooms are a space. Dad was annoyed because Murdo was lying down but so what if he was lying down if it was his room? Surely he could be in his room? Dad went to his and Aunt Maureen went to hers so why couldnt Murdo? It had been raining the last couple of days so what else was there to do? Ye couldnt go in the garden. Ye had to stay in yer room or else go to the lounge, except if ye did somebody else might be there so ye had to say hullo and start talking. And obviously ye couldnt play the music: obviously.

He didnt want to read anyway he was sick of it.

Uncle John spoke about an Indian village they visited, a real one someplace where they had wooden houses. Indian descendants showed them historical things and they felt it creepy but not the ones showing them, they didnt bat an eyelid.

So what, that would have been Murdo, exactly the same.

That prayer on the leaflet at Mum's funeral. The minister read it out. Oh Thou who are present in every place and from Whose love no space or distance can ever separate us. Grant us to know that those who are absent from one another are still present with Thee. Ha ha. Was Murdo supposed to cry? Memories memories. Ye cry about the past and memories are the past. If the person is with ye then she is with ye so how come the tears? No tears. That is crap. Let Jesus take the strain. Ha ha.

Screams from the basement. Tortured screams. Dig deep beneath the floor, going down beyond the foundations, way way down, down into the dark earth that used to be lush fields and dirt trails; the black soil ye rub between yer fingers where the maggots are, places where Indians camped, where they buried their dead.

Dad didnt cry either. People felt sorry for him. Why not Murdo? If things were tough for Dad, it was the same for him. Poor Dad. What about Murdo! Grant us to know that those who are absent from one another are still present with Thee. That is like ha ha.

Rows, moans and grumbles all the time having to think about him. Why not him about Murdo? Who was the father and who was the boy? Murdo was the boy and Dad was Dad. How come he was to feel sorry for him? It was bloody nuts. The son shouldnt have to feel sorry for the father. Jesus didnt feel sorry for God.

The son wants to get there but the father is there already. The father is always there and the son never is. That was Dad, Dad Dad Dad. He sat beside Murdo at the funeral and listened to the minister. Everything the minister said Dad heard like it was a real conversation and not just a sermon. Murdo didnt listen at all. It was Dad the minister was saying it for anyway, and when people listened they listened for the poor man, the poor poor man, what is going to happen to him? Is he going to be okay? Or else go mad! Maybe he will. People do go mad. Mum was there in the coffin. Imagine that. People fling themselves on the coffin. Imagine Dad. Dad could have done it, he could have jumped on the coffin. And Murdo saving him, it would have been Murdo: Dad Dad dont jump, dont jump, come back, come back. All the people looking, Oh look at Tom Macarthur, he's mad; that is grief, he is mad with grief. So who is going to save him?

Bloody Murdo that's who. Dad took pills.Unless he had stopped. Maybe he had. People take pills to calm down. Then they forget them and go crazy. Dad didnt. He just had silences. His silences went on and on. He went to his room. What did he do in his room? He read books. Anything else? Stared out the window. Dad could sit at the window and see out. He was at the front of the house so he saw the street. If Murdo wanted to see out he stood up on a chair and reached higher. All he saw was the sky. Although he liked the sky. The sky was good in Alabama.

A chap at the door.

Murdo got up and opened to Aunt Maureen. Brought you something! She passed him a muffin on a plate and a mug of tea. Low pressure all over, she said, right from the coast. All along they got it torrential.

Oh well.

Aunt Maureen nodded, and smiled. Murdo held the muffin and the mug of tea. Thanks Aunt Maureen!

He placed them on the bedside table and made to close the door.

But Aunt Maureen wagged her finger at him. Now son you ask good questions and I got one for you: you reckon they could cure cancer?

Cure cancer?

They go spending millions on weapons and guns going into other people's countries. So why not look after their own huh? Shouldnt that come first? Whoever will do that? You think there is someone but there aint; no sir, black, brown or white. That aint their prerogative. Forget medicine. That aint what they do with our tax money. That's for something else huh. Well, I get cross about that son, I do. We were talking about it in church. Things just aint right. That's what people are saying. That was the talk, like a discussion? that is what you would call it. You enjoy a talk son that was a talk.

Aunt Maureen reached to grasp him by the wrist. Her hand was light and he could have brushed it away. She had a thin hand, thin fingers and the flesh felt silky. She said: That is one beautiful name, Eilidh. That the old language of Scotland Murdo?

Yeah, it's Gaelic.

Well it is beautiful, it is beautiful. Aunt Maureen nodded then she smiled and shook her head slowly. You maybe think about next Sunday son huh?

. . .

If you want to come with us to church you would be so very welcome.

Oh.

Your Dad is coming.

Dad! Is he?

Aunt Maureen smiled. It's a welcoming church Murdo. She touched him on the wrist: Now do I get a hug from you or what!

Murdo stepped to her and they hugged. She returned upstairs.

Murdo closed the door. No matter what she was the very very best. Life was just like whatever, who cares, except Aunt Maureen. Whatever else happened.

The rain teeming down. Murdo was up in the chair peering out the window. It was the sky. The rain was there but sometimes it seemed to merge. Aunt Maureen said it got in everywhere. Talking about the rain. The roof wasnt good any more but she didnt want Uncle John clambering up to mend it. He was good at jobs about the house but she worried about him falling off and breaking his neck. All the time she worried about him. Oh I'm not going to bed until he comes home. Same as Mum. It was Dad she waited for.

She did! Oh Murdo here's yer meal. Where's yours Mum? Oh I'm waiting for your father.

Ha ha.

That was something. It was great seeing. He loved seeing it. Dad walking in the door and Mum seeing him walk in the door. And she always did. That was her in the hospice. She always saw him walk in the door. How come?

She was watching for him. While Murdo was there. Murdo was talking to her and she was watching for Dad. Is that not something? What is that?

What it was. Murdo didnt know what it was.

Although he did. Mum loved Dad. Ha ha. She loved Murdo too.

Listening to stuff. No music and the sounds. Inside yer head like gas pipes, zzzzzz.

Thoughts go back thoughts go back, way way back. It was true but. That was a family.

The worst for Dad was Murdo dead and him alive. That was the worst of all. For Dad it was. The very worst imaginable. He wouldnt want to be alive.

But as soon as they got home he was leaving school. Dad had to understand that. If he didnt then he didnt understand anything. Murdo was not staying for one last year. He was not staying for one last day. He was not doing good and was never ever going to.

Never ever. How come Mum thought he could? That was Mum. Mum was Mum, she was a mother. She thought he was brainy. He wasnt. People were good at their lessons. He wasnt! He was just bloody hopeless, he needed other stuff or the same stuff done different. That was it with teachers: Oh I think I know what it is but it's different to what ye think.

Oh God, like gas pipes inside yer head, that last time when he was leaving, he didnt look, at Mum, he didnt look at her. He was not able to. He walked out the room.

He needed away, to get away. Leave and love. I leave but I love.

Oh hullo son, how are ye? Fine. How's yer Mum? Fine. Fine fine fine; everything

★

He had $90. Uncle John and Dad gave him it to spend. He didnt. He kept the lot. He got through the whole day at the Gathering without spending a penny. It couldnt have happened without Clara Hopkins. She gave him like two meals for the price of one, and he didnt even pay for that. Dad was supposed to give him pocket money but didnt. This was not because he was mean. Maybe he was mean but that wasnt why he forgot the pocket money. He just forgot. Murdo should have told him but didnt.

That $40 was food money. If ye took away the food money how much had Dad given him? Nothing. Uncle John's $50 was the pocket money. If there was emergencies, that is what it was for, like Lafayette and buses, how to get there, that was an emergency. Take away that and he had nothing.

Not in the whole world. This is why he had to leave school. He needed his own money. Not to buy toys. To get by in the world. Ye couldnt get by without money. So if yer parents didnt give ye it. Ye had to work or else rob a bank. Uncle John and Aunt Maureen were ordinary people. They had a nice house but that was like from years ago when they bought it; three jobs and all what they did. Murdo knew that. He wasnt daft. All that stuff about growing up. Ye wanted to but people didnt let ye. Ye had to find it all out yerself. Murdo knew about saving money. Everything was saving money. That was poor people the wide world over.

So it was rob a bank.

Where would ye go if ye did? There were good places to hide in Alabama; the same back home. Guys talked about that. For Murdo the best place wasnt England or Ireland. For robbing a bank the best escape was sailing a boat around Ardlamont Point and up by Crinan. That is how Murdo would go because who would expect it? Nobody. They would all think oh Glasgow and then like a train to England. For Murdo it was like get past Islay but not to Ireland, it was Canada or Greenland. The Atlantic Ocean. All ye needed was a boat and ye could get a boat.

Oh but $90 wasnt enough. Lafayette was bus tickets and an accordeon; snacks and juice, bottles of water. That was what it meant for going. Ye needed money. A lot of money. How much was an accordeon was a daft question. Ye could get a cheap one or an expensive one, or something inbetween. The pawnshop in Allentown had one that was not bad-looking. Ye would only know when ye played it, if the reeds were damaged or whatever. If he went on the Friday he could meet with Sarah and the family and get a lift down.

These were the thoughts.

★

He wandered upstairs to see what was happening. Aunt Maureen was in the kitchen. Murdo stood with her watching the Weather Channel. Rain's off, she said.

Murdo hesitated then returned downstairs, lifted his jacket and headed back up, knelt at the front door to put on his boots. Dad appeared from out his room. Where ye off to? he asked.

Eh just round the block Dad like I mean I was eh. . .

Okay if I come with ye?

. . .

Eh, is it okay?

Of course.

Murdo waited for him to get ready. Aunt Maureen appeared from the kitchen. You boys going out a walk huh?

Yeah.

Good thinking; rain's coming on later.

You could come? said Murdo.

Thanks son. I got things to do.

It would be good if ye did.

Oh now I would Murdo but I just dont have the time now huh I got things to do.

Dad had arrived and stood to the side while she was speaking. Now she opened the door for them and waited until they were beyond the garden path onto the pavement then she waved to them. Farther along the street Murdo turned to see her still there by the door. She waved again and he waved in reply. Dad also waved. Dad said, She likes to see us getting out!

Yeah. Murdo smiled.

Which way?

I was just going eh. . . Murdo pointed to the next corner and shrugged.

Anywhere in particular? asked Dad.

No.

They continued walking. Pools of water lay around but it was warm and quite a stuffy feel to everything. Before long Dad took off his jacket and walked with it slung across his shoulder. He had noticed a certain smell. Might be hickory or maple, he said, ye get them here. Different types of plants and trees. Different wild life too. Quite an interesting place Alabama.

Yeah, said Murdo.

Dad seemed cheery. Maybe something nice had happened. What

was nice for Dad? Unless going home next Tuesday. Maybe he wanted to go and was glad it was coming. In some ways it was okay but in other ways not.

In most ways not.

Was there even one was okay? A horrible day here was better than a good day there. The truth is there werent any good days back home. Even if there were so what? If they were good what happened? Nothing. Good days and bad days were the same; just like nothing at all.

So if Dad had emigrated back when he was a boy then they would have been here and Murdo wouldnt have had to go home because this would have been home. Except Murdo wouldnt have been here because Dad and Mum would never have met and married, so bla bla bla, him and Eilidh: a different mother means different children and they would have been American, whoever they were. Dad would have married an American woman like maybe Linda so that would have been them.

Murdo was going to say something to Dad about it but didnt. It was good just walking, and Dad was enjoying that too. He was noticing wee things in walking and drew attention to the flags on houses and the similarity of the gardens and garages. He was interested in the actual houses and when they were built then he seemed to be guessing the number of rooms in particular ones, and the idea that most houses were on the level like what ye called bungalows back home, maybe with basements; so if a basement might have had two rooms, three rooms or whatever, maybe just one big games room with things like pool tables or their own wee bars or whatever. There werent as many "add-ons" as back home, said Dad, where people had added extensions to their houses to make them bigger.

He spoke about other stuff too but Murdo didnt catch it all, something about his job and the kind of job Uncle John did, and things to do with working, and he also spoke about next year and how it would be "life after school" for Murdo. It was funny the way Dad said it but there wasnt anything he could say back. The truth is he didnt hear much at all because he was not listening, not to everything. Things were calm and that brought its own sound. Hardly a breeze at all, no traffic. Peace and quiet. This was a great place for walking just like for yer head so ye didnt have to really think. It was weird how ye felt yer own walking made echoes, although it didnt make any echoes.

Maybe the dampness, a kind of dampness, it maybe had something to do with how calm it was. Maybe calm before the storm. Rain was due later. Water deadens sound. Or changes it. The rain dampening the earth and a noise becomes more thudding or thick. Rain on a roof, heavy rain, not heavy but not going away, insistent, incessant. In a garden towards the end of the street an elderly woman was bent over tending plants inside plant-holders; she was wearing a large straw hat, an apron and trousers tucked into wellington boots. Puddles of water. She raised her head to see them properly. Murdo thought Dad didnt notice her but he called, Hullo.

She didnt respond. Murdo wasnt surprised but it was a wee bit disappointing too like as if she knew they were foreign and wasnt interested in knowing about them. She returned to what she was doing.

It would have been good if Aunt Maureen spent more time in the garden. She mostly worked about the house. "Pottering" is how she described it. Gardens were open air and would have been better for her.

When they reached the red-brick church with the square tower and the pillars there were younger women and small children by a side door entrance. Round the corner was the bus-stop listing information on times and destinations. Probably a bus from here would connect to the downtown area where they had a main bus station. Murdo had wanted to check this out but Dad tagging along made it awkward. When they approached the bus-stop Murdo said, Look Dad a bus-stop. I wonder where the buses go?

Dad also was interested. They paused by the information listing. Shuttle? Murdo asked, What is that Dad "shuttle"?

A shuttle bus, it shuttles ye from one place to the other. Back and forth.

Yeah but where?

Downtown probably, or else the shopping mall – this is the road.

Murdo scanned the information for a few moments longer.

Dad was looking at the sky and checked his watch. Okay? he said.

Yeah, it's just interesting seeing the buses.

It's going to rain later.

They continued walking. The traffic was heavy; big long trucks that tooted and had flags and fancy decorations round the driver's cabin. Some traveled the length and breadth of the whole country.

The actual cars were like back home, and not like television or the movies where ye saw the straight-line ones with the big long bonnets. One difference here was the different styles of pick-up trucks. Dad was looking at them too, maybe thinking about his driver's licence and if he had brought it what would have happened?

Lafayette, Louisiana! Ha ha.

No chance. Even if Dad had brought it. He would never have hired a car all that time. Although for one weekend, yes, maybe. He could have afforded that. Leave Friday, back Sunday. Or else Saturday, if they picked up the car early Saturday morning, did the gig Saturday night then delivered it back Sunday morning. They would have managed that. The route was dead easy and like straight-forwards, Dad would have done it no bother at all. It would have been brilliant. How brilliant, ye could imagine, just amazing! It didnt matter anyway. Although it did, in a way.

The Tennessee Valley in a couple of days. Dad talked about it like it was exciting, and it was exciting. Friends of Uncle John and Aunt Maureen were going with them too; an older couple who were at the Gathering. If possible they would all stay overnight. Be nice if we did, said Dad.

Yeah, said Murdo. Although he wasnt going with them. Really. That was that. He wasnt. And it was relaxing to know.

Imagine horses and a wagon train.

Car after car after car, trucks followed trucks. But that traffic was okay, wherever it all was going: nowhere; round and round, back and forward; who cares where it was going except the people inside, the ones doing the driving, their families all waiting for them to come home.

It was true but. Murdo was not going with them: the Tennessee Valley, he was not going. That was that.

Dad was talking away. I felt a couple of drops, he said.

I didnt, said Murdo.

I think we should head for the mall.

Just now?

Yeah, said Dad, it's not too far. We could grab a sandwich and you could check out the music store. D'ye fancy?

Eh. . .

It's definitely going to rain. If it's very heavy we can get a taxi home. Dad shrugged. Be nice to look about, get a coffee. Fancy it?

Eh. . .

You're not that bothered! Dad smiled.

No I mean if you are eh just like if you think.

If I think?

Yeah well. . .

So you're not bothered?

No but Dad if you are then fine, fine. If you want to go. I mean I dont mind. Murdo stopped walking.

Dad had stopped before him, and he said, So it's not yer preference?

I dont mind.

So will we head back or what? I take it you're happy to head back? Your preference son, what is your preference? Obviously ye've got a preference.

A preference?

What do ye want to do? Dad sighed. I'm asking what ye want to do?

Just whatever.

Right, okay. Dad smiled with his eyes closed. Okay, he said, and that was that, they headed back.

Close of day. Nothing. Murdo was glad. Not close of day but nearly. Close of day was Thursday evening when Uncle John returned from work, and after the meal, when everybody had gone to bed: that was close of day. The day after was Friday. Friday was Friday.

★

Early that Thursday evening Murdo was downstairs studying the Road Atlas book. Uncle John had phoned to say he would not be home until seven o'clock. So they wouldnt be eating until half past, at least. Aunt Maureen would have served the evening meal before then but Dad and Murdo were happy to wait. She worried about him. Not because he was ill but the life he led at sixty-eight years of age: up by 6.30 every morning, out the door by 7.15; a fifty-mile drive five days a week and every other Saturday, plus emergency call-outs. But that was that and if ever he retired what would he do? He laughed about it but Aunt Maureen didnt.

Most of the Tennessee Valley preparations had been done by her during the past couple of days. They planned to leave early and were prepared for an overnight stop; perhaps even two, Friday and Saturday, depending how things went. Dad told Murdo to pack extra in case they did. Of course he was packing extra but for where he was going himself. So when he said, Okay Dad, it wasnt ordinary conversational talking it was like a lie, an actual lie, each time Dad spoke to him.

Except the only thing: it was right what he was doing. He was not going with them. If he did that was him for the rest of his life. For everything. Although he was telling lies to do it, it was the right thing. So so right it was not even a decision. It fitted.

The route from Allentown to Lafayette missed out Mobile

altogether. The road went down the side of the Mississippi River down through Vicksburg, small roads to Jackson where Sarah's father wanted her to go to college. Maybe he could hitch some parts and save money. No. He just needed more money. $90 was not enough. He needed more, a lot more – another $100, maybe $150 like if it was an accordeon on top of the bus-fares. If he could save money he would but how could he do that? Unless if he hitched part of the way. Why not? People did. At home they did. They did here too; ye saw it on the movies although then it was like the Horror Channel; chainsaw massacres and vampires ripping ye limb from limb. It depended on Allentown. Everything was fine if he got a lift down with Sarah's family, and the loan of an accordeon too; maybe the turquoise if Queen Monzee-ay thought it was okay. If not, it was just money, he needed money.

But like pocket money anyway. Imagine the pocket money Dad owed him! He never gave him any! Ha ha.

It was true but. Dad forgot. He wasnt mean, he was just like forgetful. It was a bloody fortune! Ever since Mum died. When ye thought about it. He would pay it back anyway. However much he took, it was borrowing, Murdo was going to borrow. It was just like a loan.

He shut the Road Atlas book. He stretched out on the bed. No music. Maybe he didnt want any. Not just now.

Aunt Maureen too, jeesoh, whenever he passed her she smiled or said something cheery about tomorrow. It was hopeless, acting like it meant something. And what did it mean? Nothing. He was just lying. Looking and speaking. Just everything. He lied and lied. Really, he was just a bloody liar. And the greatest people in the world, that was Aunt Maureen and it was Uncle John too.

He got up from the bed and opened the door, waited for the all-clear then upstairs to the bathroom. He shut the door and snibbed it. The bathroom mirror.

He didnt mean to see his face but he did. So he had to look, to really look and really just jeesoh, his stomach. He splashed cold water on his face and the back of his neck, to get fresh.

He didnt like his eyes. What was his eyes? He didnt like them. His eyes were not, they were not something. He needed to smile. It wasnt a smile. Ha ha. Not a smile.

Strange about lips, that wee bit on the upper one shaped like a V and that wee valley bit up to between the nostrils. That was yer body and how it worked. Things fitted. That was like tunes and how ye made one up, this note came before that note, and ye just went with it and then looked at it later and shaped them all out, making it smooth, making "it" smooth. "It" was one urge all the way through.

Maybe he needed a shave. Maybe he didnt. He didnt have to, unless he thought so. Seeing his face. He wanted Eilidh and Mum to be there.

He made a smile. It was his smile.

He didnt have as many pimples. Probably the sun. His face and neck were red but hardly any suntan on his body. Maybe he had a body that didnt go brown. Some people's bodies stayed white, or else just red.

He did a thing and everybody else was affected. Ye look in the mirror and see other people. They are seeing you. Ye see yer own face but these other folk too, how come they are all there? You make a decision but it is their life too.

They know what you are thinking. They say it to ye: Oh I know what you're thinking. Nothing gets hidden. Nothing can be hidden. Ye cannay even tell a lie because the truth is always there and somebody knows, somebody knows. Dad is close and Mum is closer, yet both are further because Eilidh is inside, she is inside, so ye cannot hide, nothing ye can do is hidden, like no private access for anything, damn bloody anything, stupid nonsense shit and porn sites, and any damn anything not caring because who cares if everybody knows, ye just say it and do it like life if that is how ye live, who cares, who hears, everybody is nobody. Except the person left behind, always a person left behind. That is the plus one.

Then about lies too, how ye could say it wasnt a total bunch of lies never-ending, not like an infinity, because if ye took away that one most basic lie, then nothing else was there, it all just disappeared. A tissue of lies. One lie made the tissue. Take away the one and there wasnt a tissue. That bigger and bigger pile of lies was really just the one: he said he was going and he was not going.

He heard a door closing. Uncle John had come home from work.

★

They didnt start eating until 8 o'clock. Uncle John opened a bottle of wine and included a wee one for Murdo. Dad just smiled. They were going home next Tuesday. Murdo's head was so full he had forgotten. He sipped the wine, it was tasty. Wine could be tasty although never quite like what ye expected. Beer was better.

He hoped Dad and Uncle John would go the last hour to the pub but they were too busy with packing and stuff; Aunt Maureen too, dotting between the house and the driveway. It suited Murdo because he could stay downstairs. Later Dad sat in the lounge by himself watching television. So that was Murdo's chance: Will I go and tell him now?

When he told Dad Dad would tell Uncle John and Aunt Maureen. They would think he was ill. Viruses were everywhere. Uncle John made jokes about medical care in America. It cost ye a body part to pay for the medical bill. Ye went in with a broken leg and the operation cost ye a liver. They would worry then come downstairs and like Oh what's wrong with ye son are ye ill? No. What's wrong? Nothing's wrong I'm just like eh

whatever.

They would see he wasnt ill. Maybe he is coming down with

251

something. He isnt ill just now but tomorrow he might be. Maybe it is a mental issue. Too much stress. Would they be upset? Yes. But not a big bit. Dad would still be going. They had other friends that were going too so they wouldnt call it off. They would just wonder.

Murdo stayed in the basement. Whatever time it was. Then Aunt Maureen had been in her own room for ages. Murdo was wanting to say goodnight to her. Maybe she was in bed reading a magazine. So it was too late.

It was, it was too late.

And Dad and Uncle John were in the lounge, probably with a beer. It would have spoiled everybody's night.

★

Next morning people were up and about on the final preparations. It was the last chance. He didnt want to see Uncle John and Aunt Maureen and waited downstairs until it was Dad in the bathroom, then waiting for him to come out, the door to open, just that moment. He didnt feel bad, just his stomach and nerves nerves nerves, that jumpiness ye get, having to do it, do something, whatever. When it did open Murdo was upstairs quietly. Dad held the door for him but Murdo said: Dad can I speak to ye a minute?

What's up? said Dad.

Nothing, just eh

Is there something wrong?

No Dad I just eh Dad I need to speak to ye. Sorry Dad I just eh. . . Murdo sniffed and returned downstairs.

Dad followed. Inside Dad closed the door over. Murdo was standing by the foot of the bed, maybe four yards away, and he felt better there and even like limbering up, like running on the spot, that was how felt. The most stupid thing but just silly silly and he had to breathe in, standing as still as he could, put his hands in his pockets and was going to start crying, Oh Dad he was going to start crying, Oh Dad.

What's up? What's up?

Dad I cant go. Murdo shook his head. Dad. . .I cant go. I cant go. I just cant. I cant. Dad I cant.

Why not?

Dad I cant. Murdo closed his eyes, lowering his head and he breathed in deeply.

Son what's up? Dad made a movement towards him and hesitated.

Dad I'm so so sorry.

Calm down.

Murdo breathed in.

What's wrong?

I just cant go Dad I'm sorry like the thought of it Dad, being away and just like being with people and the whole day and everything, just sitting there and everything like all the talking and everything, everything, Dad I dont eh I dont. . . Dad I'm so sorry, I'm so so sorry; but I just feel I need to opt out, I need to opt out.

Dad was nodding his head.

Dad I'm so sorry I'm so so sorry. Dad. . .

Dad put his arm round Murdo's shoulder. Dont worry, he said.

I'm so so sorry.

Dont worry.

They stood for several moments; Murdo gazing at the floor, shoulders hunched and his hands in his pockets and it was like he couldnay raise his head, not able to look at Dad, he felt so bad like just going away forever, just forever.

Take it easy, said Dad. He patted Murdo on the shoulder. Ye okay?

Yeah.

They'll be disappointed.

I'm so sorry.

Dont worry. If ye change yer mind. . .we'll, be another half hour. Okay?

Murdo nodded.

Dad left the room and it was over. Everything. Murdo listened to his footsteps.

Aunt Maureen would be upset especially. But so would Uncle John. Dad was going but, that was something. They wouldnt have to worry either like how sometimes Murdo and Dad like if they werent talking or there was bad feeling between them. Without Murdo it wasnt a worry.

But he didnt want to see them right away, and he sat down on the edge of the bed. Soon after he heard the 4x4 doors slamming shut and rushed upstairs, but they were still packing stuff into the boot. Uncle John called to him: Alright son!

Yeah, thanks.

Uncle John smiled, he continued the packing. Murdo went between the door from the dining area into the patio and the driveway outside the house, helping Dad pass him various bags and items. At one point Dad seemed irritated but maybe he wasnt. Aunt Maureen arrived with her last two bags which she put in on the floor by the rear passenger seat, then made to enter. She looked twice when she saw him. Hey Murdo! she said. She brandished her right fist: You'll wish you had come!

Murdo smiled.

Dad said nothing but was looking straight at Murdo. Uncle John walked to the driver's door. Now Dad looked set to say something but didnt.

Murdo returned the look, before shifting stance. He folded his arms. Dad walked to the front passenger side and pulled open the door. Uncle John gave Murdo a short salute: Be midnight the time we're home Murdo boy. If we're staying on we'll phone.

We'll phone either way, said Dad.

Murdo nodded.

Aunt Maureen had opened the rear passenger window. You know where there's food son huh!

Yeah.

Dont burn the house down! Uncle John chuckled.

Dad was inside now, and closed the door. Murdo walked forwards. Once Uncle John had switched on the engine Dad let down the window to say, Don't lock yerself out. Whatever ye do!

No.

I mean if ye go out a walk.

Murdo nodded. Have a good time, he said, then stepped back.

The 4x4 pulled outside onto the street. Murdo walked to the side then behind, waving, then returned up the driveway. He watched the car until it disappeared round the bend towards the main road. He stood there an extra moment. Maybe they would have forgotten something. The longer they didnt show the more unlikely it was.

How much distance does a car travel in five minutes? Thirty miles an hour is fifteen for a half hour, is seven and a half for fifteen, is five for two and a half: two and a half miles in five minutes.

Murdo returned downstairs and sorted through his clothes and essentials, packing quickly. Past eight o'clock and he needed to move fast. The buses was the problem. The thing with America was how big it was. Ye dont think that until ye see it on the Road Atlas book pages and work out the time it takes to get from place to place. Jackson looked quite near but it was hours away passing through Birmingham then change up to Allentown, he would have to change someplace. A car would go faster because ye could choose yer roads and drive as long as ye wanted without having to stop at wee towns to let people off and on, or else change buses. He packed the two CDs, the USA Road Atlas plus a book for reading.

That was him now. He lifted his jacket, had a last look round then went upstairs to the bathroom. Would he need a towel? Yes but the one Aunt Maureen had given him took up a lot of space. He went into her linen cupboard and lifted a small one for hands.

He knew where Dad kept the emergency money. Six hundred dollars. Murdo took four $50 notes which was the very very minimum. Everything depended. $200 was not enough if he didnt get any lifts and had to pay full bus-fares there and back. Plus accordeon. But he couldnt take anything more.

From the fridge he used the cheese and cold meat to make four sandwiches. Aunt Maureen wouldnt worry. She would be glad he took it. As many slices as necessary. He gathered some fruit together and found her store of brown paperbags.

Next was Aunt Maureen's notepad to write a letter to her and Uncle John, and one to Dad too, just apologising and saying about the gig, and he would be back on Sunday but would phone and not to worry. Then the telephone rang, it kept ringing. Murdo walked to the hallway but didnt lift it. Maybe Dad from Uncle John's cell phone. Probably it was. Jeesoh. It rang again. He went to lift it this time but left it, he just left it. He couldnt speak to anybody. When he checked the time it was after half past eight. How many miles was that?

Maybe he should have answered the phone. So now they would worry. If it was Dad. Maybe it wasnt, but if it was. If it was he would worry. He would ask Uncle John to turn back, to see things were okay. He would need to. That was Dad, that is what he would do. No he wouldnt. Maybe, maybe he would. Murdo wrote down the telephone number and house address in the back page of the Road Atlas book, and again on a scrap of notepaper which he put into the rucksack, and a third time on another scrap of notepaper which he stuck into his jeans pocket.

He positioned the two letters on the kitchen counter, propped up against mugs. He checked the patio door was locked and drew the curtains, then last call to the bathroom, last look round the house. He opened the front door. Nothing else. He stepped outside and closed it.

The street was quiet. Murdo walked quickly to the corner and all the way along past the red-brick church, and to the bus-stop on the main road.

He was the only one there. Five minutes and a bus arrived. The doors opened and he stepped up, and held coins at the ready. The driver ignored him. The doors closed and the driver continued to ignore him, then jerked his thumb back the way. So Murdo was not to pay money, or what? The driver accelerated, still ignoring him. Grumpy drivers, that was like home. Murdo walked to the nearest empty seat. Only two other people were on the bus but more got on eventually, and a few who looked like students.

The bus went right into the downtown area. Murdo ate a banana while crossing the road to the bus station. On a wall inside was a large map marked with the main bus routes which he studied, working it out the best way, tied into the route to Allentown, Mississippi.

He was prepared for expensive tickets but it was extortionate, and even more extortionate if he had gone west to begin with. The trouble there was keeping sideways rather than going north to Memphis; he did not want to go back there. It felt like bad luck or something; although what was luck, ye make yer own in this life. People said that.

FIVE

South of Birmingham the bus was full: he sat on the aisle seat. On the inside was a wee thin guy. What age? Thirties maybe, worrying about whatever and looking agitated. Something bad was going to happen! He hardly noticed Murdo at all, he had his phone out, scrolling down, checking messages, scrolling down. Then he put it away and brought it back out again, then kept it in his hand and stared out the window.

Murdo was tired now and just glad to be sitting there and like going to sleep if he felt like it, if he could. The wee guy had closed his eyes too and looked to be dozing then was awake again checking the phone and chewing the edge of his right thumbnail, and muttering: The goddam buses dont move. Want them to move they dont move. Aint my fault man. People blame me. It aint me. It aint me man.

He half turned to Murdo as if surprised to see him and wondering like Oh am I talking inside my head or out?

Murdo stared ahead. He wouldnt have minded a snooze. But the bus had been going a while and if he missed the connection it was a disaster. Buses didnt wait. If ye made it fine but if ye didnt ye didnt. There were other stops along the road and ye had to be careful. Other people would have felt the same the way they were watching roundabout.

The wee guy closed his eyes now and ye could see the worry there on his forehead. He began muttering again, moving his head in such a way he could have been speaking to Murdo: Fucking bus driver man he aint no bus driver. Got a brother's a bus driver never drove so slow. What you think he's doing man I'll tell you what he's doing. Forty em pee aitch is what he's doing. You think I dont know? I know man; fucking been there man I been there.

What like driving? asked Murdo. Ye mean ye were driving?

The wee thin guy stared at him. Aint my fault; they blame me. Aint me man.

Murdo said, What are ye late?

Late. Yeah. The guy shifted to see out the window then shook his head, glanced at the phone.

Murdo waited for him to say something more. He didnt. Murdo had his book out from the rucksack and tried to concentrate. A couple of folk had laptops open. A few with phones and a couple reading books. Two guys were talking together, loudly.

People were just ordinary, worrying about ordinary stuff. That was this wee guy, whatever it was. Funny how people could blame ye for things that had nothing to do with ye. That happened to Murdo in Glasgow once, he was waiting at the train station and a foreign woman came up and started shouting at him. People were staring. They thought he had done something like stolen her bag. Probably she was ill. He tried to talk to her but she didnt let him. He had to walk away. There was nothing else he could do. These things happened. Ye wondered about other people, if it happened to them too or was it just like maybe who knows, who knows, it couldnt just be him.

Murdo dozed. When he awoke the wee thin guy had gone. The bus was stationary and only a quarter full. Outside people walked about, smoking and just stretching their legs. A few stood by the side luggage compartment awaiting the driver. Murdo was uncomfortable and sweaty but if he went for a walk what would happen? Imagine it went away without him. He moved into the window seat, rested his head against the glass, the feel of it cool against his forehead. He took the last orange from the rucksack and peeled it. It was good and juicy. Juicy oranges are just the best. He had a couple of sandwiches but was saving them. He wiped his fingers on his jeans.

Then the wee guy was there and glowering at him. Murdo moved immediately, out from the window seat into the aisle one. The guy shoved a small carrier bag into the overheard luggage rack, then squeezed in past Murdo, muttering as he went: I was at the bathroom, what you cant go to the bathroom!

I didnt know you were coming back, said Murdo.

You dont reserve no seats here.

Well I know that I mean I paid a ticket. Murdo shook his head.

Oh yeah you paid a ticket like what you think I dont?

No. I'm not saying that.

We all pay the fucking ticket man. The guy shifted on his seat, gazing out the window and doing the muttering again, We all pay the fucking ticket. He took out his phone.

I didnt know ye were coming back, said Murdo. Like if ye had just said to me ye know I mean like I would have kept yer seat. Ye didnay have to worry.

The guy turned to Murdo. He stared at him. Murdo shrugged. The guy glanced back out the window, seeing down to the main luggage compartment on the side of the coach. He stared down at whatever it was then nudged Murdo, pointing to where the tops of people's heads were visible: Look at that now see that, he is leaving. He is father of that baby and he is leaving. Look man see his girl, she's got the baby in her arms man this is them man and he is leaving, that is what he is doing; and she dont want to see it, dont want him to go man. Look. . .

The guy shifted on the seat enough for Murdo to lean and see out. He saw a young man and a young woman holding a baby. They stood apart, he held a bag and was ready to board the bus.

She saying to him write, write. That's what she's saying, write write. He wont write man. He'll phone. That's what he'll do. Six month down the line man know what I'm saying? Hey conchita I ees sorry man.

Yeah, said Murdo.

I been there man I been there.

Soon the passengers had returned and the coach was back on the interstate. Murdo wished he could doze but it was best not to. He didnt want to in case like whatever, just whatever. The bus was moving and he would get there. People got to where they were going. Sooner or later they did. If it was sooner it was sooner which meant sooner than expected. "Sooner". Nothing was sooner anyway, just later. Things were always later. Sooner was later than now.

In Jackson Murdo got up from his seat. The wee thin guy was staying on until wherever. Cheerio, said Murdo. The guy raised his arm in a short salute.

Less than an hour later he was back in Allentown, and glad to be back, passing through the waiting room and out into the main street. He crossed to the old-time Wild West shop and the pawn-shop. The accordeon was not in the window. The ashtray was still on the window ledge; a quarter-smoked cigarette lay on it. Murdo peered through both windows. Guitars were the main instruments, including a beautiful-looking bass. Murdo liked bass guitars. How come? Just something about them. He didnt have one, but if he did. It would just be good having one.

Two saxophones and a clarinet; harmonicas that looked special. The shop door opened, triggering a security chime; a familiar tune. An older woman stepped out. She was quite big and Murdo made way for her. She stood by the doorway, lifted the quarter-smoked cigarette from the ashtray, soon had it alight, puffed a cloud of smoke, folding an arm and resting the other elbow on it, puffing again and watching folk pass by. She said to Murdo, How are you today?

Fine.

Aint it just so peaceful! She patted her bosom as though experiencing heartburn.

Yeah. Murdo gazed into the window.

So so peaceful, she said. I give praise to Jesus.

Murdo smiled and resumed walking, along towards Sarah's family store. It was more than a mile away, maybe two. When he arrived he stepped up onto the porch and pushed open the door. At the cashier's desk an older woman stared at him. An elderly man was about to be served. Murdo waited behind him. The elderly man waved him on ahead, but impatiently so ye felt like saying No thanks. But Murdo said, Thanks. I was wondering if Sarah was here? he asked the woman.

If Sarah was here? No, she aint here.

Is she at home?

I dont know. I cant say where she is.

Thanks, said Murdo although he felt like saying Ha ha, but what good would that have done? He heard the elderly man say, What'd he ask for?

He closed the door behind him and continued round the side of the building to the house. There was no one around. Then a boy about twelve or thirteen years old appeared. Who you looking for?

Uh – Joel.

Joel?

Or Sarah?

Oh. The boy nodded. They aint here; they gone away.

D'you know when they'll be back?

No I dont. Joel's ma now she'll tell you.

Thanks.

Sure.

Murdo thumped again on the door. There was a bell. He rang this too but nothing. Nobody was in. He stepped to peer in the window. The boy was still watching and called: She aint there?

Murdo tried the door again.

You try the back? Usually they're to the back.

Thanks. Murdo stepped back to the pavement and saw a man approach. Murdo waited. The man said: You got business there? The man looked him up and down. What you doing here?

Nothing.

Nothing!

Well like just friends. I thought they'd be in.

They aint in.

Aw. Murdo stared back at the house.

You know these people?

Yeah.

Who d'you know, Henry? You know Henry?

He's Sarah's Dad. It's really Sarah and Joel I know.

Okay. Okay. . . The man was staring at Murdo. Henry's up in Clarksdale, he said. He'll be back later. The rest gone to Louisiana, gone with Queen Monzee-ay.

Aw jees.

Big music festival.

Yeah.

Is that a problem?

No. I was just hoping to go with them. I thought maybe like I would catch them before they went.

Right.

Is Lafayette far?

The man shrugged. Hit the I-55 take a right through Baton Rouge, that's the I-10 – which way you facing? The man peered sideways. You got a car?

A car?

You aint got a car?

No.

Right. You come on the bus here?

Yeah.

Okay.

Actually I was wondering, do people ever hitch? I mean like hitch-hiking?

Hitching a ride?

Yeah.

You come on the bus here. You take one out of here. Okay? Dont you go hitching.

Okay.

The man waited while Murdo adjusted the rucksack and walked on. Murdo glanced back at him. Thanks, he said.

The man nodded, but hadnt moved. Murdo should have said to tell Henry. Probably he would. Definitely he would. He glanced back but the man wasnt there. It was all very well saying not to hitch a lift but if ye didnt have money and ye had to get someplace what else did ye do? apart from walk! A mile here and a mile back. It was the time ye spent too. This was the afternoon already! Time time time, ye just like always were having to watch the bloody time. He began striding.

Less than a minute later a small truck pulled up alongside him and it was the same man. The passenger side window rolled down and he called: Hey. Alright? Come in here, I'll take you. The bus station?

Yeah.

I'll take you. The man gestured Murdo inside.

Aw ye dont have to!

No. The man laughed a moment. No, he said, I dont. Come on in.

Murdo hesitated a moment. No, really, it's okay, but thanks. I'm just going to like. . .thanks, I'm fine walking.

The man smiled.

I'm fine walking.

You sure about that?

Yeah I mean. . . Murdo shrugged. Thanks.

Okay. The window closed and the man drove off.

That was funny. Murdo was nervous. It wasnt anything. He was but, just like – nervous. Although a lift, if he had wanted one. Although it wasnt far to the bus station. Only he had to move fast. He strode on.

Outside the pawnshop he faced into the window while checking his money. The original $290 sounded a fortune but once ye spent money on bus-fares it wasnt so much. Then an accordeon, jeesoh.

267

Money didnt last. The one displayed here had no price tag that he could remember.

Entering the shop set off the security chime. A part security grille was fixed round the counter. So people couldnt jump over and grab the stuff. Plenty interesting: rifles, knives, handguns, tools and some brilliant electronic stuff like if he had the money: phones, tablets and headsets; good stuff, plus all the musical instruments; diamonds, rings and jewelry things. Two men were at one section examining power tools and heavy-looking outside equipment. Nobody was serving. Then from the rear room came the same older woman as before, the smell of tobacco strong on her. Hi, she said. You buying today?

Eh well maybe.

We got a good sale on some fine quality goods. You interested in buying?

Yeah well the accordeon, there was an accordeon.

Oh, yeah.

I saw it in the window a few days ago.

You certainly did. That most beautiful accordeon.

It was down in price, said Murdo.

Mm. If we still got it. The woman vanished into the rear. She soon returned lugging the accordeon. I got it! she said. She hoisted it onto the counter and stood a moment to regain her breath. She smiled, admiring it, then looked to see Murdo. Selling for eighty-five dollars only now can you believe it? This most beautiful beautiful thing. That is a sale. Was a hundred and twenty-five and we've reduced that price to sell to you this very day.

Can I try it?

The woman smiled, but had not understood him. Murdo gestured at the accordeon. Can I try it?

Oh my dear why surely you can try it! Of course you can try it. The woman opened the wire grille. Murdo lifted it through to examine. It belonged to a proper musician, she said, a real proper musician. He was a smart man too. Yes he was.

Murdo slipped the strap on over his shoulders. The woman watched with interest. He played a little, listening and getting the feel of it. It's not too bad, he said.

The woman smiled but uncertainly. Was a hundred and twenty-five and we've reduced that price to you.

It's actually not as good as it looks, said Murdo.

Eighty-five dollars. The woman smiled.

Has it got a case?

A case? Oh now, she said. Eventually she returned with one from the rear. She laid it on the counter and made out the receipt even although he hadnt said he was buying. The case had a separate price tag. The woman glanced over at the two men checking out the tools, then took the price tag off the case, and said quietly, Eighty-five dollars and the box goes with it.

Thanks.

She smiled. You play something for me? Something nice?

Murdo adjusted the strap and began on "The Bluebell Polka". The woman was taken aback. She maybe expected a novice. Murdo had been playing this since he was a boy. It was one of the first he learned properly and was just about the first request he ever got from old people, beginning from his granny and grandpa when they were alive.

The pawnshop woman watched and listened. Oh my dear, she said, that is God's gift, that is just God's gift.

The two men were looking over too. Murdo played into a quite popular slow tune, and a particular arrangement he had been trying recently. It got an emotion he liked, just something good.

He ended the playing. Okay, he said, that's fine. He opened the box then shrugged off the accordeon, laid it in the case. The buckle fastening was strong enough although maybe a little tightening would have helped. The woman was watching. That thing is heavy, she said, passing him the receipt.

Yeah. Murdo brought the money from his pocket. Once he had the change of two $50s he crossed the street to the bus station.

That was him now. That was the trip worthwhile. It didnt matter about Sarah's family all being away, he would just pay the full bus-fare money and that was that. Even if he changed his mind, it was too late.

Allentown bus station: he felt comfortable just walking in the door. The woman behind the ticket and information counter was the same as before. She looked at Murdo. Maybe she recognized him.

The bus to Jackson was busy but the one from there to Baton Rouge was only a third full, so a double seat to himself; it was great. He had one sandwich left. He also had an apple and a banana. The banana skin had gone black but fine inside when peeled. He ate it then brought out the book he was reading, and laid it on the pull-down tray. He settled back, closing his eyes. It was not a great accordeon but it was okay. He smoothed his hand over the box, then opened it to see inside. No point lifting it out.

He was still hungry. Maybe he would eat the sandwich. It was late now and still a while to travel.

The worry was the bus from Baton Rouge to Lafayette; how many were there and how late did they run? The trip back to Allentown had been costly in money and in time. But it was necessary, and the accordeon was okay, not bad. He was lucky getting it for eighty-five dollars. When he was buying it he was thinking of pounds, so really it was only like ten for fifteen is four for six is sixty-four quid. Eighty-five dollars was sixty-four quid, so it was a good buy.

Definitely no point lifting it out the case, although he fancied seeing it. He would have to stand in the aisle to pull it on. Maybe he could! Busking the bus. People did it on trains.

He was sitting on the right side so he could see the Mississippi River. By his reckoning the road went down that way and at some stage had to cross it. Maybe not.

A tune was in his head; boats and the sea. A sailor's tune from Canada. The Mississippi River was supposed to be wide in places with boats going up and down, and even had wee islands in it, making ye think of home. He missed seeing the water. That was something. He hadnt thought of that. He lifted the book off the pull-down tray but laid it down again. It was true. Alabama had only that wee bit of coast. Louisiana was different, it looked amazing with all these wee islands. There were more than seven hundred in Scotland but how many in Louisiana! Even more? Maybe.

Buses were good. Going someplace where ye werent. Ye werent someplace and were passing through. Ye had never been and never would be. These places where ye werent. Ye werent already, so just being there. I want to be in that place because I'm not there.

> I came to the place
> where the lone children lay

Murdo's usual thing was not talking. There were things to talk about but he didnt want to. The more ye did the more there was to tell. Ye heard yerself and it hardly sounded like you at all. Ye were telling the truth but it seemed like a story ye had made up.

Why would ye lie about that kind of stuff? Sometimes it seemed like boasting. Imagine boasting about somebody dying. People did that. Yer mother died and they are like Oh wait till ye hear about me. Then you are like What are you talking about I've had two people. Oh yer sister died as well! So then they know something even worse again. My fucking dog died. Oh sorry to hear it. Then they ask ye about the actual people and dont listen when ye tell them. Ye see their eyes looking away.

What did Dad think about? People think about stuff. Him thinking about Eilidh, whatever he thought; Clara Hopkins singing, if he listened, where the lone children lay

> how sweetly I sleep here alone.

Ye imagine Eilidh and just like whatever. What is that? That makes ye cry, never mind on a bloody bus and all that damn stupid school crap like in school the Guidance Teacher. Dad was like, Oh you've got to talk.

What about?

Who did Dad talk to? He even fell out with his brother, then Uncle John losing his temper in the restaurant, whatever that was, tickets.

This leaving wasnt the worst thing Murdo had ever done. Pretty bad but not the worst. His life was different to the lives of other folk. He had pals back home but he wasnt like them. Everything that went on he had to deal with. Who else was there? Only Dad.

They were stuck with one another.

For Dad it was only Mum. She was the only one. Who else? Nobody. So real love. After that what could there be? Nothing. That would be Dad till he died. Never the same love again.

What if he never told her? The man doesnt tell the woman he loves. Then she dies and that is it finished. It might have been the same for Dad. Maybe he never knew he loved her until after she was dead. Only then he realized the truth. The love he had was a real love, she was it, and he never told her. That would have been the worst. It explained things about Dad. One night he did something daft and didnt come home. He never said what it was. When he phoned he sounded drunk. Maybe he was. It hadnt happened before and Murdo thought it was funny. Dad kept apologising but at the same time was dead serious. He stayed the night in Glasgow, probably at Uncle Robert's because where else? although they werent talking, so how come?

In the early days Mum kept walking round the ward and the day-room; round and round she went. It made her feel she was trying, and if she could keep on trying ye never know; wonder drugs and new inventions.

So that was that.

Taking the money was the worst. Aunt Maureen would be disappointed. He took the money huh, how much did he take? Two hundred dollars. Jeesoh, two hundred. It was a loan but for

the accordeon and getting there on the bus. People didnt want ye
hitching so what were ye supposed to do? Says it's a loan huh. My
Lord! How much we talking there? $200. Well ye have to do it
because with the price of bus-fares added to the accordeon.

Dad would be like, Ha ha. An accordeon! Ha ha. What happened
to listening and learning! Use yer ears and the brains in yer body.

Right Dad okay and not just them in my head. Somebody once
told Murdo he had fast fingers. You've got fast fingers son. Not fast
fingers, brainy fingers. His brains were everywhere. Nerves were
brain-ends and fingers were full of them. Fingers needed to be fast
so they were fast. They werent fast to begin with. They had to be
fast for the song. The song made them fast. They were part of it
and couldnt not be. Even if they tried they couldnt be slow. If they
were it would be a different tune! That was fingers!

Dad didnt get it because he didnt "hear" music. They say that
about some people, how they dont hear notes connected to one
another, just a pile of things all scattered about haphazard.

The $200 was a loan and he would pay it back. He needed that
accordeon and had to buy it. If he could have paid it himself he
would have. He couldnt because he couldnt.

Oh jees, the feeling in his stomach.

What was that, nothing, staring out the window, what at, nothing.
The two letters. They wouldnt have found them yet. Unless they
came home early. Why? To make sure he was okay. So he didnt
get up to mischief. A naughty boy. They were supposed to be going
away for one night or else two. But now it was one night because
of him. Dad would never stay away longer, he would just be
worrying. They all would. Oh maybe he'll burn the house down!
Then Dad would read the letter.

Jees.

Aunt Maureen would stick up for Murdo. Oh now he's a boy
he just wants adventures.

That was true. What was wrong with adventures? Where would
ye rather be: sitting on a porch reading a book or else doing a gig

with Queen Monzee-ay? Oh Louisiana, dont you cry for me, there's a banjo on my knee; what was that song?

Dad would be like, Oh he doesnt even know where Lafayette is! He thinks it is next to Chattanooga!

But what did Dad know. Murdo had the Road Atlas book anyway. Aunt Maureen gave him it. She gave him it. He didnt steal it!

Oh but he doesnt listen he doesnt listen! That's why he's behind at school. He doesnt listen and he skips away and he disappears for whole days at a time. Where does he go! Glasgow? Who knows.

No, he stays in his room all day playing music!

Coming up for seventeen and repeating a year. The oldest pupil in the school. How would they like that? Nobody would like that. Uncle John said it too when Murdo told him, I dont fancy that.

It was true. Who would fancy it? Nobody. Just stupid rubbish.

Who cares anyway. Who can be bothered. Imagine being bothered. It was all just stupid.

At least he had written the letters. That was good and Aunt Maureen would think it was good. Uncle John too. It was just Dad.

It didnt matter now because it was too late. It was finished.

That was something, all finished, yer family, it is only you. That is that and no more.

In Baton Rouge it was an hour and a half wait and he was hungry. He had one last apple. He ate it on a bench outside the bus station. Just great getting fresh air. He held the rucksack over one shoulder; on his lap the Road Map Atlas. The accordeon was by his feet and he wished he could bring it out the case. He needed to play. Why couldnt he? It was peaceful; people hanging about waiting for a bus, smoking, quiet talking. Maybe he could. People would want a tune. Maybe they wouldnt. The bus people wouldnt let him. They would if it was out on the street. How could they stop him? Maybe it was against the law. He laid his hand on the case.

A woman was here, sitting about three feet away on the other side of the bench. Not old at all. Maybe in her mid twenties. She had her phone in her hand but was not looking at it, she was just gazing up the way. The night sky.

Other people were like travellers from foreign places, quite small people too, how the women wore leggings a particular way; maybe from Pakistan or India although could it have been South America, maybe. Some folk didnt seem to be traveling, just having a rest. Maybe they couldnt afford a ticket. Ye had to watch what ye spent every minute of the day. If Murdo hadnt made the sandwiches in Aunt Maureen's house that would have been fifteen dollars at least. Would his money last? He didnt know, and wouldnt know until after the gig. That was Sunday morning, whatever was happening then. If Sarah's family could give him a lift up to Jackson or someplace where he could make a good bus connection. It would save money if they did. But if they couldnt?

Ye had to watch for emergencies. Ye couldnt go spending money in cafés. Even if ye were hungry. It would just depend. People said "emergencies" but what were "emergencies"? If ye were starving. But if ye were starving and had money and didnt eat. So then it wasnt like an emergency, not a real one. Otherwise ye would just spend the money. But then ye saved money by walking instead of going on a bus and ye bought food with the money. Ye would be entitled to because you saved it yourself by walking. It would be your money for just like whatever, whatever ye wanted to spend it on.

What about the woman on the bench? Maybe it was the same for her. Did she have luggage? Murdo couldnt see a proper suitcase, only a big sort of handbag thing. She was tired-looking, bored maybe, sitting here for hours. If she had been. Probably she had. People just waited around. So probably a tune would be good, if he played one. People would enjoy it. She would too. She glanced at him. Jeesoh. She didnt catch his eye but she did glimpse him, definitely. Really, she did.

She was looking at him now, almost like not staring but nearly. She had seen him looking at her. Murdo shifted position. His face was pure red now he knew it was. Although she wouldnt maybe know, not in the shadows. Where you headed? she said.

He looked at her and looked away, then back to her.

Where you headed? she asked again.

Aw eh Lafayette.

She squinted at him.

Murdo spoke slowly, I'm eh. . .I'm headed to Lafayette, the town Lafayette. He raised the Road Atlas book and pointed at the open page. Louisiana, he said.

The woman leaned a little closer to see where he was pointing. The perfume smell from her and the T-shirt she was wearing, the tops of her boobs and even like nipples standing out. Jeesoh but they were, just like

They were. He moved slightly away from her in case she had seen him, and would think he was trying to look and he wasnt, it was just like how ye couldnt not, ye couldnt, ye just had to see, if ye looked at her, because if ye did ye saw them. Murdo scratched the side of his head. Straight run from here, she said.

Thanks.

Uh huh. She breathed sharply in through her mouth; maybe she wasnt feeling good or was worried about something. Was she waiting for him to speak? Maybe she was. People got nervous in bus stations. They could panic when a bus was due to leave, jumping up trying to see the schedule and stuff. Also when the police were there. They had been in an hour ago checking who was here, looked at Murdo too. That was weird. How come they looked at him? He didnt smile. Uncle John told him that about the cops, never look at them if they are looking at you and never ever say anything funny – like trying to make a joke or something. Never ever do that.

Not only were buses expensive the actual prices changed. He heard people talking, they went online and saw daily deals and special offers. One day it was $40 the next it was $70, and that was the same journey. How come? Even walking from one town to the next would save money. Then if ye hitched a lift for one clear stretch of the journey, that would save a good few dollars and that would be great, that would buy ye a meal. Then if yer luck was in and the driver was going farther on, and didnt mind taking ye.

How come he hadnt taken a lift off the guy in Allentown? How come? How come he didnt take the lift! Jeesoh!

Probably nothing. Or else what? Ye just had to be careful. Things ye pick up about people. Ye dont know them and ye meet them and think to yerself, I'm getting out of here. That was it with traveling, like buses or whatever, hitching, ye were never sure and had to be so so wary. Murdo turned to the woman on the bench. No eh I was just wondering, he said, about something like about traveling, just about hitching.

She gazed at him.

About hitching a lift, he said, I mean do ye ever hitch a lift or like people ye know I mean do they ever hitch a lift?

What? She frowned but with a kind of a smile.

No eh

What did you say?

No eh I just eh I was wondering about hitching. . . He could not speak further; his face was red again, and his throat felt like it had seized up. She was glaring at him. You making a joke? she said and she was so angry.

Murdo stared at her.

You making a joke at me? she cried. Dont you dare make a joke at me. Dont you dare!

But I'm not, I'm not. I only mean like if ye dont have money, if people dont have money and have to like hitch I mean if ye dont have money, that's all I'm saying.

I got money! What you think I'm trying to steal your money? I aint stealing no goddam money, your money not nobody else's money. I aint no thief! What are you saying to me?

Nothing. Nothing at all.

You think I'm stealing your money?

No! Not at all, I'm not saying anything at all.

The woman lifted her bag and got up from the bench.

I'm not saying anything, said Murdo.

She walked off to a bench on the other side of the bus station entrance. Murdo stared at the ground. Just horrible and stupid. He raised his head. An older woman was watching him. Just so stupid. How did it happen? Total misunderstandings. That was voices, people saying the same words but their voices different, so different.

When it came time for the bus the woman was still sitting on the other bench, she held her phone in her hand but wasnt looking at it. Murdo gathered his rucksack and accordeon-case. She hardly moved. She must have been staying there, probably waiting for another bus. Murdo was glad she was not going on his. It was selfish but that is what he felt. He hoped she had money and was not just sitting there because she had no place to go. Although if she didnt, what if she didnt? This bus was the last of the night through Lafayette.

It was full by the time Murdo climbed aboard. The driver had jammed the accordeon-case into the side of the luggage compartment; it wouldnt budge an inch. He kept hold of his rucksack. Some people preferred aisle seats. This man was one of them. Murdo squeezed past him into the window seat. He was wearing a denim jacket, jeans and a greasy-looking baseball cap, just sitting there staring to the front.

It had begun raining again, pattering the bus windows, making people peer out. Murdo was glad to be inside. He hoped she was too. Could she have been homeless? Ye werent sure with people at bus stations. She was young. What age was she?

People's lives and the things that happen. If ye are a girl and dont have money or a place to go. Maybe she didnt. So if she was a prostitute. She could have been. Whatever lives people have. Girls especially. For being a prostitute too, they had to be something;

good-looking, good shapes, if ye think of shapes. They had to be something.

The lights were off now and he was glad the guy on the aisle seat wasnt reading. It was good in the dark just to be sitting, just sitting there; beyond relaxing. He was tired. More than tired.

How come? What had he done? Nothing. Taking buses and walking places. But if he went to sleep, imagine sleeping, then ye wake up! Whereabouts? Miles away. Miles and miles. Three thousand miles divided by whatever, that was days.

The man in the aisle was talking to him. Going to Galveston. You know Galveston?

The man hadnt changed his position a fraction, except maybe his eyes moved. Smelling of tobacco and whatever else. He spoke again: Job down there. Nephew's doing the hiring and firing. Brother's boy.

Aw. Murdo nodded.

Brother dont like me none. The man's eyes moved again. He maybe waited for Murdo to say something. Got that song, "Galveston". Galveston Galveston. You know that song?

I'm not sure.

The man nodded, staring at the seat in front. Kinda nice.

I'm going to Lafayette, said Murdo.

Oh yeah. . .

Murdo might have said about the gig but he didnt. People were people and had their own lives. You have something and they have something. Everybody ye meet. He shouldnt even have said that, Lafayette, who cares.

Guys in front were loud and sounded drunk. Murdo saw the tops of their heads shifting about, speaking about poker. Somebody won a lot of money and somebody else lost too much for a game that was supposed to be with friends. How could ye be friends if ye took all their money? Working offshore.

So that was oil workers same as Declan Pike, going back to work. Maybe they knew him. Imagine they did. Ye met guys on a

bus in a foreign country with millions and millions of people, and
when ye said somebody's name they knew him. Murdo was gazing
out the bus window. Then a large neon sign, and he turned his
head following it, swivelling on his seat:

LAFAYETTE INTERNATIONAL FESTIVAL
BIENVENUE FESTIVAL INTERNATIONAL DE LOUISIANE

Ahead were the lights of the town itself. Murdo settled back on
the seat and was about to say something to the man next to him
but didnt. Soon the bus arrived in Lafayette. Murdo lifted the
rucksack and moved out. Cheerio, he said.

So long, said the man.

★

He had expected most of the passengers to be leaving the bus but
only six of them did. The driver dragged out the accordeon-case.
Murdo checked inside: the accordeon was fine. He set off walking
from the bus station into the festival area. It was quite a distance.
Along the way he lifted leaflets, flyers and a free map of the festival
site. He stopped under a street light to read through the stuff,
searching for the Queen Monzee-ay gig and there she was in the
main festival programme, but listed as one of the guests in "Lancey's
Cajun All-Stars", a lunchtime gig. That didnt sound right. According
to Sarah's message the venue was the Jay Cee Lounge and the gig
was late evening. Queen Monzee-ay was supposed to be opening
for a band called the Zadik Strollers. He couldnt find the Jay Cee
Lounge even listed as a festival venue. Then he found its address
in the index to the map but there was no proper information. He
shoved the stuff into his rucksack, lifted the accordeon-case.

People were gobbling takeaways and drinking beer. Everywhere
ye looked. Hamburgers and stuff. He needed to eat. When did he
last eat? Ages ago. Baton Rouge, an apple. He ate his last sandwich

on the bus, the last one. That was past the Mississippi River; he couldnt even remember eating it, he just ate it. He had money. If ye were starving, ye had to spend it. He was starving. Even an actual restaurant, he could spend money for that except he wasnt going to. Plenty foodstalls were here. At one the menu was brilliant how it was written for the song: Jambalay, Crawfish pie, Fillet gumbo. Hot Sos to Taste. Po-boy, what was Po Boy? I am just a po boy.

That was the trouble, not knowing what stuff was. In one place a girl was serving hamburgers, hotdogs and VGBugs. VGBugs. Maybe veggie. Murdo would eat it. Same as Dad. Dad ate anything. Murdo was the same. He waited by the counter. The girl served somebody to the side of him. Maybe she didnt notice him. He stood another couple of minutes. The girl served two other women. That was that, deliberate, because she had seen him, she was just ignoring him. He left the stall and continued walking. He was enjoying the sights and sounds anyway. Although it would have been nice to sit down. He was quite tired. He was used to lugging about the accordeon but at the same time a seat would have been good.

People were dancing going along the street, brightly lit in the dark. A real mix. Guys wore cowboy hats, waistcoats and jeans. Women wore everything, shorts and short skirts; sandals, fancy-coloured cowboy boots, high heels, long skirts, jeans, whatever. Plenty young folk.

He found a public payphone near a grass square and had enough change to try it but there wasnt enough light to decipher the instructions. He sat the accordeon-case by his feet, lifted the receiver and dialed the number. Nothing. Put in the money and dialed the number. Nothing. Dialed the number and put in the money. Nothing. He tried to speak to an operator, but nobody. Ye couldnt speak to anybody and ye couldnt read any damn thing. No wonder Dad had got angry trying to phone Uncle John. This was a night-mare. If ye couldnay read the damn instructions it was just stupid.

He would have to ask somebody how to do it but that was

tricky late at night. What time was it anyway? He returned to the main festival area where there was more light. He needed a sit-down; a proper rest. He was starving too, jeesoh. Nowhere to go either.

Cops. Funny how ye see cops; ye always seem to.

That was a thought, nowhere to go.

He didnt have any place. If he had expected to meet Sarah walking about, that was so so unlikely. Not now anyway. Places were closing for the night. Some already had. Sarah had offered about staying the night with family friends but it could only happen if he made contact, and he didnt have any contact number, no address, no nothing. That was just silly, not thinking about that. But so what if he had? It was Sarah should have done it.

Foodsmells. A foodstall with good lighting. Nobody queued. The guy working there wore an apron and a baseball cap. He stood behind the high counter phone in hand. Murdo walked over, laid down the accordeon-case. A sign said "Traditional cuisine de loui-siane". The menu was in Spanish, English and French; hand-written and scrawled, and difficult to read. Murdo studied it, trying to find something easy.

The guy was waiting and watching. Eventually he turned to read the menu himself. He said something to Murdo in Spanish, then in English, You want something?

Eh like a hamburger? a hot dog?

The guy shrugged, pointed at the menu.

Murdo tried to read it again but he couldnt. He just could not decipher the actual writing. Have you got any hamburgers or hot dogs? he asked.

Hot dog is cat fish, said the guy.

Murdo looked at him.

No hot dog, cat fish. The guy smiled and pointed to a place on the menu. Catfish. Is cheap and drink goes for the deal.

Murdo saw the price. Please, yeah, thanks.

You want catfish?

Please yeah.

Sure.

Murdo watched him scoop the food from the containers and dish it onto the paper plate: rice, onions, relish and lettuce too, and bits of tomato; thin strips of onion; plenty lettuce, rice. The guy smiled. Hungry eh?

Yeah.

What drink you want?

Do ye have orange juice?

The guy sighed. No orange juice. He gestured at the glass-fronted, chilled drinks cabinet. You want coke? We got 7 Up, orange fizzy.

You got tea?

No tea. Fizzy. Coke, Doctor Pepper. We got 7 Up.

Have ye got water?

Sure, water. The guy got him a bottle of water. He pointed at the accordeon-case: Hey man you play?

Yeah.

Good, good. The guy smiled, and hesitated, then added: Me too.

You too?

Si, I uh. . .

What the accordeon? you play the accordeon?

Si, I play.

Murdo grinned. The guy stood the bottle of water on the counter next to the paper plate. He straightened his baseball cap, waved round the foodstall. I got kids man you know, I earn money: got to earn money. He made a mournful face, but chuckled. He wagged his finger at Murdo. One day!

Murdo chuckled. Me too. He paid a $10 bill over the high counter, lifted napkins then collected the change; three single dollars and coins. A tips jar was there. Murdo dropped in the coins, stuck the dollars into his jeans pocket.

The foodstall guy frowned at him. Hey man!

Yeah? Murdo smiled.

The guy gestured sharply with his hand. How much you put in there?

Pardon?

How much? You put in there, how much?

Eh?

The guy wagged his finger at Murdo. You put in thirty-five cents! Is change I give you, thirty-five cents. No, is not good. The guy pointed at the tips jar: Put in a dollar man put in a dollar.

A dollar? Murdo looked at him.

One dollar. The guy shook his head. A dollar man, you know.

Murdo sniffed and took out a dollar, he shoved it into the tips jar.

The guy shrugged. Is what you do man.

Murdo nodded, he put the bottle of water in his rucksack, lifted the paper plate and the plastic fork. The guy said, Salsa?

No thanks. Murdo turned to leave.

The guy raised his hand to stop him. Hey you will be glad I tell you. You gotta tip a guy man.

Okay.

Yeah. Adiós.

Okay. Murdo walked on, and continued where the pavement led out of the lighted area and farther along where there was grass, like a little park, and two old-fashioned benches about twenty yards apart which were both empty. He chose the first, laid down the accordeon-case, swung off the rucksack and plonked down on the bench, utterly knackered. His first seat since when-ever, the bus!

Then he opened the food, used the fork to break up the fish. It was tough and the fork was made of soft plastic.

He had heard of catfish but just really the name. It was a good-sized solid fish. Did it look like a cat? He lifted it up in his fingers. It was quite stiff, ye could hold it and just eat it. He took the first bite. And it was tasty, jees, a real mouthful. He used the fork to get some of the relish: onions were in it and a liquidy kind of stuff. He coughed and swallowed a mouthful of water. Usually he liked it peppery. It was chopped-up red chillies. He tried some of the relish on his finger. Very hot, but tasty. He was eating everything.

Even the lettuce. Lettuce was good; he liked it. He never used to. Now he did.

Another customer at the foodstall, a wee man. Him and the guy that worked there were chatting, laughing together. Probably they knew each other and were speaking in Spanish. Hot dog cat fish. Ha ha ha. Maybe laughing at Murdo. A dollar tip. So what? Ha ha. He was enjoying the food. He ate the lot, wiped his fingers and sat an extra five minutes sipping the water then was onto his feet again. He kept the napkins and stuffed the rubbish into a bin which was about overflowing. It was getting cold. Not cold so much as cool. He had other clothes in the rucksack, if it got like cold as in really really cold where ye were shivering and not able to get warm. This was just cool. Not really cold at all. He pulled on the rucksack, gripped the accordeon-case handle, then was walking again. Where? Where was he going? He walked a while, not thinking about stuff, or not seeming to think about stuff; maybe he was but not registering what it was; just like whatever, a mix of stuff. His mind did that like one thing to another, just leaping about, stupid. Because where was he going? Maybe there was someplace. Where? He would see it when he got there! His feet would lead him. People said that, Oh my feet led me. Ye closed yer eyes: Right feet, on ye go, then they tripped up and ye fell on yer face.

Later he laid down the accordeon-case and cupped his hands, blew into them. He stood for a while. The streets were quiet, very very. He was by the entrance to a venue now closed for the night. He felt like he had been walking for hours. Had he ever stopped? Yes, to eat a fish. He sat on a bench and ate a fish. His hands were still greasy.

He just had to keep walking. It was important. Why? Just because. Because what? Something would happen. What? Something. Definitely.

One thing was the toilet: he hadnt been since Baton Rouge. Whatever they called it here, washroom, restroom. But if ye couldnt find one? What did ye do if ye couldnt find one? An actual lavatory.

Ye couldnt take a chance and just do it someplace because if ye got caught, like the cops or somebody just seeing ye and shooting ye down in cold blood.

He lifted the accordeon-case and continued walking.

But if ye couldnt find one and didnt have a choice like if ye were bursting and really needed to go, like really really, ye were desperate, then ye had to, because ye had no choice ye had no choice.

The next street corner. He would get to there. Then the one after that, he would just walk to there, jeesoh. Could he do another one?

Probably there werent any toilets. He had the festival street map in the rucksack but was wary of taking it out to read. Nobody was walking. If anybody came along and saw ye with a map they would know ye were a stranger and that wasnt good, that was risky.

Maybe turning back was best.

Where was he?

Ha ha.

That happened; ye turned a corner then another and another and ye wound up lost. But it wasnt good to stand still.

Ye dont do anything standing still. Ye have to walk. Murdo did, just forwards, but then maybe not, maybe best just

What? Thinking about it first. Was it best to go back? Where to, the bus station! Ha ha.

That was the trouble, he wasnt thinking, he wasnt thinking at all he was just like – whatever, just whatever, walking, walking and walking.

Whereabouts? Where was he?

Ye aye hoped ye were on a square so ye turned a corner and followed a straight line backwards or forwards and then ye would be out but what if the streets went at an angle so then ye went wherever, north instead of west. Angle lines are straight. Even the line of a circle! When is a circle not a circle? Please sir infinity. Please sir three right sides, a point a point a point.

Maybe he was lost. Was he lost? Maybe he was. Not lost but just away from everything. Not everything, just everything that is like

He walked closely by the wall of a building where the light was a little better.

A block farther on the pavement became more shadowy; this building of an older type with ordinary doorways and in one was an edge of something

like a body

like wrapped in a blanket, a body.

It was. A tuft of hair poking out. A man's head. Jeesoh. A man's head; a man asleep, African-American, snoozing, but ye couldnt hear him, ye couldnt hear his breath.

Murdo had stepped aside along by the edge of the kerb, turning the next corner and walking fast, faster, just in case of whatever, guys sneaking up and jumping ye, and on into another street, wee and narrow. Dark and like pitch black even; and not a sound. He was not worried; definitely not worried but just like where was he going where was he going! Jeesoh. Having to take the chance but this was for a pee, he could pee, jees, it was so so dark. He stepped in at the side of where it was, set down the accordeon-case, stepped a little way off and urinated wherever wherever, into the street just, hoping, hoping, doing it as fast as fast made possible, just like – oh God. . .

Then grabbing the accordeon-case he was quickly walking walking yes thank God, thank God, thank you God, keeping to the outside edge of the kerb and away from the wall.

He glanced into doorways and spaces where a body could hide or even just sit to keep out the road like if ye had to if it was raining, just to shelter.

Way along he saw two figures. The cops here had guns and holsters, sticks and handcuffs and that other thing they had that reminded ye of a ball and chain for knocking off people's heads. That spiked ball thing like dangling at the end of a chain; they used them back in the olden days, knights in armour, and swung them round and round then crash, knocking the head off yer shoulders. The cops here were tough and killed people. Dont ever make jokes. Then a voice, somebody shouting at somebody, farther along the street. Then an actual person across the street. Somebody, Jesus Christ, Murdo walked fast on. Leaning against the wall or just a shadow maybe a shadow. Creepy. Dont stop. Along another street and onto a wider street there was grass. And a certain building. Grass and a certain building. And there the public telephone he tried to use earlier. It was, it was the same public telephone. The grass was the same grass square. On the other side of there was the catfish foodstall now with the shutters drawn, and the benches, and the road that took ye back to the main festival area. Thank God.

He walked round the other side where there was a little bit more light, and a bench. But two people were there already. He kept going; farther along there was one empty. It was. He set down the accordeon-case and the rucksack at one end of it, he sat down.

Later his head was full of stuff, but away in the distance someplace and ye had to grapple to discover what it was. Spots of light down the end of a tunnel. Then ye were at the end and nothing except feeling kind of cold, yer body. He shouldnt have been cold but he was and his teeth did the rapid shiver-click he used to get as a boy, trembling out the bath and Mum wrapping the towel round ye: dih dih dih dih dih dih dih, dih dih dih dih dih dih dih, oh Mummy Mummy Mummy. Are ye cold? I'm freezing I'm freezing I'm freezing.

Not freezing, but cold. He opened his rucksack and brought out his other top, took off his jacket and pulled it over the one he was already wearing then put the jacket back on. He had spare socks. Yes he did. He could put them on too. Maybe later. He sat a moment, then extracted the belt from his jeans and tied it through the handle of the accordeon-case and the rucksack to connect round his wrist, so if anybody tried to snatch them it would alert him. He could even doze off and be safe, although he didnt want to; risky stuff. First thing in the morning he would phone home. If they were back. Of course they were back. They were back right now. They never would have stayed overnight. Then the letter. Dad would have read it! They all would know. He says he will phone, thank God. Then it would be Dad, Oh why hasnt he phoned, he said he would phone.

Ye said ye would phone and ye didnt! Yes Dad but if ye dont have yer own and there arent any landlines that work.

He tried to phone and the damn bloody thing didnt work. It wasnt his fault. How could it be? If it didnt work it didnt work, people couldnt bloody use it, they couldnt use it. Jeesoh. Jees, jees. Ye said ye would phone. Yes but. Yes but.

He folded his arms in tightly, hunching in his shoulders, bent forwards, elbows resting on his thighs, rocking back and forwards a little bit but stopping that and just hunching in and hunching in, the heat in, keeping the heat in like trapping it, trapping yer heat, oh mammy daddy mammy daddy mammy daddy, then shoving his hands in his pockets, leaning forwards.

Later again he was awake so he must have dozed; definitely. He looked to the sky. Probably about whatever. Who knows. Three o'clock maybe.

The bottle of water. He unscrewed the lid and sipped.

He should have brought a blanket, he was quite shivery. Aunt Maureen's big towel. He brought a wee one instead. He was shivery and it was cold, it was, jees like jees jees jees, really. Getting up and stamping his feet was what he felt like doing but he didnt, he just sat there tighter in, in, not wanting to move at all because even the slightest most minute fraction would take the heat from his body. Socks could be gloves. Socks and towels for warmth for warm, heat warming, body warming, and extra socks and yer teeth drrr-rrrr drrrrrrr drrrrrrr drrrrrrr, that was ringing not shivering ringing ringing, ring ring, ring ring

Oh hullo Dad.

It was just round and round and round, things things things and whatever the tunes would be then they would be that, whatever they were, tunes shivery and doh doh doh, doh.

A mental sort of a doze. What like was it? Horrible. That was him, for however long he had no idea except cutting off consciousness if ye can say that, something dark and switched off.

Except when he woke it was the real nightmare, this guy staring at him; some madman. A bloody madman. Just a fucking scary scary madman staring at him on the side of the bench farthest away just sitting there, less than two feet away oh Jesus Christ scary scary scary, he was scary, he was scary scary, just like a real real scary guy. That is the truth. Murdo kept looking at him. The one thing maybe was holding his gaze. Not looking away. But straight into his eyes just looking. Because then what could he do? Nothing, not with Murdo looking straight straight at him,

and while he did he was pulling the belt out through the accordeon-case handle and the rucksack straps, then coiling it into a rucksack compartment, and rising to his feet still looking at the guy, and now off the bench he backed away, gripping the accordeon-case and rucksack in either hand, and he set off walking in a kind of curve so like if the guy tried anything Murdo would see him. Beyond the foodstall he crossed over the street, round a corner and crossed another one and round another one but then was on a main street and he kept along this.

Murdo didnt feel like a coward. So what if he was? Guys had knives. Some of them did, hidden in the blankets like if they were homeless and sleeping rough, they were ready to fight. So if somebody went to get them they would leap out with the knife and stick it right into them. Ye couldnay blame them either. Things happened. In Glasgow ye had them begging on the street, they sat on the pavement even if it was raining; ye saw their trousers soaked. Some from foreign countries. They didnt have any money. Nothing. How even did they get to Scotland? It was incredible. A lassie he knew put a £5 note into one of their paper cups. Murdo didnt see it himself, a guy told him. They were up in Glasgow and were just like walking down the street and she saw a beggar and she went and put in a £5 note. A beggar. A fiver. That was lassies. No guy ever would give a fiver. It was just like incredible.

It was safe now. He still had his money. He counted it. The guy couldnt have robbed him. But if the dollar notes had slipped out his pocket? While he was hunched up dozing?

Imagine they had! What would he have done? He would have had to go back. He would have had to. So if the guy was still there? Okay. It didnt matter because it was the money so he would have had to go. What choice? None. To get his money, if that was it, he would have gone, he would have had to.

Anyway, it didnt matter.

A sandwich and a carton of hot tea! If he could find a 24/7 store. Maybe a garage; garages had shops. One foodvan he passed was advertising OPEN ALL NIGHT but it was closed. An all-night foodvan that closed during the night.

Although it was morning. Nearly. The quality of light. That smell of dampness. A fresh morning. How near was the sea?

Tonight was the gig. Amazing to think. Because he was here. Dad would be sleeping or else awake worrying. But that was that.

More people around; early workers, morning strollers, a couple with dogs. Maybe somebody the same as him, nowhere to go and just walking about. Homeless people. Murdo was one.

Then an amazing foodsmell, a wee café-style restaurant open for business bloody hell it was just oh man what a smell, just this beautiful foodsmell like aroma through a wee kind of alleyway and music coming from inside, a lone voice singing; a French guy and a French song; just him and the guitar jeesoh, bloody beautiful. What was he doing! Everything and nothing. Murdo stopped about thirty yards from the café entrance, listening. Food in the song too – le plat de fricassée. Just beautiful that nice nice guitar. What was he doing! Hardly any damn thing at all! How do ye get that? How do ye just make it like that? How is it people can do that? They just like do it, they do the song, they sit and they have the guitar like they just

What an amazing-mazing thing! Murdo didnt want it to end, he strode on fast before it did. Because too he needed to play, he really did. Things press on ye. Tonight was tonight. One of the flyers showed Queen Monzee-ay featured as a guest at an afternoon Cajun session, traditional style, but no information on the evening gig. That was okay. The venue was a regular Zydeco and Blues Club and he had the street address. Things went on there all the time and he would find it. It was only the playing, he needed to play. Time was going and he needed to play.

Okay there was no actual place but if it was dry he could play anywhere. So anywhere becomes a place.

The wee grass square. What was wrong with the wee grass square? If the maniac was there so what if it was daylight. People were out and about. What could he do? Nothing. Not in daylight, not in front of witnesses. And like the cops too, if they were there, they would just shoot him.

Murdo felt fine. Not much sleep but okay. Imagine Dad. What happened what happened are ye okay are ye okay! Yes Dad. Why didnt ye phone why didnt ye phone! A bloody grass square ye spent the night! Did anything bad happen? No Dad just this scary maniac.

But he wasnt a scary maniac. He was scary but not a maniac; a scary guy. A lot of guys are scary. They can be. Ye just have to tell them, Fuck off, away and scare somebody else.

★

He found a store. It sold sandwiches and hot donuts. No hot tea but hot coffee and a bottle of water for later. A turkey salad sandwich for the best value. Turkey wasnt tasty but it filled ye up, and that was what ye wanted. People looked in bins. Imagine looking in bins. Oh there's an old crust.

Murdo would have eaten the sandwich while walking but the accordeon-case made it tricky.

Ahead was a bus-stop. He put down the accordeon-case then took off the rucksack and placed it next to it, and sighed, and floated somewhere off, off

then opened the sandwich packet and scoffed everything. The coffee was scalding! He laid the carton on the pavement.

He stood at this bus-stop for a while. No buses came. He was glad of that. What if one had come? Maybe he could have got on it, gone to the terminus and back. Worth it for the comfy seat. Maybe he could play them a tune. Good to get the fingers moving. The driver would be like Oh good, that'll cheer people up. First thing in the morning everybody is all sad, going to school, going to work. Slavery. Oh here's a nice waltz and ye dance along. Loudspeakers at street corners.

Murdo eventually gathered up the stuff and headed along the road. Ye could play while ye walked, strolling players, who'll come a-waltzing with me, waltzing Matilda. A waltz can be sad.

But how come? If ye are dancing. Could ye dance and be sad? Maybe ye could. But if ye have a girlfriend and are dancing with her, how could it be sad! Although if it was yer last time together, if she was seeing somebody else and it was yer last time, yer last waltz. Or if it was yer girlfriend dancing with you but like thinking about somebody else.

But it didnt matter. You were playing the tune. So you would be happy. Even if it was a sad tune, so what? Okay bawl yer eyes out but I'm happy, I'm just the musician.

None of it mattered except you got it right. Queen Monzee-ay was thinking drums and bass but did she need it? Maybe not, it was up to her. Maybe it didnt matter. Their guitarist was the best according to Sarah. Usually he rehearsed with them but couldnt last Sunday. He was away someplace with his own band; he played in two different ones. So probably he was good.

For Queen Monzee-ay the bonus was Murdo's accordeon. He wasnt being big-headed. She said it herself and it was true. Two accordeons made it exciting. She was powerful, so so powerful, and the whole thing, like jeesoh he just needed to play, needed to get his fingers moving he was rusty rusty, so so rusty, just rusty. His fingers were like carrots.

The payphone!

Here he was. He rested the accordeon-case against the wall and read the instructions, coins at the ready. He finished dialing the number, and waited. Nothing the first time but the second time it rang Aunt Maureen answered. Aunt Maureen herself. Murdo smiled.

Yeah? she said. Who's calling there?

Aunt Maureen it's me, Murdo.

Murdo?

Yeah.

Murdo!

Yeah, how are ye Aunt Maureen?

Oh now Murdo.

Sorry for phoning so early. I'm just wondering about my Dad, is he there?

No – my Lord! Murdo he aint now he's gone. Murdo, he's gone.

Pardon?

He aint here. Forty-five minutes they've been gone son, they've gone to Birmingham. Your Uncle John is driving him down there right now. Right now son, they are driving right now. You hearing me? Your father is catching a bus and he's going to meet you son.

. . .

You hearing me? Meeting up with that musician fellow now what d'you call him was singing at the Gathering huh, the Irish fellow, your Dad got him now, Uncle John got him the number.

. . .

You hearing me son? You in Louisiana? Is that where you are?

Yes.

You got him so worried.

Is he okay?

He's okay. Murdo now you should have phoned: last night like you said. We waited and waited.

I couldnt.

We waited.

Yeah but I couldnt, I couldnt Aunt Maureen I dont have one I mean. . .

You said you would.

Yeah but just like a landline and I couldnt get through and

Didnt sleep a wink hardly at all then first thing this morning him and your Uncle John. My Lord Murdo. . .

Yeah but the phone wasnt working, I couldnt get it to work and it was very late.

You took the money son. Why'd you take the money? I could have given you money. You didnt ask! Why didnt you ask me? You should have asked me son.

I just needed it. Aunt Maureen I'm going to pay it back, it's just like a loan I mean I'll pay it back.

Well it aint the money Murdo. Tom is so worried. Where'd you sleep? You eating? What you doing son? In Louisiana, what you doing there?

Murdo didnt answer. Aunt Maureen began repeating bits of what she had said and more that related to it but Murdo couldnt take it in properly – as much as he tried, he tried.

He needed the phone call to finish. He had to finish it. She was talking on and he cut in: Aunt Maureen! Aunt Maureen. . .

When she paused he said, I've got friends here Aunt Maureen. They're musicians and I'm staying with them so dont anybody worry. I'm completely fine I mean like I'm just phoning to tell ye.

I would have given you money son, if only you said.

I know you would have Aunt Maureen I mean so like I'll see ye soon. I'll see ye soon. 'Bye!

Oh son you'll take care now?

Of course. Of course. Okay Aunt Maureen I'll see ye soon.

Oh Murdo.

'Bye. He replaced the receiver, maybe not cutting her off. Probably he had. He stood a moment. He would see her soon anyway. He looked one way then the other. He just wasnt sure about stuff. But how could he be? He couldnt phone back.

He started walking then stopped along the pavement to look back. The accordeon-case. Inside the case the accordeon. Where he had left it by the wall next to the public phone. He was about twenty steps away. Imagine leaving it.

But weird seeing it. What was it? Just nothing. A machine. It was him made it work. The handle of the accordeon-case fitted snugly in his hand. It was no effort to lift it. He could have smiled, but whatever, crossing the road to the wee grass square and to the same bench as last night.

The scary guy was gone and the bench was empty. Although maybe it was "his" bench, if he was a homeless guy and that was where he usually slept. He scared him away so he could get "his" bench back. Probably he wouldnt recognize Murdo if he saw him again.

The sun was good, even this early. Blue sky was great. Back home it was clouds, clouds and grey clouds; purple clouds, red clouds, orange clouds; yellow clouds and almost black clouds, palest blue clouds, almost white clouds.

He took the leaflets and flyers out of the rucksack and checked through once again for information on the Jay Cee Lounge gig. All he could find was Queen Monzee-ay featured among "Lancey's Cajun All-Stars" in an event scheduled for lunchtime. Sometimes "All-Stars" was a label for anybody available on the day. Murdo put away the leaflets and flyers and opened the case. He pulled on the accordeon, adjusted the straps and began on a thing that got the fingers moving. He had Queen Monzee-ay's set in his head and needed to go in and work but not too fast. Ye could go too fast. Sometimes ye did and it was a waste of time. It didnay work and ye had to blank it all out, and go for it again. Okay if he had been playing like usual like every day, then it would have been easy. But if ye werent playing regularly ye lost the feel and did things that were only there to guide ye in. Once ye were in ye dumped them. Ye just had to judge it, and go with it, and move fast: push it push it push it and not be scared.

Not a great accordeon but it would do. It would be his American one; he would leave it at Uncle John's house, then the next time him and Dad were there he could use it again.

This was a public place and people were walking now, and walking was moving, moving to the beat, dogs this way and that. Kids there too. Ye got it anywhere. Joggers, strollers; fast power-walkers, shoulders going and Murdo moved on with a kind of two-step thing in line from what he had been hearing off the two CDs, the bare thing itself then thickening it out – making it thick was how he thought of it: beginning on the bare thing then over and over and over, opening it out but bringing in what else could be there and that was crucial.

If he had had a guitar he would have played in a rhythm the way he did for Chess Hopkins. Just to get himself in. Once in that was that. Here he didnt have the guitar, he went with the fingers, where the fingers led him, geared towards the tunes he had been listening to these last many days.

Where did it take ye? Wherever, just wherever. Ye didnt know till there ye were, and that was that in the best kind of playing, the best kind of players. Queen Monzee-ay would be leading and you would know which way to follow, you would find it. You go that way how you think, you go that way how you think, how you think, oh jees yeah on ye go, just like whatever, whatever. Ye could shiver in that kind of playing; and hearing it in other musicians. After it ye needed a gap, not talking to people; the audience were there and however they heard it, okay, but you needed to disappear.

However long Murdo was playing on the bench he didnt know but it felt good and his fingers were fine just moving from what he had been hearing these past days down the basement. It was his learning, whatever that was, it was his to work from. That was enough. Once the band was in he would be in. Queen Monzee-ay was leading the way. He would be with her, he would be with her. She knew he would. That was all she wanted. She was only asking for that.

A crashing noise from the catfish foodstall. A woman had unlocked the shutters and pushed them up. The guy's wife maybe. He was home with the kids as in turn and turn about. Two jobs, sometimes three. The husband and wife too. One worked then came home. Then the other one went out. One night and one day.

Murdo took off the accordeon. It was a beautiful beautiful morning. He walked a few paces exercising his shoulders and arms, swigged from the bottle of water. Two people were already at the foodstall counter, waiting for the woman to serve them. Nearby the bench three birds pecking into the grass by the verge; crumbs in the dirt, birds look for crumbs; people too. The bird with the human face. Maybe it was there. Aunt Maureen thinking of him. Thinking was worrying. She was worrying. She didnt have to. Aunt Maureen! You do not have to worry! Murdo is alive-alive-oh! Where is that bird! Away and tell Aunt Maureen! Murdo says dont worry.

It was true but. People worry, why do people worry? Dad would just be

oh jees, Dad.

But what could he do? nothing. Dad was coming and that was that because Dad was Dad and Dad just like whatever: that was Dad. Murdo shut his eyes, only a moment: he pulled on the accordeon. Dad was a worrier. People were worriers. Other people werent. Murdo settled the accordeon then stood still and sang a song for Dad:

> I was born and raised in Glasgow
> in a Glasgow tenement
> and when people spoke of my bonny land
> I didnt know what they meant

For I have seen the Highlands
I have seen the low,
And I will brag of my native land,
Wherever I may go.

On the shores of foreign brothers
we'll lay no robber's hand
all we ask is to toil and live
in our own native land.

The song for Dad was a song for Dad's own father – Murdo's
grandpa. That was Grandpa Macarthur and he used to sing it himself.
Oh and he was a grumpy old guy right enough, who kicked the
cat when he lost his temper and wouldnay emigrate to America
when people wanted him to. Murdo didnt sing it like grandpa who
sang it in a certain way like how he explained it, his own country
wasnt his own country:

when people spoke of my bonny land
I didnt know what they meant

because rich people had it all, and tried to keep out the poor
people who didnt get the chance to see it and were stuck in filthy
stone buildings and filthy stone streets, never allowed out to see
the mountains and lochs and great places, woods and sea and sandy
beaches and like whatever, rich people had it all, kings and queens
and millionaires, landowners and robbers. Grandpa stood to sing it
but he always talked, he stopped and talked and granny would give
him a row. Sing if ye're going to sing! We dont want a lecture!
People laughing, Mum and Dad.

Murdo sang it. They were all there. Everybody. Eilidh was laughing.
Grandpa liked Eilidh, he always liked Eilidh, he *smiled* with her.

He liked Murdo too. "Just you sing son, you sing!" Murdo sang.
He wanted to sing! And that was the song; so what. He was just
glad about stuff, just about being here. Today was today and here
he was. Tonight was the gig and just everything was like everything.

When he finished the song he went straight into a jig, capering about.

People were watching. A few adults, kids and toddlers. A wee girl in a football jersey came forwards. She was like eight years old and the jersey she wore showed the colours of Barcelona FC. Kids wore the same jersey back in Scotland. She held out a dollar. His empty coffee carton was there on the bench. Murdo winked at the girl and nodded towards it. Beyond her he saw the mother smile. The girl dropped in the dollar, stepped back and returned swiftly to her parents. Other people stopped. A few looked foreign and were taking pictures. A couple of guys and lassies roundabout his own age stayed for two songs. The accordeon brought them. Not his voice!

He played on, maybe three quarters of an hour. It was so worthwhile just doing it, and out of nothing. He hadnt meant to do anything like that. It was just everything! A whole combination of stuff. He took his time putting away the accordeon and getting his stuff together. He was keen to see how much money was in the old coffee carton but didnt want to look when people were watching. Then he was able to count it: $11.70. Ye would call it a wage. His first wage in America. This was it! That was like two sandwich meals or one big one, two catfish. It was just brilliant.

If Dad had been there. Not like to hear Murdo play but to realize that he could earn money for doing it. It wasnt just a boy growing up like a wee hobby. He was a musician and musicians earned money. It was like a job. Ye do it and ye keep doing it. If ye stop playing ye stop playing. So ye cant stop, ye have to play play play. If ye go wrong ye get the chance to make it right. But the chance only comes in the playing. If ye dont stick with it ye dont get it, ye dont right the wrong.

That is what it is; that is what happens. People watching wont notice, unless they are musicians and pick it out. Like how Chess Hopkins knew when Murdo moved the wrong way on "Bonaparte's Retreat" but pulled it back, and nobody knew. Except Chess. But that let Chess relax and run with his own thing, because he knew he could trust Murdo. Murdo was up to the task. So that allowed Chess to make room for Clara. He was freed up from the fiddle, and did back-up vocal for her. Murdo provided that. Him on guitar set Chess free to give Clara what she needed. Murdo on guitar meant Clara could sing.

It made ye laugh but it was true. That was how it worked. Declan Pike saw that. That was the compliment he gave Murdo at the Gathering, You got her singing son: that was what Declan said.

Bands can do that. The exact same with Queen Monzee-ay. The exact same. She could rely on Murdo. She knew she could, she bloody knew. That was how come she wanted him, right from the start, from the second tune he played on the porch back in Allentown! That was the whole damn thing, she could relax and just like play, just go and go wherever, wherever. Jees, sometimes. . .it made ye angry. It made Murdo angry. It made Murdo so so angry.

What? What did?

Something, just bloody something. He walked on fast. Where to? Just someplace he just bloody was angry. He needed something to eat. As if he could ever let her down! Ha ha fucking ha, fucking ha, ha ha. Queen Monzee-ay for God sake, never ever, never ever. He felt like crying jeesoh, jeesoh man, he walked fast, lugging the accordeon-case.

★

Early afternoon he found the road out to where the Jay Cee Lounge was located. It seemed a long way away. He wondered whether to walk it there just to see the place and make sure of finding it later. He didnt have to be there until nine o'clock tonight; eight o'clock to be on the safe side.

He returned to the main festival area. Already there were crowds of people. Maybe because it was Saturday. Exciting. And music

301

music all the way, begun from the Cajun beat but Zydeco in there too and the French connection in both. It was interesting. And made sense too with Queen Monzee-ay and Aunt Edna each speaking French. He headed for the lunchtime venue.

The poster read "Lancey's Cajun All-Stars" but her name was missing. He stood outside listening for several minutes. He didnt want to pay money to go in if she wasnt playing.

Then he discovered the sign saying "entrée gratuite/free admission".

Inside people wandered around; an all-aged audience, including old people and family groups; children playing and chasing one another. Some tourists too, phones out and photographs. Mostly white people but a few black and all like ordinary together; the usual with clothes, all different outfits, cowboy hats and short trousers. Then the music itself! Jeesoh. Folk were just dancing, dancing along the sides of the space and the gap between here and the seated area which held maybe five to seven hundred people. Plenty seats taken but plenty available.

Murdo threaded his way through behind the rear of the seated area and found a spot to stand with a clear view of the band: Queen Monzee-ay on her cream-coloured accordeon, just a member of the band and nothing special; seated to the side of Lancey himself, on fiddle and lead vocal. Then a bass guitar and drums; electric guitar, acoustic guitar and triangle. No Sarah.

Lancey also had an accordeon next to his chair. He sang directly to Queen Monzee-ay and she sang in reply to him. Both sang in French and called to each other in high-pitched voices. It was rocking along and fun all the way. Some in the audience laughed at quips the musicians made, so they knew French. Others were foreign, were maybe Chinese and Japanese and from countries in Europe or wherever.

The audience laughed at something Lancey was saying, then loud applause; whistling and cheering. It was for Queen Monzee-ay. She gave a wave to the audience. They were all appreciating her.

They all seemed to know who she was. Everybody. All clapping her, including the band, who were all quite old themselves. Murdo hadnt noticed until now. Maybe they were genuine all-stars.

Queen Monzee-ay was leaning to chat a moment with the bass guitarist and drummer while Lancey was pointing to folk in the audience he knew and some were known musicians too. He spoke in French and repeated some of it in English.

It was brilliant. This is what Murdo felt, so strongly. He was just lucky. So so lucky. If only this! It was another world. An amazing-mazing thing. Lancey introduced the next song, tradeesheeonalll. People got up to dance to the front and down the sides. A few stood having a smoke and chatting, moved aside to allow the dancers space.

With the dancing going other spare seats became available, including at the very back row and Murdo found one fast. He placed the accordeon-case by his feet and removed the rucksack altogether. He sat a moment then breathed out slowly, at last, just being able to *breathe*. Not worrying about stuff. Hearing the music, watching the band.

All the different styles too, and seeing the dancers; everything, just relaxed, here he was and everything was okay.

That was a thing here how folk were relaxed, just like chatting, whatever. Even with the band playing. Back home there were guys Murdo played with got irritated by people talking. But what is wrong in people talking? They are having fun, and being friendly. What is wrong with being friendly!

Aunt Edna! Jees! Aunt Edna! She was on the edge of the third front row, way down from Murdo but on the same side, next to a guy in a cowboy hat which was black and studded.

Aunt Edna had that upright way about her. Even sitting down. Her and the cowboy guy were making comments, their heads turning to each other, cheery comments and laughing. Sarah was farther along from her, sitting next to a guy. Joel was there too, but Murdo didnt recognize the guy sitting beside Sarah.

He was sitting beside her. He was with her. Seeing how close they were sitting, he definitely was. Murdo raised himself up from the seat to get a clearer view. The guy was close in to her. Even like their shoulders touching; they looked like they were. Squeezed in. Although other people were too. It was funny but. Not funny, it just meant – whatever. What did it mean? It meant like they were sitting close together and it was as close, closer, than her and Joel. Joel was on the other side and there was a big space between them, and he was her brother. So ha ha. Whatever that was. It meant something; whatever it meant, that is what it meant.

While the next song was being introduced, Aunt Edna and the guy in the black studded cowboy hat got up and strolled to the smoking area. Aunt Edna was a smoker but the guy wasnt, he was just keeping her company.

Aunt Edna turned to gaze in Murdo's direction but would never see him unless he waved. He didnt wave. He didnt, otherwise

He didnt feel like talking.

Ye think things and they are stupid.

Sarah was saying something to the guy, half turned to him, and their faces like close, how could faces be so close? Obviously they couldnt. If yer face was as close as that ye would have been touching, touching faces: touching faces is kissing. What else is kissing?

Murdo sat back on the seat.

Things that are daft. This is life. Ye think things. Just stupid. Girls are girls and guys are just like, just the usual.

How could he go home? He didnt have enough money. The bus cost too much. He would have to hitch. He would hitch. The road out of Lafayette was okay for hitching, it wasnt like a real interstate where ye couldnt stand. Hitch it to Baton Rouge and then up the way to Jackson and over to Birmingham, although Birmingham, ye wanted to pass it by because of that damn church and what happened to the girls, where they were killed; that bloody bomb, that was like America, that was America, that was ha ha ha, killing and bombing and battering and just bloody horrible and he wanted away, away away away, he wanted away.

Murdo crouched forwards, arms folded and resting on his knees, just how he was feeling was the stupidity, just like stupidity. Murdo and stupidity. Dad would say it. Life. Murdo's life. Stupidity. Talk about stupidity, that was him, he was just daft. Daft. Some guys got lassies but he didnay; beautiful lassies, he didnay get any. He didnay. He had a girlfriend before and she went with another guy. Imagine that. Just like

That is what happened. That guy had sex with her and Murdo didnt. That was the truth and he knew it for a fact. She had sex with him but not with Murdo. How come? Ye just like – ye have to think, ye have to think. . .ye have to, ye just like worry worry, ye worry about it, if ye've done something wrong, something like whatever; if it is your fault, ye wonder, or maybe like if ye are gay, so it is like maybe I'm gay and that is what it is, like if the lassie doesnay fancy ye, how come? if ye are gay, maybe ye are. The guy in the toilet. Then him in Allentown offering a lift, jeesoh, how come? How come these guys

like if it was a real lift, how come Murdo didnt take it? Ye wonder about that. How come he didnay take the lift? If ye want to hitch it then somebody offers and ye dont take it. How come?

Just something. Something. Probably nothing; probably he was a good guy and just helpful. He knew Sarah's father. It would just be stupid, just Murdo like how – whatever, he was daft, he did daft things, said the wrong things. Grow up, why didnt he?

Ye got sick of it, sick of yerself. Everything was mixed up. The guy was trying to be helpful and ye said no. He was black. So if he was white? Was that something? People were white, or else black. Sarah was black and American. Murdo was white and Scottish. White and Scottish. He twisted on his seat, pulling on the rucksack, set to leave. He breathed in and it made a snorting sound. He closed his eyes and sat there, and settled the breathing, forcing it measured, measured; one two three; one, one; one two three, one two three. He breathed in.

He gripped the handle of the accordeon-case but didnt get up off the seat, he just breathed in; breathing in, breathing out, breathing in, breathing out, because he didnt want to get up off the seat but just stay there and nothing. None of it was like anything; nothing at all; everything was something else. He let go the handle of the accordeon-case and slunk even further down, still on the edge of the seat. He shouldnt have put the rucksack on but he had and he couldnt take it back off without getting up off the seat and he didnt want to in case anybody saw him. He wasnt going to the gig tonight, he was not going. Never.

What is life? "Life"? When Mum died her face changed. Her actual face and like the shape of it, the cheekbones maybe. It wasnt Mum's face. Was that pain? Maybe it was. Twisted up with pain. Heavy heavy morphine drugs. They gave her morphine. Somebody said that. Who told them? Why not Murdo? If you are the son how come they dont tell you? Oh Mum is dying, maybe ye can find out for yerself. Oh well. Life is life. Sarah and she's got a boyfriend. What did Queen Monzee-ay think? There was Murdo and there was whoever. People see ye. Ye get these thoughts about people too, that they know what you are thinking. They say it to ye: Oh I know what you're thinking. But do they? They cant see into yer brain. So if a guy looks at ye and he is gay then is that you? Maybe it is, so if ye are, so what? Dad is like Oh ye have to do this and ye have to do that. It was just daft bloody nonsense, so if ye were gay, however life is, so what, it is all just plus 1, everybody and nothing. It was all just stupid. Ye look in the mirror and see other people. Because they are seeing you. Ye see yer own face but these other folk too, how come they are all there? They say something so you have to go along with it. You make a decision but it is their life too.

If it had been night-time he could have got up and walked out and nobody would know. Here the sky was blue, the sun was shining, Saturday afternoon and the broadest daylight ever ye could get. On stage Lancey introduced another one and on they went, him on fiddle, another waltz oh but sad sad sad bloody sad, that voice this morning, the French guy doing the French song, how did he get that sadness it made ye bloody cry just so so sad. Stupid stupid stuff, that was music and just fuck, how they got that sadness. How do they do it? Musicians just get it. Some get it, Queen Monzee-ay in her playing, sitting there, the all-stars, she was just staring; where she was staring, ye would never ever know. Never. Never never. She was sitting there staring off, and that sad waltz rhythm. What was she staring at? Nothing, only her eyes were open. She was the centre. Ye knew it. Ye had to watch her. Murdo had never seen anybody, never seen anybody, whatever she was she was just, she was just like what, the minute-most minute

Murdo was onto his feet now gripping the accordeon-case handle, not looking to the front but squeezing his way sideways out. He could not stay because people would see him. Out from the row of chairs Aunt Edna was standing with the guy in the black studded hat. They were to the side of the space away from the seated area and people milled around next to her. She had glanced in Murdo's direction but wouldnt have seen him if he didnt do anything. He waved to her. Aunt Edna, he had to. She saw him coming and laughed a real laugh, introduced him to the older man in the black studded cowboy hat; a musician. Diego Narciso. Murdo had never heard of him.

Aunt Edna spoke in Spanish to the man, and Queen Monzee-ay's name was mentioned, then added to Murdo: I told Diego you aint ever heard of him Murdo, he says you got no education!

Diego extended his hand to Murdo and they shook hands, and clapped Murdo on the shoulder. Hey Murdo: you play with Queen Monzee-ay?

Murdo grinned.

Good. Diego nodded, turned to one of four young guys who were standing not far away, and spoke with him in Spanish. The four listened to Diego, seeing Murdo and the accordeon-case.

Aunt Edna put her arm round him drawing him to her, and

whispered: He is telling them about you. These young ones are his band, they play tonight Murdo. Diego is very famous here: one of the finest players – from Texas but you know like Mexico? Aunt Edna kissed Murdo on the cheek. People will be very pleased to see you here. Aunt Edna pointed over to where Sarah was sitting. You see Sarah and Joel there? Gene too. You know Gene? sitting with Sarah, a fine guitarist Murdo, he plays with you tonight.

Aunt Edna broke off to join the applause for the end of a song, then dropped her cigarette to the ground, and tried to crush it beneath the heel of her boot, but it kept burning. Murdo stepped on it. The band leader Lancey was telling the audience in a mixture of French and English that Queen Monzee-ay would now play one of her own songs. Lancey bowed to her. This song also from our tradition, Zydeco tradition. Zydeco, Haricot, Queen Monzee-ay! La maestra, magnifica, Queen of Zydeco music!

There was applause. Aunt Edna shook her head. Oh he dont know, she said, he dont know.

Diego touched her hand. Miss Kwankwan, he said.

Aunt Edna shook her head again. She saw Murdo looking and smiled, but only a moment, and he didnt know what it was, if he had missed something. Queen Monzee-ay had remained seated and she replied to Lancey's introduction with good humour: Merci Lancey, full of beans as usual! Full of shit as usual!

The audience laughed.

Okay, she said, I sing one of my own songs here, and ask Sarah – Sarah! Queen Monzee-ay beckoned Sarah forwards: My beautiful granddaughter!

Murdo shuffled sideways at the mention of her name, keeping out of view behind people.

Come play alongside your beautiful grandmother! called Queen Monzee-ay.

Sarah stood up. Gave the guy beside her one of these jokey type of looks between couples, and a wee punch on his arm. She walked along and up onto the stage, donned her rubboard. During the applause from the audience Queen Monzee-ay squinting in Murdo's direction, but it wasnt Murdo it was Diego, she had recognized Diego, and she laughed: Señor Narciso!

She pointed him out to the audience: Mesdames et m'sieurs, un bad hombre in from San Antonio! Diego Narciso: the one and only!

People were surprised and pleased, including Lancey and the band members who shifted and strained forward to see him. Diego took off the cowboy hat and did a sweeping bow with it.

Diego is playing someplace. I dont know! Queen Monzee-ay called to him: Diego! Appearing today! Where and when?

Diego dismissed the question. Queen Monzee-ay smiled. Sometime today!

But the four young guys from his band moved fast; one went to the edge of the platform where he raised a pile of flyers in one hand. He shouted: Esta noche! Las siete y media! Tonight is seven o'clock! Place is Scene Kiosque à Musique!

The other three had bundles of flyers and began passing them out to the audience. Diego shook his head but was smiling. He exchanged words with Aunt Edna.

Then Queen Monzee-ay led Lancey's band on one of her good fast songs and members of the audience were up onto the floor dancing. She played it on the porch back in Allentown and it was good seeing how she was doing it here. Murdo would have stayed beyond the opening minute except he had to leave before the song, and when it ended, and Sarah came down from the stage.

Aunt Edna was engrossed in the performance and he could have escaped except he couldnt, not without saying; he couldnt do that. Aunt Edna, he said, I've got to go now.

To go Murdo?

Eh it's eh, my father. He's coming like eh so I'm going to have to go and meet him. Murdo smiled and turned to leave.

Aunt Edna hesitated. They'll be disappointed you've gone.

Yeah but I'll be there tonight. I just have to go just now. But I'll eh – it's just like my father eh. . .

Things okay with you Murdo?

Yeah.

Aunt Edna gestured at the front row. Joel's sitting there. And Gene – you know Gene?

Yeah but I just need to go.

How is your father son, how's he doing?

He's fine. He's fine. If ye just tell eh Queen Monzee-ay like I mean I will be there.

Okay Murdo.

Thanks, said Murdo and turned to leave. Two guys from Diego's band were watching him; they made to speak. One was the guy who had shouted the information earlier. He put his hand out, gesturing at the accordeon-case. Hey! You play with Queen Monzee-ay? Tonight like the Jay Cee, you play with her?

Yeah. Murdo nodded and stepped on. The guy put his hand forwards quickly, pointing at himself. Esteban, he said, then pointing at the other guy: Santiago.

Murdo waited. Santiago grinned, reached to shake hands. Esteban indicated the other two members of the band who were handing out flyers to some of the audience. We four, we are with Diego. Esteban shrugged. We play with him, concert.

Santiago jabbed his finger at Murdo's chest. Queen Monzee-ay? You play?

Yeah.

Your name?

Murdo.

Murrdo! Santiago nodded. Murrdo! Comp ticket! Santiago handed him a ticket. Is tonight. You come maybe?

Yeah.

Is comp ticket.

Thanks.

Seven o'clock, said Esteban. You are late, we are early. You come.

Yeah, thanks. Murdo shoved the comp ticket and a flyer into his jeans pocket and walked off fast, through the dancers and fringe audience, heading for the rear exit.

★

In the wee grass square the benches remained occupied. He had been waiting for one to become free. He checked for dog shit then sat on the grass, his back to a bush. Later he was awake, his head bent forwards. When he moved it it made a weird crunching noise in his ears. His neck was sore. He rubbed it with his right hand. The accordeon-case and rucksack were secured to his left wrist with his belt. His bum was numb. He must have been sleeping. Probably he had been. He looked for his bottle of water, swallowed a mouthful. He slackened off the belt and inserted it back through the loops on his jeans. How long had he been here? An hour and a half maybe. Late after-noon and warm.

No wonder he was tired. His last sleep was Thursday into Friday and tonight was Saturday into Sunday. The gig was set for 9 p.m. but probably didnt start until half past. So by the time he got to bed. Wherever that was. Back here. Unless the friends of Sarah's family were still offering.

He was hungry. The same foodstall was there and that was a place. An actual café would have been better, so he could wash his hands and face. They had these festival-type WC cubicles but they didnt have washing facilities. The toilet he had to use was too gross even to talk about like diarrhoea, totally disgusting, the pong was just like the worst imaginable. Whoever used it last must have been ill.

The idea of a shower. This was Saturday and he had been wearing the same stuff since Thursday. People going between venues would see him as a tramp. Maybe he was. Murdo lifted the rucksack and pulled it on, lifted the accordeon-case, and started walking. Where to? Ha ha.

Unless if he went to Diego Narciso's gig. He checked out the flyer again. It was like a major concert! Murdo had never even heard of him. The trouble was it started at seven, so then it was like getting to the Jay Cee Lounge in time for the nine o'clock kick-off, although nine o'clock might mean nine thirty. The guys in Diego's band said it would be okay for time but would it? Maybe it wouldnt, and he couldnt be late. Because he definitely was doing the gig with Queen Monzee-ay. He thought he wasnt but now he was. For definite. It didnt matter about Sarah. She was nice and that was that. He was foreign and she was nice to him. So then it was like Oh she must love me. Stupid shit and his own stupid fault because he was so damn stupid, damn bloody daft, that was all.

Only how come she touched him? That was the one thing. She did touch him. So if ye touch somebody. Girls touch a guy and it is like nothing to her but for the guy it is like the guy is getting touched. So ye shiver! Ye just shiver. Sarah touched him and he shivered. How come? Like if a lassie has a boyfriend, well, touch him but dont touch somebody else if ye have a boyfriend already.

It didnt matter anyway.

Turn a corner and bumping into Dad: imagine. Where have you been? Walking about. Sleeping on the grass. What!?! Yeah well how long does money last like I mean Lafayette to Huntsville, plus accordeon? Could ye even buy a return it was so damn expensive? Maybe ye couldnt.

Dad would find him. Nose in the air, sniff sniff: he went thataway. Good that Declan Pike was there. Dad got stressed with people but Declan was different, Declan knew about stuff. The Jay Cee Lounge for Zydeco and Blues. Probably he knew it already. Probably he had been there. Your boy is doing a gig with Queen Monzee-ay so he will be there, he will be there. It's an honour. Declan would tell him. Declan would know.

The foodstall was ahead: same place same guy. He approached

the counter, settling the accordeon-case on the ground. The guy waited for the order. Murdo smiled. Could I have the fish again eh the catfish?

Catfish, you want catfish?

Please, yeah.

The guy went into one of the food compartments, got a catfish fillet and tossed it onto the hotplate. You want hot sauce?

Yeah. And what goes with it, is that rice?

Rice, sure. The guy spooned hot sauce onto the fish and began the frying.

Murdo studied the different side foods. I think it was salad you gave me the last time.

Salad, si.

Are ye busy? asked Murdo.

The guy grunted something and turned from him to see the listed meals and meal deals.

Murdo thought to say something again but the guy waved him aside. Another customer was there, a big man wearing short trousers. The foodstall guy took his order. Obviously he didnt remember Murdo. But the festival was busy and thousands of people were here. A bottle of coke and a packet of doritos. That was the customer's order, and he dropped coins into the tips jar.

The foodstall guy watched the man open the packet of doritos with his teeth while heading along to the main festival area. He yawned and shifted a step, looked at the catfish, flipped it over. He folded his arms and stared way over Murdo's head.

Murdo turned to see the grass square and the people going about. After several moments he said to the guy: I'm playing tonight eh. . .doing a gig.

The foodstall guy glanced at Murdo who gestured at the accordeon-case. The guy turned to rearrange something on the shelves behind him, wiped his hands on a dishtowel.

We dont go on until after nine o'clock, said Murdo.

Mm. The guy used the dishtowel to wipe along the counter top then ripped the cellophane surround from a pile of paper plates. He extracted one and set it on the counter. What drink you want?

You've not got any orange juice?

No orange juice.

You have water?

Si water. The guy lifted the catfish up off the hotplate, and slid it aboard the plate. He picked a bottle of water from out the glass-fronted cupboard: You want salad?

Please, yeah. Murdo had taken the flyer for Diego's gig from his pocket and read the details. I'm going to a gig, he said, this other gig. It starts at seven. Scene Kiosque à Musique.

The guy was pronging out the lettuce and tomato. While he did that Murdo read aloud from the flyer. The guy jerked his head to the left, spooning a dollop of rice to the plate. Diego Narciso, added Murdo, he plays kind of

Huh?

The gig eh, Scene Kiosque à Musique.

Diego Narciso? said the guy.

Yeah.

Is Diego Narciso? You are going al concierto Diego?

Yeah.

Whohh! The guy laid down the paper plate and patted himself on the chest. Diego! I listen to him, I play his music. Here. . .! He reached for his phone. See Diego, his music!

You like him?

Si I like him, si: Diego! The foodstall guy laughed.

I've got a ticket.

Good! Lucky.

I actually met him. This afternoon.

The guy squinted, listening. Murdo passed him a $10 note. The guy took it and held it a moment. I met him this afternoon, said Murdo. I mean I was like introduced to him. That's how I got the ticket. . . Murdo brought out the comp ticket and looked at it, then showed it to the guy.

The guy studied it and replied, Is backstage.

Yeah.

The guy nodded and half turned from Murdo to collect the change from the till. He laid the money on the counter in front of Murdo. He smiled, lifted the dishtowel and flicked at the hotplate.

Murdo let the money lie. The truth is, he said, I cant actually go. I dont have enough time. Because like my own gig, where I'm playing, I've got to be there for something like eight o'clock. Diego's gig is seven o'clock.

The foodstall guy was listening but not maybe understanding.

Murdo said, I mean you could go. He reached over the counter, gesturing with the comp ticket. You take it.

The guy smiled, shaking his head.

Honest. You take it. It's a comp. No money. Just take it.

No.

No?

The guy shook his head. No. Gracias.

Murdo said, I know you are working just now but could you not get somebody to maybe let ye away or whatever?

The guy didnt answer. He moved back from the counter and involved himself somewhere beneath it. Murdo waited but that was that. He lifted his change from the counter and put a dollar bill into the tips jar, stuck the bottle of water in his pocket and lifted the plate of food.

He walked along past the bench from last night. There was space at one end but he didnt want to sit there. He kept going to the next and sat down there.

Back at the foodstall the guy stepped outside for a smoke, had lit his cigarette and just stood there gazing into space. He had the phone in one hand but wasnt looking at it.

But it wasnt Murdo's fault, whatever it was. Having to work there instead of playing music. Being married with his wife and kids, having to work at that job. Night-shifts and long hours; her days, him nights. Whose fault was that? Who was the guy blaming,

Murdo? How come? If ye want to play music and ye dont. Who do ye blame? If ye blame somebody, who is it? Cooking grub for folk. Murdo would have hated that. Then if it was you hungry and you had to cook for them. Who wants to do that! Just like a servant. So a guy comes up to ye and asks for a hamburger. But it's you wants the hamburger. And you've got to cook it for him. Ye would be angry. Aw here ye are and ye would just bloody throw it at him, there's yer fucking hamburger, catch. No wonder ye got angry, anybody would. Ye would be in a daze all day dreaming and just like fantasizing; one day this and that. But then it is day after day after day here's a hamburger, no hamburger, catfish. That guy loved Diego. Murdo didnt know who he was. It wasnt his fault. That was life. Murdo should have left the ticket on the counter and went away. Then the foodstall guy, whatever he done with it was up to him. Dump it or keep it, go ahead, instead of blaming Murdo. A guy gave him the ticket. Whose fault was that? A guy from Diego's band. It wasnt Murdo's fault. Only offering him the ticket. Maybe he shouldnt have. How come? It made the person feel low.

But a present? The ticket was a present. He gave the guy a present. A present is a present. What is wrong with a present? Why didnt he just take the ticket then he could have ripped it up afterwards, or sold it. He could have sold the thing! Who cares. It was like being too proud. Oh I'm not taking a present off you, who do ye think ye are. Oh ye play accordeon, well ha ha, so do I. That was like school, just daft nonsense.

★

The end of the road widened out near a railway line and Murdo saw the Jay Cee Lounge way across the other side, no longer a road, just a free-standing building on an open stretch, with a large parking place to the front. Quite a few vehicles were parked. A big man was by the door; African-American and dressed like a cowboy;

the hat and waistcoat, jeans and boots. Murdo paused to switch hands on the accordeon-case. There was nowhere else he could be headed except to the club entrance. The man watched him until he arrived then held up his hand to stop him: Where you going?

Murdo would have had to push past him to enter. To one side of the doorway was a large glossy poster advertising The Zadik Strollers and Special Guest Queen Monzee-ay: $15 cover. To the other side of the doorway was a cardboard notice: RU25? The doorman pointed at the RU25? notice, crooked his right forefinger: ID. ID!

Murdo looked up again at the notice and at the poster.

You are way too young, said the doorman. I need some ID.

I've not got any.

Not got any?

I'm not American.

The doorman stared at Murdo and at the accordeon-case. I got to see some ID. You are way too young.

Do ye mean like a passport? If it's my passport like I mean I left it at home. Murdo pointed to the poster. I'm playing with Queen Monzee-ay.

Other people were coming forward and the doorman waved them on into the club. They glanced at Murdo. Murdo repeated it, quietly: I'm playing with Queen Monzee-ay.

What do you say? Playing with Queen Monzee-ay? The doorman pointed to the name on the poster. You playing with her?

Yeah.

The doorman nodded, he sniffed and said: Okay. Now I will know if you aint. Understand what I'm saying. I will know and I will come looking.

I am playing with her.

I hear you boy I hear you. The doorman pointed his right forefinger at Murdo's nose. You go in there and you stay put. You dont do nothing. You hear me? No beer no nothing. You dont leave that stage area. Old man tending bar see you doing something man he will shoot you. Old Vinnie man you know who he is! He gotta shotgun man he will shoot you.

The doorman stared at Murdo until eventually Murdo nodded. The doorman said, Okay. He shaped his hand like a pistol, directing Murdo into an L-shaped lobby. Taped music played; a rhythm and blues thing that was so measured and so just moving ahead; piano, sax and drums, one voice: baby dont turn me down, baby let me hold your hand, dont turn me down. A few people were here; a cloakroom and attendant. Murdo passed along, lugging the accordeon-case, rucksack over his shoulders.

Two women were by a small table taking tickets and issuing tickets. A $15 cover. They looked at Murdo and he made to pay across a $20 note and get the $5 change, thinking just like save hassle, save hassle. One of the women smiled, jerked her thumb sideways. Thanks, he said, putting the money back into his pocket. He heard them laugh, probably about him. A white boy, or just because he was young, whatever, playing with Queen Monzee-ay, who cares. It didnt matter. Through the doorway now into the main hall, by the side of a long bar. And it was hard not walking to the beat, in the singer's own rhythm, feeling like a clown, please dont turn me down baby,

> please let me hold your hand,
> baby let me hold your hand
> and if I hold your hand

The platform stage was set up; instruments in place, and ready for use. Mainly black people but not only. The place was half full already and they werent due to begin for another hour. Nobody paid Murdo any attention, except for the bartender who was quite old-looking and wearing a hat, not a cowboy one but like a gangster or a businessman. Murdo realized he was watching him, beneath the rim of the hat hiding his eyes while opening bottles of beer for a customer.

Then he moved his head and it was for Murdo, nodding him

along and to the side there. Murdo saw a door, leading backstage. By the other side of the stage, way to the opposite end of the space from the bar, were tables along the wall. Two were side by side. Aunt Edna and Joel were there with Sarah's parents. No sign of Sarah or Queen Monzee-ay. He was glad not to see Sarah.

He headed to where the bartender indicated, through the door into a corridor. Along here the music faded. Murdo stood in half light, a blue light. He didnt want any more. It would have been on him and he wanted shadows. Sometimes ye felt like hiding. Although he knew why he was here. Coming all this way. Maybe he was daft. So what? Maybe he did mistake the situation. Who fucking cares, if everything was stupid and everything was crap and so damn bloody horrible, who cares, people looking and everybody knowing. Stupid shit. He heard music and it was good. Faint music but good, just fading how it fades; breath going from the body, breath entering the body. Murdo heard and it was a waltz. Probably in his own head. When he was playing his mind stayed out of it; same with listening, ye hear it but ye dont; it enters through the skin, yer actual skin, the pores in yer skin.

Imagine silence. Everybody shuts up at the exact same moment. Suddenly nothing.

Murdo opened his eyes. He saw faded posters and old-style photographs lining either wall; signed photographs. Great musicians down through the years. He wandered along seeing the faces and reading the names: Boozoo Chavis, Clifton Chenier, Little Walter, Queen Monzee-ay, Beau Jocque, Professor Longhair, Queen Ida, Lightnin' Slim. Then he put the accordeon-case down for a wee minute, looked back to the door into the main area. He saw the light there and didnt want ever to go back. Oh jees never and he was just wanting to cry, that is what he wanted. Right here. It was this right here. Even the smell. Old and fusty, damp. The atmosphere was just like thick. That is what it was: thick; the most most wonderful ever imaginable. Ye could never ever imagine it. That was the shiver. Nothing like anything except itself. Oh jees, he was just looking forwards to playing, he was just wanting to play, just like so so wanting to play, taking yer hand. What else? Nothing, only holding me, please please let me.

How come he was here? To bloody play. It was his life. Sarah was Sarah and that was her – Gene, who cares about Gene. People have their own life. This was Murdo's. Nobody else's. Not Dad's. Not nobody. Whatever he did was him. Ye just go ahead, this is what ye did and ye just bloody lived. That was that, like Mum, that was Mum, ye just wanted to cry and he always did and that was that he bloody cried, standing there in the corridor so had to wait there, wherever Sarah was, if she came out a room and saw him.

He was controlling it. He managed this by not doing anything until the water stopped flowing. It stopped flowing because he didnt do anything. He didnt try to stop it. He didnt try anything. That was the best way. And he didnt wipe his eyes because that just smeared and left streaks, yer eyes went red and people noticed. Who cares anyway. That is people, whatever they do, that is up to them. Ye cannot hide, who can hide, nobody.

He lifted the accordeon-case. Ahead was the emergency exit door and it was ajar, enough to peer through. The smell of tobacco, cigarette smoke. Queen Monzee-ay was outside on a wooden dining chair. He pushed open the door.

It was a small patio, more like a wooden platform; big enough for about four chairs. Queen Monzee-ay sat drinking tea, gazing over a wide empty area that looked like it had been a place for factories or warehouses but now was cleared of everything except the concrete foundations: she was gazing to the evening sky; a redness there that was quite amazing. Where did that lead? Away west, wherever that was, the Pacific Ocean. But what ye knew about was tomorrow, that it would be a beautiful day, the very best; the sky was telling ye.

She seemed not to know he was there, until then she spoke, barely so much as moving her lips: Hey Mister Murdo you going to play with me?

Murdo grinned. He kept grinning.

You going to play with me?

That would be great.

What you been doing all day?

Walking about.

You didnt stop and say hullo this afternoon now why was that? Edna said you were there and Sarah went looking. You disappeared.

Queen Monzee-ay shifted on her chair, she studied him. Murdo lowered his gaze, switched hands on the accordeon-case handle. She massaged the side of her back a moment then lifted her bag from the floor, pointed to the emergency exit door. Get a chair from in there, she said.

Murdo did as she bade. When he returned and was seated she gestured at the accordeon-case. Let me see that thing.

Murdo brought out the accordeon. Queen Monzee-ay looked at it. I dont like its face, she said. It play okay?

Not bad.

I got you the turquoise.

Did ye! Aw! Thanks! Thanks! Really I mean thanks, thanks.

Queen Monzee-ay chuckled. You like that one huh?

Yeah I do, yeah. Yeah, I do.

Yeah, that old turquoise got a history. . . Hey now you make Diego's show?

No.

Okay. Queen Monzee-ay nodded. They were wanting you there, Diego's boys, wanting you to hear what they do. I would have gone myself but these venues got no place proper to sit Murdo and I got this back.

She rubbed at her back and at her sides again. And a weird thing happened: Queen Monzee-ay was looking away to the front some-place but at the same time was talking to him or seemed to be. Except he couldnt hear anything, if she was speaking it was so quietly, hardly at all, like saving her breath.

Also the light, her facing to the sunset and him seated behind her, not able to see her face properly. This wee patio was a special place. A place so quiet ye could go to sleep, sitting right here. And if ye were weary, really really weary, and Murdo was weary, just so so weary, if he even had a mind, if he had one

The chair screeched on the wood. His chair, on the wooden floor.

Diego would have been good for you to hear, said Queen Monzee-ay. Got his own style of playing but he goes rocking along.

Mm.

Life in us old timers huh? Come over here, she said. Murdo dragged his chair closer. Queen Monzee-ay reached to touch his left wrist and she stroked it. Sarah said you would come. And Miss Edna said it too. Oh he'll be here, that is what she said.

Queen Monzee-ay held onto Murdo's left hand and he couldnt have taken it away, and she kept looking at him until he raised his head to meet her eyes properly. He smiled. You laughing? she asked. What you laughing at Murdo?

Murdo chuckled.

Boy you laughing at me! You are too young to be laughing at me! Queen Monzee-ay made a fierce face at him. You know who my people are!

No.

You dont know who my people are!

Queen Monzee-ay kept a hold of his hand and he could not withdraw it; he would have preferred to. He didnt like being held by people. Although it was her and she was different. What you got to say for yourself? she asked, and Murdo could not raise his head. He studied the floor, the spars of wood, chipped and one edge rotted away. Queen Monzee-ay continued: You got to talk son. Women like a man to talk. Not all the time but some of the time. You got to talk some of the time Murdo.

Sorry.

What you mean sorry? Dont you be sorry.

Murdo put his right hand to his eyes, shielding them.

Hey now, ssh, let me say about Sarah, you met her mom who is Carrie. Carrie is my own daughter but she aint like me. You think I'm tough! I aint tough, not one little bit. Carrie is tough. But now Sarah, Sarah is sweet and she is my girl, she tells me everything.

Murdo took his hand from his brow. Queen Monzee-ay was peering at him. I know about your sister. I know about your Mother. I know how hard it's been; I know it son. My Sarah tells me. Sarah is my girl; my most close friend – next to Edna.

Murdo smiled.

You laughing again! Miss Edna make you laugh! Hey now people quake with Edna! I'm talking men, rough tough men! She is Miss Kwankwan, you know who that is!

Murdo looked at her.

Woah, they walk in fear boy, you know what fear is! Queen Monzee-ay let go his hand, she tilted her head and squinted at him: What name do you call me?

Eh.

Queen Monzee-ay waited a moment. Murdo was frowning, thinking about this, until she said, Yeah Murdo, you got it now: you dont call me nothing.

No but

You dont.

Well because it's hard to say like I mean Queen and ye're not my grandmother.

No now I aint your grandmother! Queen Monzee-ay glared. You call me Miss Monzee-ay.

Murdo smiled.

Say it.

Miss Monzee-ay.

Monzee-ay, she said. No secret there son it's my own family name. Aint Cajun. Dont go mixing that up; Edna wont speak to you ever, not ever. We got our French they got theirs, we were here first son. We didnt come from no Canada. You know about that?

Murdo was looking at her. Queen Monzee-ay reached to the

other side of her chair, lifted a cigarette pack and extracted one, flicked the lighter to light it, and inhaled.

Murdo said, I'm not sure what ye mean.

No, they aint big on history here. Queen Monzee-ay exhaled smoke. You got to make your own space in this country Murdo. People dont give you that. You got to take it. You're American. White is American.

Murdo looked at her. Queen Monzee-ay raised her hand. White smooths the way, she said. Makes it easier for you. Black dont make nothing easy. We make a space we take a space. Queen Monzee-ay studied him, and smiled. It aint against you son. How long you in this country?

Two weeks.

Two weeks. My Lord, two weeks. You got it already. You walked in that door and here you are. That is the most amazing thing ever could happen. You come in our home. Our family. Queen Monzee-ay smiled, shaking her head.

Yeah but you invited me. Murdo shrugged.

Okay but you got to come. Someone invites you you got to come. You got invited and you came. That is what you did. You came. People dont do that. Folks want to give them something and they wont take it. They dont take nothing, only they will grab it. When you aint looking, they will push you out the road; they will stab you and they will beat you. Queen Monzee-ay paused in talking. She said, What you got to give they dont want. They take what they want. You know what I'm talking about?

Yes.

Queen Monzee-ay nodded. Now we got a little time left son and I will see you soon.

Thanks.

You do one tonight? Huh Murdo, want to do one?

Do one, yeah!

Okay.

Murdo grinned.

Go talk to Sarah and Gene about where you play now I dont want to be falling over your feet.

Well ye wont.

No. Queen Monzee-ay chuckled.

I only mean like I wont get in yer way.

I know you wont. I know that. She pointed round the side of the building. Go round there, she said, then pointed to the rucksack and the accordeon-case: Leave them in the truck. Joel'll bring you the turquoise.

Thanks.

Murdo walked closeby the wall of the building and this brought him out near the carpark which was busy now. A queue had formed by the club entrance. The big cowboy doorman was exchanging comments with people, having a laugh while ushering them in. Murdo saw Sarah standing near Joel's pick-up truck. The guy was there too, leaning against the side of a car parked next to it. Sarah was talking, moving about and waving her hands in that excited way she did. But how could ye not look at her? Any guy at all. Ye would. She had a tough way about her till ye knew her then she wasnt. He would never have come except for her. It was her, that was why he came.

Queen Monzee-ay thought he could talk to her. That was just stupid. Although he had to. It didnt matter anyway. He gripped the accordeon-case. More people queuing and cars arriving. Sarah saw him and waved, and came forwards. Murdo was already walking towards her. She called to him: I knew you would come Murdo!

She put her arm round his waist and leaned into him like a cuddle. He was still holding the accordeon-case. I knew you would, she said.

Yeah, he said and smiled. I went to yer house yesterday.

We left early morning.

Yeah the afternoon it was.

You came in the afternoon? Oh but you should have called.

I didnt have yer phone number. Ye forgot to give me it!

I did? Oh my God.

It doesnt matter anyway, I dont have a phone.

Oh Murdo.

No, well, I mean. . .

I am so sorry!

No like I was going to Allentown anyway so. . .I needed an accordeon.

But we were bringing one for you!

. . .

We were bringing one for you Murdo.

Murdo smiled. He said, It's just I needed to rehearse a bit so like I knew there was one in the pawnshop.

Sarah gazed at him.

You come by bus? asked Gene.

Murdo didnt look at Gene. Then he did look at him. He was just ordinary, looking back at him, expecting him just to say what it was, whatever: I came by bus, yeah. Murdo nodded.

Sarah made to touch his hand. Murdo shifted position slightly. It was the wrong Lafayette, he said.

Pardon me? said Sarah.

There's all these different Lafayettes like on the map. . .? Ye didnt tell me which one. So the one I thought was in the state of Georgia. Near Chattanooga.

Oh God.

Then I found out it was the state of Louisiana. It was another Lafayette altogether. Lucky I had a map.

What about your Dad? Didnt he know?

What?

Where Lafayette was? Didnt he know?

No. No, he didnt – well I didnt ask him. I mean I did and I didnt. What I mean is like well I didnt tell him. I didnt tell him I was coming.

Sarah was puzzled.

He would just have said no.

Oh Murdo.

Murdo shrugged. My Dad is just like. . . I didnt tell him because there was no point.

He'll be worried.

Yeah well maybe, but he doesnt have to be. Murdo sniffed and shook his head. He knows I'm here now anyway so it doesnt matter. He's coming.

Oh that's good, said Sarah.

Murdo looked at her. He lifted the accordeon-case and gestured with it. Yer Gran said to leave my stuff in the truck.

Hey. . . Gene took the accordeon-case from him, opened the boot of the car next to the truck. Safer in here, he said.

He settled the accordeon-case inside. Murdo passed him the rucksack. Thanks, he said.

You bet. We better get ready.

Yeah. Sarah smiled at Murdo, then touched his hand. It is so good you came.

Yeah, he said. It is, it's great. He pointed at the venue. What a brilliant place!

Sarah laughed.

Gene said, The old Jay Cee; cant ask for more!

Sarah walked on in front. Gene hesitated, waiting for Murdo. Murdo also hesitated, so then Gene walked on, following Sarah around the side of the building, across the little platform and in through the emergency exit door. Before entering Gene turned to Murdo: You know the Zadiks?

No.

We got their drums and bass man they are tight, they are tight. Yeah.

They're playing with us? asked Murdo.

Yeah.

Brilliant.

Yeah. Gene grinned.

Along the corridor Gene and Murdo waited ahead of Sarah. Behind her Queen Monzee-ay sat in the tiny room where she and Sarah dressed. Soon Joel appeared down by the entrance into the main area, and paused there with his hand on the door handle. He grinned seeing Murdo: Hey Murdo!

And he gestured at them to come forward. Gene walked on, then Murdo, with Sarah immediately behind, and out into the main area. They had to pass the bartender, the old guy with the hat who stood there with his arms folded. By now the club was more than half full and all tables taken. They stepped up onto the stage and into their positions. Joel had set out their instruments. Murdo pulled on the turquoise accordeon and tinkered with it. Gene was tuning his guitar and Sarah was leaning to talk to somebody down from the stage whoever that was, Murdo didnt see and wouldnt see, was avoiding the slightest eye contact with the audience and anybody in it. It was just something, he didnt do it. Getting into his own space. Although if Dad was there. Maybe he was. It would be good if he was. It didnt matter about stuff anyway because that was that. Although he felt like laughing, laugh laugh, hoh di hoh; he touched the keys: that particular sound the turquoise had, jees, yes, beautiful. Okay. That was that, his teeth clicked, they were clicking. Oh well, that was teeth, teeth clicked. The drummer and bass guitar from the Zadiks were onto the stage and chatting to Sarah. Probably they knew her. Of course they did. Everybody did! Queen Monzee-ay's granddaughter. Murdo saw them looking at him, and he nodded; they smiled in reply. So whatever. The time it was now, ha ha, he looked at the ceiling. Sarah was by the edge of the stage talking to somebody, whoever, Murdo looked to the rear, the drummer getting ready, the bass talking to Gene.

Then a silence, scattered applause. Murdo glanced around. Queen Monzee-ay had appeared at the backstage doorway. The old bartender held her accordeon and waited with it. She was wearing

a type of gown that made ye think of Africa. She s
upright way the same as Aunt Edna. When she came
did it like a march, hands at her side and pausing only
up onto the stage. This was one of the greatest moments
life. The musicians as well as the audience applauded ⎯ ⎯ she
raised slightly the right side of her dress, and stepped up onstage.
Murdo laughed suddenly but stopped. Greatest moments ever, in
his entire life. He felt this as strongly as ever he could feel anything.
Queen Monzee-ay circled the front of the stage, still in a march,
gazing out at the audience. She paused by the centre mic, and
raised her forearms. Now the bartender stepped up and handed
the accordeon to her, her accordeon, the fanciest ever ye saw, just
this beautiful beautiful amazing-mazing thing. Queen Monzee-ay
said: Thank you Vinnie, and he returned offstage. She stepped behind
the mic while pulling it on and adjusting the straps; she was staring
out at the audience like ensnaring them, looking straight into their
eyes because then what could they do? nothing, nobody could do
a damn thing because she was in control, this was Queen Monzee-ay,
and she was looking straight at them, she was the one, she was the
hero. She was, just the best ever; ever.

Did she wink? Maybe she did. She gave a beckoning wave, drawing
everybody in, into my parlour, and delivered the opening lines of
the track "C'est Moi" – one written by my sister, Queen Ida.

And she delivered the opening lines as a statement: Come listen
to my story; I come from Louisiane.

And she looked around the audience, then she said, I play my
music on an old accordeon. And she stepped back, but still to the
mic she sang in close:

Ooo la la.

And all of the musicians and very many members of the audience
responded in a shout:

Je suis comsois

People were onto the floor immediately. Queen Monzee-ay sang on from then. Sarah on le frottoir, Murdo accordeon, Gene on that strong-sounding blues guitar. On backing vocals Sarah, Murdo and the Zadiks drummer who also called line-end responses to Queen Monzee-ay in that jokey style, in French as well as English. The Zadiks bass played with great shoulder movements, like a tough guy walking, all the time looking to Queen Monzee-ay. Him and the drummer gave a fullness but a fighting rhythm that was just like the best because here she was, this was her, here in this very space, she was the tough guy walking, she was the one, she was Queen Monzee-ay. It was like what she had said about Aunt Edna: really it was her, she was the one made the tough guys quake, she was the Lady.

Once ye got it that was that. Murdo played in to the bass, so this best-sounding rhythm section; bass, drums and accordeon, freeing up Gene firing off on lead guitar, and freeing up Sarah too so she could play in to Queen Monzee-ay which was how Queen Monzee-ay wanted it herself. Sarah's laughing eyes.

She did not smile with the other musicians unless called for in the track. So ye were just like totally in the music all the time, ye didnt see anything else except them in their music while you were in yours and all what it was doing: making sure of the next thing along, where it came and how it came, including the bits inbetween like the "silences", except measured. So if it is like silence how can it be measured? Ha ha, the Zadiks bass and drummer knew, so did Murdo.

Each track played had been on the CDs. No surprises. Queen Monzee-ay introduced the first of her own, "L'air frais fait du bien", going back to when Murdo first played it on her back porch, and again that morning in the wee grass square. Yeah, she said, glancing back to the drummer: fresh air does you good. Serve it with weed soup man, c'est potage. Passez-moi le poivre!

The drummer responded: Le dîner est servi, where is the croutons!

The title was the line ending the chorus. The dancers paused in the dancing to yell: L'air frais fait du bien.

And the drummer called: Where is the croutons! It was just daft but total fun.

Two more of her own followed: on the first Murdo did something a little different and for part of it Queen Monzee-ay stepped aside to shift focus onto him. Next along was "Gens comme vous et moi", and this was different again. She raised her hand for quiet, and introduced it by telling about where she came from, to do with an island closeby the town of Natchitoches. She spoke in English and in French. The Creole people were her people, a French-speaking people from way before the Cajuns came. She directed this to the audience and for some it was special. If it was yer own family history how come people didnt know? People who were sitting stood to hear her and among them were Aunt Edna and Carrie at the family table.

Also Diego Narciso. Diego had arrived and was standing between the wall and the family table, obscured by people milling around the dancing area. His band were there too, watching from the side of the dancing area. How long they had been there who knows.

On the CD version Queen Monzee-ay sang part English, part French. Now she sang entirely in French and it brought the weary sadness even closer.

Maybe not sad, only weary; ye were picking yerself up and carrying on. This was the song; we pick ourselves up and we carry on, you and me and people like me: "Gens comme vous et moi".

Sarah stayed close to Queen Monzee-ay, moving step to step in total concentration. Somebody so close to you, so so close, so close you would have to be crying, just such a hero, such a fighter, ye couldnt do anything else. She was glowing! Love and pride, ha ha. She didnt cry. Murdo would have cried. Murdo was a crier. Sarah wasnt. Maybe it was men, women just whatever.

Towards the end of the song Queen Monzee-ay faded on vocal,

not like she had lost her voice, but that there was no voice left in the song, and she took it through an extra verse on accordeon alone, and she finished alone, the other musicians just watching her.

The audience applauded and Queen Monzee-ay bowed a little. This was the fifth song in. Queen Monzee-ay twirled a step and grinned. Hey! she was pointing offstage: Y'all know this cowboy?

People turned to see, and some recognised Diego.

Hey hombre! called Queen Monzee-ay.

He doffed the black studded cowboy hat in the same sweeping move he had used earlier in the day. The difference here was in Queen Monzee-ay. She had her hands on her hips in a swaggering stance, and she stepped from foot to foot. It looked like a dance step but it might have been an aid to her back, if she was experiencing any slight pain because her next move was to rub at the side of her hip. But she laughed, wagging her right forefinger at the floor space next to her and the mic. Hey Señor, Señor Narciso: you do one for us!

Diego was shaking his head, dismissing the idea.

Diego! I am ordering you, tout de suite, je suis pressé. Si hombre you come: now!

Laughter from the audience and band members. It was play-acting and it was funny and obvious how well they knew each other. Diego gave a tired gesture and looked to his band, then shrugged and got to his feet. Loud cheers and whistles from the audience. He lifted his accordeon from beneath the family table, and strolled forwards. His band stepped onstage without instruments. Vicenté and Esteban came to where Murdo stood. Vicenté shook hands with him and Esteban patted his shoulder. Hey Moordo, he whispered, we sing here eh.

They needed in to the mic. Murdo stepped away. Diego was in discussion with the Zadiks bass and drummer, and Queen Monzee-ay too. The bass nodded, passed his guitar to Santiago and the drummer vacated his place to Roberto. Diego moved to the centre mic, adjusting his accordeon. Murdo followed the two Zadiks musicians to the side of the stage, and caught sight of Dad way back at the bar, staring right at him. Declan Pike stood alongside drinking beer. Murdo hoped Dad was drinking one too but acted as though he hadnt seen him, like he didnt know he was there.

Onstage Diego had given a nod of the head and went straight into a song called "Margarita" which he sang entirely in Spanish, vocal backing from Vicenté and Esteban into the same mic with much whooping and on-the-spot stamping feet. Behind them Queen Monzee-ay marched across stage and back in short marching steps to the beat. She knew the song well. He was turning to play to her and calling to her in Spanish and she replied in Spanish, in French and in English. The life the fun the excitement. No time for anything else. Murdo punched the air. The Zadiks drummer glanced at him. Sorry, said Murdo. The guy was smiling. Murdo shrugged, smiled back at him.

Although things had changed with Dad being there it was like so what so what, things hadnt really changed at all. Him being there didnt have to make things awkward. It didnt have to do anything at all. Unless like if Dad wanted it to. Murdo was part of it and that was that. Santiago on bass was signaling to him, and the signal was clear in the raised eyebrows and changing facial expressions, What do you think what do you think?

And Murdo signaled a reply – a big grin and wee punching movement with his right fist – I think it is great I think it is great.

Jees and it was great. And real strong applause for Diego and the guys. They only stayed for the one. That was manners.

Queen Monzee-ay stepped to reclaim the mic. She and Diego kissed cheeks. She clapped him from the stage. Her own musicians returned. Murdo followed the Zadiks musicians back onstage where they retrieved the bass guitar and drums.

Murdo winked to Santiago and Roberto. Solid, he said.

Soleed. . .! Santiago grinned and slapped him on the shoulder.

Queen Monzee-ay waited by the mic until they had gone and

the audience quietened while the musicians prepared: Forget the Conjunto cowboy, she said, this here is my band. And I am one lucky lady. J'ai des bons amis, très bons amis, très très bons. Queen Monzee-ay looked behind to Sarah, Gene and Murdo, then at the bass and drums. Two of these Zadiks here, wonderful musicians, all the way from Opelousas, I taught them everything they know. Yeah – showed them the fast road outa there!

The bass, the drummer and the other Zadiks jeered. Queen Monzee-ay glared at them. Okay boys okay.

She continued: Ça me fait beaucoup de plaisir. Some young friends here with me this evening, young Gene there, geetar maestro; come all the way from Vicksburg Mississippi.

Gene stepped forward to acknowledge this. She gestured at Murdo who just grinned, watching her. Mister Murdo there, she said, and paused. What you laughing at! This boy laughs at nothing! Come all the way from someplace. Where?

There was a silence

Queen Monzee-ay turned to Murdo: Where you come from boy?

The bus station! he called.

Laughter from the audience and band members. Queen Monzee-ay chuckled and blew him a kiss. Yeah, she said, Murdo is my boy. Also here with me, from Allentown Mississippi, my own sweet grand-daughter Sarah, daughter of my daughter. Come forward girl!

From the family table there were extra cheers. Brought her own fan club, said Queen Monzee-ay. Okay! She stepped back from the mic now and began the next number, and followed with another; both uptempo. During the end applause she leaned to speak off-mic to Murdo: You do one for us now Murdo? Huh, you got something?

Yeah.

We all will pick up on it.

Okay.

Queen Monzee-ay spoke into the mic: Only one thing better than one accordeon is two accordeons: deux cœurs qui battent à l'unisson! Murdo here is going to lead the way on this next one now Murdo: what you going to play for us?

"I'm on the Wonder"?

Queen Monzee-ay looked at him. Son you can you play anything. You play anything you want.

Yeah, I'll play "I'm on the Wonder".

You want to play "I'm on a Wonder"?

Yeah.

Then that is nice, that is nice.

But you take vocal, you know the vocal?

Sure. I can take vocal. Queen Monzee-ay spoke into the mic: We'll do now "I'm on a Wonder", song by old brother Clifton. She stepped aside, and whispered, Take as long as you need on the opening; give folks here a chance to catch up. You been listening to Beau Jocque?

Beau Jocque, yeah.

Yeah, she said, and passed on the information to the others.

Sarah gave him a half wave and he smiled to her. He was by the centre mic. The audience waited and that was that; he started in and it was the straight blues. This was the song he could only play, whatever people thought, it didnt matter, he could play only this, and how Beau Jocque played it, going in that same way, doing it from this morning on that bench and the whole damn nightmare, from there, and where to? wherever: wherever it was leading. Queen Monzee-ay was waiting, Sarah and the guys closeby.

Murdo repeated the opening and was swaying, swaying sideways, allowing Queen Monzee-ay to the mic, and she edged into it, pulling in the band.

And that was them. It was all there in the song and playing of the song. There was nothing other, not any place. He was there in it and didnt have "to feel like he was" because he was; and not "feel like a musician" amongst other musicians because he was one. He was just Murdo and this was Murdo. So what? It didnt matter anything else, he would play whatever, anything;

and just say whatever, whatever he felt like saying; he was a musician and so what, that was all. He knew it and had done for such a long long while and was so weary weary but on ye go, ye just go on, that is that, picking yerself up, here he was. Whoever else was there that was them, it was up to them. Dad could do what he wanted to do. It was his business so he could just go ahead. It was up to him. Sarah too, she was great and never a word against her. It is just how it was. Oh Murdo, when she said Oh Murdo. She knew it too. Oh Murdo. That is just like another world, Oh Murdo, if it was another world and they were in it, but they werent, they were just bumping into each other, and maybe having fun.

He was glad when the song ended. It had ended. He brought it to a close. It was his to do that. His to begin, his to end. Queen Monzee-ay waited a moment for the audience and while they were clapping she gave Murdo a kiss, their noses touching over the boxes, which was fun, and people laughed. Murdo heard them – heard them clapping, heard them laughing – he wasnt looking hardly, only at one point he did, smiling like a thanks, whatever the thanks was and what it was for, whatever, it was just everything, him and them all, he was only a part of it, just like everybody. Then Queen Monzee-ay, he was gazing at her, seeing her give one of her glares into the mic, grabbing a silence: the last song was over now here was this one: Hey, hey, hush now, mes enfants; mes petits-enfants. . . And she chuckled looking all roundabout at everybody, ones sitting, ones standing and all along by the bar, everybody just waiting. She whispered: Quel âge me donnes-tu? You think I'm past it! She glared at everybody, at the band and everybody else: You think I'm past it! Réfléchez bien avant de répondre!

There was laughter. Okay now, she said, we play one more; one more outa here, taking the fast road to Texas, wishing Diego and his boys fond farewells home – on se reverra bientôt. Song by sister Ida, "I-10 Express".

When they left the stage people were wanting to talk with Queen Monzee-ay and Sarah stayed alongside her. Gene was with the musicians. Dad wasnt there. Murdo had thought he might be. A couple of people were looking at him and it was like ye didnt know what to do, where to look if ye saw them and they saw you seeing them. He was glad to go backstage along the corridor. He had a quick wash in the wee dressing room – before Sarah and Queen Monzee-ay came. Then he stepped outside, down from the wooden platform. He stood with his back to the wall.

It was dark and peaceful, with a mild breeze. Across was the wide empty area; no lighting there, the old foundations now unseen, whatever it had been in the past. Earlier he heard the sound of a train, long drawn out from someplace not too far away. Louisiana. It was good just standing there and thinking that. Ye heard it in songs but not much and he didnt know much. Without anybody there it was like just him, it was him there and the old place, old foundations and whatever it was, Louisiana. He didnt have to be here but he was, he came and this was him, here from the inside out, whatever it was, it made him feel something. But what? He didnt know, he just liked it, and that blues there in his napper:

> I'm on the wonder
> tell me why you wanna walk away
> I dont wanna come back home
> Lord knows I love you
> but I'm living in misery

Ye had to be old to sing it. Or did ye? He wasnt living in misery. Brains just make the connection. That was brains, what do brains do, if they are for something, like ye have brains, we all have brains and what do they tell ye! Nothing, just like conduits; the mother-board; algorithm of algorithms. Ye still have to do it.

Dad being here was like from another world. The world of "the real Murdo". Not his own world but the one where everything else went on, where Murdo was just whatever. Dad joined them together. With Dad here it was "the real Murdo".

Time to go back inside. Only he didnt want to go back inside, talking with people and whatever, he just wasnt able to. To be being with people. He didnt want to be with people, only like being swallowed up if he could be swallowed up he wanted to be swallowed up. Jees. The darkness, the old foundations. Oh God.

Wherever Dad was. Outside with the smokers, Declan Pike was a smoker.

It would be hard for Dad saying hullo, with Sarah's family, he wouldnt want to be pushy. Oh sorry for that time about Sunday lunch, we had to get our bus.

Murdo had to go inside. He had to go inside. Anything else was stupid. Imagine walking, walking, away in the darkness, Lord knows I love you, where would ye go? Anywhere.

He opened the side exit door and returned through the backstage corridor, aware of the old posters and photographs. He paused by the door out to the main hall and pushed it ajar. Nobody here, jees. He exited. But Santiago and the guys from Diego Narciso's band were at the side, like as if waiting for him, they were, saw him and came toward him, excited and wanting to talk. But there wasnt time for that because Dad was over by the main door entrance and gazing across.

Murdo turned in the other direction, as though casually, crossing the floor to Sarah's family table where he was greeted as a friend of the family, which he was anyway. He found a place on the fringe of their table. Gene was sitting close to Sarah who was telling them about some wee incident to do with the gig, and they were laughing about it. Murdo didnt get it, but didnt try to. He was glad just to sit and keep out the road, listen to the taped music. He would have to talk to Dad but not now. The truth is he was tired. His stomach too, his stomach was kind of

Nerves. He needed the toilet. But a shit! Jees, where? This was the worst. He stared at the floor to out-think it, stared at the floor. Things in considering, in considering. Stuff. Things. Two hundred dollars. Pay it back. Obviously he would, that was obvious. He still had some of it left. Everything else he would pay back. Everything, just like everything everything.

There was nowhere to go except sit here. Although it was up to him to go to Dad. Dad would never come to him. Sarah's family table, he wouldnt intrude. Bad manners is how he would see it.

Oh well. He yawned. It was true but he needed a sleep. That was one thing. Oh but his stomach. Nerves again.

The taped music: the same guy singing as before, a nice swinging blues with piano, sax and drums. Ye could picture the old bartender as the piano player, and if ye interrupted him playing, Where's my gun till I fucking shoot ye.

Queen Monzee-ay had appeared, over by the backstage door in her ordinary clothes; ready to leave. She was signing flyers and tickets and people were taking photographs. Her and the family were going for a meal someplace. Murdo was welcome. He knew he was but it wouldnt happen. It wouldnt happen because with Dad it would be something else.

Somebody poked him in the shoulder: Esteban from Diego's band; he whispered: Moordo, come. Beer for you.

Murdo grinned. Esteban gestured to where the other guys were standing waiting for him. Vicenté clapped him on the shoulder. Hey Moordo!

The other two were Santiago and Roberto and it was high-fives: Moordo!

That was about all they could say, Moordo. Murdo liked "Moordo". Moordo was better than Murdo. Santiago lifted the bottle of beer from the floor, poured it into a polystyrene cup and passed him it. Esteban said, Eh Moordo, you play with a white people band?

Do ye mean like in my own country? In Scotland do ye mean?

Si, Scotland.

Yeah.

Irish music uh? asked Vicenté.

Well Scottish.

Scotteesh! Santiago laughed and whispered something in Spanish to Roberto.

You didnt come to our gig, said Esteban.

No eh the time wasnt good.

Okay.

Moordo, you know Conjunto? asked Vicenté. Conjunto?

No.

You know Tejano? Tejano music?

Tex-Mex? said Esteban.

No.

Vicenté said, You hear us with Diego, is Conjunto. Vicenté pointed to the other three. We are Conjunto band. Looking for people.

No people, said Esteban quickly. Un accordeonista.

Si, said Vicenté, one accordeon. You want to play with us?

What?

Esteban said, Come with us in our band Moordo. We here.

You play with us? asked Vicenté. We have gigs.

Murdo grinned, he glanced from one to the other, and sipped the beer which was a kind of lager and sharp-tasting.

Santiago reached to clap him on the shoulder. Moordo! he said. He had a phone in his hand and gestured with it to take a photograph. Eh Moordo. . . He took one of Murdo.

You come with us, added Esteban.

Vicenté said, You did not sleep any place. They tell us, last night. This night come with us in motel.

Murdo grinned.

Santiago clenched his fist. You accordeon! Heyy!

Tomorrow we go early, said Vicenté.

Early early, said Esteban.

We go home. Vicenté said, You come with us. You play with us man. You wanna play with us?

Santiago pointed to the ceiling and wagged his finger at Murdo. Dios mío! Un accordeonista.

Is true, said Esteban. We need and you are here.

Murdo laughed but smothered it fast. Yeah, he said, but I dont have anything I mean like clothes and stuff, I've only got eh I mean hardly anything.

Vicenté spoke in Spanish to Santiago and Roberto, then to Murdo: You need clothes, we got clothes.

Santiago said, Si clothes, clothes.

Roberto now spoke in Spanish to the others and they laughed. Roberto high-fived Murdo who didnt know what it was about.

Is your accordeon, said Esteban. Roberto says no you – dont give shit for you!

Aw! Murdo chuckled.

Vicenté said, We are good band you know. Hey we got gigs man.

Gigs! Santiago clenched his fist, punched the air.

Murdo raised the polystyrene cup to his mouth, sipped the beer. Joel appeared by his side and whispered, Hey man.

Hi, said Murdo. Across at the bar he saw Dad watching, but acted like he didnt know, and sipped again at the beer. The others were watching him and looking at Joel. Joel said, They ask you the big question? They been talking about you all night man they want you playing the oompah ooompah stuff. Joel winked. Like you are white, they think that is cool man. Joel snapped his fingers: Get more women that way.

Esteban and Vicenté laughed.

Cómo? said Santiago.

Esteban and Vicenté translated for him and Roberto. Roberto made a shrieking noise, pointing at Vicenté. Esteban said, Is true, Vicenté, he dont get no woman!

Seis meses! said Santiago.

Vicenté formed the shape of a pistol with his right hand, pointed at Santiago's head and made the sound of an exploding gun: Pwohhh! Pwohhh!

Aahh. Santiago staggered, kidding on he had been shot. The others laughed, Murdo too — it was funny, Santiago was funny.

Joel said quietly. Hey Murdo I gotta go.

What?

We all are leaving, gran and everybody. You want to come say hullo? Joel smiled. Hullo, goodbye?

Jees!

And it was noticeable that the tables were full again. A couple of the Zadik Strollers band were onstage footering with the instruments and preparing. They were the headline show, about to start, and people were returning from the interval. Murdo was about to follow Joel who had continued along towards the backstage area but Vicenté was tugging at his arm. Moordo you come with us; we got beds beds beds, bathrooms, shower rooms.

Bars, added Santiago.

More bars, said Esteban. Diego got one big suite. We got two rooms, two rooms, space for you.

Thanks, said Murdo.

Then tomorrow early, nos vamos.

Nos vamos, we leave early, early early, said Vicenté.

Vicenté and the guys were waiting for him to say something. Murdo saw Dad and Declan Pike coming toward him. Declan made a punching movement in salute. Murdo smiled. My father, he said, it's my father. He indicated Dad who was behind Declan. Declan arrived first and gripped Murdo's wrist: Sensational man! Sensational! Where d'you learn Zydeco music? you get that in Scotland! He laughed.

Dad was hanging back. Murdo smiled at him by Declan's shoulder. Hey Dad. . .

Okay son? Dad reached to him, and they shook hands. Dad said, It was good.

Yeah?

Dad smiled. Murdo leaned closed to him. Sorry Dad, he said. I'm so sorry.

Ssh, said Dad.

Diego's band were talking in Spanish together. Santiago said something and the others laughed and looked from Dad to Murdo.

Murdo scratched his head and added, Diego's band eh. . .

Exactly! Declan chuckled. Now what I want to know boy: how did you do that? Diego Narciso. Declan growled: Thirty years man and boy and I aint ever seen Diego Narciso man in the flesh man know what I'm saying, he dont stray farther north than Austin! Declan kissed Murdo on the cheek. It was a smacker and Murdo wiped at it.

Declan laughed.

Esteban and Vicenté were talking together and attempting to draw Murdo into it but it was impossible and just too much, they all seemed to be talking and other people were there like the Zadiks bass guitarist passing by and giving him a wee salute, and Murdo could have said cheerio to him too but it was outside especially where he needed to be and he said to Dad, I've got to say cheerio to people. Queen Monzee-ay Dad, like I mean she's leaving and eh. . . Murdo glanced at Vicenté and the band.

Yeah of course, said Dad.

Murdo began walking towards the main hall exit at once, but Vicenté and the guys followed on, and behind them Dad and Declan. Vicenté called: So man you got place tonight with us, okay, we got beds, bathrooms. Tomorrow night is rehearse. Go in studio, okay?

Studio! said Santiago.

Declan was looking from one to the other. Dad too, attending to it all but not knowing what was happening except maybe the word "tomorrow". Declan said to him: Room with us too Tom, huh? Murdo?

Of course! What d'ye mean? Dad frowned and glanced at Murdo. What a room? Ye mean a bed? Of course a bed, of course. Ye dont have to ask something like that son we got an extra one in.

Murdo nodded. They passed along the L-shaped lobby. Dad said, I'm picking something up here son and I'm no sure what it is.

. . .

Eh?

Murdo didnt reply, but continued walking. When they stepped outside Declan made a V-sign of peace with his right two fingers, and brought out the cigarette pack, extracted a cigarette and had it in his mouth before leaving the building. The big cowboy doorman watched them exit. Dad said quietly: What the boys there were saying son. . . Eh? What were they saying?

Nothing Dad I mean can we talk about it after?

Dad looked at him.

Over in the parking area Gene was helping Joel with the roadie stuff, loading the pick-up truck. Queen Monzee-ay was by the corner of the building surrounded by a wee crowd. Some of her CDs had been available and she was signing them and saying hullo. Sarah and Aunt Edna were to the side of her, with Diego Narciso and Sarah's parents. Murdo went to them. Dad followed, and Declan came too. Sarah patted Murdo on the arm. You going with the guys? she said.

Aunt Edna chuckled. Set Texas on fire huh?

Dad had overheard. Declan too. Murdo had to say something. Diego's band, he said.

Diego's band? said Declan.

Well not like Diego I mean like his band, the guys playing with him.

What. . .? Dad said.

Dad was staring at him. Murdo sniffed and looked away. He said to Sarah: You going home now?

Sarah was about to reply but Aunt Edna cut her off: Murdo, we are going to eat. And you are most welcome to come along with us. Aunt Edna said to Dad: You like salt cod sir? We are going to eat salt cod.

Sarah raised her eyebrows. It's like chewing rubber Murdo honest to God.

Aunt Edna chuckled.

You going home after that? he asked Sarah.

Right now, yeah.

Oh. . . Murdo smiled, after a moment.

She touched his wrist.

No, he said, I just eh. . . He nodded. Vicenté and the guys had come from the entrance and were chatting with Diego. Santiago especially, doing most of the talking.

You okay? asked Sarah.

Yeah.

Aunt Edna spoke to Dad, pointing her forefinger at him: These boys are good.

Playing with Diego. . .! Declan smiled. Oh yeah.

Dad didnt know what was happening. It was obvious the way he was looking. Murdo avoided him and said to Declan, It's the guys themselves. They've got their own band. Murdo sniffed. They think I'll fit.

Declan said, Well sure you'll fit son. You will fit right in there.

Murdo shrugged, glancing at Dad.

They're all related, said Aunt Edna.

Declan growled: Where they come from everybody's related.

Queen Monzee-ay had appeared next to Aunt Edna and Sarah. She had taken her cigarettes from her bag, passed one to Aunt Edna. She said to Dad, Your son should go.

Dad looked at her as though he didnt know what she meant, but he should have by this time because of what people were saying. Murdo said, Dad what it is their own accordeon's been playing with another band and the guys are looking for another one who'll just be there with them so they can get some proper rehearsal in.

Sarah grinned. Murdo smiled at her.

Aunt Edna said, I like San Antonio; river walking, honky tonking.

Diego and the guys had come forward to hear what was being said. Diego and Santiago exchanged words in Spanish. Santiago pointed at Dad. Diego stared at Dad. Aunt Edna whispered to Queen Monzee-ay and it may have been in French, then spoke quietly to Diego who nodded and raised the black studded cowboy hat to scratch at the side of his head. He peered at his wristwatch. Queen Monzee-ay said to him: The boys got some gigs lined up huh?

Vicenté called the answer: Si señora we got Matamoros through Nogales. El Paso, Mexicali.

Declan said, Conjunto circuit huh?

Si, si! So you know is for Murdo, we want him come play with us. Be good for him; good for us.

Yeah. Yeah, said Declan. He glanced at Dad although most were looking to Declan. Dad hadnt spoken a word hardly. It was like people had forgotten to include him. But Dad would speak. He was just taking things in. Dad did that. He would say it soon enough. Whatever. Him and not anybody else. Dad didnt care about anybody else, if people were looking or what. If he thought something he would say it, and it didnt matter about other stuff.

Murdo waited. Sarah was watching him. He smiled a moment then looked at Dad. Dad just shrugged. Murdo stared at the ground.

What are they talking about son? Dad said, We're going home on Tuesday. Do you know what they're talking about?

Dad was not smiling. Murdo could have. Dad spoke directly to Declan. I dont know what people are talking about.

Declan coughed and cleared his throat and probably would have spat except so many people were there. He was a fine musician. People here didnt know that. Murdo could have told them. To the side it looked like Aunt Edna was going to say something but she didnt. Vicenté and the guys were looking at him. And Dad, and Dad said, What's happening here? Eh? Murdo we're going home on Tuesday. Am I missing something here?

Murdo stared at him.

Eh? Murdo?

Yeah Dad well like if I could maybe stay on a wee bit.

What do ye mean?

Well maybe I could just stay and like, play with the guys, like if I could just stay on and maybe. . .

I dont know what ye're talking about.

If I could just stay on and maybe. . .

Son we're here on holiday. Dad smiled. This is a holiday.

Dad. . .

Sarah was watching, standing closeby Aunt Edna. In the background Diego and the band also were listening; Esteban and Vicenté translating for Diego, Santiago, and Roberto.

Dad said, It's a holiday.

Murdo said, It's not a holiday.

Yes it is.

Dad it's not. It's not.

I'm not talking about this here.

Dad, it's not a holiday.

Aye it's a holiday of course it's a holiday. Dad addressed Queen Monzee-ay. It is a holiday, he said. You know that, like a vacation. We're here on vacation.

Queen Monzee-ay didnt reply.

Murdo said, Dad I'm sorry.

What about?

Murdo noticed Sarah's attention distracted by her parents over by the pick-up truck, there with Joel and Gene and waiting to leave. Sarah signaled to them.

What about? said Dad.

Eh, well. Murdo sniffed.

What are ye sorry about?

Nothing. I'm just like thinking maybe I would I mean eh just stay here and just like play with the guys. And come home after.

Dad was staring at him. The others were all intent on what was happening but keeping their distance. Declan too, now smoking a cigarette and standing back a couple of paces.

Murdo said, Sorry Dad.

Son ye cant. It's not possible. Ye cannay just stay here. It is not possible.

Yeah but if I do the gigs and came home afterwards?

It is not possible.

But Dad.

Ye've got to listen to me here son it is not possible. Ye're sixteen years of age.

Nearly seventeen Dad I'm coming up for seventeen.

Ye're sixteen years of age. Dad glanced at Declan. Declan it isnay possible!

Declan sighed and nodded. It is kinda complicated, like the bureaucracy son know what I'm saying? it's all in there, red tape and like man. . . Declan shook his head, dragged on his cigarette.

Dad said wearily, Visas and work permits, Social Security cards, Green Cards. Ye've no even got yer passport son I mean ye left it at Uncle John's. Ye left yer passport. Dad peered at Queen Monzee-ay. The boy forgot his passport!

Well he dont need one for Texas, said Queen Monzee-ay.

No! said Sarah.

Declan chuckled, and growled, You don't need no passport for Texas.

Diego said to Esteban: Texas? Passport?

What I'm saying is it's ID for everything. He needs permission. Dad glanced at Murdo: Permission son ye need permission.

Aunt Edna muttered: Permission, toujours.

At the side Esteban and Vicenté were explaining things to Diego in Spanish. Santiago and Roberto were listening closely. Diego nodded. He strolled the few paces to Dad, and stood directly in front of him. Dad stared at him. Diego returned the stare, then he tapped Dad on the shoulder. Hey, he said, Moordo's father. Amigo.

Declan said, Murdo's father is Tom, his name is Tom.

Tom, amigo. Diego laid his hands on both Dad's shoulders: I get permission. For Moordo. I get permission. I get permission now. He turned to Murdo, still with his hands on Dad's shoulders: Moordo hey – Moordo, el musico talentoso.

Murdo smiled, then stopped it.

Diego said: Moordo! You need permission. I give this permission to you. I Diego Narciso, citizen San Antonio in state of Tejas – Texas – all power vested in me, ever and ever forever eternal.

Diego took his hands from Dad's shoulders, stepped back a pace, tapped himself on the chest and wagged his forefinger at Murdo: Moordo! I give to you permission.

Diego faced Tom again, and he signed with his right hand as in a Papal dispensation: All power vested in me I do permit your son, Moordo, y una accordeon, do in hell what he wanna do, okay? Okay.

Dad stared at him. Declan chuckled, and others too, but Dad wasnt smiling and he still didnt answer.

Okay? asked Diego.

Dad still did not smile.

Hay un bar cerca de aqui, said Diego. We may celebrate? Tom, you drink beer with me?

Diego placed both hands onto Dad's shoulders again, staring into his eyes. It was fun but it wasnt. Dad was not good. Dad was trapped. Diego was not smiling so much now. He said: Hey, Tom, boys look out for your son. Dont worry. Got gigs, got money. Your son is okay. In San Antonio is good, good with us. Family is there, I am there. Your son is very safe señor. Is all okay. He got place there. My family, they family; all people and friends. Diego shrugged, indicating Santiago: Crazy one is my nephew, son of my little brother.

Diego nodded to Dad, he smiled a moment then turned to Queen Monzee-ay and Aunt Edna and blew them a kiss. He signaled the band and clapped his hands together sharply: Okay we leave, hurry, say with Moordo for morning; all detail, motel. Hurry. Car keys? Esteban!

Esteban came forwards.

A beer, food.

Si Diego.

Diego's team had two vehicles; a huge pick-up and a huge 4x4. Queen Monzee-ay and Aunt Edna walked with him part of the way and they were talking and laughing. Another guy was driving the 4x4 and he stood by the passenger side waiting. When Diego arrived the man opened the door for him and closed it afterwards.

Santiago was driving the pick-up truck and the other three were traveling with him. Esteban returned for a final word with Murdo, he clasped his hand firmly and said quietly, Tomorrow we come seven o'clock. Okay?

Seven o'clock?

Early early, yes. We come for you. Okay?

Murdo nodded.

Esteban whispered. You say to your father?

Yeah.

Yeah? said Esteban.

Yeah. Murdo nodded.

Okay. Esteban smiled at him a moment longer, then clenched his fist and returned to the pick-up. The others were waiting. They exchanged waves with Murdo from there.

Queen Monzee-ay pulled a wrap more tightly round herself. You find it chilly? she said to Aunt Edna. I find it chilly. Brr.

Cold huh? Stars in the sky, said Aunt Edna.

Declan said to Queen Monzee-ay: Miss Monzee-ay tonight was special and you are very very special. Declan reached to shake her hand.

Thank you sir, said Queen Monzee-ay.

Declan is a musician, said Murdo.

I know, she said.

Declan smiled.

But ye are, said Murdo, ye're brilliant.

Well now. Declan nodded.

Sarah's father was beckoning to them. It was like the final call and Murdo turned from them then turned back again. Eh Murdo! Aunt Edna held her arms out to him for a quick cuddle, but she gave him a longer one. You take care now ya hear!

Then Queen Monzee-ay for another cuddle but this was briefer, hardly at all. Oh we touched noses already, she said, we dont need no heavy hugging! Then she spoke quietly: Now we will be seeing you Murdo okay? You got all the info now huh! She glanced at Sarah who grinned. Emails and stuff, you got that?

Yeah, said Sarah.

Murdo nodded.

Yeah and you know where we're living.

Murdo smiled.

Okay, she said, and put her arm round his waist and smiled to Aunt Edna: This boy laughs at the drop of a hat.

Murdo stared at her.

You are my boy, she said. You think I will forget that? I will not forget it.

Yeah.

Yeah. Queen Monzee-ay nodded. Yeah. She smiled and kept walking.

Aunt Edna called back: We are going for something to eat! Callaloo Kitchen! Mes enfants, Edna goes ethnic, we eat salt fish.

Murdo watched them walk to the vehicles. Sarah was there beside him. They exchanged looks. Sarah smiled. They started toward the carpark area, but keeping a yard apart. Sarah said, It's wonderful you came. We needed you.

Well ye didnt really.

We did, you know we did.

He snorted.

Sarah stopped and put her hand onto his wrist. Murdo. . .

Ha ha! he said. The idea I wouldn't come!

She kept a hold of his wrist. Oh Murdo.

He was trying to take his wrist away. Sarah let him do it. He looked away from her. Of course I would come. Of course. Ye just eh. . . I mean. . . Murdo had gone red, the reddest. His eyes closed a moment, he wasnt smiling. Sarah was watching him.

What? she said. Murdo, what?

Nothing.

Oh Murdo.

I just. . . Murdo stopped to breathe. What age is Gene?

Sarah gazed at him.

No, he said, I was just eh. . .

He's twenty.

Is that his car I mean like is it his?

It's old Murdo.

He frowned at her.

Well yeah! she said. Of course it is! My God!

They had stopped walking now, inside the carpark area. Queen Monzee-ay and Aunt Edna had entered the rear seats of one car. Sarah's mother stepped into the front passenger side and her father into the driver's seat. Gene and Joel were closeby.

Sarah whispered, You okay?

. . .

Murdo?

Yeah, I just feel a bit stupid.

Oh Murdo.

I do. He shook his head and sighed. Then he smiled. Are you still going to that college thing?

Yeah!

He chuckled and was maybe about to say more but she reached for his hand and pressed it. I got to go Murdo. I got to go now. You'll stay in touch huh?

Yeah.

You got to.

I will.

People will want to know.

Murdo nodded. Sarah hesitated then leaned to him, put her arm round his waist and kissed him on the side of the face. Murdo remained, after she had gone in Gene's car; she didnt look back. Her family's car now moved off. Her father tooted the horn. The rear passenger window was down, Aunt Edna peering out. Murdo grinned, he waved to her, he waved to Queen Monzee-ay although he couldnt see her, she was on the other side.

Joel was there by the side of the pick-up and signaling him: Hey Murdo! You forgot something there?

Murdo frowned, he went forwards. It was the rucksack, Joel had his rucksack and accordeon-case, he brought them from the rear of the truck and passed them to him.

Jeesoh!

Joel clapped him on the shoulder then entered the driver's side. We'll see you sometime huh?

Definitely.

You going with the guys?

I think so, yeah.

Yeah. Joel nodded, switched on the engine.

Murdo stepped back. He pulled the rucksack on over his shoulders, lifted the accordeon-case, watching the pick-up roll forwards. Joel had his hand out the side window, a wave. Murdo waved in reply.

At the entrance to the Jay Cee Lounge Dad stood to the side of Declan. Declan was chatting to the cowboy doorman, smoking a cigarette with him. Murdo walked to stand next to Dad. That's them all away, he said.

Yeah, said Dad.

When the cab arrived Dad made to lift the accordeon-case but Murdo kept a grip on it, settled it into the boot next to the rucksack. He got into the rear passenger seat, and Dad in the other. Declan sat next to the driver who was a white guy and knew all about the oil industry and maybe worked in it himself at one time or else knew people who did. Him and Declan spoke about working offshore and named actual rigs and famous guys who worked on them. Quite interesting stuff – Dad was listening – but Murdo was just tired, probably he dozed most of the way.

★

Dad had the key to the room which was on the ground level. A couple of chairs were along from the door. Inside two single beds and a double. The double was nearest the door and had Declan's stuff on it. Him and Dad had six-packs of beer in the room. Declan lifted one and returned outside for a smoke.

Dad sat on the edge of the bed nearest the opposite wall. So the one in the middle was for Murdo. He yawned, lowered the rucksack and accordeon-case down on the floor between the two, and sat on the edge of his, elbows on his knees and hands clasped, gazing at the floor. Ye hungry? said Dad, after a moment.

Yeah! Murdo smiled.

There's sandwiches in the fridge.

Great. Murdo continued to sit there.

Tired?

Yeah.

I'll not ask what ye've been up to! Ye can understand but I was worried.

Yeah Dad, I'm sorry.

I dont mean for ye to apologize, I'm just saying.

I'll pay back the money.

It doesnay matter about the money.

Well I will.

Murdo it's not an issue. It's just how I worry, ye know. I'm yer father. I cannay help it. People worry.

Dad I phoned Aunt Maureen.

I know, it was good ye did.

354

Murdo sighed, he leaned to drag over the rucksack.

Dad watched him a moment. We have to talk about things. I mean ye must know it cant happen. They're not going to change their rules for ye son, they're not going do that.

I'm not asking them to.

It doesnay matter what Diego said. It would be great if things worked that way, but they dont.

Murdo had unzipped the main rucksack compartment and was poking around inside. He yawned then rose from the bed with his toilet bag and some clothes.

Son ye've got to let me speak.

Dad I need a shower.

No. They've all been speaking except me.

Well I've not been speaking either.

Okay so now's the time.

Yeah but if I can shower first. We can talk after. Dad there will be time.

No there wont. You'll come out the shower and fall into bed, I know what like ye are after a gig.

Murdo groaned.

Hey, I'm not the baddy here. It's just I'm worried. Come on, sit down a minute.

I would rather stand.

They're all in the right and it's me in the wrong.

Ye're not in the wrong Dad.

Of course I am. I'm the only one saying no! no! ye're too young, how will ye manage! Dad shook his head. Seriously, he said. Nay wonder I get irritated. They go home and sleep at night. I dont. How can I? How can I?

Dad!

No. I just lie there, worrying. Bloody Mexico! You're no going to Mexico Murdo I dont want ye going there.

Dad it's Texas.

It's Mexico. That's what they mean when they say the Valley.

Dad they mean the border, the Mexican border.

In America it's the Mexican border, not if ye're in Mexico; it's the American border over there. Whatever it is it's a border. Ye step from there to there. It's a line son not a place.

I thought it was a river.

Dad looked at him. It's a nightmare. That's what it is: killings and murders; dope smugglers, private armies. I've got to tell ye what I think – ye might no like it – it's a fantasy.

Dad what's a fantasy?

This; what ye're talking about.

It's everybody else as well.

Yeah – except me, everybody except me. They all know and I dont. I'll tell ye something son people here go about in a stupor. They dont seem to know anything. Dad walked a couple of steps, shaking his head. Seriously, he said, it's kind of strange. They dont seem to know anything at all about what goes on in the world; politics and history. Geography! What a joke! It's a bloody dream world; that's what they're living in.

Dad we're only talking about music.

Oh are we! Is that what we're talking about? I've been with Declan all day, away and tell him that. He's a musician too if ye remember.

Of course I remember, he's a brilliant guitarist.

Yeah well. . .

Dad, he is.

Dad shrugged. I'm no disputing it. Actually it makes my case. How come he works offshore? Eh? He hardly does any gigs at all. He's not even part-time, he's just once in a blue moon. That was a one-off last Saturday. And how much do ye think he got paid for it?

It's not my business.

Seriously, how much? Think about it son. I'm talking the practicalities.

Murdo shrugged.

How much did Queen Monzee-ay get paid for tonight?

Aw Dad.

No. I'm only asking the question. Ye've got to. Never mind you and the girl and the other guys. Did ye ever hear about the big opera star that came to Glasgow for a one-off concert and got paid a million dollars? D'ye know what the orchestra got? Bugger all. Nothing. None of the orchestra got paid a penny.

What d'ye mean?

I'm not meaning anything except what I'm saying. If that was Queen Monzee-ay's only gig in the past six months, how much did she get paid?

Murdo frowned.

And is that to last her another six months?

I dont know what ye mean.

Is that how long it'll take her to get another gig?

Dad she's retired.

Dont fall for that one, retired, it's only rich people retire son the rest of us stagger on. It's just people wont give ye the right wage for the job. They want somebody young because they dont have to pay them so much. So you're left twiddling yer thumbs. What I'm saying is it's a struggle and a fight, a total fight.

Queen Monzee-ay fights.

Sure she does. All I'm saying is ye've got to ask these questions. How does she get by? Is she on an old age pension?

I dont know Dad how do I know! Murdo shook his head. Jeesoh Dad.

I'm only asking.

The family has the store. That's her store. She bought it when she was making money.

Right, replied Dad, okay. So that keeps her going. What about the rest of the family?

How do I know?

I'm only asking.

Well Dad ye're better asking her. I'm no being cheeky.

I know ye're not. Dad nodded. It is interesting but, when ye think about it in that way. Likes of the Gathering, when Declan played the gig, nobody paid to get in. Did ye notice?

They paid at the entrance.

That was for the actual Gathering Murdo. That was yer ticket for the whole thing. Everything that was there. That was what ye paid for. All the games and prizes and the kids' competitions, bouncy castles, everything. Yer entrance ticket paid the lot. The dance too. That dance band, how much did they get paid? Add in yer traveling costs and the rest of it. These guys needed a truck for all their sound equipment. Plus they had two roadies.

The roadies were their pals.

It doesnay mean they dont get paid. They will. Then there were seven guys in the band. Seven guys! Motel costs, petrol, food. People have got to eat and that needs paying. Dad smiled. Ye've got to pay for food ye know. People dont give ye it for nothing.

Murdo stared at him.

Dad smiled for a moment. They dont, he said.

Murdo nodded. I made eleven dollars and seventy cents busking this morning.

Ye were busking!

Yeah.

Busking?

Yeah Dad why not. Eleven seventy, it was enough for a meal, more than enough. Murdo shrugged, and made to enter the bathroom, but he paused and said, I know people need to work like in an ordinary job Dad I know that. That was always Mum, that was her. Stick in at school and go to college. It was so as I could get a job and then I could like relax and play music and not have to worry about the next meal. I mean, I know that Dad. Murdo sighed.

Dad had his hands in his pockets. He glanced at the front door, then back at Murdo and he said quietly, How much did Diego Narciso get paid for tonight?

No Dad.

For talking's sake?

No Dad no; jeesoh!

Come on, what? A hundred dollars, a thousand dollars, ten thousand dollars? What?

How do I know?

How many people went to the gig?

Murdo shook his head and stepped inside the bathroom doorway.

Just work it out, said Dad.

I dont want to work it out. I need to shower and go to my bed. The guys are coming early.

Dad stared at him.

Seven or something.

So ye're going with them? Dad smiled. I'm not that bad surely.

. . .

Eh? That ye want to run away. Am I that bad? Really, am I? Dad was still smiling. He shrugged. I think I'm entitled to ask that.

Dad

No, well. . . Dad shrugged. We've been through a lot together.

Murdo gazed at him.

Eventually Dad said, I need to ask Declan something. Dad held up his hand. Just a minute son, if ye dont mind. He opened the outside door. Declan, he said, will ye come in a minute? Just for a minute.

Declan appeared in the doorway, gripping a bottle of beer by the neck. You want the heavy-weights in on this?

Naw just eh, we're trying to bring some clarity into this.

Oh yeah so you got me, yeah. . . Declan yawned.

No I just mean like the practicalities, getting by as a musician.

Are you serious!

Just the basics I'm talking about; earning a wage and so on.

Declan held up his hand to stop him. Dont speak to me about no basics man, I been to Georgia on a fast train. Declan planked himself down on the edge of the double bed. You're asking me man I'm the wrong guy. I would have cut off my nose to play with them guys Tom. Sure I would. Declan growled: Clara never got paid for nothing in her entire life, except baking cakes. Chess gigged, she stayed home.

That just makes the point, said Dad.

Folks need to live Tom I aint gonna deny that. They went gig to gig, same like most of us.

Hand to mouth, said Dad.

Hand to mouth is okay brother. Diego's boys got a head start. You think he wont give them a leg-up? You heard him man they are family. He puts the word in they'll find work everywhere. Like you go to the west coast man, their kind of music, they'll get gigs. Hell Tom old Diego could fill a stadium. You come to Houston when him and the band are playing, his own band! Hey, ever hear of Lydia Mendoza? Houston lady man, born and bred.

Declan swigged beer from the bottle. He settled back on the bed lying full stretch with one hand behind his head, raised a little on the pillow. He swallowed the last of it and lifted a fresh one from the pack.

Murdo said, I need to shower Dad.

Hang on a minute.

Please Dad I'm really tired. Thursday was my last sleep. Murdo made to close the bathroom door. Does anybody need before I go? he said.

No sir, replied Declan, but go fast.

Dad shook his head.

Murdo smiled. See when ye think about it Dad: it's all I do, is music; really, I don't do anything else.

Ye can do it in Scotland.

Yeah, or here. I can do it here. Murdo closed the bathroom door behind him. He stood inside, looking about. Folded white towels, wee bits of soap. He had his own shampoo.

★

Next morning he was roused by Dad. Dad was over him shaking his shoulder, and whispering, Half six son ye better get up.

Murdo was dressed in moments. Dad collected the remaining sandwiches from the fridge. Declan was asleep when they left the room. Sun and blue sky, a beautiful morning. They sat eating sandwiches on the two chairs by the wall, listening to the whooshing traffic noises. A main road was not faraway, and visible between buildings; big trucks passed every few seconds. Murdo said, I think that's the interstate road.

Mm.

Murdo glanced at him.

I do have a kind of sensitive question: ye got anything left out the two hundred dollars?

It was actually two hundred and ninety dollars. Ye gave me forty at the Gathering and Uncle John gave me fifty.

Uncle John gave ye fifty?

Yeah.

Dad chuckled.

I didnay spend anything.

Ye just saved it?

Yeah. Apart from bus-fares I've hardly bought a thing, except the accordeon. That pawnshop in Allentown Dad, I saw it that time we were there.

So have ye anything left?

Well only a bit.

Dad smiled. So what like's the accordeon?

Aw no bad, fine, it's alright. Eighty-five dollars. They reduced it from a hundred and twenty-five. It's paying itself already, like I mean if ye count the busking. It's not a bad sound either, although it might not look much.

Not look much! Ye kidding! It's a beauty!

Well. . . Murdo smiled.

Seriously. It just glistens!

Murdo looked at him.

Even from the side of the bar, said Dad, from where I was standing. Yer playing I mean it was just. . . God! I'll tell ye something too, people were knocked out; Declan too, you might not have noticed. But see that slow one ye did, the one where ye took the lead. Ye could have heard a pin drop. Did ye hear that audience? Eh! Did ye hear them! God son that was something, and that accordeon too, it was just sparkling and glistening and God! just part of it the way ye were playing. It was just special, like you, you are special.

Aw Dad.

I'm telling ye.

Dad

You are. You've got to stop this modesty nonsense.

Dad I'm not modest. That's the last thing I am is modest. It's just that you're talking about another accordeon, you're talking about the turquoise one. That isnay it. That belongs to Queen Monzee-ay. She just brought it for me to use. Mine's is in the accordeon-case. And really. . . Murdo chuckled. It's fine but I mean, it's okay, it's actually alright.

Let me see it.

Murdo got up and opened the door quietly. Declan's bed was empty and the bathroom door closed, he was in having a shower. He collected the accordeon-case. He chapped the bathroom door on his way back out: Morning Declan!

No reply.

Outside he closed over the room door. Declan's in the shower, he said.

Glad to hear it, said Dad.

Murdo sat down on the chair and held the case on his lap, and opened it. The turquoise was inside. It was the turquoise. Murdo frowned at it, the turquoise. They had forgotten to change it. Joel should have done it. Joel had forgotten to. He should have changed it after the gig and he didnay. Joel was supposed to collect it and take it to the pick-up truck. Murdo had left the turquoise onstage with the other instruments. So he should have taken it. He did take it. He must have put it into the accordeon-case by mistake, and brought out Murdo's own one. He must have brought out Murdo's own one. How come? It's the wrong accordeon, he said.

What?

It's the wrong accordeon. Murdo shook his head and made to lift it out, but left it instead. Joel must have seen the pawnshop one when he opened the case. It was Murdo's case, so when he opened it he must have seen the accordeon. So he had to take it out to put in the turquoise. So he took it out, then he put it in, the turquoise. Murdo stared at it. He looked at Dad. Dad, he said, they've gave me it. Dad. . .

What?

Dad. Murdo started greeting.

Dad leaned over to him.

Murdo clenched shut his eyelids trying to stop it he just couldnt stop it, couldnt stop bloody greeting. I'm just bloody greeting, he said, I'm just bloody greeting Dad always bloody greeting.

Aw son dont worry. Dad put his arm round his shoulders. Dont worry.

But Murdo was shaking with it and had to stop just bloody stop greeting, always greeting. I'm sorry Dad.

Dont be, no; no son dont be

I'm always bloody greeting. I'm always bloody greeting Dad I cannay stop bloody greeting just myself like Dad in the bloody bathroom I just start greeting, Dad, I'm just greeting all the time. All the time.

Me too, said Dad. Me too. Jesus Christ me too. Dad was shaking his head.

Murdo blew his nose. I just cannay get over it like I just I dont know what it is – just Mum I mean – and Murdo was greeting again. He stopped and blew his nose. Ah God.

Dad was nodding his head.

It's Queen Monzee-ay. It's her, she's gave me it. She's took mine and gave me hers. Murdo took another tissue from his pocket and blew his nose. I'm sick of greeting Dad I'm sick of it.

Oh Christ.

I'm not as bad as I was but it's still bad. Are you the same?

Yeah. Dad wiped his eyes.

Murdo shook his head. Ye know like this, Queen Monzee-ay giving me the accordeon and you asking about how much ye get paid and like I know what ye're meaning about last night too how I never got paid.

But I wasnt meaning that. I wasnt meaning that.

I'm only saying how maybe she got paid and we didnay, me and Gene and Sarah.

But I wasnt meaning that!

Yeah but

I wasnt.

I thought ye were Dad sorry. But it's this side of music I like, where ye just meet people and become friends. Then ye dont see them again till maybe six months later like doing a gig and ye bump into them. And like all the stories about who played with who and all the old-time guys and the old-time events and festivals that all used to be there. It's just special Dad, it doesnay matter who. But did ye see how he bowed to her, how he bowed to her?

What?

Diego. How he bowed to Queen Monzee-ay. Did ye not see him?

No. . .

Dad he bowed to her, Diego bowed to her.

Dad nodded. He got up and turned away.

★

About 7.20 a.m. Murdo was hanging about the carpark area watching the entrance off the side street. He turned back to the motel. His backpack and accordeon-case were by the room door. Declan was on the same chair as last night, scribbling address information and contact numbers onto a notepage. He finished and stood to his feet. Okay Murdo!

Declan gave him the notepage. Now that's my address, that's my email address and this here's my cell phone number.

Ye on Facebook?

No son I aint and aint going to be. But I can sure pick up a phone, any time, offshore, inshore; any time. But if you got to come dont you wait. You come son, that is what you do. You leave a message and you just come.

That's great.

Houston's real close. You got your Atlas there huh? Declan grinned.

Yeah.

San Antone; you could walk it!

The front door opened and Dad stepped outside; he listened while Declan was talking to Murdo: Where you're going people dont worry so much. Like officialdom? Not once you're in. It's good down there. Good music, good food, good people. Dont worry like your age now that dont matter. You want to work you can work. Other stuff is trickier. Your Dad is right to worry there, but it'll be okay, you'll be okay. Declan glanced at Dad. He's got friends here Tom.

I hear ye, said Dad.

Declan nodded. He gazed at Murdo and Dad, then he stepped

a few paces to the side, got his cigarette pack and strolled down to the carpark area, lighting a cigarette as he went.

Dad gave Murdo another notepage of instructions. I'm not being fussy, he said, it's all numbers and stuff and ye'll need it.

Thanks Dad. Murdo stuck the page in his pocket.

Be careful with it.

Yeah.

It's all yer contacts!

Okay Dad.

Now phone Uncle John this evening Murdo ye buy a phone ye get connected and ye bloody phone, okay? Dad sighed.

Definitely.

We need yer address. So it's the first thing ye do, okay?

Okay Dad.

Have ye got enough?

Do ye mean like money?

Everything.

Yeah. Murdo shrugged.

Like what? What have ye got?

The basics.

The basics?

Yeah Dad the basics.

Have ye got a change?

Jeesoh.

I mean like shoes and jeans?

Yeah.

Have ye? I thought ye had only one pair of jeans?

I've got a pair of joggers.

Have ye got another top?

Dad

I've got to ask these things, you forget.

Dad the guys are going to give me a loan of clothes.

A loan of clothes? A loan of clothes?

Yeah. Murdo smiled.

Dad stared a moment. He returned into the room.

The traffic noises were loud now. Murdo looked towards the main road. A Sunday morning as early as this yet it was busy. Big trucks were there too, quite a line of them, wherever they all were going.

Hey Murdo! Declan had glanced back at him, pointing at his wristwatch, then at the door into the room.

Murdo nodded. He opened the room door. Dad was sitting on the edge of the bed. He looked up at Murdo. Okay?

Yeah Dad.

Dad smiled. Where did ye sleep last night by the way? I've been feart to ask.

Well the bus was late in, coming from Baton Rouge, it was nearly midnight.

So where did ye go?

Eh well I had to walk it from the bus station, just looking about and so on because like Sarah and her family, I was supposed to be meeting up with them but because the bus was so late in it was too late. I got a place quite near the festival, not too far away, a wee grass square and with benches, and I got a bench; there was an all-night foodstall there too so it was like ye know, cups of tea and so on. I had a good meal there, fish and chips, it was good.

Fish and chips?

Yeah.

So ye slept on the bench?

Yeah.

Right, ye slept on a bench.

Well Dad it was too late for anything.

Dad nodded.

So. . . Murdo paused. He heard music, he glanced at the door a fraction before the knock. Declan called from outside: That's Diego and the boys.

Murdo grinned. Dad was watching him. It's eh. . . Murdo gestured at the door and walked to op   it. Dad got up from the bed and Murdo held the door open for him. Outside Murdo lifted his rucksack and accordeon-case. Dad moved to give him a cuddle. Take care now, he said.

Of course.

The two vehicles had parked in the carpark area and different music came from each. Murdo carried the rucksack and accordeon-case, walking to meet them. Dad and Declan followed. Dad said, Listen son they can give ye an address ask them for an address, they must know where they're going.

Murdo grinned at Declan.

Seriously, said Dad.

Santiago was driving the pick-up. Esteban was beside him, waved his hand out the window: Hey Moordo!

Diego let down the window of the 4x4 and saluted Dad and Declan. Esteban got out the truck and took the accordeon-case from Murdo carefully positioning it in with the other instruments, luggage and equipment.

Murdo reached to shake hands with Declan. Declan gave him a quick slap slap cuddle, then stuck some notes into a top pocket on his jacket. Murdo tried to shrug it off. Honest I dont need it!

Declan growled: Hey boy, you pay me back sometime.

Aw thanks Declan. Murdo smiled at Dad. Okay Dad?

Yeah, said Dad. He palmed Murdo a small wad of notes.

Aw Dad! Murdo grinned.

Yeah aw Dad, he said. Make sure ye get that phone.

Of course.

Dad and Murdo shook hands again. Esteban opened a rear door in the truck and he got in there leaving the front passenger seat available. Santiago chuckled. Moordo!

Murdo got in the front leaving the door open for Dad to speak. Vicenté and Roberto slapped him on the shoulder.

Dad was saying, If ye can't phone the night then phone tomorrow. Just dont worry about it. Dont let anything put ye off, never ever. Know what I mean son never ever.

Santiago hadnt switched off the engine and now he released the handbrake.

Dad said, Dont lose contact whatever ye do. Aunt Maureen will never forgive ye. Neither will I. Then yer passport. I dont know what to say about yer passport. If ye get it or leave it with Uncle John, ye just keep it in yer front pocket at all times and never ever take it out or leave it any place. Never.

Santiago glanced at him and shrugged.

It's the most important thing of all, said Dad, it is just so so crucial son ye keep it in yer trouser pocket at all times. Never ever take it out or leave it any place. Know what I mean son yer passport's yer passport. Never take it out yer pocket.

Okay Dad.

And phone phone phone.

Right.

Santiago was gazing at Dad, his foot on the accelerator pedal, the truck inching along.

Dad nodded. Okay, he said and shut the door.

Gracias, said Santiago.

Murdo saw that Diego had got out of the 4x4 and Declan walked to meet him. Then Dad. They spoke together. Dad stood with his hands in his pockets.

Santiago said to Murdo, Your father hey!

Yeah.

Santiago made a sad face, then shrugged like there was nothing to be done. Soon Diego was in his car and they were moving ahead. Santiago reversed out and set off after them. Dad standing there with Declan. Murdo waved. Santiago lowered the side window for him, and Murdo waved out in a better way. Dad and Declan walked after them, then stopped by the carpark exit. Declan was waving. Maybe Dad was. Murdo couldnt see properly in the side mirror. That was that. Santiago switched on the music, a good accordeon; kind of jaunty, probably Conjunto.